LEGACY
OF DORN

D0869498

More Space Marines from Black Library

THE DEVASTATION OF BAAL
A Blood Angels novel by Guy Haley

ASHES OF PROSPERO
A Space Wolves novel by Gav Thorpe

WAR OF SECRETS
A Dark Angels novel by Phil Kelly

OF HONOUR AND IRON
An Ultramarines novel by Ian St. Martin

SPACE MARINE
L E G E N D S

LEMARTES
David Annandale

AZRAEL
Gav Thorpe

SHRIKE
George Mann

CASSIUS
Ben Counter

RAGNAR BLACKMANE
Aaron Dembski-Bowden

THE EYE OF EZEKIEL
A Dark Angels novel by C Z Dunn

SCYTHES OF THE EMPEROR
A Scythes of the Emperor anthology by L J Goulding

SHIELD OF BAAL
A Blood Angels novel by Josh Reynolds,
Joe Parrino and Braden Campbell

THE WAR FOR RYNN'S WORLD
A Crimson Fists novel by Steve Parker & Mike Lee

LEGACY OF DORN

MIKE LEE

BLACK LIBRARY

A BLACK LIBRARY PUBLICATION

First published in 2018.
This edition published in Great Britain in 2018 by
Black Library,
Games Workshop Ltd.,
Willow Road,
Nottingham, NG7 2WS, UK.

10 9 8 7 6 5 4 3 2 1

Produced by Games Workshop in Nottingham.
Cover illustration by Mikhail Savier.

A CIP record for this book is available from the British Library.

ISBN 13: 978 1 78496 777 2

See Black Library on the internet at

blacklibrary.com

Find out more about Games Workshop
and the world of Warhammer 40,000 at

games-workshop.com

Printed and bound by CPI Group (UK) Ltd, Croydon, CR0 4YY

It is the 41st millennium. For more than a hundred centuries the Emperor has sat immobile on the Golden Throne of Earth. He is the Master of Mankind by the will of the gods, and master of a million worlds by the might of His inexhaustible armies. He is a rotting carcass writhing invisibly with power from the Dark Age of Technology. He is the Carrion Lord of the Imperium for whom a thousand souls are sacrificed every day, so that He may never truly die.

Yet even in His deathless state, the Emperor continues His eternal vigilance. Mighty battlefleets cross the daemon-infested miasma of the warp, the only route between distant stars, their way lit by the Astronomican, the psychic manifestation of the Emperor's will. Vast armies give battle in His name on uncounted worlds. Greatest amongst His soldiers are the Adeptus Astartes, the Space Marines, bioengineered super-warriors. Their comrades in arms are legion: the Astra Militarum and countless planetary defence forces, the ever-vigilant Inquisition and the tech-priests of the Adeptus Mechanicus to name only a few. But for all their multitudes, they are barely enough to hold off the ever-present threat from aliens, heretics, mutants – and worse.

To be a man in such times is to be one amongst untold billions. It is to live in the cruellest and most bloody regime imaginable. These are the tales of those times. Forget the power of technology and science, for so much has been forgotten, never to be re-learned. Forget the promise of progress and understanding, for in the grim dark future there is only war. There is no peace amongst the stars, only an eternity of carnage and slaughter, and the laughter of thirsting gods.

'My orders arrived in the dead of night, hand-delivered by messenger from New Rynn City, halfway around the world. *Invasion imminent.* I read the words again and again, my tired mind trying to make sense of them. I remember holding the heavy parchment in my hands, tilting the page up to the light, as though my eyes were somehow deceiving me.

'For months, the ork horde that had come howling out of Charadon had been a distant menace, leaving a trail of horror and ruin across the worlds of the frontier. Rynn's World hadn't been attacked in centuries. We had our angels, the Crimson Fists, to protect us. *The greenskins wouldn't dare,* I thought.

'I knew nothing of Snagrod then. No one outside the Arx Tyrannus did. I could not imagine the horrors to come.'

– Antonia Mitra, *The Shieldbearers*

PART ONE
THE BROKEN TOWER

SACRIFICES

ZONA URBIS, MINESSA
DAY 1

Ships were dying in the starry skies above Rynn's World. An hour ago they had been mere pinpricks of searing orange light, flickering for a fraction of an instant in the vast sea of night; once or twice a minute at first, then growing steadily in size and number as the fighting moved inexorably closer to the planet. Now they were smudges of fire that lingered for long seconds across the heavens, nearly bright enough to cast shadows across the ferrocrete landing pad of the city's urban defence headquarters. Very soon now, the explosions would fade altogether, and the first telltale streaks of ork landing craft would start their plunge through the agri-world's atmosphere.

Alert sirens were wailing across the small city of Minessa, ordering its terrified citizens and tens of thousands of refugees into hastily built shelters, and summoning the young soldiers of the local planetary defence forces to their posts. The western edge of the vast landing pad was a riot of shouted orders and grumbling petrochem engines as red-faced sergeants turned their platoons out of barracks and herded them onto transports bound for the city walls. Boots pounded across the ferrocrete as messengers and staff aides raced to and from the headquarters building with hastily drafted orders for the city's Rynnsguard regiments. Horns shrilled as staff cars tried to weave their way through the chaos, carrying sleep-deprived officers summoned from their beds across town.

All of them gave way before blue-armoured giants striding purposefully from the headquarters building towards the Thunderhawk gunship idling at the far end of the pad.

The leader of the three Crimson Fists was helmetless, his Phobos-pattern bolter locked into travel stays on the side of his backpack. His armour was ancient but dutifully tended, its midnight-blue surface marked at shoulder and breast with oath ribbons and battle honours that bore witness to millennia of war across the length and breadth of the Imperium of Man. Veteran Sergeant Sandor Galleas bore the silver skull of the Ordo Xenos' Deathwatch at his left shoulder and the ivory Crux Terminatus at his knee. His gauntlets were the colour of fresh-spilled blood, marking him as a member of the Chapter's elite Crusade Company. A holstered bolt pistol and a power sword in an ornate scabbard hung from his waist.

Galleas pressed a red fingertip to the vox-bead below his right ear. Unlike most Space Marines, he had a lean, pale face, with a sharp nose and deep-set eyes the colour of polished jade, framed by a head of short, curly black hair. 'Brother Zephran!' he called over the vox. 'How long until lift-off?'

The Thunderhawk's pilot responded at once, his deep voice buzzing in the sergeant's head. *'The Chosen have stowed all baggage, and I've concluded the pre-flight litanies. We can leave at any time, brother.'*

Three Rynnsguard officers followed in Galleas' wake, hands pressed to their peaked caps and greatcoats flapping around their ankles as they hurried to keep up with the veteran sergeant's ground-eating strides. Their leader was a young man with dark eyes and a duellist's moustache, his cheeks red from the late winter chill.

'You can't possibly go!' Colonel Sebastian Ybarra said, shouting over the din. He had the rigid bearing and sharp enunciation of a low-country aristocrat, born to one of the wealthy agri-barons who ran the combines that stretched across most of Calliona's arable plains. The regimental shoulder boards on his greatcoat seemed two sizes too large for his narrow shoulders, and his handsome face was almost rigid with panic. 'We're still finishing work on the inner redoubts, and the guns at the southern bastion aren't properly calibrated! We need more time–'

'The time for preparations is past,' Galleas replied brusquely. 'In another hour, perhaps less, the city will be under attack.' He keyed the vox-bead again. 'Brother Tauros, I don't see our Rhino stowed aboard the Thunderhawk. Where in the black hells are you?'

'Valentus, Salazar and I are on our way back from the southern bastion,' Tauros replied. The veteran, a Crimson Fist of more than five hundred years' service, sounded entirely unconcerned by the prospect of an impending ork invasion. *'The regimental enginseers needed a little persuading, but we convinced them to forego the Rites of Calibration and let us configure the gun batteries by hand.'*

'Chapter Master Kantor expects us in New Rynn City *right now.'*

'*But before that, he ordered us to supervise defensive prepa-rations for the city,*' Tauros pointed out. '*There's no virtue in leaving a job unfinished, brother, especially not on the eve of battle.*'

Galleas scowled. They'd only had six days to mobilise the local Rynnsguard regiments and restore fortifications that hadn't seen use in nearly a thousand years. The Space Marines had pushed the troops hard, working them around the clock to get the city ready, and while they'd performed some certifiable miracles getting the ancient defence sys-tems back online, there would still be a great many crucial tasks left undone by the time the greenskins arrived. Such was the way of war. 'If you're not back here in five min-utes, you're *driving* the Rhino to the capital. Understood?'

Tauros chuckled. '*We'll be there, brother.*'

'I don't understand,' Colonel Ybarra persisted. Six days before, he'd been a privileged son of a wealthy family, mark-ing time in an inherited commission with the Rynnsguard, and the ork Waaagh! sweeping across the eastern frontier had been little more than a troubling rumour. 'I thought we were supposed to have forty hours' warning or more from the time the xenos arrived insystem!'

The sergeant's scowl deepened. 'It would appear that the Arch-Arsonist of Charadon has surprised us yet again,' he snapped, heading for the trio of Crimson Fists who waited, boltguns in hand, at the foot of the Thunderhawk's star-board hatch.

Titus Juno nodded his head in greeting as Galleas approached. Like his sergeant, Juno was bareheaded, his broad, rugged features as blunt and unyielding as Magalan granite. Two silver service studs glittered coldly from his scarred forehead, just below the line of his close-cropped black hair. Like Galleas, he wore the silver skull of the Deathwatch upon his left shoulder, and a short, heavy sword hung at his left hip. The parchment ribbons of purity seals fluttered angrily in the wind generated by the Thunderhawk's idling turbines.

'Another few minutes and I think Amador here was going to start swimming for Sorocco without us,' he called out.

'We're wasting time!' Claudio Amador said hotly. He stood to Juno's right, his trigger hand twitching irritably on the grip of his boltgun. Chains of polished ork tusks hung from both pauldrons, and his breastplate was crowded with battle honours and badges of valour. Amador fancied himself a warrior in the same mould as the fearless Alessio Cortez, captain of the Chapter's Fourth Company, and took great pride in his war trophies. 'The orks could be over New Rynn City at any moment. Am I the only one who grasps this?'

'We remain constantly in awe of your tactical prowess,' Timon Royas grumbled. Standing at Juno's left, Royas' helmeted head was constantly in motion, scanning the chaos of the landing field for potential threats. A veteran of two hundred years and countless bloody battles, he too wore the silver Deathwatch skull on his left shoulder, and had spent more time with the secretive order than nearly any other Space Marine in the Chapter. Galleas often wondered if that was the reason for his cynical nature and razor-edged tongue.

'Where are Caron, Olivar and Rodrigo?' Galleas demanded.

'On board, checking to make sure we haven't left any gear behind,' Juno replied. 'Tauros, Valentus and Salazar seem to have disappeared with the Rhino.'

'They're on the way,' Galleas replied, sounding nearly as impatient as Amador.

Royas fixed Colonel Ybarra with a baleful red stare. 'Does the popinjay think he's coming with us?' he growled.

The colonel's eyes went wide. If a man had spoken to him thus, it would have meant an immediate demand of satisfaction, and sabres or pistols on the parade field at dawn. As it was, the young officer drew himself up to his meagre height and met the Space Marine's eyes. 'I am an Ybarra,' he said, with much affronted dignity. 'I know very well where my duty lies.'

'Then I suggest you see to it,' Galleas said coldly. He turned to Ybarra. 'The city is no longer our concern, colonel. Our work here is done.'

Ybarra's aides blanched at the tone in Galleas' voice. The young colonel's hands clenched at his sides. The full weight of his responsibility seemed to settle on his narrow shoulders, and for a moment it looked as though it might break him. He drew a deep breath. 'H-how long are we expected to hold out?'

Galleas looked down at the man. Ybarra and his troops had never seen a greenskin before. They'd never even seen real combat. If they had, they would have understood the grim truth. Every man, woman and child in Minessa was doomed. The cold calculations of war dictated that the defence of the planet would be focused on the Arx Tyrannus, the Crimson Fists Chapter monastery, and New Rynn City, where the majority of the planet's populace was located. The rest of the planet's scattered cities would have to fight alone as best they could, drawing off and killing as much of the greenskin horde as possible before they were overwhelmed. Given the magnitude of what they faced, there was no other alternative.

'A month, perhaps. Six weeks at the most.'

The young officer considered this, nodding slowly. He drew another deep breath, summoning his resolve. 'We will not fail you, my lord,' he said gravely. 'Is… is there any last wisdom you can share before you go?'

A familiar snarl of petrochem engines caught Galleas' attention. He glanced across the landing field and saw the squad's Rhino nosing past the line of trucks at the south gate and heading their way. His mind was already hundreds of kilometres away, contemplating the squad's dispositions once they reached the capital.

'Fight the xenos with every weapon at your disposal,' Galleas said. 'Make them pay for every square metre with blood. Fight until the ammunition is gone, until the walls are breached and the guns have fallen silent.' He turned, heading for the Thunderhawk's open hatch.

'After that, colonel, all that remains is to die with honour.'

The ork Waaagh! had struck the Loki Sector without warning, catching even the Chapter's psychic Librarians completely by surprise. Snagrod, the infamous Arch-Arsonist of Chara-don, had fought countless battles against Imperial forces during his brief and brutal rise to power, and had learned much of his foe's tactics and strategies. Uniting the fractious ork tribes along the Loki Sector's eastern border, Snagrod struck at listening posts and astropathic relays across the frontier, crippling the Imperial communications and early warning network. By the time news of the Waaagh! reached Rynn's World, much of the eastern frontier had been lost, and the ork vanguard had reached the planet of Badland-ing, just a few short weeks' travel away.

The Crimson Fists reacted swiftly and decisively to the sudden threat. Chapter Master Pedro Kantor despatched the

Third Company, along with scouts from the Tenth, to gather information on the strength of the ork horde at Badlanding and to delay their advance while he warned the rest of the Segmentum. But the undertaking had ended in disaster; during a surgical strike on the greenskins' long-range communication network, an impetuous Space Marine Scout had given away the location of the main force and drawn the wrath of the entire horde down upon them. Of the eighty-four Crimson Fists that had gone to Badlanding, only twenty-eight returned, most with wounds severe enough to require the attention of the Chapter's Apothecaries. Captain Ashor Drakken, the commander of the Third Company, was counted among the slain, having lost his life attempting to rescue a wounded battle-brother.

The news of the Third Company's near-destruction at Badlanding was a terrible blow to the Chapter, but worse was yet to come. Intercepted ork communications warned that Snagrod, enraged by the Crimson Fists' attack, intended to turn the full wrath of his Waaagh! on Rynn's World.

There had been less than a week to make ready for the greenskin attack. Second Company, along with the surviving Crimson Fists of Third Company and the Chapter's elite Terminators, were sent to defend the capital at New Rynn City. Veteran squads from the Crusade Company were despatched to cities like Minessa to oversee defensive preparations. Meanwhile, the Chapter's powerful space fleet, commanded by the vaunted Ceval Ranparre, had formed a defensive cordon around Rynn's World to contest the arrival of the ork invasion fleet. Ranparre was pragmatic about the fleet's odds against the xenos, whose ships outnumbered the system defence forces many times over. It would be impossible to stop Snagrod's horde from reaching the planet, but the fleet would harry them the entire way from the jump point at the edge of the system. The space battle had been expected to last up to four days, providing the planet's defenders with ample warning to complete their final preparations.

But Snagrod had outmanoeuvred them once again.

Galleas frowned down at the status report from the Strategium at the Arx Tyrannus. 'The ork fleet jumped into the system just a hundred and fifty thousand kilometres from Rynn's World,' he announced, raising his voice to be heard over the muted roar of the gunship's thrusters.

Heads turned inside the Thunderhawk's red-lit troop compartment. Juno and Amador had disengaged from their crash harnesses and were making last-minute checks of their wargear. Yezim Olivar sat in his harness with his helmet on his knees, head bowed in prayer. Unlike his brothers, Olivar's war-plate was decorated not with battle honours, but with oaths of moment and parchment pages from the *Lectitio Divinitatus*, the holy book of the Imperial Cult. The rest of the squad had been deep in meditation, taking the time between duties to rest, as veteran soldiers had been wont to do since the days of ancient Terra.

Mikael Tauros glanced over at Galleas. The veteran had removed his helmet as well, revealing a bald head and a blunt face tattooed with the Imperial aquila. 'That's madness,' he said.

Royas grunted from the far side of the troop compartment. 'What else would you expect from greenskin filth?'

Brother Valentus leaned forward in his harness, slowly shaking his polished metal head. His face and much of the bone beneath had been burned away by tyranid bio-acid during an undertaking to a space hulk a hundred and fifty years ago, requiring steel prosthetics and a pair of glowing augmetic eyes. Both arms and one leg were bionic replacements as well, left behind on battlefields scattered across the Segmentum. His squad mates had taken to calling him Brother Dreadnought Valentus as a result, a title the scarred veteran bore with equanimity.

'*It is poor tactics,*' he said, his voice grating from a vox grille set into his gorget. '*At such a distance, the orks stand to lose as many ships to jump mishaps as they will to incoming fire.*'

Galleas blanked the data-slate and set it in a cradle by his seat. 'Snagrod's fleet was even larger than we believed,' he said grimly. 'Hundreds of greenskin ships were destroyed on re-entry from the warp, but hundreds more emerged into real space just three hours from the planet, right in the midst of Ranparre's defensive cordon.' He shook his head. 'Casualties were heavy on both sides, but our ships were outnumbered nearly a hundred to one. The last report from Ranparre's flagship said that the frigate *Crusader* and a number of escorts were going to try to break through the ork formations and make for the Segmentum naval headquarters at Kar Duniash to summon aid. Once *Crusader* was safely away, Ranparre and the remnants of the fleet intended to seek an honourable death amongst the foe.'

The squad took the news in stunned silence. The deck of the Thunderhawk tilted beneath them, its thrusters rising in pitch. The gunship was turning in on its final approach to New Rynn City. The distant rumble of the capital's anti-aircraft batteries could be felt through the transport's armoured hull.

Ibrahim Salazar broke the silence at last. 'The whole fleet... gone?' he said. A member of the Crusade Company for little more than seventy-five years, he was the youngest member of the squad. 'I can't believe it.'

'*First Badlanding, and now this,*' Valentus said. '*These are dark times for the Chapter, brothers. Dark times indeed.*'

Even Galleas could not help but feel a cold sense of foreboding at Valentus' words, but he refused to give in to it. 'We all knew that the void battle would be a grim one,' he told his squad. 'But the fight for Rynn's World has only just begun. Snagrod doesn't realise it yet, but he has attacked our home world at the worst possible time. Nearly the entire Chapter was gathered here for the Founding Day ceremonies just a few weeks past, and now we stand ready to bring our full strength to bear on the greenskin horde.

'The Chapter Master and more than six hundred of our brothers hold the Arx Tyrannus. Second Company holds New Rynn City, supported by three-quarters of the Crusade Company and the survivors of the Third. Kantor knows that Snagrod will send the vast majority of his horde against the fortress-monastery, where our brothers will slaughter the xenos filth by the thousands. The Arx Tyrannus is warded by layers of void shielding that are proof against the heaviest orbital bombardment, and there is enough ammunition buried within the mountain to keep the guns firing continuously for *years*.

'Eventually, once the chasms surrounding the Arx Tyrannus have been filled with greenskin dead, the horde will grow impatient with their lack of progress and start looking for easier prey instead. Then our turn will come, and we'll have to hold Snagrod's horde outside the walls of New Rynn City. Then Kantor will go on the offensive, clearing the orks from around the fortress-monastery with a series of counter-attacks, launching strikes against the xenos outside the capital. If the horde turns its attention back to the Arx Tyrannus, then *we* will go on the offensive. Between fortress and city we will grind Snagrod's horde to bits.'

Tauros chuckled. 'I didn't realise you were privy to the Chapter Master's strategy meetings.'

'You all know I served with Kantor as a Tactical Marine when he was captain of Fourth Company,' Galleas replied. 'He was a mentor to me, and taught me everything I know about fighting greenskins.' He leaned forward, his expression fierce. 'The Arx Tyrannus is key, brothers. Mark my words. The fortress-monastery cannot be taken. It's too well-sited up in the mountains, and too well-defended. As long as we hold it, Snagrod's horde cannot prevail. When ships from Kar Duniash finally arrive, months from now, they will find the Waaagh! broken and the Arch-Arsonist's head resting on a spike atop the Conqueror's Gate.'

Galleas' words had the desired effect. Amador let out a triumphant yell, and Salazar and Rodrigo followed suit. The bleak mood inside the troop compartment had been dispelled. Tauros, the old veteran, gave Galleas an approving nod and leaned back in his crash harness.

Moments later the Thunderhawk touched down on a crowded landing pad outside the Cassar, a secondary Chapter fortress situated in the Zona Regis, a governmental preserve located on an island roughly in the centre of the city. The squad gathered up their wargear and fell into formation as the gunship's assault ramp lowered to the ferrocrete.

The Crimson Fists trotted down the ramp into the midst of a raging warzone. The air shook with the percussive beat of anti-aircraft guns, and streams of green and red tracer fire etched glowing arcs across the night sky. The guttural roar of ork attack craft echoed from the city's outer districts, followed by the reverberating blasts of rockets and heavy bombs. Angry yellow flames lit the horizon to the north and east, silhouetting dozens of towering columns of smoke and debris. All the while, high overhead, the fiery arcs of thousands of xenos landing craft plunged towards the planet's surface.

The awful, overpowering din sank into Galleas' reinforced bones and set his powerful hearts racing. He looked eastwards, past the flames and the ribbons of smoke, his gene-enhanced vision searching for a point along the distant peaks of the Hellblade Mountains. A fierce grin lit the veteran sergeant's face.

'Look there, brothers!' he said proudly, pointing to the horizon. Thin filaments of angry, white light were rising heavenward, slowly at first, but gathering speed with every passing moment. 'The Arx Tyrannus has opened fire! Now the battle's truly begun!'

The Space Marines watched as scores of heavy ship-killer missiles blasted from silos around the fortress-monastery and clawed their way into the night sky, heading for Snagrod's orbiting fleet.

'That's for Third Company!' Amador shouted, raising his fist to the sky. 'Vengeance for the fallen!'

'Vengeance for the fallen!' Salazar echoed, and soon Caron took up the cry. More missiles were launching now, following on the heels of the first wave. Soon there would be a whole new constellation of dying ships hanging in the sky above the planet.

Brother Rodrigo, a legendary sniper during his time with Tenth Company, took a step forward. He peered intently at a spot on the horizon. 'What's that?'

After a moment, Galleas saw it too. One of the silver contrails was curving, twisting into a corkscrew path above where the fortress-monastery stood. For a moment, it looked as though it might right itself and soar skyward – but then, with a final sharp twist, its armour-piercing nose dropped, and the missile plunged earthward like a fiery spear.

For a fleeting instant, nothing seemed to happen – but then the mountains were limned in an expanding globe of furious, white light. Thousands of metres across, the fireball continued to swell, roiling up into the heavens and darkening to a deep, angry red.

A full minute later the sound of the blast swept over the city: a rumbling roar that swelled in volume until it blotted out the thunder of the city's own guns. Windows shattered across the Zona Regis and the Space Marines themselves were staggered by the sheer, awful force of the noise.

It was a sound like the end of the world.

CHAPTER ONE

INTO THE BREACH

ZONA 13 COMMERCIA, NEW RYNN CITY
DAY 86

'*I say again, we have a breach in Zona Thirteen Commercia, opposite the sector command post!*' The young captain was struggling to remain calm and in control, but his voice was growing louder and more shrill by the moment. '*They're pouring into the gap! Blessed Emperor, we need help!*'

The Rhino's troop compartment tilted crazily underneath Galleas as the armoured personnel carrier rolled over the edge of a rubble pile. Salazar cursed loudly on the far side of the vehicle's forward bulkhead, gunning the labouring engine. Loose rock and bits of structural metal rumbled and crunched beneath the right tread, pounding the underside of the transport. Reflexively, the veteran sergeant leaned back against the bulkhead as far as he could go, and Tauros, Juno, Rodrigo and Caron did the same. A moment later they cleared the pile, levelling out on the far side with a teeth-jarring crash, and then the Rhino was off again, clawing its way down the debris-choked lane.

'Stand fast,' Galleas said into his helmet vox. 'We are en route to your position now. Hold the greenskins at the breach. Do you understand? Do not let them gain a foothold on the far side of the wall.'

'They're tearing us to pieces! We've got to pull back–'

Galleas bared his teeth. 'We are two minutes from your position!' he snarled. 'Contain that breach, captain, or by Dorn the xenos will be the *least* of your worries!'

Screams and sounds of gunfire punctuated the static coming over the vox. The Rynnsguard captain stammered and started to reply, but his words were lost beneath a strident beeping in Galleas' helmet. A crimson sigil flashed at the margin of his helmet display: a priority transmission from the command post at the Cassar.

'*Galleas, this is Deguerro.*' The Librarian's voice was a dull monotone, leached of vitality by psychic exertion and the constant demands of the grinding siege. When Pedro Kantor and the Arx Tyrannus had been lost on the first night of the invasion, Captain Drigo Alvez, commander of Second Company, found himself in command of the last two hundred and eighteen Crimson Fists left on the planet. More than two and a half months later, Alvez was gone too, having fallen in battle trying to hold the Verona Gate. Now a veteran sergeant led what was left of Second, and responsibility for the defence of New Rynn City fell squarely on the shoulders of Epistolary Deguerro, who had been one of Alvez's aides.

Galleas still saw the expanding ball of fire every time he closed his eyes. The roar of the fateful blast seemed to echo in his ears. The Chapter Master and more than six hundred brothers, warriors he'd known for nearly his entire life, gone in the blink of an eye. Ten thousand years of history, lost forever. He'd witnessed it with his own eyes, and yet it still didn't seem possible.

'*Galleas, can you hear me?*'

The veteran sergeant shook himself from his reverie. His mind had been wandering for seconds at a time lately. He reckoned it was due to lack of food and sleep; both had been in short supply since the invasion had begun. 'I read you, brother,' he answered quickly, focusing his mind on the present.

'*The orks are attacking in strength at Zona Twenty-four Industria. Veteran Squad Savales is heavily engaged at Zona Twenty-eight. Can you assist?*'

Galleas took a deep breath, calming his mind. 'Negative. We are containing a breach in Zona Thirteen. Suggest you despatch one of the reserve squads.'

The Rhino hit another patch of rubble, bouncing the entire squad high enough that the tops of their helmets hit the troop compartment's armoured ceiling. No one, not even the acerbic Royas, made so much as a grunt. The squad was in deep meditation, preparing themselves for the next desperate fight.

'*All reserves are already committed,*' came Deguerro's grim reply. '*Notify the Cassar when the breach is contained. There is only the Emperor.*'

'He is our shield and protector,' Galleas replied dully. The command sigil vanished. Calling up a map of the sector from memory, the sergeant gauged how close they were to the breach, then opened the squad vox-channel. 'One minute,' he told his brothers. 'Weapons check.'

His battle-brothers roused themselves, their hands moving with thoughtless, mechanical precision as they checked ammo loads and loosened combat knives in their sheaths.

Their armour was battered and dust-stained from months of constant fighting, and many of their cherished battle honours had been torn or burned away. Snagrod's unrelenting assault was grinding them down a bit at a time. Soon there would be nothing left.

An amber vox-sigil was blinking on Galleas' vox display. *The Rynnsguard captain*, he reminded himself. Instead of switching back to the local defence net, however, his attention was drawn to another sigil entirely, and the operation that even now was occurring just outside the city.

For days there had been rumours that Deguerro and the other Librarians had sensed a shifting in the fates surrounding not just New Rynn City, but the entire planet as well. Someone was coming, someone momentous, who could well make the difference between victory and defeat. The psykers could not determine who this person was, but every battle-brother in the city dared to hope it was Pedro Kantor, the Chapter Master himself.

The odds that Kantor had survived the cataclysmic loss of the Arx Tyrannus – and then traversed hundreds of kilometres of ork-infested territory on foot to reach the city – were nothing short of astronomical. Yet it was enough to persuade Deguerro and Sergeant Huron Grim, the acting commander of Second Company, to send no less than four squads – nearly their entire reserve – via tunnel to Jadeberry Hill, to see if the portents were true. The undertaking was risky in the extreme; the hill was well beyond any friendly support, so the longer that Grim and his four squads remained there, the greater the chance that they would be cut off and overwhelmed. If they were lost, it would seal the fate of city and Chapter alike.

Galleas hesitated a moment longer, then selected the

Second Company icon. At once, shouted orders and the hammer of boltgun fire reverberated in his ears.

'*Suppressing fire! I want suppressing fire on those greenskins now!*'

'*Keep them back, brothers! Don't let them reach the hill!*'

'*Squad Davelos is down to two magazines per brother. Permission to draw knives and charge?*'

'*Denied! We hold here, brothers! For Kantor! For Dorn!*'

Galleas switched off the link. Grim and the reserves had been out on Jadeberry Hill for hours now. They couldn't last much longer, Galleas knew. But would the sergeant withdraw before it was too late? At what point would Grim decide there was no further reason to hope?

If I were out there, Galleas thought, *what would I do?*

The Rhino slewed around a corner, treads screeching across the ferrocrete. The sounds of battle, which had been growing steadily over the throaty roar of the transport's engines, suddenly intensified. Galleas heard the distinctive boom of heavy artillery and the angry crackle of lasgun fire. And above it all, rising and falling in a constant, surf-like roar, the war cries of thousands of angry greenskins.

Almost at once, the front of the Rhino rang with shell hits. The transport's engine roared, sending it hurtling forwards another thirty metres before Salazar hit the brakes and brought the armoured vehicle to a slewing, skidding stop. A half-second later the rear assault ramp deployed, crashing heavily to the ground just to Galleas' left. Smoke and screams poured into the troop compartment.

The squad was already moving, their bodies operating on hard-wired instinct and centuries of experience. Galleas surged to his feet, hands tightening on the grip of his bolter. 'Formation Delta!' he called out. 'Deploy left! Let's move!'

Galleas emerged into dull, reddish-yellow light. Even in mid-afternoon, the planet's twin suns shone from behind a thick haze of dirt and ash – the pulverised remnants of the Chapter monastery and the mountain it had rested upon. It had hung like a pall over the city for months, stinging the eyes and coating the throats of human and Crimson Fist alike. Salazar had driven the Rhino onto the eastern edge of a broad, rubble-strewn square, bordered on three sides by half-destroyed hab units, and on the fourth by the thirty-metre curtain wall that protected this quadrant of the inner city. A battery of wheeled Medusa siege guns were deployed in a rough line just a dozen metres away, their blunt snouts elevated to lob their thousand-kilogram high-explosive shells over the curtain wall and onto the xenos horde beyond. The panicked gunners were working feverishly with a portable winch to feed the massive guns from a pallet of shells close by.

The veteran sergeant exited the transport and cut to the left, bolter clutched to his chest as he spun on his heel and dashed along the transport's side. The Rhino was stopped at an angle to the edge of the square, its blunt nose facing towards the breach on the western side. Further off to Galleas' right, a field medicae station had been set up in the shadow of one of the ruined buildings. Scores of wounded lay outside the crowded surgical tents, attended by exhausted orderlies who assessed their injuries and determined who was too far gone to save. The grim-faced attendants seemed oblivious to the stray rounds that buzzed past their hunched shoulders or struck sparks from the ferrocrete around them. To the left of the medicae station, almost at the north wall of the square, sat a trio of command tents and a radio tent that constituted the headquarters of the local Rynnsguard regiments. A steady stream of messengers ran between the command tents and the radio tent as the regimental officers fought to hold this section of the city for just a few hours more.

With the Arx Tyrannus gone, Snagrod had turned his full attention on New Rynn City, and the onslaught had been terrible. Landing craft were crashed into the outer walls, opening the way for the horde, and from there it had been nothing but bitter, bloody urban fighting as the defenders were pushed back towards the city centre. The Rynnsguard had fought like cornered lions, making the greenskins pay for each metre in blood, but the hated xenos just kept coming, undaunted by their staggering losses. The Crimson Fists – now little more than two companies strong – were relegated to defending critical points, or in the case of the veteran squads, employed as mobile 'fire brigades' to contain breaches or cover the withdrawal of trapped units. For Galleas and his squad, the last few weeks had been one desperate battle after another, fighting day and night to hold back the tide.

The greenskins held more than two-thirds of the city now. This was the second-to-last defensive wall, just eight kilometres from the Residentia Ultris, the wealthy districts that lined the river around the Zona Regis. Soon the defenders would have nowhere left to go.

Galleas paused at the front of the Rhino while the rest of the squad formed a narrow wedge behind him. Amador took position at his left shoulder, Juno at his right. Tauros was in the centre of the wedge where the old veteran could keep an eye on everyone else.

'Remember the protocol,' Galleas warned, as he did before every fight. One of the first things Captain Alvez had done upon assuming responsibility for what was left of the Chapter was instituting the Ceres Protocol, a code of behaviour that placed the survival of the Chapter above the demands of honour or revenge. There would be no doomed charges, no stubborn last stands or bloody self-sacrifices in the name of righteous wrath. Whether they wanted to or not, the Crimson Fists would swallow their despair and their rage and fight to defend the city until the bitter end.

Galleas stared across the smoke-wreathed square. Half a dozen Chimera armoured transports had been drawn up in a loose semi-circle, facing a breach in the curtain wall some ten metres across. The remains of a Rynnsguard regiment filled the gaps between the vehicles, crouching behind makeshift barricades of rubble and flakboard and blasting away with their lasguns at the howling mob of greenskins trying to force their way into the square. The Chimeras' turret multilasers were hammering away at the xenos, their barrels shimmering with heat, but the orks kept coming, clawing over heaps of piled corpses to try to reach the wavering troops. Slugs from the greenskins' crude guns ricocheted from the personnel carriers' armoured sides, buzzing like marsh hornets through the hazy air.

Dead and wounded Rynnsguard soldiers lay on the rubble-strewn ferrocrete behind the Chimeras, and the faces of the surviving troops were grimy masks of panic and fear. It was a look that Galleas had seen many times over the past three months. The soldiers were at the limits of their endurance. One sharp blow and the whole formation could shatter.

Just at that moment, a ragged mob of greenskins reached the barricades near the centre of the Rynnsguard line. Bellowing like bull grox, they chopped at barricade and men alike with huge, howling chainaxes, ripping through stone and flesh with equal ease. Ork guns rattled, spraying the human troops with heavy slugs at point-blank range. Blood and flesh made a fine mist in the dusty air.

The Rynnsguard squads nearest the orks fell back, screaming in terror and firing as they went. Their flight sent ripples all along the line as the rest of the defenders started to waver.

The sight of the hated xenos scorched the fog from Galleas' mind. Rage burned pure and terrible in his breast.

'For Kantor! For Dorn!' Galleas cried. The veteran sergeant broke into a run, firing as he went, and his squad charged at his back. 'Death to the greenskins!'

Boltguns hammered, the distinctive double bang of the mass-reactive shells echoing across the square. Galleas and his squad were Sternguard veterans, specialists at ranged combat; they fired single shots to conserve their dwindling stores of ammunition, and every one found its lethal mark. Orks toppled with their heads blown away or their vital organs shredded. The barricade was cleared in a single volley, and the retreating troops hesitated. Heads turned, questing faces seeking the source of their salvation.

Galleas put a bolt through the throat of another greenskin. Switching his bolter to his left hand, he reached for the power sword at his hip. It was called Night's Edge, an ancient blade and a relic of the Chapter – perhaps one of the last of its kind left on Rynn's World. The sword blazed with holy fire, its energy field crackling hungrily in the dust-laden air.

'There is only the Emperor!' the sergeant shouted, his booming voice carrying across the battlefield.

'*He is our shield and our protector!*' the squad replied.

The fierce oath galvanised the exhausted Rynnsguard. At the sight of the Emperor's Angels of Death, they regained their courage and surged forward again, lasguns blazing at the enemy.

Another wave of greenskins reached the barricade, guns roaring. Heavy slugs rang from Galleas' war-plate. Men screamed and fell, hands grasping at their wounds. Juno drew his short sword and Amador followed suit, brandishing his combat knife and bellowing a challenge at the xenos. As one, the Crimson Fists put on a burst of speed and vaulted the corpse-strewn barricade, plunging blade first into the teeth of the oncoming horde.

Night's Edge carved a burning arc through two howling greenskins, slicing crude armour and splitting torsos with ease. Galleas fired point-blank at snarling ork faces, so close that the rounds had already struck home before their rocket motors could ignite. Crude axes and cleavers of sharpened hull metal hammered at his thick pauldrons and breast-plate, but the sergeant's sacred wargear turned powerful blows aside. As the greenskins fell, Galleas pushed deeper into the mob, driving the wedge towards the breach in the curtain wall one bloody step at a time.

An ork lunged at Galleas from his right, brandishing a chainaxe; there was a flash of razor-edged adamantium and the ork's head parted from his shoulders mid-stride. Titus Juno stepped over the twitching body and ducked the swing of another xenos in the same motion. His gleaming blade flickered again, sure and certain, finding a chink in the ork's armour and spearing its heart. One of the very best melee fighters in the Chapter, Juno was in his element here, reading the swirling battle like a regicide board and plotting his attacks four moves in advance. He killed with an executioner's precision, swiftly and dispassionately, trusting his armour to withstand the few blows he couldn't parry or dodge.

If Juno was a cold and calculating engine of death, Amador was more akin to a frenzied grox. Roaring a constant stream of rage and hate at the xenos, he crashed headlong into them, stabbing and slashing with his monomolecular knife. He sliced tendons and opened throats, speared eyes and severed spines, his armour splashed with layers of sticky gore. He was a butcher, rendering his foes into piles of split bones and ragged meat.

Behind the tip of the wedge, the rest of the squad fired their bolters to left and right, keeping the squad's flanks clear. Lasgun fire from the barricade added to the carnage, striking the greenskins in the side and rear as they tried to circle behind the Space Marines. The orks' attack faltered as the xenos were torn between attacking the Adeptus Astartes in their midst or throwing themselves at the Rynnsguard barricade.

The squad was less than thirty metres from the breach now. Bolter fire and volleys from the barricade had divided the greenskins, and their bloodthirsty cries were growing more frustrated and confused with every passing moment. Galleas knew his squad had the upper hand, having seen this sort of fight play out countless times over the past three months. He and his squad would plug the breach, keeping the rest of the xenos at bay while the Rynnsguard counterattacked and finished off the orks on this side of the wall. After that, one of the Chimeras would be rushed forward to physically block the hole in the wall until a civilian labour gang could be found to seal it up with rubble. By then, Galleas and his brothers would be long gone, rushing to the next crisis point along the struggling Imperial line.

An ork cleaver smashed against the side of Galleas' helm. He staggered a step, but as the greenskin lunged for his throat he shot it in the knee, blowing the ork's leg off. The brute fell forward onto Night's Edge, the point of the power sword spearing the greenskin through its open mouth and bursting from the back of its skull. The sergeant fired twice more, dropping the two orks next in line before wrenching the burning blade free. A red sigil flashed in his helmet display, warning him that the bolter's box magazine was down to its last nine shots.

Now the greenskins' war cries were turning to shouts of despair as their attack lost its momentum and their numbers dwindled. The xenos were close to their breaking point.

'Forward, brothers!' the sergeant cried – and a deep-throated roar answered from the crowded depths of the breach.

More greenskins came pouring from the jagged hole in the curtain wall, driven forcibly into the square by the source of the bestial war cry. The xenos mob surged towards Galleas again, all but shoved against the deadly blades at the front of the wedge. The sergeant struck the head from one bellowing ork and shot another in the chest, but his attention was focused on the massive figure emerging from the breach just twenty metres away.

The ork warboss was huge, easily twice the size of the greenskin brutes on the near side of the wall. His broad chest and shoulders were armoured in rough plates of midnight blue, carved from the wreck of a Crimson Fists tank, and a chain of scorched human hands hung about his corded neck. Tattoos of curling flames in dark ink wound their way up the ork's powerful forearms and climbed the side of his leering face. Beneath a dull, riveted metal plate that covered the warboss' misshapen forehead, red beady eyes fixed balefully on Galleas and his squad. A ragged red banner, painted with the crude image of a burning human, rose on a metal pole from the ork's back. Three Crimson Fists helmets, their surfaces blackened by intense heat, hung from the top of the warboss' banner pole.

Rottshrek! Galleas' hearts burned with rage at the sight of the giant ork. One of Snagrod's chief lieutenants, Rottshrek's cunning and cruelty were well known to the city's beleaguered defenders. His death would be a rare, bright moment in the dark days of the city's siege.

Galleas raised Night's Edge in challenge. 'Hear me, monster!' he shouted. 'I am Sandor Galleas of the Crimson Fists! Come and face me, if you dare!'

Rottshrek glared down at the veteran sergeant. His thick lips drew back in a malevolent grin. Raising a giant chain-axe in one hand and a massive belt-fed gun in the other, the warboss threw back his horned head and roared.

'*WAAAAAAAAAAAAAAGHHHH!!!*'

The orks on the near side of the wall took up the cry at once, bellowing until the smoke-filled skies trembled at the sound. Undaunted, Galleas pressed forward, opening the throat of one howling ork and shooting another through the eye.

'Rottshrek is mine!' Galleas called out to his brothers, readying himself for the warboss' charge.

But Rottshrek did not move. The warboss stood at the mouth of the breach, grinning cruelly, axe still raised – not in challenge, Galleas suddenly realised, but as a signal to the rest of the mob.

A chorus of spitting, sulphurous roars arced high overhead. Galleas glanced upwards and saw a mob of orks cross the top of the curtain wall on long tails of billowing smoke and orange flame. The greenskins wore massive rockets strapped to their backs, which hurled them like poorly aimed thunderbolts onto the rear of the Imperial lines. Long handled grenades tumbled from the rocket troopers' hands, followed by chattering bursts from their belt-fed guns. Blasts ripped through the ranks of the Rynnsguard platoons, shredding men with clouds of high-velocity shrapnel. A Chimera exploded as a grenade found a weak spot on its upper deck, detonating its fuel cells.

The rocket troops landed amongst the stunned Rynnsguard, laughing like daemons as they riddled men with bullets or chopped them down with hatchets. Several of the orks' rocket packs exploded like bombs, which sowed further carnage through the Imperial troops. Burning fuel splashed over the tightly packed men, setting many alight.

Surrounded by orks on all sides, Galleas watched help-lessly as the Rynnsguard fell back from the rocket troops' surprise assault. The tide of battle had turned in a single instant, and now the Crimson Fists were trapped.

CHAPTER TWO

ALL IS LOST

ZONA 13 COMMERCIA, NEW RYNN CITY
DAY 86

The Rynnsguard fled in panic, and the ork mobs set off after them, howling for blood. The greenskins leapt the barricades and poured in a green flood through the gaps between the Chimeras. Others turned their attention to the transports, battering at them with their crude weapons and wedging grenades into wheel wells and under turrets. One of the vehicles was immobilised and caught fire almost at once; those of the crew who managed to throw open the hatches and escape the flames were torn to pieces by the orks.

Rottshrek bellowed in triumph and shouted orders in the greenskins' bestial tongue. The xenos closest to Galleas and his squad roared in reply and charged the Crimson Fists from all sides. The warboss himself surged from the breach, a cadre of armoured, flamethrower-wielding orks lumbering along in his wake.

Galleas shot a charging greenskin in the throat. 'Formation

Epsilon!' he barked, and the veterans immediately shifted from a wedge into a hollow diamond with Tauros in the centre. Boltguns hammered in all directions, cutting down the closest orks, but for every xenos slain, two more were ready to take its place. Still more greenskins were pouring from the breach now, a tide of alien filth spreading inexorably across the square.

'*What do we do, brother?*' Tauros called over the vox. '*Fall back to the Rhino, or hold our ground here?*'

'I say we make our stand here!' Amador cried. He caught a lunging ork beneath the chin with his combat knife and shouldered its twitching body aside. 'The wall is lost. All we can do now is die with honour, and try to take Rottshrek with us!'

'*We can still reach the transport,*' Valentus countered. He was now at the point of the diamond facing the distant Rhino. '*The Ceres Protocol demands that we survive by any means necessary, brother, and you well know it.*'

Juno stepped aside from the sweep of a greenskin's axe and stabbed his attacker in the eye. 'Rottshrek is coming for us,' he said, his voice as calm as if he were training at the Arx Tyrannus. 'If we kill him, it might throw the ork attack in this sector into confusion.'

'*Or it might not.*'

Juno shrugged. 'The warboss would be dead either way.'

Galleas ducked the swipe of a chainaxe. Night's Edge opened the greenskin's belly and emptied its guts onto the pavement. The ork staggered, but did not fall. Screaming in rage, the xenos made to swing again, and Galleas shot it in the throat. *Six rounds left,* he thought grimly.

Another few seconds and Rottshrek would be on top of them. His greenskin retinue were already adjusting the settings on their fearsome-looking flamethrowers, intensifying the flame until it could cut through armour like a blowtorch.

Attack the warboss, or retreat? It was hardly a choice, as far as Galleas was concerned. Unfortunately, it wasn't his to make.

'Back to the Rhino!' he commanded bitterly. 'Double pace!'

Amador shouted in protest. The squad began to move, but the hot-headed Space Marine hesitated, glaring at the oncoming warboss. A gap opened in the formation.

'Amador! *Move!*' Galleas snapped. A greenskin tried to take advantage of the opening to get inside the formation, but the veteran sergeant stopped him with two boltgun rounds to the chest. *Four rounds left.*

A pair of orks leapt on Amador, trying to grapple his arms and pull him down. The Crimson Fist killed one with an elbow to the side of the head, then slashed open the throat of the second. He spread his arms to Rottshrek in invitation. 'Come and get me!' he bellowed angrily. 'Here I am, xenos! What are you waiting for?'

Cursing, Galleas locked his bolter into a travel stay on his backpack and lunged for Amador, grabbing the Space Marine by the edge of his pauldron. 'I gave you an order, brother!' he yelled, dragging Amador back. 'Get into formation before you get the rest of us killed!'

Amador shouted angrily and tore free of Galleas' grip, but did as he was told. Rottshrek was just ten metres away now, shoving his way through the press.

The Crimson Fists withdrew quickly, Valentus clearing the path with his boltgun and a few carefully tossed grenades. Resistance at the barricade had collapsed, and the surviving

Chimeras were falling back as well, gunning their engines and driving over anything in their path. The greenskins closed in around the Space Marines from three sides, firing point-blank with their crude guns. Slugs buzzed through the formation. Galleas was hit repeatedly, but the curved plates of his armour turned the impacts aside.

Orks rushed at the rear of the formation again and again, trying to force their way in amongst the Space Marines, but their strength and speed was a poor match for the veterans' skill. They passed through a gap in the abandoned barricade, stepping over the bloody corpses of orks and men. Galleas split the skull of a howling greenskin and chanced a quick glance over his shoulder. The orks still surrounded them, but the Rhino was now just eighteen metres away.

'Salazar, when we get to the transport, get inside and get the engine going,' Galleas said over the vox. 'We'll hold outside the ramp until you're ready to move–'

Rottshrek interrupted him with a bellowed command. With a coughing roar and half a dozen twisting columns of smoke, the surviving orks with rocket packs leapt into the sky around Galleas' squad and fell into the formation's midst.

The greenskins cackled like fiends, blazing away with their guns as they came down on the Crimson Fists. Galleas saw Juno hit by a burst of ork slugs; the warrior staggered beneath the impacts but still managed to sever the head of one ork as it flashed by. The rocket pack, now completely unguided, dived into the ferrocrete and exploded right behind Galleas. Red-hot shrapnel rang off the sergeant's armour, and the blast knocked him from his feet.

Galleas landed hard, taking the impact on his armoured shoulder. He rolled left, purely on reflex, noting absently that the back of his arms and legs were on fire from the burning rocket fuel. An ork leapt atop him, brandishing an axe; the sergeant buried Night's Edge in the greenskin's side and kicked the corpse away.

Another fiery blast roared over Galleas, this time from further away. He rolled to his feet and greenskins came at him from all sides, hacking at him with cleavers and blasting away with their guns. A slug struck him in the cheek, half-wrenching his head around; heavy blows smashed into his back and side, and another glanced from the silver aquila on his chest. Hands grabbed at his pauldrons and backpack, trying to pull him from his feet. Snarling an oath, Galleas lashed out with Night's Edge, severing limbs and splitting skulls. The surviving orks fell back a step, and he charged to the right, shouldering a stunned xenos aside and widening the space around him further.

The Crimson Fists' defensive formation had been broken by the unexpected assault. Other greenskins had seen their chance and rushed into the gaps, dividing the Space Marines further. Now each of the veterans fought alone, surrounded by orks.

Rottshrek and his bodyguards were almost on top of them. A grim sense of foreboding stole over Galleas, but the veteran angrily pushed the feeling aside. 'Keep moving!' he yelled over the vox. 'Look to your brothers and get to the Rhino!'

Galleas saw Juno start moving first, cutting a path through the mob towards the waiting transport. Tauros moved next, followed by Salazar. The sergeant turned, searching for Amador, but the brash Space Marine was nowhere to be seen. Cursing, Galleas fell back, unclipping his bolter again. He caught sight of Royas, struggling to make headway against a trio of orks, and shot one of the greenskins in the head. *Three rounds.*

Olivar was close by, intoning the Litanies of Hate as he held four axe-wielding orks at bay. Galleas headed in his direction, coming up behind one of the orks and splitting him from shoulder to waist. When the greenskins spun to face the new threat, Olivar killed another with his knife. The sergeant indicated the Rhino with the point of his sword and Olivar nodded, his recitation of the litany never skipping a beat. Together, the two Crimson Fists began to fight their way across the square.

Juno reached them within moments, carving his way through a pair of orks. Galleas spied Valentus a few metres away, grappling with a massive greenskin. Taking aim, he put a bolt-round into the side of the ork's head. *Two rounds.*

Five metres away, Salazar cut down an ork with his bolter and shouldered another aside. Shouting an oath, he forced his way through the press of orks and reached the side of the transport. Tossing his boltgun onto the Rhino's top deck, he began to pull himself up to the driver's hatch.

'Get to the ramp!' Galleas ordered the squad. 'Move!'

He pushed forward, blocking an ork's cleaver with the side of his bolter and stabbing the xenos through the chest. Juno shouted a warning. 'Look out!'

The sergeant glanced back over his shoulder – and saw Rottshrek, less than ten metres away. Beside the warboss was a hulking ork wearing thick goggles and carrying a massive energy weapon linked by thick cables to a ramshackle power supply on the greenskin's back. Grinning madly, the ork levelled the gun at the Rhino.

Galleas brought up his boltgun and fired in a single motion. His aim was true, and the mass-reactive shell sped right at the ork's forehead – only to vanish in a flash of light as the round impacted against a force field a metre short of the target.

The ork let out a deranged laugh and pulled the trigger. There was a crackle of ozone, and a searing, blue-white arc of lightning carved its way through the melee and struck the front of the Rhino. The blast reverberated across the square like a thunderclap, ripping the front quarter of the transport open and melting one of its tracks. Salazar was blown clear, his armoured form disappearing in a spray of molten fragments.

Rottshrek bellowed in triumph. Now there would be no escape.

The warboss charged. He came upon Veteran Brother Caron, fighting valiantly against three determined green-skins. Galleas shouted a warning, but it was too late. Rottshrek raised his combi-weapon and fired, unleashing a stream of slugs that cut down two of Caron's attackers and smashed into the Space Marine's side. Caron staggered, stunned by the impacts, and the warboss' giant axe bit into his neck. The massive blade pierced the ancient war-plate in a burst of sparks and bright, arterial blood, and the centuries-old veteran collapsed, mortally wounded.

Three of the warboss' bodyguards rushed forward, eager to join in the kill – only to be cut down in a savage burst of boltgun fire. Veteran Brother Pellas Rodrigo rounded on Rottshrek, his bolter levelled at the warboss' face. At less than ten metres, Rodrigo could not possibly miss. He pulled the trigger – but the bolter's magazine was dry. Tossing the weapon aside, Rodrigo broke into a run, his combat knife ready.

Snarling, Rottshrek brought his combi-weapon around

and triggered its flamethrower attachment, bathing Rodrigo in a blast of jellied flame. The veteran staggered, screaming in agony as the burning fuel seeped past the armour's ceramite plates and melted through vulnerable joints and seams. Yet Rodrigo still came on, driving his maimed body forward with the force of his righteous rage. He managed another dozen steps before his knees gave way, toppling his burning body onto the ferrocrete.

The mob of orks surged around Galleas, forcing their way between him and his squad mates. Within moments they were isolated again and fighting for their lives. Soon, they would all be overwhelmed.

Galleas was just ten metres from the wrecked Rhino. He drove himself towards it, killing every ork in his path. He could hear Rottshrek bellowing behind him, and heavy footfalls pounding the ferrocrete. He had, at best, just a few moments before the warboss was upon him. The sergeant quickly selected the vox-sigil for the Cassar.

'Epistolary Deguerro, this is Veteran Sergeant Galleas. Containment has failed. Repeat, containment has failed. The orks have broken through. Advise you withdraw all remaining troops to the Residentia Ultris while there is still time.'

His duty fulfilled, Galleas switched channels once more. The battle at Jadeberry Hill reverberated in his ears.

'They're getting too close! We can't hold them!'

'Squad Estrelas is down to its last five rounds.'

'No one is coming! We've got to pull back!'

Galleas' spirits fell. The psykers had been wrong after all.

He reached the front of the transport. Ork slugs slammed into his back and legs; he stumbled against the Rhino's armoured prow, but did not fall. Readying his bolter, he stepped around the front corner of the vehicle and scanned the eastern side of the square. The orks were rampaging through the medicae tents, slaughtering the wounded. The tents of the command post had been shredded, and the regimental officers lay in bloody heaps on the ground.

The siege gun battery had been abandoned, its gunners having taken flight as soon as the barricade fell. The portable winch still stood next to the pallet of massive artillery shells.

A shadow fell over Galleas. He could hear the ragged whine of the warboss' chainaxe.

The sergeant calmly raised his bolter. *One round left.*

The axe crashed into his back. Galleas pulled the trigger. As he did so, the voice of Huron Grim rang in his ear.

'There's someone at the bottom of the hill–'

The rest was lost as Galleas' shell hit the nose of one of the artillery rounds and the world vanished in a blaze of light.

CHAPTER THREE

HOUSEHOLD GODS

ZONA 13 COMMERCIA, NEW RYNN CITY
DAY –

Darkness. An absolute emptiness: weightless, depthless, silent. It is the first thing he is aware of after the blast.

Is this death? Galleas wonders dimly.

And then the pain hits, crashing down on him out of the black-ness like a mountainous wave on a moonless sea. He has never felt such agony before, not even during his time as an aspirant, when his body was remade in Rogal Dorn's image.

The wave crushes him, driving him under.

It is like when he was a child, lying on a boat at night out on the Bitter Sea. He learns to ride the waves, enduring each ter-rible crest for the relative peace of the trough on the far side. Between waves, he tries to think, to make sense of the darkness.

He cannot move. He cannot tell if he is upright or prone. After a time he wonders whether his body exists at all, or if his awareness has simply been decanted into something else entirely. He wonders if this is what the ancients feel, the Dreadnoughts slumbering in their vaults beneath the Arx Tyrannus. But then he remembers that the Chapter monastery is gone, and the ancients along with it.

Ages pass. The waves grow further apart. His senses start to return. He becomes aware of his extremities, and then the armour encasing them. Slowly, patiently, he tries to move his fingers. That's when he learns how broken he truly is.

He is blind. He is deaf. Most of his bones are shattered. Blast effect, he thinks. Hydrostatic shock. His armour withstood the blast, but not the flesh beneath.

He meditates. He calms his mind. He rides the waves, and he waits.

The world shifts. Something tugs at his armour. Once. Twice. His mind reacts, commanding his body to strike, but his limbs do not respond. The helplessness he feels is worse than terror, worse than shame. It nearly overwhelms him.

The tugging stops. For the first time, he is grateful for the emptiness.

There is a blaze of light, startling in its intensity. After so long in darkness, the sensory input nearly overwhelms him. He struggles to breathe, to focus, to think past the cascade of jangling nerves and take in this new source of data.

His helmet display is resetting. Vague sounds – sounds! – impinge on his mind. He cannot make out what they mean. They are just blurry tones, rising and falling in his ears.

Shades of dark blue and iron grey swim before his eyes. It takes a moment to realise that he is staring up at an overcast sky, lit by the icy glow of a full moon.

Vague figures rear above him. He feels a tug on his armour. Combat reflexes make his muscles twitch and his bones ache.

The figures are speaking. The tones are sharp. They are arguing with one another, he realises. Arguing over him.

His eyes adjust, and the figures take on form. They are human, not ork. A man and a woman, clad in battered flak armour, the Rynnsguard crest on their shoulders. His eyes go automatically to their collars. She is an infantry officer, a lieutenant, and he a medic.

He's nothing like us, *the medic's lips say.* It won't do any good.

The lieutenant scowls. He's the best chance we've got. *She reaches over him, grabbing the medic by the arm. Tendons stand out along the back of her hand.* If you don't give it to him, I will.

He doesn't understand what they are talking about, and doesn't particularly care. He tries to speak, to ask them about his brothers, but his throat is dry as leather.

He concentrates on his right hand. His fingers twitch, sending waves of pain along his arm.

The pain becomes agony. The wave rises above him. He fights it this time, riding the crest for as long as he can.

His hand grips the lieutenant's wrist–

Galleas woke to the sound of voices.

'His vital humours haven't changed in three days. Something must be wrong with the suit's life signs monitor–'

'It's not a *suit*. Show some respect. That's aquila-pattern power armour. Six thousand years old, forged by the holy artificers at Arcadia Planitia. It's *sacred*.'

'It's *damaged*. Surely even you can see that?'

'Well, superficially, perhaps, but I assure you, its machine-spirit is strong.'

'I need more than assurances, Oros. I need to be *certain*. Our lives depend on it.'

The veteran sergeant opened his eyes. Instead of sky, he saw a network of rusting conduits and cracked ferrocrete, covered in patches of black mould. A wall of peeling flakboard rose to his right. Shadows danced across its surface, stirred by the ruddy glow of candlelight.

Two men stood at his feet, locked in a heated debate. One was the medic he'd seen before, a young Rynnsworlder with pinched features and intense, dark eyes. The other was a red-robed enginseer, his features hidden behind a black respirator mask. The enginseer's servo-arm was tucked behind his shoulder, and his gloved hands were held nervously against his chest. The lenses of the mask glowed with a pale, yellow light.

'I-I'm only a novitiate,' he protested, staring down at Galleas. 'I know none of the proper rites.'

The medic frowned. 'I'm not asking for ceremony, Oros. I just want you to inspect the life signs monitor and make adjustments if necessary.'

The enginseer wrung his hands. After a moment, he sighed and bent over Galleas. Long, segmented mechadendrites extended from sockets along the novitiate's back. 'Omnissiah forgive me,' he murmured, reaching for an access panel at the Space Marine's waist.

'Touch my wargear, enginseer, and the Omnissiah will be the least of your concerns,' Galleas rasped.

Oros recoiled, mechadendrites lashing in surprise. '*Deus Machina!* He's alive!'

The medic was no less shocked. 'Get the lieutenant,' he hissed. 'Hurry!'

Galleas paid little mind as the enginseer scurried off into the darkness. His attention had already turned inwards, gauging the condition of his battered body. His bones ached, but everything seemed to be in its proper place. His fingers and toes obeyed his commands. There was a faint, medicinal taste in his mouth. His neuroglottis identified it as a combination of antivirals, electrolyte boosters and synthetic healing stimulants: typical field medicines for injured Rynnsguard soldiers, but wasted on one such as he.

The status sigils on his helmet display were normal. His armour was not damaged, despite what the medic believed. Frowning in irritation, he slowly sat upright and took in his surroundings, his enhanced senses easily penetrating the gloom.

From the damp on the walls and the ambient temperature, he surmised he was below ground – likely a sub-level of one of the city's hab units. Dust hung thick in the dank air, and heaps of broken ferrocrete and other debris littered the floor. Much of the candlelight came from the top of a large crate near the wall to Galleas' left. A gaudy plastek icon of the Emperor – likely a hab resident's household god – formed the centrepiece of a shrine atop the crate's dented surface. A middle-aged priest in stained Ecclesiarchal robes knelt in the grit before the altar. As Galleas stirred, the priest turned to face him and bent his head in supplication, making the sign of the aquila over his heart.

The medic visibly gathered his resolve and took a step towards Galleas. 'Emperor be praised,' he said hesitantly. 'I am Regimental Field Medic Vega, my lord. How do you feel?'

Galleas ignored the man. He glanced about, searching the floor around him for his weapons, but they were nowhere to be found. Even his bolt pistol was gone, no doubt torn from its holster by the force of the blast. Dismayed, he blinked at the icon set on the margin on his helmet display, switching over to the vox settings and choosing the sigil for the Cassar. 'This is Veteran Sergeant Galleas, calling the Cassar. Respond.' A roar of static and spikes of howling feedback were the only reply.

Vega stepped closer. His uniform and armour were filthy, the tough fabric reeking of mildew and old sweat. He had a long face, shadowed by dark stubble, and his cheeks were hollowed by hunger and fatigue. 'Are… are you well?'

Galleas turned his attention on the medic. 'Where is this place? What am I doing here?'

Vega blanched at the sharp tone in the sergeant's voice. 'We're in a hab unit in Zona Thirteen Commercia,' he answered quickly. 'Just a few hundred metres from Leonis Square, where we found you.' He gestured past Galleas' shoulder. 'It's a wonder we got to the three of you before the xenos did.'

Galleas whirled. A pair of blue-armoured forms were stretched out amid the puddles and the heaps of broken ferrocrete. Olivar and Juno, he saw at once. They were unmoving, and the lenses of their helmets were dark.

Grimacing in pain, the veteran sergeant half-walked, half-crawled to where his brothers lay. Vega hastened after him, his weary face apprehensive.

'They still live,' he told Galleas. 'Just barely, I think. Their humours are… Well, they're unlike anything I've seen before.'

Galleas knelt beside Juno and rolled him partially onto his side in order to check the suit's power plant. As he expected, the impact of the blast had overloaded the suit's machine-spirit and forced it into slumber. The sergeant cleared his mind and performed the Rite of Awakening, touching the system runes in the proscribed order to restore the spirit to wakefulness. Next, he checked the suit's auto-dispensary. The vials were all full, but not of the nerve blockers and healing stimulants he expected.

He turned back to Vega. 'What is the meaning of this?' he growled, pointing to the vials. 'These are *human* medicines.'

'It was all we had,' a hard voice said. 'And no offence, but it looked as though you needed them.'

A woman in grimy flak armour and a Rynnsguard uniform stepped through an open doorway to Galleas' right. She was of average height for a human and lean as a whipcord, with black hair cropped in a military cut and stern, aristocratic features. She wore a laspistol and an officer's sabre at her hip, and a cut-down lascarbine was slung over her shoulder. The woman was accompanied by Enginseer Oros and another soldier: a stocky, middle-aged sergeant with flinty eyes and a rough, weathered face. He carried a laspistol of his own and a battle-scarred combat shotgun cradled in his left arm.

Galleas recognised the lieutenant at once. *If you don't give it to him, I will.*

'This was your doing?'

If the lieutenant was intimidated at all by Galleas' forbidding tone, she didn't show it. 'If you're asking who gave the order, then yes,' she said coolly.

There was a deep hum, more felt than heard, as Juno's armour woke. Galleas turned to Olivar next. His purity seals and the parchment page upon his shoulder were tattered and scorched. The polished silver aquila upon his chest glimmered beneath a thin layer of dust and ash.

Like Juno's, Olivar's helm was dark. A jagged chunk of metal was embedded in the right eye socket, surrounded by a thick crust of dried blood.

'He is weak, but stable,' Vega said. 'I… thought it best to leave the shrapnel in. I am no chirurgeon, and if it's pressing on his brain–'

Galleas took hold of the piece of shrapnel and tore it free. Blood and viscera welled up in the shattered lens socket. He dropped the chunk of metal at Vega's feet and set about reviving Olivar's armour.

'We tried to help as best we could,' the lieutenant said. 'You were all badly injured, and your auto-dispensaries were empty. So we gave you what we had, and brought you someplace secure where you could recover.'

'A waste of time and resources,' Galleas declared. 'We would have recovered well enough on our own.'

The lieutenant's jaw clenched as she bit back an angry reply. Her sergeant caught the look on her face and cleared his throat. 'Begging your pardon, my lord, but not if the scavengers had got to you first. From the looks of things, you'd been out there since the breach.'

'What of it? Another few hours at most, and we would have been able–'

'The breach was eleven days ago,' the lieutenant shot back. 'Believe me, it's a genuine miracle any of you are still alive.'

'Emperor be praised,' the priest intoned. '*Deus gloriosa!*'

The news took Galleas aback. *Eleven days, locked in darkness? The blast came closer to killing me than I thought.*

The lieutenant stared at the priest. After a moment she sighed, pinching at the corners of her eyes with a dirt-streaked hand.

'My apologies,' she said to Galleas. 'The past few weeks have been… difficult.' She straightened, turning back to face the towering Space Marine. 'I am Lieutenant Antonia Mitra, Second Platoon, Forty-Second Territorial Infantry

Regiment.' Mitra nodded at the stocky, older Rynnsguard. 'This is Kazimir, my platoon sergeant. You've already met Oros and Vega. The holy man is Preacher Gomez.'

'Where are the others?' Galleas asked.

Mitra gestured towards the doorway. 'I've got twenty-four men left. They're covering the approaches to the sub-level.'

The Crimson Fist shook his head. 'My squad. Where are the rest of my brothers?'

'The rest?' Mitra frowned. 'We only found the three of you.'

'How many are missing, my lord?' Kazimir asked.

Galleas paused. In his mind's eye, he saw Rottshrek's axe chopping into Caron's neck. Rodrigo, staggering, wreathed in clinging flames.

'Five. There are five others still out there.'

Mitra gave Kazimir a questioning look. The older man shrugged.

'It was dark, and we were moving fast,' Kazimir said. 'We might have missed them.'

'Damn it, sergeant–'

Galleas cut them off. 'Why are you still here?' he demanded.

Mitra's eyes narrowed as she gazed up at the Space Marine. 'I'm sorry?'

'When it was clear that the breach couldn't be contained, I contacted the Cassar and recommended an immediate withdrawal. If that was eleven days ago, what are you still doing here?'

Mitra's frown deepened. Sergeant Kazimir shifted uncomfortably and looked away.

'We were holding a section of wall in Zona Twenty-one when the order came down from the Cassar,' Mitra said.

'We tried to pull out, but the damned orks had got in behind us and cut us off.' Her expression grew haunted. 'Most of the regiment was destroyed trying to break out. We hid in the ruins and have been trying to stay alive ever since.'

Kazimir nodded. 'We knew the sector headquarters was in Zona Thirteen, so we came here looking for supplies. We found you instead.'

'It was the will of the divine Emperor,' Gomez said with conviction. 'I am sure of it!'

The preacher's words reminded Galleas of the Librarians' premonitions in the hours before the breach. 'Some of my brethren were outside the city, waiting for someone very important at Jadeberry Hill. Do you know what happened?'

Mitra snorted. 'We're planetary defence forces. No one ever tells us anything.'

Kazimir cleared his throat. 'Come to that, we still don't know what to call you, my lord.'

Galleas straightened. 'Veteran Sergeant Sandor Galleas, a battle-brother of the Crusade Company.' He indicated his brethren. 'This is Veteran Brother Juno, and Veteran Brother Olivar.'

Juno moved, shaking his head slowly and trying to sit up. Olivar let out a long, low groan.

At that moment, the darkness rang with warning shouts and the snarl of lasgun fire, followed by guttural war cries and the hammering of ork guns.

Sergeant Kazimir turned and dashed for the doorway without a word, unlimbering his shotgun as he went. Lieutenant Mitra cursed under her breath.

'They've found us,' she said, her expression bleak.

CHAPTER FOUR

A DUTY TO THE LIVING

ZONA 13 COMMERCIA, NEW RYNN CITY
DAY 97

Galleas looked over to the doorway, where Sergeant Kazimir leaned out into the darkness. He appeared to be listening intently. The fighting was growing more furious by the moment, punctuated by grenade blasts and the screams of dying greenskins.

'Those aren't runts,' Kazimir said grimly. 'It's a proper mob, and a big one.'

Galleas had reached the same conclusion, his enhanced senses and superbly conditioned mind sifting through the noise of battle to identify voices, weapons, numbers and distance. 'Thirty orks, perhaps six dead or wounded so far,' the veteran sergeant declared. 'Where are our weapons?'

'Back at the square,' Lieutenant Mitra said tersely. She unslung her lascarbine and checked its power load. 'Buried under bodies or blown to bits for all I know.'

'You didn't think to check?' Galleas said angrily.

'I was too busy worrying about how I was going to move

three very injured, very *heavy* Space Marines out of the square and into cover before daybreak,' Mitra shot back. 'Would you rather I'd left one of your brothers behind and brought your weapons instead?'

'Don't be ridiculous,' Juno growled. 'Of course we'd rather have the weapons.'

'There is this,' Preacher Gomez said. He turned and picked up a cloth-wrapped bundle from the altar. 'I found it near the wrecked transport. No doubt it belongs to you, my lord.'

He unwrapped the bundle with a deft movement, revealing Night's Edge. The power sword's polished blade gleamed hungrily in the ruddy candlelight. Galleas took the relic from the preacher's outstretched hands and thumbed its activation rune, feeling whole once more.

'We've got to move,' Kazimir warned. 'If this keeps up we'll bring the whole district down on our heads.'

Juno started for the door. 'I'll deal with this,' he said darkly.

Mitra stared at him. 'How, for Throne's sake? You don't have any weapons.'

'The orks have enough to spare,' Juno answered. 'I'll just help myself to a few of theirs.'

'I'm coming with you,' Olivar grated. The veteran was trying to stand, one hand pressed to his ruined eye.

'No,' Galleas commanded. To Mitra, he said, 'Is there a way out of here?'

The lieutenant nodded. 'Through the maintenance tunnels. There's an entrance just outside and to the right.'

'You want us to *run* from these animals?' Juno growled.

'We're still bound by the Ceres Protocol,' Galleas countered. 'Our deaths must serve the Chapter, not ourselves. And make no mistake, if we stay here, we die.' He gestured to Olivar. 'Now help your brother. We're getting out of here.'

For a moment, it looked as though Juno might protest. He glared at Galleas, struggling with his desire to spill xenos blood. At last he relented, shaking his head in frustration, and went to join Olivar.

Galleas sighed inwardly. He knew all too well what Juno was feeling. But duty had to come first. He turned to Mitra. 'Order the withdrawal. I'll go with Kazimir and buy you as much time as I can.' Without waiting for the lieutenant to reply, he nodded to the Rynnsguard sergeant and followed him through the doorway.

He emerged into a long, low-ceilinged corridor that stretched off into cave-like darkness to Galleas' left and right. The sounds of fighting were reverberating down the corridor from the left, lit by staccato flashes of lasgun fire. Galleas' auto-senses adjusted to the darkness at once, revealing a passageway choked with stacks of crates and piles of fallen debris.

Kazimir set off down the corridor in a low run, shoulders hunched and shotgun tucked tight against his chest, weaving amongst the crates and heaps of broken ferrocrete using the brief pulses of weapons fire as illumination. Galleas followed easily in his wake, making a mental map of the fallback route as he went.

The passageway ran for nearly a hundred metres, passing a number of side-branches that led to different blocks within the hab unit. At one point Kazimir signalled for a halt, then fished a small torch from one of his fatigue pockets. Switching on the light, he pointed out the fine line of a tripwire strung across the corridor. The wire ran to a clutch of krak grenades fixed to the bottom of a support pillar. The sergeant pointed to a splash of red paint on the pillar. 'Watch for that mark on the way back,' he warned. 'If the

Emperor is with us, that charge will bring the whole ceiling down. Just be sure you're nowhere close when it goes off.'

Galleas grunted in approval, committing the location to memory with a somatic prompt. His body would know to step over the wire even if his conscious mind was preoccupied with other tasks.

The passageway ended at a perpendicular corridor. Now the sounds of combat came from the right, and the air was thick with the noxious stink of ork gunpowder. Kazimir paused at the corner, peered to the right, and muttered an angry curse. As Galleas approached, the human ducked around the corner and started shouting at someone on the other side.

'Why in the name of the Holy Throne aren't you at the forward barricade, Corporal Vila?'

A young man's voice shouted back. 'We held as long as we could, sergeant, but there were too many of them! We must have dropped a dozen, but they were getting set for a charge. I told Miraz to toss a couple of grenades, and then we fell back.'

'You were to fall back to the second barricade, corporal, not all the way back here!'

Galleas turned the corner. The passageway was largely identical to the one he had just left, though here the Rynnsguard troops had gone to some effort to create firing positions and barricades out of the available debris. Eight metres further on, one squad was huddled against a low wall of broken ferrocrete and structural steel. The soldiers were a mix of men and women, young and middle-aged, most with the leathery skin and deep-set eyes of combine workers. They stared at him with a kind of weary dread as he came striding up the corridor, his power sword crackling like a brand.

Corporal Vila was a young, handsome man with quick, dark eyes and a roguish moustache that hinted at an easy life in the city. He was tucked up tight against a large slab of ferrocrete, and an unlit cigarillo was clenched in his teeth. His expression was earnest, but his eyes were calculating as he stared up at the glowering Kazimir.

'Lorca and Torres were running low on ammo packs, so we fell back here for an ammo count. We'd just finished up and were getting ready to reinforce Ismail when you showed up.'

Sergeant Kazimir was unconvinced. He surveyed the rest of the squad. 'Any casualties?'

'Torres was hit just before we pulled out.'

'And you *left* him there?'

'He went down. There was nothing we could do for him.'

Kazimir shook his head. 'We're pulling out. Rendezvous with the lieutenant at the entrance to the maintenance tunnels. And mind the tripwire on the way back!'

Vila grinned around the cigarillo. 'Not to worry, sergeant!' He scrambled to his feet and dashed off down the passageway, leaving the rest of his squad to gather their gear and stumble after him. Kazimir waited until the last of the squad was on his feet, then turned and continued up the corridor.

The sounds of battle grew louder now with every step Galleas took. Thirty metres further on, they reached a much larger barricade of ferrocrete and rubble-filled crates. There was another Rynnsguard squad there, stubbornly trading fire with a furious greenskin mob on the far side. A hail of ork bullets chewed at the edges of the rubble pile and the xenos corpses splayed across it, kicking up sprays of blood and pulverised stone. Two dead soldiers lay stretched out on the floor behind the barricade; a third soldier, bleeding from a wound in his shoulder, was feverishly stripping the dead of weapons and ammunition.

A sputtering ork grenade came spinning over the barricade as Kazimir and Galleas approached. It hit the floor and bounced once before a small, slender figure pounced on it and hurled it back in the orks' faces. The grenade exploded a second later, amid guttural shouts and orkish screams on the far side of the rubble pile.

The grenade thrower turned at Kazimir's approach. Galleas saw it was a young woman with delicate, almost doll-like features and bright, pitiless blue eyes. She carried a heavy combat knife sheathed at her hip, and wore a string of ork tusks around her neck.

Kazimir knelt beside her. 'How you holding together, corporal?'

'I've got two dead, and we're running low on power packs,' Ismail shouted back. 'Where in the cold hells are Vila and second squad? The greenskins are almost on top of us!'

'Get your people ready to move,' Kazimir told her. 'When you're ready, toss some grenades and we'll pull back to the main corridor.'

Ismail gave him a bleak grin. 'Sure, sergeant. If you can talk the orks into giving us a couple more of theirs I'll see what I can do.'

Galleas took in the tactical situation with a glance and switched off his power sword. He strode past Kazimir and up to the barricade, his midnight-blue armour nearly invisible in the darkness of the corridor. A dozen ork bodies filled the corridor on the opposite side of the barrier, torn by shrapnel or pierced by lasgun fire. Twenty metres further back, a large mob of greenskins was blasting away at the barricade with their oversized guns and working up their courage for another frontal assault.

'Pull your soldiers back, Sergeant Kazimir,' he said. 'I will hold the xenos filth here while you make your escape.'

Kazimir knew better than to argue. 'Very good, my lord.' He grabbed Ismail by the shoulder and hauled her onto her feet. 'Get your people moving, corporal! Go!'

Ismail's squad needed little encouragement. At the corporal's command, the soldiers fired off a last volley at the greenskins, then fell back from the barricade and ran down the passageway. Kazimir went last, backing his way along the corridor with his shotgun at the ready.

The orks howled in fury as the lasgun bolts tore through their ranks. Two fell dead with smoking holes in their skulls. The rest emptied their guns at the barricade and broke into a maddened charge.

Galleas felt his hearts quicken as the enemy drew near. His hand tightened on the hilt of his blade.

Remember the protocol, he told himself.

Bloodthirsty howls shook the air as the first orks reached the barricade. Beady eyes glinting, slavering jaws agape, they scrambled over the broken ferrocrete in search of easy prey.

Galleas kindled Night's Edge, filling the corridor with a blaze of angry light. 'For Kantor! For Dorn!' he roared. 'Vengeance for the fallen!'

The power sword carved a burning arc through the dank air, severing arms and splitting skulls. Steaming blood spattered the corridor walls. Three greenskins died in as many seconds, and the rest bellowed like panicked grox before the veteran sergeant's furious attack. Galleas surged forward, blood singing through his veins, hungry for the chance to slaughter his foes.

Here the greenskins' numbers worked against them. The corridor was only wide enough for three orks to move abreast, and they tripped one another up trying to clear the shifting rubble of the makeshift barricade. The front rank of xenos was driven onto the shifting rubble by the mass of greenskins pushing from behind, all but forcing them onto Galleas' sword. Bodies piled one atop another along the barrier, the stones beneath growing slick and treacherous with gore.

Standing alone against the horde, Galleas was the image of a stalwart son of Dorn. He would not yield so much as a centimetre to the orks, and when the pile of bodies became a barrier of its own, he climbed onto the broken ferrocrete to continue the fight.

Ork slugs began to gouge the walls of the corridor and buzz past Galleas' head. The greenskins further down the passageway had started to fire over the heads of those in front. The unaimed fire did more harm to the xenos than good, killing several of the greenskins and frustrating the rest.

Finally, it became too much. The orks fell back from the barricade, pushing now against those jammed into the corridor behind them. The sudden retreat provided Galleas with a fresh opportunity for carnage. Like a starving man contemplating a feast, he started to work his way across the tangle of bodies on the far side of the barricade.

A volley of slugs struck Galleas in rapid succession, bouncing off the curved surfaces of his pauldrons or flattening against his breastplate. He was a much easier target now without the barricade to shield him.

Dead greenskins were piled in the corridor almost knee-deep; Galleas reckoned he'd killed nearly a score of the xenos in the space of less than five minutes, but the rest of the mob showed no signs of retreating. The hailstorm of heavy slugs never slackened. The veteran sergeant knew in the back of his mind that sooner or later, one of those bullets would strike a vulnerable joint or a weak spot in his armour, and his fate would be sealed. At that moment, consumed by hatred and the need for revenge, it seemed like a cheap price to pay.

Remember the protocol.

Galleas hesitated, torn between the demands of honour and vengeance. *The survival of the Chapter must come first.*

The orks continued to retreat, opening a corpse-choked space between them and Galleas. Gritting his teeth, the Space Marine ripped a clutch of grenades from a dead ork's belt, pulled the pins and threw them after the flee-ing greenskins. By the time they detonated amid the rear ranks of the struggling xenos, he had deactivated Night's Edge and was running the other way, back across the aban-doned barricade.

The greenskins recovered from the thunderous blasts within moments, pushing the dead and wounded aside and charging after Galleas. Ork slugs filled the corridor, more than a few striking the Crimson Fist as he ran. Again, his sacred wargear turned aside the heavy rounds, and Gal-leas offered a short prayer to the armour's machine-spirit as he rounded the corner and headed for the entrance to the maintenance tunnels at the far end of the passageway.

His hopes that the night-blind orks might miss the branch corridor in their haste proved to be short-lived; within moments the sounds of pursuit echoed down the passageway after Galleas, followed by another fusillade of shots. Slugs droned past his helmet and smacked into his armoured backpack.

The veteran sergeant was just two metres short of the tripwire when an ork bullet struck him in the back of the knee. Searing pain lanced up his right leg, mitigated only slightly by the weak nerve blocker his suit's auto-dispensary fed into his bloodstream. Galleas fell, hands outstretched, his analytical mind gauging the precise distance between himself and the invisible metal wire stretching across the passageway. At the last moment, he launched himself forward with his left foot, clearing the wire with millimetres to spare and tucking into a shoulder roll on the far side.

Galleas lurched to his feet and kept going, blocking the pain of his injured knee from his mind. An icon flashed at the margins of his helmet display, warning him of damage to the joint actuator. He pressed on, the orks gaining ground now by the moment.

He was halfway down the corridor when the greenskins hit the tripwire. Four blasts in quick succession ripped through the passageway, and then the whole hab unit seemed to shake as the support column collapsed and brought part of the ceiling down with it.

Galleas stumbled for a second time as the floor bucked beneath his feet. A grinding roar, like an avalanche, raced along the passageway after him. He picked up speed, running blindly through a billowing cloud of dust.

The sound of the collapsing corridor rose to a bone-shaking crescendo, and then abruptly ceased. Galleas ran on for a few metres more, then risked a glance over his shoulder to gauge the devastation.

The pall of dust was still settling, but the veteran sergeant's enhanced vision was keen enough to discern a jumble of massive ferrocrete slabs slanting at steep angles across the passageway. Dozens of greenskins had been crushed in the collapse. Within moments, however, angry shouts echoed through the murk, and more orks could be seen forcing their way through gaps between the fallen slabs.

The blast hadn't sealed the corridor as Kazimir had hoped. At best, it had bought Galleas' brothers and the beleaguered Rynnsguard no more than a minute before the xenos were upon them again.

The doorway to the maintenance tunnels was just another ten metres down the passageway. Galleas burst through the half-open doorway, nearly pitching Sergeant Kazimir down a narrow flight of curving metal stairs on the other side.

'What are you still doing here?' the veteran sergeant demanded. The air inside the stairwell was dank, smelling of old stone and river mud. Galleas gripped the door's rusting metal handle and tried to push it shut. The hinges squealed in protest, refusing to budge.

'Someone had to stay behind and show you the way,' Kazimir replied. 'How else did you expect to find us?'

Galleas put his shoulder to the door and braced one foot against the opposite wall. 'Footprints,' he growled, throwing his full weight against the metal barrier. 'Thermal traces. Scent. Just... like... the orks.'

The rusted hinges screeched. Then, centimetre by centimetre, they began to give. Over the piercing squeal of metal, Galleas heard the guttural howls of greenskins and the swelling thunder of hob-nailed boots. Kazimir heard it, too. The Rynnsguard sergeant pulled a frag grenade from his belt, primed it, and tossed it through the narrowing gap between door and jamb. It went off with a muffled thud just as the portal clanged shut.

There wasn't a lock, as far as Galleas could see. Frowning,

he activated Night's Edge. As the first greenskins began hammering on the other side of the door, he brought the flat of the power sword up to the topmost hinge. The metal blistered and then started to soften at the touch of the weapon's power field. Galleas quickly did the same to the middle and bottom hinges, effectively welding them shut.

'Will it hold?' Kazimir asked.

A terrible, clanging racket filled the stairwell, and half a dozen bullet impacts dimpled the near side of the door. Howls of pain and anger sounded in the corridor.

'Not for long,' Galleas said grimly. 'Go, Sergeant Kazimir. Quickly!'

Kazimir nodded and set off down the stairs, with Galleas close behind. A dreadful racket of fists, cleavers and slugs filled the stairwell as they descended, the noise rising in volume as the bloodthirsty xenos piled up on the far side of the tunnel door.

The smells of mud and rust grew stronger the lower they went. Galleas knew from his hypno-briefings at the Cassar that the city's maintenance tunnels lay atop an extensive storm drain network, which channelled the heavy spring rains into the river that cut through the heart of the city. He reckoned they were thirty metres below ground when they reached the bottom of the stairs and emerged into a dimly lit tunnel lined with pipes and power conduits.

Corporal Ismail and half of her squad were kneeling in the rusty slime a metre along the tunnel to Galleas' left, their lasguns trained on the stairwell door. Kazimir saw them and spat a sulphurous curse.

'Ismail, what part of *withdraw* don't you understand?' he barked.

'You expected me to leave the two of you to get away

from the greenskins on your own?' the hard-eyed corporal shot back.

Kazimir jerked a thumb at Galleas. 'He's a *Space Marine*, you halfwit. He's worth a regiment of you lot.'

Ismail's sharp reply was lost in a series of loud blasts that echoed down the stairway. Galleas heard the tunnel door hit the far wall of the upper stairwell with a muted clang.

'The orks have broken through,' he snapped. *'Move.'*

The Rynnsguard obeyed without thinking, galvanised by the veteran sergeant's commanding voice. Ismail and her half-squad pulled out first, loping off down the tunnel with Kazimir close behind. Galleas set off at a brisk walk, keeping pace with the retreating soldiers and scanning the passageway ahead for anything he could use to further delay the pursuing orks.

Within moments the tunnel rang with hoarse shouts and the clangour of hob-nailed boots as the greenskins came charging down the metal stairs. Up ahead, the Rynnsguard came to a branching tunnel and turned right. It wouldn't confuse the orks – the humans' trail was easy to follow through the slime of the tunnel floor – but at least it took them out of the immediate line of fire.

This was not a race they could win, Galleas knew. The human soldiers were too slow, and the orks were relentless when their blood was up. That left just one option.

Galleas considered the tactical situation and studied Ismail and her troops. Three of the Rynnsguard would be sufficient, he calculated, provided they had enough grenades.

Sergeant Kazimir had come to the same conclusion as well. He slowed his pace, falling back until he was alongside the Space Marine. 'There's a bridge up ahead where the tunnel crosses one of the storm drains,' he said quietly. 'I'll take two of Ismail's men and hold the greenskins there.'

The orks were in the tunnel now. Their heavy footfalls splashed through the slime as they ran after their prey. *Fifty metres*, Galleas reckoned. They had a minute, perhaps less, and then the xenos would be upon them.

'Show me this bridge.'

Kazimir picked up the pace. They covered another thirty metres before the orks reached the branching tunnel behind them. The orks' howls rose in volume, and wild shots came buzzing out of the gloom.

Galleas' auto-senses detected a subtle change in air pressure just ahead. Moments later, the tunnel ended at a sheer man-made chasm spanned by a narrow, rusting metal bridge. The Space Marine peered over the bridge's corroded railing and caught the faint glimmer of stagnant water thirty metres below.

Ismail and her soldiers were already halfway across the bridge, their heavy tread sending shivers along the decaying arch. Kazimir crouched beside Galleas, his shotgun ready. He nodded at the tunnel mouth on the far end of the span. 'We can hold the greenskins there for a good long while,' he said. 'More than enough time for you and the others to get away.'

Galleas nodded thoughtfully. 'Go, sergeant. I will cross once you've reached the other side.'

Kazimir gave the Crimson Fist a questioning look, but he knew better than to argue. With a curt nod, he trotted out onto the bridge.

An ork slug hit the back of Galleas' left pauldron, striking sparks from the silver Deathwatch skull and ricocheting off into the darkness. The veteran sergeant turned to face the xenos, his power sword blazing. The greenskins were just forty metres away now. His preternatural vision could make out the glint of their beady eyes and the yellow sheen of their tusks in the faint light.

Galleas glanced over his shoulder. Kazimir was just reaching the other end of the span. Satisfied, the Space Marine took a careful, deliberate step backwards, onto the bridge.

Slugs droned out of the gloom, ringing against his breastplate. Bolts of searing, red light flicked back as Ismail's soldiers returned fire from the other side of the chasm. Standing tall amidst the crossfire, Galleas raised Night's Edge in challenge. The orks answered with a savage cry and rushed to meet him.

He chopped down with the power sword, cutting cleanly through the bridge's railing and biting deep into the base of the span to his right. Molten metal dripped sluggishly from the cut, flickering brightly in the darkness. Galleas pulled his sword free and struck again, this time on the bridge's left side. The weakened span groaned under the blows.

The veteran sergeant fell back with measured strides, careful to keep his weight centred along the spine of the bridge. The orks were far less cautious. They burst from the tunnel onto the narrow span, shouldering past one another for the chance to be the first to trade blows with Galleas. The decking shuddered beneath their heavy tread.

The first greenskin to reach Galleas was wielding a snarling chainaxe; as the ork's first blow fell, the Space Marine caught the haft of the axe with his free hand and severed the foe's legs with a sweep of his sword. The xenos fell hard, bellowing in pain before being trampled by the rest of the mob.

A lasgun bolt took one of the orks in the throat. The

greenskin staggered, sagging against the bridge railing. There was a groan of tortured metal that rose to an angry shriek as the rail gave way, toppling the dying xenos into the chasm.

Galleas kept retreating, slashing at the orks with swift, precise cuts. His power sword cut through crude ork blades and into the dense flesh beyond, crippling limbs instead of killing outright. The rest of the mob kept coming, piling onto the narrow span. The tortured squeals of twisting metal were lost beneath the xenos' bloodthirsty shouts, but Galleas could feel the decking starting to tilt beneath his feet.

An ork thrust at him with a chisel-edged blade; he knocked the blow aside with his armoured gauntlet and stabbed the xenos through its open jaws. Another ork staggered as it was hit by a pair of lasgun bolts, and Galleas finished it off with a blow to the side of its head. *Five more metres*, he reckoned, measuring the length of the span from memory. *Four good strides–*

The decking shuddered and tilted sharply, falling away with gathering speed. Too late, the orks realised their peril as the overwrought bridge finally gave way. Furious shouts and terrified screams rang against the walls of the chasm as scores of greenskins plummeted to their deaths in the shallow water below.

Galleas reached out with his free hand and grabbed the left-most bridge rail as the world seemed to fall away before him. A half-second later the decking hit the wall of the chasm with a thunderous crash and hung there, quivering, suspended by the intact but twisted metal anchors on the Rynnsguard side.

The veteran sergeant watched the last of the orks fall,

taking a grim joy in their frustrated cries. He stood perpendicular to the chasm wall, knees slightly bent, the magnetised soles of his boots gripping the metal decking of the bridge. Servos whined, taking up some of the strain on his armoured form.

Galleas glanced back over his shoulder, gauging the distance to the tunnel above. Sergeant Kazimir was peering over the edge, his eyes wide with shock. 'By the Golden Throne,' he murmured, shaking his head in disbelief.

It took Galleas several minutes of slow and careful movements to turn himself about and climb to the tunnel mouth. The gravity made the going difficult, but he'd coped with worse climbing along spacecraft hulls in any of a hundred different boarding actions.

The Rynnsguard soldiers stared at him in stunned silence as he emerged from the chasm. Galleas deactivated the magnets in his boots and continued down the tunnel without a word, his auto-senses sampling the air for the scents of Lieutenant Mitra and his battle-brothers. Kazimir and the others followed at his heels, whispering quietly amongst themselves.

Galleas paid them little mind. His thoughts were ranging far ahead, past the immediate step of rendezvousing with Juno, Olivar and the others. There was much to be done if they hoped to make it to the Cassar and continue the fight against the invaders.

CHAPTER FIVE

AMONGST THE DEAD

ZONA 13 COMMERCIA, NEW RYNN CITY
DAY 97

Lieutenant Mitra and her troops hadn't gone far. Galleas caught up with them after less than a kilometre, tracking them through the tunnels to a drain management substation underneath the eastern commercia district. Juno stood watch at the station entrance, a twisted length of thick metal pipe clutched in his right hand.

'Any signs of pursuit?' Juno asked hopefully.

Galleas shook his head. 'I left the greenskins back at the bridge.'

'Pity.'

Behind Galleas, Sergeant Kazimir spoke quietly to Corporal Ismail and her half-squad, and the soldiers sank wearily to the tunnel floor.

'How's Olivar?'

'In need of an Apothecary, obviously,' Juno replied. 'Think we'll find one between here and the Cassar?'

Galleas shook his head, brushing past Juno and entering the substation. Kazimir followed silently in his wake.

The drain management substation was not much more than a square room a dozen paces on a side, lit by the fitful glow of a pair of failing lumen strips. Huge, rumbling drainpipes ran from floor to ceiling along the far wall, connected to a series of oil-streaked water pumps and hydraulic valves. Servitors manned control stations along the walls to left and right, struggling feebly to perform their programmed tasks despite months of neglect. Dark green patches of mould spotted their metal casings and spread lividly across segments of exposed skin.

Lieutenant Mitra and what remained of her platoon filled most of the room. The soldiers sat or sprawled on the damp floor, their faces slack with exhaustion. Mitra leaned against one of the water pumps at the far end of the room, her arms tightly folded across the front of her flak vest. Her pale face turned hopefully to Galleas as he strode into the room.

The veteran sergeant surveyed the crowded chamber, seeking Brother Olivar. The Crimson Fist sat with his back to the corner, his damaged helmet at his feet. Olivar had heavy brows and a hooked nose that gave him a dour look at the best of times; now the entire right side of his face was crusted in old blood, and the skin around the ruined eye socket had been chewed to tatters by shrapnel and fragments of broken lens. His face drawn with pain, Olivar probed gingerly at pieces of broken lens crystal jutting from the ghastly wound.

Galleas gritted his teeth. The injury might have killed a lesser man outright. As it was, the damage was so extensive that not even Olivar's superhuman healing ability could fully cope with it.

'How do you fare, brother?' he asked gently.

Olivar's good eye focused on his sergeant. He drew a pained breath. 'I am alive,' the veteran said simply.

Mitra stirred from her spot on the wall. 'What about the greenskins?' she asked.

'They are no longer a threat,' Galleas said over his shoulder. 'Not for the moment, at least.'

The lieutenant nodded absently, eyes blinking as she tried to focus her thoughts through a haze of fatigue. 'There will be more,' she said. 'There's *always* more.' Mitra indicated her troops with a nod of her head. 'We're down to our last power packs,' she said. 'We need to keep moving. Find a place to hide–'

'Then go,' Olivar spat. The wounded Space Marine struggled to his feet, hands pressed to the walls for support. 'Find some hole to cower in while the xenos ravage your world!' The veteran's deep voice rose in anger. 'We are the sons of Dorn! While we live, we *fight!*'

Galleas expected Mitra to quail before Olivar's fury. Instead, her eyes blazed with anger. 'The only reason you're alive right now is because of us!' she snapped. Too exhausted and too wrung out to fear the consequences, she stepped up to the towering Olivar and jabbed a grimy finger at his ruined face. 'Another few days and the scavengers would have found the lot of you. You know what would have happened then? I can tell you. I've watched it happen more times than I can count.'

For a moment, Olivar stared down at Mitra in shock. His fists slowly clenched. 'You insolent–'

'Enough, brother.' Galleas stepped between them, forcing Mitra to ease back. Tension crackled in the confines of the substation – even Juno and Corporal Ismail had noticed, coming back inside to see what was wrong. The Rynnsguard troopers watched the confrontation in stunned silence, their hands close to the grips of their lasguns. It was clear that they were close to breaking point, their nerves frayed raw by the terrors of the past few days. If Olivar lashed out at Mitra, there was no telling what might happen.

The veteran sergeant turned to face Olivar. 'Lieutenant Mitra is right,' he said, loud enough so that everyone in the room could hear. 'It took courage to do what they did for us, and we owe them our thanks. Save your wrath for the xenos, and remember your duty to Rynn's World and the Chapter.'

Olivar glared at Galleas, his bloodied face a mask of rage. For a moment it looked as though he might protest – or worse, give vent to his anger despite what his sergeant said. But then he bent, and picked his damaged helmet off the floor. Slowly, deliberately, he slipped the battered helm over his head and locked it into place. The single lens glowed to baleful life.

'I need no reminder of who I am,' Olivar growled. 'Do *you*, brother?'

Galleas held Olivar's stare without flinching. 'We're not going to hide,' he told Olivar. 'We're going back to Leonis Square. Right now.'

Now it was Mitra's turn to be shocked. 'You can't,' she said. 'It's mid-afternoon. The whole area is swarming with greenskins.'

Galleas glanced over his shoulder at Mitra. 'We must. If the three of us survived the blast, then it's likely that the others survived as well.'

'There weren't any others,' Mitra protested. 'We *looked*.'

'They might have been buried under greenskins,' Galleas said. 'Did you dig through the bodies?'

Mitra grimaced. 'Of course not. Even if we'd wanted to, there just wasn't time.'

'Then we must see for ourselves,' Galleas declared. 'Share out your remaining power packs, lieutenant. We move in five minutes.'

'We?' Mitra exclaimed. 'You can't be serious.'

'I'm not given to humour, lieutenant,' Galleas said coldly. 'Your platoon will serve as lookouts, and will provide assistance in case any survivors are too injured to move.'

The lieutenant shook her head. The strain of the past few days was evident on her face. 'My lord, please. The risks–'

'They are my brothers,' Galleas said in a steely voice. 'The risks do not concern me.'

'You don't understand what it's like out there–'

Galleas turned. 'Lieutenant, I was fighting the Emperor's wars more than two hundred and fifty years before you were born.' He glared down at Mitra. 'Pray tell me what it is I fail to understand here.'

The lieutenant held the Space Marine's unblinking stare for a long moment, her jaw clenched and her expression bleak. Galleas understood her concerns all too well. It would take some time to search the corpse-choked square, and they would be dangerously exposed. If the xenos discovered them, it would be Mitra and her troops who would suffer the most.

Such is war, the veteran sergeant thought. *All of us risk losing more than we can bear.*

'Four minutes, thirty-five seconds,' Galleas said, his tone implacable.

The sounds of fighting were well to the north now, Galleas reckoned, perhaps only a handful of kilometres from the river. The crackle of thousands of lasguns sounded like fat sizzling in a fire, punctuated by the heavy drumbeat of ork guns and the crash of artillery. Beneath it all, so deep as to be more felt than heard, was the muted roar of hundreds of thousands of greenskins, clamouring for blood and fire. The sky beyond the ruined buildings north of Leonis Square was hidden behind a shifting veil of black smoke and swirling brown dust.

Mitra had led them on a tense dash down rubble-strewn streets to a burned-out hab unit at the very edge of the square. The Rynnsguard troopers formed a perimeter to watch out for scavengers as Galleas and his brothers studied the objective from the ruins of a second-storey gallery.

The square, nearly thirty metres across, was a scene of gruesome carnage. Human and ork corpses, some little more than charred husks, covered almost every square metre of the open space. The stench of rotting flesh and the rancid vegetable stink of dead greenskins hung heavy in the air. Three small, spindly-legged xenos were poking through the remains, pulling tusks from the bodies of their larger kin and chittering malevolently to one another.

'Show me where you found us,' Galleas murmured.

Lieutenant Mitra edged up to the shattered window frame. 'You were there,' she said, pointing down at the tangle of bodies with a gloved finger. 'Your brother – the one carrying the pipe – was eight metres further east and a little to the south. The other was just a little north of you, about three metres. You were all resting on your back, more or less facing the wreck.'

She was referring to the Rhino. The squad's armoured personnel carrier had been flipped on its side by the blast, and judging from the scorch marks, had burned for some time afterwards. With that as a reference point, and using mnemonic rotes to reconstruct their positions at the point of detonation, he reckoned they had been hurled almost fifteen metres by the exploding shells. That gave him a baseline to estimate the positions of the rest of his squad.

'Anything?' Galleas asked over the vox. Even here, above ground, the signal was fouled with static and squeals of interference. Tactical transmissions – short range and mostly line-of-sight – were strong enough to overcome the noise, but he couldn't pick up anything from the Cassar.

Juno scrutinised the corpse-choked square from the shadows of a broken window a few metres to Galleas' right. 'I think I see my sword,' he reported.

'Never mind the damned sword,' Olivar growled. He stood by another window at the far end of the gallery. 'What about our brothers?'

'Can't see them anywhere,' Juno replied. 'No sign of Rottshrek either, come to that.'

Galleas gritted his teeth. He had noticed that as well. Hundreds of orks had died when the pallet of shells had exploded, ripped apart by high-velocity shrapnel or pulped by the shockwave that had swept across the square – but the vile warboss was not among them. Perhaps the ork engineer's force field – or simple, fiendish luck – had spared the hulking greenskin from the blast. 'Olivar?'

'Nothing,' the half-blind Space Marine admitted reluctantly. 'Do you think the orks–'

'If the xenos found the others, they would have discovered us as well. Thus,' Galleas said, speaking through his vox-grille for Mitra's benefit, 'our brothers must still be out there, buried under the dead.' He glanced over at the lieutenant. 'I have determined a number of potential locations, based on the force of the blast. We will eliminate the scavengers and conduct a careful search.'

'How?' Mitra peered down at the greenskin runts and frowned. 'There's no cover. We can't get close enough for knives, and we don't have any other silent weapons.'

Galleas chuckled coldly. 'The Adeptus Astartes are instruments of war, lieutenant,' he said. 'We are trained to kill with far more than just bolter and blade.' He bent and picked up a fist-sized chunk of ferrocrete, testing its weight in his hand. 'Juno, take the runt in the middle. Olivar, the one on the right.'

The veteran sergeant watched and waited while his brothers armed themselves. Out in the square, the runts had paused amid the rotting corpses, showing off their grisly trophies. He expertly gauged the distance to his target. He drew back his arm. 'Now!'

The Space Marines struck as one, hands snapping forward. Heavy chunks of debris fell like thunderbolts on the unsuspecting runts. Two were killed instantly, their skulls crushed like eggs.

Olivar's rock missed its target by a finger's breadth, buzzing past the scavenger's ear. 'Damnation!' he hissed over the vox.

The third runt, its pointy face spattered with blood, gaped in shock at the corpses of its pack-mates. It hesitated for a half-second, torn between the urge to flee and the temptation to grab the gory treasures gripped in the dead scavengers' fists. Terror trumped greed a moment later. The xenos let out a squeal and turned to run, but it was too late. A fourth hunk of debris crunched into the back of its skull, knocking the greenskin face-first into the pile of alien dead.

Juno dusted off his crimson gauntlets, admiring his handiwork. *'We need to get you another eye, Brother Olivar,'* he chided. *'Maybe if we find Brother Valentus out there, he'll loan you one of his?'*

Galleas cut off Olivar's heated reply. 'Time is wasting, brothers,' he said sternly. 'Let's move!' Without hesitation the veteran sergeant leapt through the broken window and dropped two storeys onto the edge of the corpse-filled square. Juno and Olivar followed, landing heavily at Galleas' side.

The veteran sergeant spoke quickly, assigning sectors for his brothers to search as he made his way to the wrecked Rhino. The rear assault ramp was still down, providing access to the troop compartment. Loose ammunition, spare magazines and other small pieces of gear had spilled from their bins during the blast and littered the compartment. As Juno and Olivar went to work, Galleas made his way inside and began quickly gathering up everything he could find.

As he filled up removable bins and fashioned webbing into makeshift carry-nets, another part of Galleas' mind was keeping track of the time and gauging how long they could afford to continue the search. Every passing minute increased the chance of discovery. If the orks caught them in the square with one or more injured brothers, their chances of escape were slim. At what point did the risk outweigh the loss?

It took seven minutes and twenty-eight seconds to collect everything from the Rhino. In truth, there wasn't a great deal left to take, Galleas noted ruefully, though at least he was able to recover the half-empty case of spare vials for their auto-dispensaries. If his brothers were still alive out in the square, the medicines would be sorely needed.

By the time he emerged from the transport, Mitra and her troops had made their way outside, taking cover behind mounds of bodies and scanning the surrounding buildings with fearful eyes. *The lieutenant was right,* he thought, gazing warily up at the hundreds of empty windows that looked down on the square. *We're too exposed out here. But what choice do I have?* He pushed the apprehension from his mind and focused on the task at hand. Juno and Olivar were several metres away, digging through heaps of greenskin dead.

'Anything?' Galleas asked urgently.

'Just dead xenos,' Juno answered.

'Move on to the next sector.'

Galleas quickly moved to the spot where he'd been standing when the blast went off, and began working his way to where he'd been found. His spirits rose as he saw the grip of his boltgun protruding from beneath a pile of greenskin bodies. Moments later, he found his bolt pistol as well. He murmured a placating prayer to their machine-spirits and kept searching. Soon, his keen eyes spotted Olivar's bolter and Juno's weapons as well.

Eleven minutes, eight seconds. The chances of discovery were growing by the moment. Galleas gazed across the field of dead and felt his guts turn to lead. *A few minutes more,* he thought grimly. He was about to tell his brothers to switch sectors again when Olivar shouted over the vox.

'I've found Valentus! He's alive!'

Galleas saw Olivar nearly twenty metres away, uncovering the prone form of Brother Valentus from beneath a pile of greenskins. The veteran sergeant hurried over, carry-nets banging against his back and legs. By the time he arrived, Olivar was kneeling beside Valentus, checking his vital humours from the readouts at the Space Marine's waist.

'Weak but stable,' Olivar reported. 'He's in a coma.'

Galleas had expected as much. Most Space Marines were able to voluntarily enter a comatose state to heal grievous injuries, but a flaw in the Crimson Fists genetic code deprived them of the sus-an membrane that made this possible. Valentus' coma was something out of his control, and would require crude methods to reverse. 'Check his auto-dispensary.'

'I have,' Olivar said. 'It's empty.'

Galleas pulled out the case with the spare vials. 'Give him one of these, and take one for yourself as well.'

Olivar took one vial but refused the other. 'There's only four left,' he pointed out. 'Someone might need one more than me.'

The veteran sergeant scowled at Olivar, but could not fault his brother's logic. He made a note to revisit the matter at a later point, when Juno called out. 'Here's Tauros!'

Galleas quickly passed over Olivar's bolter and one of the carry-nets. 'Get Valentus on his feet and keep looking,' he said quickly, and then dashed to Juno's side. *Twelve minutes, fifteen seconds.*

Tauros was comatose as well, facedown under a heap of corpses. By the time Galleas passed over Juno's weapons and one of the stimm vials, Olivar had discovered Royas and Salazar close by. Valentus was beginning to stir, his augmetic limbs twitching slightly. Galleas put the veteran to work searching for lost wargear while he passed out more stimm vials from their steadily dwindling supply.

Tauros and Royas were back on their feet within moments, moving slowly but surely despite their injuries. Both found their boltguns fairly close to hand. Galleas watched his squad rise from the dead with a grim sense of triumph.

He had always been taught that there was no honour in a bloodless victory, but at that moment he was prepared to disagree.

It took another two full minutes to find Amador, working from the assumption that he'd been close to Rottshrek when the explosion occurred. He'd landed amongst the bodies of several of the warboss' bodyguards, one hand still tightly gripping a greenskin's severed head. Galleas gave Amador the last of their stimm vials and tossed the empty box aside.

After a long moment, Amador let out a low groan and slowly sat upright. Dazedly, he surveyed the battlefield, then glanced up at Galleas. 'What happened?' he asked hoarsely. 'Where's Rottshrek?'

Before Galleas could reply, the roar of petrochem engines could be heard approaching the square from the east. *We're out of time.*

The veteran sergeant turned and signalled to Mitra to get her troops out of sight, back down the street from whence they came. 'Follow the Rynnsguard!' he said, pulling Amador onto his feet. 'Move!'

Galleas brought up his bolter and dug a fresh drum out of the carry-net at his hip. He surveyed the square as he reloaded, checking to make sure the rest of the squad was falling back in good order. That's when he saw Olivar, still kneeling beside Salazar's prone form. Valentus stood guard over the two Crimson Fists, his bolter held against his breastplate.

Keeping a wary eye on the western end of the square, Galleas ran to where Salazar lay. 'I thought I told you to get moving,' he said, glancing questioningly at Olivar.

It was Salazar who answered. 'There seems to be a problem with my legs, brother,' he said, his voice tight with pain.

'There's a piece of shrapnel in his back,' Olivar said grimly. 'It's pressing on his spinal cord, or it might have severed it completely. I can't tell.'

'It doesn't much matter,' Salazar said. 'I can't walk either way.'

The engines were close now: five hundred metres, maybe less. Four large vehicles, Galleas reckoned, which meant anywhere from forty to sixty greenskins.

'Take his arms,' the veteran sergeant told Valentus and Olivar. 'We'll carry him–'

'With all due respect, brother, no, you damned well won't.' Salazar gripped Olivar's shoulder. 'Just give me my weapon and prop me up so I've got a good field of fire. I'll cover your withdrawal.'

Galleas shook his head stubbornly. 'This isn't up for debate, Salazar! I'm not leaving you here to die.'

'Yes, you are.' Grunting with pain, Salazar used his arms to push himself upright. 'I'm half-dead already. Carrying me will just slow you down, and I won't have that. Give me my weapon, and get out of here.'

'The protocol–'

'The protocol forbids unnecessary risks. I'm risking all three of you right now just having this debate.' Salazar's voice grew strained. 'Go.'

Galleas looked to the west. He could see the exhaust of the ork vehicles billowing over the tops of the burned-out hab units just a few blocks away. His earlier sense of triumph now felt like a cruel jest.

'Give Brother Salazar his boltgun,' he said.

Valentus handed over Salazar's weapon. '*Twenty rounds left,*' he said.

Salazar nodded. 'I'll put them to good use.' With his free

hand, he pushed himself backwards, until his shoulders were resting against a heap of greenskin bodies. 'The xenos filth will know they fought a Sternguard by the time I'm done.'

Olivar set a combat knife where Salazar could reach it, and then laid a hand on the crippled veteran's pauldron. 'The God-Emperor keep you, brother. In this life, and the next.' Then he withdrew, heading back across the square with Valentus close behind.

Galleas reached into his carry-net and drew out two grenades. 'Take these.'

Salazar took the explosives and laid them in his lap. He readied his bolter and looked out across the square, where the orks would soon appear.

'Less than a hundred years in the Crusade Company,' Salazar sighed. 'By the Throne. I'd only just begun.' He shook his head. 'I hoped to see my name written in the annals, but that day will never come. It's all just ashes now.'

'The pages will be rewritten, brother,' Galleas said with feeling. 'The Chapter will be reborn. And by Dorn, what you do here today will be remembered. I swear it.'

Salazar looked up at his sergeant. The orks were very close now. 'Thank you, brother,' he said quietly. 'Now get the hell out of here and let me get to work.'

With a heavy heart, Galleas turned and left his brother behind. It was a short run across the square and into the concealing darkness of the hab unit.

The rest of his squad was waiting for him a few dozen metres down the street. Lieutenant Mitra stood in their midst, staring past Galleas to where Salazar waited for the xenos. Her expression was bleak.

'Where do we go from here?' she asked.

The roar of ork engines echoed from the western side of the square. Salazar's boltgun answered, single shots ringing out against the onrushing horde.

'Back to the Cassar,' Galleas said, turning his face to the smoke-laden sky. 'Back to the war.'

CHAPTER SIX

HIGH GROUND

ZONA 13 COMMERCIA, NEW RYNN CITY
DAY 97

They worked their way across the ruined district in silence, the Space Marines moving from cover to cover while Lieutenant Mitra's soldiers spread out to defend their flanks and rear. More than once Galleas and his brothers had to go to ground as bands of greenskins went roaring down the rubble-filled roads in smoke-belching buggies or heavily armed trucks. It was galling to let the enemy pass unchallenged, but there was nothing to be done, Galleas knew, not if they hoped to reach the Cassar undetected.

It took nearly four hours to cover as many kilometres, working north and west through the district in the general direction of the river. The sun was sinking behind the ruined buildings to the west, suffusing the hazy sky with shades of sullen purple, livid red and fiery orange, and creating deep pools of shadow amid the tumbled ruins on the far side of the buildings. Beyond the field of twisted metal and broken ferrocrete rose a ten-storey hab unit, its reddish-brown flanks blackened with streaks of soot and pocked by the impacts of energy beams and artillery shells.

Mitra crouched down beside the remains of a wall and nodded in the direction of the hab unit. 'That's the highest ground in this part of the district,' she said, taking a sip from the water bottle at her belt. 'There's no telling how stable it is, but if we can make it to the top you should be able to see all the way to the river.'

Galleas studied the battered hab unit and nodded curtly. 'It will serve,' he said at last. By his reckoning, they were only two kilometres from the curtain wall protecting the Residentia Ultris; from the top of the hab unit he would be able to observe the orks' dispositions between them and the wall, and plot a route that would take them through the enemy lines to one of the wall's smaller gates. *A difficult passage, but not impossible,* he reasoned. The greenskins would be exhausted after a long day of assaults against the wall, and once darkness fell most would withdraw to their camps, which experience told him would be a few kilometres south of where he was now. By the time the Imperials were ready to make their move, at the darkest part of the night, there would be few greenskins between them and the wall.

Assuming we can cross two hundred metres of rubble and make it to the upper floors of the hab unit undetected, Galleas thought, studying the debris field stretching between them and the distant building.

'We will wait here until full dark,' the veteran sergeant said to Mitra. 'Another ten or twelve minutes from now. You and your troops may rest until then.'

Galleas left Mitra and went to join the rest of his squad. The Imperials had taken cover in the wreckage of a large, ruined grocery, sitting or crouching amid toppled shelves and dust-stained counters. Mitra's two squads, under Sergeant Kazimir's watchful eye, had clustered along the eastern wall of the shop and left the rest of the space to the Adeptus Astartes. Tauros, Valentus, Juno and Olivar formed a tight knot near the centre of the shop, nearly hidden behind tall piles of fallen debris, while Royas and Amador stood watch to the south and west. Mitra had offered to post some of her own troops as sentries and give the wounded Space Marines a chance to rest, but Galleas had gruffly declined.

The veteran sergeant picked his way silently over the shifting piles of debris and crouched down beside his brothers. 'Tauros, Juno, I want you on point when we move. I doubt the greenskins will be watching the approaches to the hab unit, but we need to be prepared for resistance just in case.'

'Why not let the Rynnsguard go ahead and scout the building for us?' Juno said. He had ripped a relatively clean patch of clothing from a withered corpse on the street outside and was using it to clean the grime from his sword. 'If we're going to be dragging them around with us, we may as well put them to use.'

Tauros completed a murmured invocation to his boltgun's machine-spirit and glanced up at Juno. 'That's like trying to open a window with a hammer,' the grizzled veteran observed wryly. 'There are better tools for the task, brother.'

Juno shrugged his massive shoulders. 'I've opened windows with worse things than hammers before.' He chuckled. 'When I was with the Deathwatch on Sundamar I put an eldar's head through four centimetres of crystalflex. *That's* how you open a window!'

Tauros sighed. 'Do those humans strike you as stealthy, efficient ork hunters, brother?'

'Not in the least,' Juno replied. 'But at the rate things are going they could stand to learn, don't you think?'

Olivar snapped a fresh drum into his boltgun and fixed Galleas with his one good eye. 'How much longer are we going to put up with this nonsense?' he demanded.

'Pay no mind to Juno, brother,' Galleas advised. 'You know how he likes to wind up Tauros.'

Olivar snorted in disgust. 'I'm not talking about Juno,' he said. The one-eyed Space Marine nodded in the direction of Mitra's platoon. 'When are we going to be rid of *them*?'

The anger in Olivar's tone surprised Galleas. *It's the pain talking,* the veteran sergeant reckoned. 'I'm not sure I understand.'

'Don't be stupid,' Olivar snapped. 'It will be hard enough for us to reach the Cassar, much less those fools. At best, they'll slow us down. At worst…'

'And what do you suggest I do? Tell the lieutenant she and her troops are on their own?'

Olivar shrugged. 'Since when do we have to explain ourselves to a platoon of Rynnsguard? Just get up and leave them. It's not as though they could keep up with us.'

Servos whirred softly as Valentus turned to regard Olivar. *'You would abandon them to their fate, brother? They won't last another week out here on their own.'*

Olivar snorted in derision. 'They're dead no matter what,' he said. 'If we keep them with us, there is a good chance they'll get some of us killed as well. Is that what you want?'

Valentus' scarred metal face was inscrutable. *'You are starting to sound like Royas,'* the old veteran said. *'Are our lives worth so much more than theirs?'*

'What kind of question is that?' Olivar replied indignantly. 'Of course they are.'

'They saved us, brother,' Galleas countered. 'We do not forget our debts. Not now. Not ever.' He stood, effectively ending the debate. 'Tauros, Juno, you move in three minutes. We will follow once you're halfway across the field.'

The two veterans nodded and went to work making final checks and venerations to their wargear. Olivar shook his head but said nothing, turning his attention back to his boltgun. Galleas moved away, his spirit troubled, and returned to his vantage point at the north wall.

Olivar had a point. From a purely military sense, if nothing else, the lives of his squad were worth far more than a platoon of Rynnsguard troops. Could he knowingly risk the lives of his brothers, each of whom were veterans of hundreds of years' service, for the sake of a handful of humans? Did the Ceres Protocol not explicitly forbid such risks?

He was still brooding over the problem minutes later, when Tauros and Juno slipped past. The veteran Space Marines moved swiftly into the shadows of the rubble field, working their way expertly from one patch of cover to the next. The sun had set, and heavy, overcast darkness was settling over the city. If there were greenskins in the hab unit across the field – and he had little doubt that there were – their poor night vision would give them a difficult time spotting even Mitra's less experienced troops.

The Rynnsguard had begun to stir in the wake of Tauros and Juno's departure. Sergeant Kazimir rose to his feet and went from one squad to the next, nudging soldiers awake with a tap of his boot and a few well-chosen words. Lieutenant Mitra had been resting against a tilted slab of ferrocrete, eyes closed, while Preacher Gomez read to her from a small, timeworn copy of the *Lectitio Divinitatus*. As the platoon readied itself with muttered oaths and the rattle of wargear, she gave a nod to Gomez and stood, her face a mask of weary determination. When she was satisfied that Kazimir had the platoon in hand, she picked up her lascarbine and went to join Galleas.

The veteran sergeant watched the platoon ready itself as Mitra approached. The humans were clumsy, slow and uncoordinated. He shook his head in faint disapproval.

If Mitra noticed, she gave no sign. 'What are your orders, my lord?'

Galleas glanced back at his squad. The Crimson Fists had formed up in silence, boltguns held across their chests as they awaited the command to advance. Olivar stared back, his expression hidden behind his damaged helm.

Just get up and leave them. They're dead anyway.

'You and your platoon will wait here,' Galleas said, 'until I and the rest of my squad are halfway across the field. Then head for the hab unit as quickly and as quietly as you can and rendezvous with us past the main entrance.'

Mitra stared out across the field. 'That will put a lot of separation between us,' she observed.

'That is the point,' Galleas replied. Without waiting for a reply, he nodded to his brothers and darted out into the debris field.

He moved to a heap of rubble less than five metres away and sank to a crouch, surveying the landscape ahead for threats and picking out his next stopping point. A route across the field took shape quickly in his mind, offering the optimal amount of cover for the speed he required. Valentus was a dark shadow off to his left, dashing silently up to a broken stretch of wall. A half-second later Royas came around to Galleas' right, settling down into a crater that left only his head and upper shoulders exposed. As soon as he was in place, Galleas moved to his next spot, a few metres further across the field. No sooner had he broken cover than Amador settled into the spot he'd just vacated, boltgun trained on the distant hab unit. Like a precision timepiece, the veterans operated in perfect harmony, each element working seamlessly as part of a deadly whole.

Galleas swept the hab unit with his bolter as he moved, expecting to see muzzle flashes at any moment. It didn't seem that the debris field was under direct observation by the xenos, but it would only take a single greenskin glancing outside at exactly the wrong moment to throw their entire plan into disarray.

It took the veterans little over three minutes to reach the middle of the field. No sooner had Galleas taken cover behind the crumpled shell of a groundcar than Tauros' voice crackled over the squad vox. *'We've reached the entrance.'*

'Any sign of xenos?'

'The air is thick with their stench,' Tauros replied. *'Smells like there's a pack of runts somewhere inside.'*

'Continue inside and find a route to the upper floors. Avoid contact with the enemy unless absolutely necessary.'

'Understood.'

Galleas glanced back the way he'd come. A hundred metres away the Rynnsguard were emerging from the burned-out grocery with Sergeant Kazimir and Corporal Ismail's squad in the lead. Hissed commands and the thud of pounding feet echoed through the darkness. The veteran sergeant gritted his teeth at the noise and broke cover, bounding to the next waypoint.

Three minutes later, Galleas had reached the foot of the

cracked stone steps leading up to the hab's main entrance. The air was bitter with the reek of melted plastek and the greasy smell of charred flesh. The rust-coloured sandstone overhang above the hab unit's entrance was stained black with soot and melted in places by the heat of greenskin flamers. The Arch-Arsonist's horde took great pleasure in burning any structure they could find, especially those with Imperial civilians still inside.

Galleas stowed his boltgun and drew Night's Edge, waving the rest of the squad forward into the building. The Crimson Fists slipped past on either side. The veteran sergeant paced after them, pausing just inside the charred entrance.

The hab unit was typical of those found in New Rynn City, with a wide atrium just past the entrance that led to an open commons area lit by a large skylight high above. Heaps of broken stone and other debris littered the gloomy interior, along with the shrivelled husks of human refugees. The Space Marines picked their way quietly through the rubble, spreading out to cover the approaches to the atrium.

Galleas took a deep breath. His enhanced senses sampled a miasma of odours. At once he detected greenskins, just as Tauros said. The spoor was fresh, less than an hour old. The scavengers had to still be somewhere in the building.

The other veterans had picked up the scent as well. Amador shook his head in disgust. *'Runts,'* he muttered over the vox. *'We're cowering down here from a bunch of runts.'*

'Focus on the mission, brother,' Galleas warned. 'Tauros?'

'There is a staircase down the gallery to the west of the atrium. We're working our way up now.'

'Understood.'

Galleas turned, searching the rubble field outside. He spotted the Rynnsguard at once, bounding by squads in fits and starts through the debris. They weren't even half-way across yet.

The veteran sergeant watched their progress, silently urging them on. Every second they were out in the open increased the chance of discovery. Galleas counted the seconds, expecting to hear the chatter of ork guns any moment.

What would the Rynnsguard do if they were discovered? Would they fall back to the grocery, or go to ground in the middle of the field? Either way, the Space Marines would only have two options: fall back and attempt to extricate the soldiers, or abandon them to their fate.

'Contact, fourth floor,' Tauros reported over the vox. 'There's a group of runts just past the staircase entrance. Do we engage?'

'Only if you can't get past,' Galleas replied.

'We can,' Tauros said. 'But what about the Rynnsguard?'

'We'll deal with that if it becomes an issue. Press on.'

'Affirmative.'

The seconds stretched past. There was nothing more from Tauros, which meant that he and Juno had slipped past the runts without difficulty. The sounds of battle had largely subsided off to the north as night took hold. Galleas fought to control his impatience. Any moment there would be thousands of orks passing through the zone, heading south – and the Rynnsguard were still almost forty metres away.

Valentus spoke over the vox. 'Sounds of movement in the commons area,' he reported. 'I can't see the source, but it must be greenskins.'

Amador responded at once. 'I'll go look–'

'Stay right where you are, brother,' Galleas ordered. 'Valentus, are they coming this way?'

'Affirmative.'

'Fall back from the entrance to the commons area and get under cover,' Galleas said. As the squad repositioned, the veteran sergeant checked on the Rynnsguard. The soldiers were strung out across two-thirds of the field now, and the lead elements had actually *stopped*, just twenty-five metres from the building. Exasperated, Galleas stepped into view at the entrance and beckoned urgently to the waiting soldiers.

To her credit, Corporal Ismail saw Galleas' signal and acted at once, rising from cover and dashing across the remaining open ground to the entrance. Her squad followed immediately, boots thudding on the ferrocrete. They came up the steps and into the atrium like a herd of stampeding grox.

'Dorn's blood!' Royas hissed over the vox. *'Are they trying to get us killed?'*

Galleas grabbed the front of Ismail's flak armour as she came alongside him, stopping her so suddenly that both feet came off the ground. 'Down the gallery to the west,' the veteran sergeant snapped. 'Look for a staircase. *Go.*' He gave her a gentle nudge in the right direction, sending her stumbling over the rubble. The rest of her squad followed, sweaty faces tense in the half-light.

'The greenskins are coming!' Valentus warned.

'Let them,' Galleas replied. He followed after Ismail's soldiers, sinking behind a heap of burned flakboard just a few metres from the gallery entrance. 'Ready your knives. We go on my command.'

The Space Marines disappeared into cover. Unable to see his foes, Galleas focused on sight and smell instead. The sound of footfalls echoed over broken stone, punctuated by the panting breaths of the greenskins. The stink of the xenos filled his nostrils.

Seconds later the pack of runts scuttled into the atrium,

chuckling evilly and hissing to one another in their vile tongue. They headed for the west gallery, drawn by the smell of human flesh. When the pack was nearly on top of him, Galleas revealed himself. Night's Edge blazed with blue fire. *'Now!'*

The greenskins recoiled from the flare of light, shielding their eyes and screeching in surprise. Galleas counted eleven of the hideous-looking runts, their crude harnesses ornamented with fresh human teeth and finger bones. His power sword flashed in a hissing arc, and two xenos heads bounced across the atrium floor.

The Crimson Fists fell upon the scavengers from all sides, striking with knife and fist. Amador charged into the middle of the pack, knocking three of the runts off their feet and slashing the throat of another. Olivar crushed the skull of one of the fallen greenskins with a chunk of rubble and spitted a second one with his knife. The third runt struggled to rise, bringing up an oversized pistol, but Valentus broke his neck with a swift kick. Royas accounted for one with a swipe of his knife and stunned another with a slap to the side of its head.

Caterwauling in terror, the surviving runts scattered in four different directions. Pistols boomed, but the shots were wild, ricocheting from the blackened walls. The veteran Space Marines hurled their combat knives, one after another, and the four xenos went down.

Seconds later, Lieutenant Mitra appeared at the building entrance, accompanied by Preacher Gomez, the medic, Vega, and Oros, the enginseer. She dashed into the atrium, lascarbine ready.

'What happened?' she said in a low voice. 'We heard shots–'

Royas bent over the splayed body of a runt and ripped his knife free from its back. He glared at Mitra and snarled, 'Your sorry excuse for soldiers–'

Galleas cut him off. 'We were discovered,' he said curtly.

The lieutenant's hands tightened on the grips of her weapon. 'What do we do?'

Kazimir appeared at the hab unit's entrance with Corporal Vila's squad in tow. Vila followed the grizzled sergeant like a whipped dog, his face a mask of resentment.

'We keep going,' Galleas said without hesitation. 'Greenskins fire off their weapons all the time. The other runts in the building aren't likely to investigate a handful of shots.'

'And if they do?' Mitra pressed.

'Then we kill them,' the Space Marine said flatly. 'Quickly and quietly. If even one gets away and alerts the horde, we won't leave this building alive.' He issued a quick set of hand signals to his battle-brothers. 'Enough questions,' he told Mitra. 'Stay close and follow me.'

He led the lieutenant and the rest of her troops down the western gallery, senses alert for any sign of greenskins. The Rynnsguard struggled to keep pace with his long strides, loping along and setting their gear to rattling again. The veteran sergeant clenched his teeth and forced himself to slow his pace. Back in the atrium, the rest of his squad held position for several moments, watching for signs of pursuit, then silently withdrew along the Rynnsguard's wake.

Galleas quickly found the stairwell at the far end of the west gallery. Its heavy metal door was jammed halfway open by the heat of a previous fire. Corporal Ismail and her squad were nowhere to be seen.

Faint sounds echoed down the stairwell from above. The

human soldiers had continued up the stairs, completely unaware of the pack of runts on the fourth floor.

Biting back a curse, Galleas drew his sword and bounded up the stairs, leaving Mitra and the others behind. He ascended swiftly, taking the steps four and five at a time, expecting to hear the screeching cries of greenskins and the thunder of guns at any moment.

He caught up to the squad on the landing between the third and fourth floors. The Rynnsguard were crouching with their backs to the wall, lasguns resting across their knees. They raised their weapons with a start as the blue-armoured giant suddenly appeared in their midst.

Galleas counted heads and frowned. 'Where is Ismail?' he hissed.

'Right here.'

The veteran sergeant glanced upwards. Ismail stood with her back to the wall, just to one side of the fourth floor stairwell door. She was cleaning the blade of her heavy knife with a filthy rag. A bloody clutch of pointed ears had joined the ork tusks hanging around her neck.

Galleas studied the young corporal. 'You were supposed to hold position at the ground floor,' he said.

'My mistake,' Ismail said, shrugging off the admonishment. 'I thought I heard sounds of enemy activity and went to investigate.'

The veteran sergeant scowled up at her. *This one is just as bad as Amador,* he thought. 'What did you find?'

'Five of the little dung-eaters,' she said simply, sheathing her knife. The bloody rag went into a bulging cargo pocket. 'Just the other side of the door.' Ismail's impassive expression faltered slightly. 'They'd... found some bodies and were having a meal.'

'Any trouble?'

Ismail's bright, blue eyes snapped back into focus. 'Trouble? No, my lord. No trouble at all.'

Mitra and the others clambered up to the third floor landing, shoulders heaving. The lieutenant took in the scene above. 'Ismail,' she panted. 'What in the Emperor's name have you got yourself into this time?'

Ismail stiffened. Galleas glanced from her to Mitra.

'It's nothing,' he told the lieutenant grudgingly. 'She... did well.'

Galleas climbed past Ismail's squad and then the corporal herself, pretending to ignore their wide-eyed expressions as he went.

He was every bit as surprised as they.

Tauros and Juno were waiting on the stairwell landing at the top floor, peering into the darkness beyond the open doorway. The older veteran turned as Galleas climbed into view.

'Upper level is clear,' Tauros reported. 'No signs of activity.'

A moment later, Galleas could see why. At some point during the siege the northern face of the building had been pounded by artillery – likely their own guns, firing from positions in the Residentia Ultris. The access corridor beyond the doorway was a tangle of fallen beams and broken, sagging walls. Large sections of the floor had collapsed, creating a deadly patchwork of jagged gaps and tilting ferrocrete slabs.

Galleas spent a full minute studying the ruined passageway, working out a route that would get him to an intact doorway several dozen metres away. Finally, he nodded. 'Single file, double spacing. Let's go.'

Tauros glanced back at Ismail and her squad. 'What about them?'

'They can take care of themselves,' Galleas told him, with considerably more confidence than he'd felt a short while ago.

He eased his way carefully through the doorway, testing the stability of the floor with each slow step. The veteran sergeant called up a subroutine on his helmet display that measured resistance on the servomotors at his knee and ankle joints. It was a trick he'd learned in the Deathwatch a half-century ago, fighting the eldar in the treacherous mountainous terrain of Ularis Prime. A micrometre of extra flexion in his knees would be enough to warn him that the ferrocrete was ready to give way beneath him.

Galleas actually felt his spirits rise as he negotiated the hazardous terrain. Ismail's handling of the runts suggested that Mitra and her troops might not be as much of a liability as he or his brothers believed. And Kazimir at least seemed to understand the importance of noise discipline. With a great deal of careful planning and not a small amount of luck, Galleas reckoned, they could reach the Imperial lines without incident.

Flexion indicators rose on the veteran sergeant's display. Structural beams groaned faintly, and a spray of ferrocrete dust hissed down from overhead. Galleas paused. He was just a handful of metres from the doorway. Looking back, he saw Tauros, Juno and then the entirety of Mitra's platoon stretched out along the corridor. The humans were following the trio of Space Marines with great care. *There might just be hope for them yet,* he mused.

After a few moments the flexion readouts stabilised. Taking a breath, Galleas eased forward.

It took two more long minutes to reach his objective. Past the doorway, the veteran sergeant glimpsed the orange flickers of distant fires.

Galleas stepped up to the threshold. The space beyond – a hab unit for a family of four in better times – was nothing but a blackened shell. An artillery round had struck the outer wall, blasting it away and knocking out the side walls separating the habs on either side. The floor was now little more than a broad ledge stretching for six metres from the doorway out into empty space.

The Crimson Fist eased through the doorway. The floor beneath his feet was still solid, despite the damage. He crept right up to the ragged edge, where the missing outer wall afforded him a panoramic view of the city centre. What he saw made his blood run cold.

Smoke still rose in places from gaps in the last curtain wall. Imperial gun emplacements along the battlements were blackened ruins, and huge packs of greenskin runts capered over the corpse-choked barricades that had been thrown up to try to stem the xenos tide. Ork camps filled the Residentia Ultris as far as the eye could see, stretching east and west in a squalid band on both sides of the fallen wall. Their cook fires flickered balefully amid the ruined villas of the city's former elite.

Between the horde and the banks of the River Rynn there was nothing but burning ruin, a hellscape of cratered rubble and smashed war machines in a slightly curved swathe nearly a kilometre across. The arc of destruction was centred on the Cassar, looming above the smoke from its position amid the Zona Regis, in the centre of the river. Through gaps in the billowing smoke, Galleas could see the broken stubs of the wide bridges that had once connected the island to the rest of the city. The retreating Imperials had blown the spans behind them, putting the rushing waters of the River Rynn between them and the invaders.

They were too late. The battle had been decided days ago, Galleas realised, while he and his brothers lay unconscious among the dead in the square. For all intents and purposes, New Rynn City had fallen to the greenskins, and they were trapped in the midst of the horde.

CHAPTER SEVEN
POINT OF NO RETURN

ZONA 13 COMMERCIA, NEW RYNN CITY
DAY 97

Darkness had fallen, but ork artillery was still firing at the Cassar. From both sides of the river, batteries of massive cannons – most scavenged from the hulls of crashed ork gunships – fired ragged salvoes in flashes of orange and white, hurling their heavy shells at the Space Marine citadel. Tonnes of steel and explosives struck the void shields surrounding the island and vanished in eerie flickers of phosphorescent light. A few shells, owing to the strange geometries of the defensive fields, were deflected away from the island at random angles, falling into the river or among the ork camps on the far side. The rumble of the barrage rolled over the Residentia Ultris and crashed against the ruined face of the hab unit, more than three kilometres away.

The island's Imperial defenders did not let the onslaught go unanswered. Earthshaker batteries pointed their tubes skyward from the Zona Regis' tree-lined parks and fired a series of short salvoes at the ork guns. Directed by Space Marine spotters high atop the Cassar, the shells nearly always found their mark, wreaking havoc amongst the xenos artillery crews and setting off carelessly stored stacks of shells.

From his vantage point, Galleas saw half a dozen squat, tracked greenskin missile launchers edge into the beaten zone between the ork camps and the river's edge. Lurching roughly over the cratered ground with eight ammo trucks in hot pursuit, the launchers were racing for a patch of relatively level ground at the edge of their effective range where they could launch their guided bombs. They reached their objective in seconds, steel treads scattering trails of sparks as the orks slewed their launchers to a stop. One rocket bomb roared off its launch rail, then another. As they rose on stuttering plumes of fire and smoke they were bracketed in streams of bolter fire from the flanks of the citadel. The bombs were halfway to their target when the Crimson Fists gunners found their mark, touching off the warheads in thunderclaps of red and orange flame. Moments later a volley of turbo-laser fire raked the launch site, chewing apart ork launchers and ammo trucks in an ear-splitting chain of explosions.

Galleas stared at the distant citadel, wreathed in flashes of weapons fire and the ghostly flickers of its void shields. He glanced at the vox readout on his helmet display and selected the icon for the Cassar. 'This is Veteran Squad Galleas calling Epistolary Deguerro,' he called. 'Respond.'

Roaring static and wave-like howls of distortion filled his ears. The interference was actually worse than it had been underground. *Not interference,* he corrected himself, *multi-spectrum jamming. Crude, but effective.* 'This is Veteran

Sergeant Galleas,' he persisted. 'I am transmitting from Zona Thirteen Commercia. Can anyone read me?' The Space Marine paused, listening intently, his hyper-keen senses sifting through the churning noise. Amidst the howling onslaught of the jamming signal and the crosscurrents of atmospheric distortion he thought he could hear a voice, but it was too faint and garbled to understand what was being said.

Galleas noted others moving in the ruined hab unit around him. Tauros and Juno moved up to either side of him, their helmeted heads swivelling slowly left and right as they surveyed the sweep of the ork camps along the river. Mitra appeared at his side a moment later, pulling a pair of field glasses from a pouch at her hip. The veteran sergeant glanced over his shoulder to see Sergeant Kazimir, Corporal Ismail and half of her squad crouching against the rear wall of the hab unit. Olivar was crossing the hab unit's uneven floor with Amador close behind. The veteran sergeant could see the tension in the set of the wounded Space Marine's shoulders.

Tauros spoke over the hammering of the guns. 'I count more than five hundred banners on this side of the river.'

'And not one of them belonging to Snagrod,' Juno observed. 'Pity.'

Mitra lowered her glasses. The lieutenant's face had gone white. 'Emperor save us,' she hissed, her voice full of dread. 'How are we supposed to get through *that*?'

Olivar gave Mitra a scornful look. Like his brothers, he had grasped the tactical situation at once. 'We're not,' he said.

Tauros straightened. 'The tunnels.' He turned to Galleas. 'The tunnels under the river–'

The veteran sergeant shook his head. 'Collapsed. Epistolary Deguerro planned to bring them down once Huron Grim and the others returned from Jadeberry Hill.' He glanced back at the embattled citadel, thinking of Grim and the last transmission he'd received, just before the blast. Was it Kantor that Grim saw at the bottom of the hill? Did the Chapter Master still live, or were the psykers mistaken? He called over the vox again, knowing in the back of his mind there was little chance the Cassar could hear him.

Mitra appeared stricken. She looked from one Space Marine to another. 'What do we do?'

Amador stepped past Tauros, almost to the very edge of the broken floor. He stared down at the greenskin camps. 'I see no reason to wait for the orks to come to us,' he said grimly. 'There are fuel dumps out there. Ammo piles. With the majority of the ork camps grouped so tightly together, it could work in our favour. A fast-moving force could cause a great deal of damage before–'

Galleas clenched his fists. 'The protocol forbids it, brother,' he said, as patiently as he could. 'Our first duty is to survive.'

'Damn the protocol!' Amador cried. The young veteran rounded on Galleas. 'You'd have us hide like rats and wait for the xenos to hunt us down? Our fates are sealed – at least let us die with what little honour we have left!'

Galleas bristled. He pointed at the Cassar. 'The Chapter–'

'The Chapter thinks we're dead already,' Olivar snapped. 'What possible difference does it make?'

The bitterness and anger in Olivar's voice brought Galleas up short. Even Tauros was shocked. The veteran Space Marine started towards Olivar. 'That's enough, brother–'

The rest was lost in the screaming roar of rocket packs and the bloodthirsty howls of greenskins.

The orks rose into view on sputtering columns of flame, the lenses of their crude goggles reflecting the red muzzle flashes of their guns. Slugs snapped through the air, chewing the flakboard walls and kicking up sprays of grit from the ferrocrete floor.

Galleas bit back a curse. The damned xenos had used the thunder of the barrage to cover their approach until the very last moment. Now the air was full of them, arcing high over the hab unit and blazing away at the exposed Imperials below.

The Crimson Fists reacted at once, returning the hailstorm of fire with precise, aimed shots from their boltguns. Dying orks corkscrewed through the air on out-of-control rocket packs or vanished in blots of flame as mass-reactive shells pierced their fuel tanks. Galleas saw Tauros stagger as a burst of ork slugs hammered against his shoulders and chest. The veteran sergeant took aim and shot another greenskin out of the air. 'Back into the corridor!' he ordered. 'Move!'

The Space Marines began to withdraw in good order, firing single shots as they edged back across the broken floor. Guttural battle cries filled the air as the surviving orks hurled sputtering grenades at the Imperials and then cut their rocket motors, plunging towards their prey.

Most of the grenades went wide of their mark, bouncing across the roof of the hab unit or disappearing through gaps in the floor. One of the club-like bombs landed less than a metre to Galleas' right. He heard a warning shout, then a flash of movement at his side as Mitra lunged for the grenade.

She wasn't going to make it. Galleas calculated angles and speeds in the blink of an eye, and knew the grenade would go off just as the lieutenant's hand closed on its grip. Without thinking, he reversed direction and got between her and the bomb. Mitra crashed into his shoulder and bounced backwards as the grenade went off, the concussion slapping Galleas in the face and lashing his armour with shrapnel. He scarcely felt either, shielded behind layers of heavy ceramite plate. At best, it was a momentary distraction – which was exactly what the greenskins intended.

Howling figures dropped down on Galleas out of the fire-shot night. The veteran sergeant bellowed an oath and brought up his bolter, blasting one of the xenos backwards with a point-blank shot to the chest. Another ork crashed heavily into his shoulder, knocking him off his feet. As he hit the floor the greenskin's gun boomed, close enough that his helmet display dimmed to compensate for the muzzle flash. The slug punched into the ferrocrete beside Galleas' head.

The ork howled and pressed its attack, raising its cleaver – only to stagger backwards as a lasgun bolt punched into its chest. Two more shots followed in quick succession, stabbing into the greenskin's vitals, and the xenos toppled slowly onto its side.

More lasgun bolts snapped across the hab unit, targeting greenskins locked in combat with the Space Marines. Galleas looked back to see Ismail dragging Mitra onto her feet while her surviving squadmates provided covering fire. One of the Rynnsguard lay in a pool of blood, his vacant eyes staring skyward.

Tauros had made it back through the doorway and into the corridor beyond. Olivar covered the doorway, firing at the xenos surrounding Juno and Amador. There were more than a dozen of the greenskins, lunging and hacking at the Space Marines from all sides.

Galleas surged to his feet. 'Fall back!' he shouted at the Rynnsguard, then reached for Night's Edge. The power sword blazed to life as he leapt into the fray.

'Olivar, cover Juno!' he commanded, heading for Amador. The veteran was taunting the xenos, daring them to come close. His combat knife dripped with greenskin blood. A trio of foes lay dead at his feet.

Juno had dealt with five of the greenskins in rapid succession. Amador seemed determined to beat his brother's score.

Galleas fell upon the orks from behind. His power sword sliced through the skin of a greenskin rocket pack. Pressurised fuel ignited at the touch of the blade's energy field, spraying him and the surrounding xenos with liquid fire. The orks scattered, screaming in pain.

Amador spun, knife poised to strike. The veteran sergeant glared at him. 'I gave you an order, brother,' he growled. 'Get back into the corridor with the rest of the squad. *Now.*'

The young veteran raised his chin defiantly. 'This is as good a place to die as any,' he shot back.

Galleas took a step forward. 'That's not for you to decide, Claudio Amador. Now fall back, double-quick, or by the Emperor I'll knock you cold and drag you out of here myself.'

Amador hesitated, and for a moment Galleas thought the young hothead was actually going to test him. Then, with a muttered curse and a sideways glance at Juno, Amador pushed past Galleas and headed for the door.

A screaming greenskin, on fire from head to toe, charged at Galleas. The veteran sergeant shot the xenos through the head. 'Juno!' he called.

'Coming!' Juno slashed an ork's throat open and then

kicked the xenos in the chest, sending it tumbling out into space. The veteran fell back at once, stepping over the bodies cut down by Olivar's deadly fire.

Galleas was the last one through the doorway, exchanging fire with the surviving orks at the far end of the hab unit, only to find himself in the middle of another fight. More orks had landed on the roof and worked their way inside, falling on the Rynnsguard from above. One of the human soldiers lay nearly at Galleas' feet with an ork cleaver buried in his skull. Another grappled with a snarling greenskin just a few metres away. Before Galleas could react, the ork lost his footing on a tilted ferrocrete slab and fell backwards through a hole in the floor, dragging his foe along with him.

A shotgun boomed, blasting an ork off its feet. Sergeant Kazimir stood amid the beleaguered Rynnsguard, holding the platoon together by force of will alone. 'Stand fast!' he roared. 'If the greenskins came here to die, then by the Emperor, we'll oblige 'em!'

Lieutenant Mitra, a bloody scrape livid across her pale cheek, led Corporal Ismail and her squad forward, firing into the mass of orks. Galleas left Olivar to cover the door and went after her. Tauros, Juno and Amador had already joined the fight, catching the xenos unawares and cutting them down with bolter and blade. The sudden appearance of the Crimson Fists turned the tide and panicked the remaining orks, who tried to flee back the way they'd come. Barely a handful got away.

Moments later, gunfire and grenade blasts echoed from the far end of the corridor. 'Valentus?' Galleas called over the vox.

'The stairwell is full of orks,' the venerable Space Marine reported.

'Can we fight our way through?'

'We're barely holding them off as it is.'

Lieutenant Mitra worked her way over to Galleas. Under fire she was calm and composed, but her expression was grave. She glanced in the direction of the gunfire. 'I don't much like the sound of that,' she said darkly.

'The orks have seized the stairwell.' Galleas nodded his head at the greenskin corpses along the corridor. 'The aerial assault was meant to distract us and fix us in place so the xenos could cut off our escape route.'

More shots rang out – this time from the opposite end of the corridor. Ork slugs ricocheted from fallen beams and ferrocrete slabs, forcing the Rynnsguard back into cover. A slug buzzed through the air close enough to make the lieutenant flinch.

'They've found another way up!' She shook her head. 'There's a lot of wreckage at that end. I don't know if the orks can get past, but they've got us in a crossfire.'

Galleas' mind raced, looking for a way out of the trap. The orks had both stairwells, and the lifts were blocked with debris. They could slip through the gaps in the floor and reach the level below, but that would buy them only a few extra minutes at best.

Mitra settled behind a chunk of ferrocrete and raised her carbine. 'I'm not going to be taken alive,' she swore. 'By the Emperor, I won't. I've seen what the orks do with their prisoners. I'll throw myself out of a window first.'

The veteran sergeant nodded. 'A wise choice–' He glanced back at the dead greenskins and froze. The answer had been right in front of him the entire time.

Mitra frowned. 'What is it?'

Galleas ran a series of calculations in his head. It could

work, he surmised. It *had* to work. 'Tauros, Juno, Olivar –
help me with these rocket packs!'

The Space Marines quickly separated seven of the crude
engines from their dead owners. Juno held one up and
eyed it dubiously. 'You can't be serious.'

A handful of wild shots careened down the corridor. The
orks at the far end were getting closer. 'It only has to work
for a few seconds,' Galleas insisted. He beckoned to the
Rynnsguard. 'Help us strap these on. Quickly!'

The soldiers were even more bemused than Juno, but
they did as they were told. Mitra helped tighten the straps
across Galleas' chest. 'Are you going to do what I think
you're going to do?'

Galleas nodded. The rocket fit awkwardly atop the
armour's backpack power unit and made it difficult to stand
upright, but it would have to do. 'It's the best chance we
have.'

'What about the rest of us?'

'We'll carry four at a time,' the veteran sergeant said. 'I've
done the calculations. The thrust-to-weight ratio should
work in our favour.'

Mitra's eyebrows rose. '*Should?*'

'You were already planning on jumping, lieutenant. Is
this truly any worse?' Galleas called over the vox. 'Valentus, Royas, block the stairwell entrance as best you can and
join us at the centre of the corridor. Hurry!'

While Valentus and Royas were being fitted with their
own rockets, Galleas had Enginseer Oros booby-trap the
remaining packs with the orks' own grenades. The fire
coming from both ends of the corridor was increasing
by the second. The Space Marines had done what they
could to block the passageway, but the greenskins were

closing in. Galleas ordered the Imperials to fall back into three adjoining hab units on the building's southern side.

Galleas stepped up to the unit's smashed window frame. A few well-placed kicks widened the opening further. Mitra and three ashen-faced soldiers crowded around him. The humans were careful not to look down at the rubble-strewn landscape below.

The veteran sergeant stowed his weapons and grabbed hold of the heavy-duty webbing across the soldiers' backs. As he tested his grip, he showed Mitra the rocket's firing lever. 'When I give you the word, activate the rocket,' he said.

'*Me?*'

'You'll note my hands are full, lieutenant.'

Mitra took a deep breath. 'All right. When do we go–'

The bellowing of orks sounded just outside the door. '*Now!*' Galleas called over the vox, and leapt into the open air.

The drop was little more than forty-six metres; a dozen metres less and the Space Marines could have made the jump unaided. Galleas and his charges fell in a steep arc, aiming for the broad plaza in front of the building's entrance. Wild screams rode the night air.

Galleas tightened his grip on the soldiers. 'Now, lieutenant!'

Mitra hit the lever. There was a loud *bang* and a roiling cloud of oily smoke erupted from the rocket exhaust, followed by a rumble that swelled to a sputtering roar as the engine came to life. Galleas jerked against the thick straps and watched warning sigils flash in his helmet display as his arms and shoulders took up the full weight of four humans in combat gear.

The rocket wasn't built to carry such a load. They fell –
but more slowly than they had before. Galleas watched the
ground rush up to meet them. He took the impact first,
releasing the humans a half-second later. A red sigil flashed,
warning him of further damage to his right knee joint. The
veteran sergeant pitched forward, bouncing across the broken stone. The rocket dragged him another twenty metres
before he could shut it down.

Galleas rolled onto his side, tearing at the straps of the
rocket pack. His ears rang, but compared to an orbital drop
the impact had been minimal. Looking back, he saw the
rest of the squad touching down with their cargoes. The
Rynnsguard were picking themselves up off the ground,
battered and scraped but otherwise unharmed.

Half a dozen monstrous, ungainly ork trucks sat outside
the entrance to the hab unit, their petrochem engines rumbling. Galleas drew his bolter and headed for the vehicles,
his brothers falling in behind him.

One of the trucks was different from the others. Generators hummed from its cargo bed, and a forest of crooked
antennas jutted from its upper deck. As the Space Marines
approached, an ork engineer leapt from the back of the
vehicle and broke into a run, screeching in panic. Royas
gunned the xenos down before it had covered more than
a metre.

Frustrated shouts and a flurry of wild shots rained down
on the Imperials from the upper floor of the hab unit.
Galleas reckoned they only had a few minutes before the
orks reached the ground floor. He gestured at the idling
trucks. 'Tauros, pick two transports and disable the rest,'
he ordered.

As the squad went to work, he approached the ork

engineer's truck and peered warily into the cargo bay. Inside was a trio of rumbling generators, linked by thick cables to a bank of odd-looking machines. He studied their flickering displays, trying to understand their function. Finally, he shook his head. 'Enginseer Oros!' he called.

Limping slightly, the tech-priest hurried over and genuflected, making the sign of the Machine-God. 'How may I serve, my lord?'

'What do you make of this?'

The enginseer extended his mechadendrites and climbed, spider-like, into the back of the truck. Murmuring a litany against the temptations of xenos tech, the priest bent over the displays.

'Frequency. Amplitude. Phase analysis.' The tech-priest nodded thoughtfully. 'This is a direction finder, my lord. It can track vox signals up to several kilometres away.'

The news shocked Galleas. 'I led them to us. I was broadcasting our location every time I tried to contact the Cassar.' *First the greenskins use our own tactics against us,* he thought. *Now our own wargear betrays us.* 'Destroy it,' he commanded.

Galleas left Oros to his task. Juno, Valentus and Amador were fixing grenades to three of the trucks' fuel tanks. 'Lieutenant Mitra!' the veteran sergeant called. He pointed at the trucks Tauros had selected. 'Get your troops aboard!'

The dull thud of explosions echoed from the upper floors of the hab unit. Oros clambered from the back of the ork truck. Moments later, the generators in the cargo bed erupted in a series of deafening blasts and a shower of orange sparks. Juno and the others primed their grenades as the captured trucks started to roll, the three Space Marines sprinting to catch up.

Galleas reached down and pulled Juno into the cargo bay

of the truck he shared with Amador, Mitra and ten of her troops. The trucks roared off into the darkness, heavy tyres crunching over piles of rubble. Behind them, the remaining trucks erupted in flames, one after another, adding to the conflagration spreading through the upper floors of the hab unit.

'We'll ride as far as Zona Eighteen and then abandon the trucks,' Galleas said. 'Then we'll double back and go to ground somewhere in Zona Fifteen.'

Mitra studied him, her face hidden in shadow. 'And after that?'

Galleas did not respond at first. He looked northwards, seeking the Cassar. The citadel rose above the hab blocks, ghostly light flickering from its void shields as the orks continued their bombardment.

'The Cassar endures,' he said at last. 'Help is coming – we know that at least one of our ships escaped the system to summon aid. Every day that passes brings Rynn's World closer to salvation.

'While the Cassar fights, so must we,' Galleas told them. 'No matter the cost.'

CHAPTER EIGHT

FIRE IN THE BLOOD

Titus Juno let out a deep, bestial growl and charged at the trio of Rynnsguard troops. He'd taken off his helmet, and his lips were drawn back in a bloodthirsty snarl. The tip of the heavy ork cleaver in his hand scraped against the basement ceiling overhead, raining an arc of fat orange sparks in his wake.

Corporal Ismail and her squad mates were slow to react to the sudden onslaught. Juno reached them in three lumbering steps and took a wide swing at the soldier to his right. The Rynnsguard was frozen, his exhausted mind trying to decide whether to parry the blow with his own cleaver or attempt to dodge out of the way. At the last moment Ismail saved him, shouldering the dazed trooper out of the reach of the blow and then leaping into Juno's path herself. With a fierce cry she swung her own cleaver with both hands, striking Juno a ringing blow on the thigh.

The Crimson Fist scarcely broke stride. He was a

nightmarish figure, looming over the desperate humans, his once-resplendent armour fouled by layers of mud, grit and grime. He felled Corporal Ismail with a backhanded blow of his cleaver just as the third soldier rushed him from the left, cleaver outstretched. Juno rounded on the man, snarling, and the soldier pulled up short. The Space Marine batted the blade from the man's hand and then dropped the Rynnsguard with a blow to his ribs.

Too late, the last remaining soldier recovered his wits. Juno was turned away from him; sensing an opportunity, the Rynnsguard lunged forward, stabbing for Juno's mid-section. But the attack came too slow. Juno caught the movement and turned, almost lazily, letting the soldier's blade pass harmlessly by. The flat of the Space Marine's cleaver rapped the trooper smartly on the side of his helmet, sending the human sprawling into the midst of a filthy puddle.

Juno placed his fists on his hips and shook his head in dismay. For a moment, the only sounds were the gasping breaths of the soldiers and the steady trickle of water through the many cracks in the basement's ceiling. 'Dead again,' the Space Marine declared. 'And nothing to show for it. How many times do we have to go over this?'

Ismail rolled into a sitting position, grimacing as she put a hand to her throbbing shoulder. The practice weapons were dulled and the soldiers' flak armour absorbed some of the impact, but the blows still hurt when they landed. 'I put a blade into your damned leg, didn't I?' she panted.

Juno glanced down at his thigh, where a dull streak through the crusted mud showed where Ismail's blow had landed. 'That? I didn't even feel it,' he said. 'I'm an *ork*, corporal. I'm big, stupid and angry. I'll pull your little knife out of my leg and pick my teeth with it after I've finished tearing you to bits.' He raised his head to address the rest of Ismail's depleted squad, who were dutifully observing the practice session from a mostly dry portion of the basement a few metres away.

'An ork is like a maddened grox. It charges the first thing that catches its attention,' he told them. 'It all comes down to numbers. One of you can hurt a greenskin. Two of you can cripple it. Three of you should be able to kill it, but you've got to work together, and you've got to *think.*' He tapped at the inside of his thigh with the point of his cleaver. 'Go for the big arteries in the legs. A quick thrust, eight or ten centimetres deep, is enough. The ork will bleed out in less than a minute, stop moving ten seconds or so after that.' He went on, rapping the side of his knee. 'Here you go after the tendons. Front or back works just as well. Cut the cords and then let gravity do the rest. Once he's down on your level, it's elbows, throat and eyes.'

Ismail shook her head, wiping sweat and gritty water from her eyes. 'It's no good. You're too damned fast.'

Juno frowned. 'I'm going no faster than a typical greenskin, corporal. And they're not going to slow down to give you a better chance to hit them. You just have to move faster.' He beckoned. 'Get up and try again.'

Ismail sighed. The Rynnsguard were filthy and haggard, their fatigues stiff with dried sweat, dirt and blood. 'For pity's sake, my lord,' she said dully. 'We've been at this for over an hour already.'

The Space Marine gave a grim chuckle. 'Do you think the orks care that you're tired, corporal? Get up. You can rest once you've killed me.'

Ismail stared up at Juno for a long moment, as though

trying to summon the strength to argue with the towering Space Marine. Her squad mates watched the exchange with a kind of weary dread, waiting to see what their leader would do.

Sergeant Kazimir broke the lengthening silence with a ragged cough. The grizzled soldier leaned forward and spat into a nearby puddle. 'How about we give Vila's squad a turn?' he suggested. 'Maybe Ismail could learn a thing or two by watching them?'

The idea drew groans from Vila's troops and sullen growls from Ismail's men. Ismail squeezed her eyes shut and clenched her fists, digging deep for some small reserve of strength. Doggedly, she gathered her feet underneath her and forced herself to stand. One by one, her squad mates followed suit.

Juno nodded approvingly. 'Right, then.' He turned and went back across the basement to his starting place. 'Remember what I told you. Work together. Go for the knees. Do it right and one or two of you should still be standing after I'm dead.'

Veteran Brother Royas eyed Juno disdainfully from the far side of the chamber as the training session began again. 'Hopeless,' he muttered, almost too low for Galleas to catch, then went back to work on a belt of shells for the clumsy ork gun at his side. Tauros, seated close by, gave Royas a sidelong look, but said nothing, his own hands busy with the fuse mechanism of an Imperial anti-tank mine. Next to him, Amador and Valentus were still as statues, lost in recuperative meditation. Olivar knelt in the far corner of the room, head bowed and fists clenched. Whenever they weren't on the move he'd taken to going off by himself and reciting the Litanies of Hate for hours on end.

Galleas sat atop a pile of rubble close to Royas with Night's Edge resting across his knees. The gauntleted fingertips of his left hand rested lightly upon the ancient blade, drawing strength from its scarred, unyielding surface. He meditated upon its six thousand years of unbroken service to the God-Emperor of Mankind and prepared himself, body and soul, for the long battles to come.

It had been just fifteen days since Jadeberry Hill and the breach at Zona Thirteen. The spring season was nearly over, and Matiluvia, the Month of Hammering Rains, was well under way. The storms would roll in from the sea in titanic waves through the afternoon and evening, shrouding the ruined city in shifting curtains of rain. The River Rynn was in full flood, swirling around the Zona Regis and lashing at its embankments. Water poured into ruined buildings and flooded the rubble-choked streets, leaving a morass of mud and filth in its wake.

The heavy rains worked in the Imperials' favour, making it all but impossible for the orks to track them through the ruins. Galleas had used the weather to his advantage as much as possible, changing position daily and scavenging for weapons and supplies along the way. He had ordered the squad to stow their boltguns and conserve their limited stocks of ammunition. In their place, the veterans and their Rynnsguard counterparts carried ork guns and the xenos' crude stick grenades. The human soldiers took to the weapons grudgingly; they were inaccurate and difficult to handle, but as long as the greenskins held the city they would never run out of shells. Tauros, Valentus and Amador had been tasked with teaching the Rynnsguard the rudiments of handling the xenos weapons effectively, but progress was frustratingly slow.

Galleas had observed much about Mitra's platoon over the past weeks, and did not care for what he saw. The soldiers were poorly trained and suffered from an appalling degree of individuality. Each squad was more or less a reflection of its leader, with no regard for doctrine or ritual. Corporal Ismail had the instincts of a hive ganger – and the skills to match – but often let her courage get the better of her. Corporal Vila, by contrast, was an opportunist and a schemer, who followed the path of least resistance wherever he could. Keeping him in line was a full-time job for Sergeant Kazimir, and it was clear there was no love lost between the two. The older man, a former sergeant in the Astra Militarum and a veteran of many offworld campaigns, held the platoon together and kept them fighting through sheer force of will.

Galleas glanced up from his meditations and sought out Lieutenant Mitra. The Rynnsguard officer sat apart from her troops, conversing quietly with Vega and Gomez. An officer by virtue of her social class, what she lacked in actual combat experience she tried to make up for with a fierce sense of duty.

After assessing the soldiers' many deficiencies, Galleas had set about correcting them through a steady regimen of lectures and training. Olivar had been scandalised by the very idea of sharing even the tiniest fraction of the Crimson Fists tactical training, but the veteran sergeant was unmoved. It was a minor sin as far as he was concerned, and entirely justified when the very survival of the Chapter was at stake.

Mitra chanced to look up from her conversation just as Galleas' attention was turned her way. The lieutenant's face was pale and haggard, shadowed in places by smudges of ash and grime. When she saw the veteran sergeant staring at her she beckoned to Vega and rose stiffly to her feet, then began picking her way around the perimeter of the chamber towards him.

Juno squared off against Ismail and her squad mates and rushed forward again, his exaggerated, ork-like movements almost comical to Space Marine eyes. But the Rynnsguard didn't wait to receive his charge this time; at Ismail's shout, the three humans went on the offensive, rushing straight at Juno and hacking at him from three sides. Ismail and one of her mates went down in moments, swept off their feet by the flat of Juno's cleaver – but then the Space Marine grudgingly sank to one knee. Galleas grunted in surprise. He hadn't even seen the crippling blow strike home. The last soldier hesitated, just out of Juno's reach, uncertain how to get inside the Space Marine's guard and finish him off.

Mitra threaded her way past the sitting Space Marines, earning a glare from Royas as she and Vega went by. 'May we have a word, my lord?' she asked as she reached Galleas' side. There was a rasp to her voice, just like Kazimir's.

'What is it, lieutenant?'

Mitra paused, considering her words carefully. 'Do you still intend on ambushing the ork convoy this evening?'

'Of course. That is the whole reason we're here.'

'Then stop this incessant training,' she demanded. 'My troops are exhausted, my lord. They haven't spent more than eight hours in the same place in the last eighteen days.'

Galleas frowned. 'We're deep within enemy territory, lieutenant. We have to keep moving to stay ahead of enemy patrols.'

'I realise that,' she said. 'Believe me. But the pace...' Mitra paused, her lips pressing together in frustration. 'We march all night, then it's wargear maintenance, lectures and training. Pausing to eat a few bites and get a few hours' sleep seems almost like an afterthought.'

The veteran sergeant stared at her. 'My brothers and I haven't eaten or slept in more than a month, lieutenant. War makes demands of us all.'

Vega cleared his throat. 'With all due respect, my lord, we are not Angels of Death, but mere mortals, with mortal failings.' The medic glanced from Mitra to Galleas and back again, clearly uncomfortable at being part of the discussion. 'There is also the matter of the rain…'

'Whether your troops are adequately dry or not is of no concern to me,' Galleas snapped.

'That's not what he means,' Mitra interjected. 'The flooding has spread raw sewage and xenos filth throughout the city. It's making us sick.'

'Were you not given antiviral treatments when you were mobilised?'

Mitra sighed. 'There wasn't time. We'd just been called up and issued our weapons when Snagrod arrived.'

'What would you have me do, lieutenant? I am capable of many things, but I cannot stop the rain.'

Mitra turned to the medic. Vega shifted uneasily. 'There is a chirurgium in Zona Twenty-three,' he said. 'It was the primary medical facility for the entire sector. There is certain to be antivirals and other useful potions there.'

'We considered raiding it for supplies weeks ago,' Mitra continued, 'but the complex was overrun by greenskins, and the risk seemed too great at the time.'

Across the basement, Juno was lurching at the last of Ismail's men like a maddened greenskin, half-crawling, half-dragging himself across the ferrocrete. The Rynnsguard soldier hesitated, wary of the heavy blade in Juno's hand.

The man's chest was heaving with exertion, and his hands had begun to tremble.

'Lieutenant, I will be frank – your soldiers' failings stem from poor training and a lack of will, and until those deficiencies are corrected they are of no use to me. The training regimen is no different than what I myself experienced as an initiate.'

'But surely not under conditions like this!' Mitra protested.

'Certainly not,' Galleas agreed. 'They were much, much worse. Only fifteen per cent of the initiates in my training cycle survived.'

Vega shook his head doggedly. 'Even machines have their limits, my lord. Push them too far, and they break.'

Galleas raised Night's Edge. The power sword's edge glimmered coldly in the lantern light. 'Some do. I grant you that. But not those forged in the hottest fires. Those endure forever.'

Vega relented with a sigh, but Mitra was not so willing to accept defeat. 'My lord, *please*,' she said. 'If you keep this up, you're going to kill them.'

'And if I don't, the greenskins most assuredly will. That is the way of war, lieutenant.' He rose, sliding Night's Edge into its scabbard. 'Now I suggest you make better use of your time and prepare for the operation this evening. We move out in three hours, twenty-two minutes.'

Across the basement there was the dull thud of a blade striking flak armour. Ismail's squad mate collapsed, hugging his ribs. Juno shook his head in disdain.

'Again,' the Space Marine said, rising to his feet.

Thunder rumbled to the east, out over the Dantine Straits – brassy, ponderous drumbeats that momentarily drowned out the noise of ork guns along the river. For the moment, the skies above the city were clear, but purple-black clouds were massing along the eastern horizon, warning of another round of heavy rains to come.

Lightning flickered, casting stark shadows across the ruined landscape of Zona Twenty-four. It was an hour past sunset. The convoy was running late, but that sort of thing was to be expected from the greenskins. Their customary lack of discipline would work in the Imperials' favour. The orks would be more reckless than usual, racing to get back to their camp before full dark.

Over the past few weeks it had become clear to Galleas that the siege of the Zona Regis was devolving into a stalemate. The Imperial forces were completely surrounded, having collapsed the underground tunnels and the network of bridges that had once provided access to the rest of the city. But the potent void shields of the Cassar were impervious to the guns of the greenskin horde, allowing Imperial artillery to create a killzone for many square kilometres along both sides of the river. Already, several mass assaults had been soundly crushed before they had even reached the river's edge; even an aerial attack by a fleet of greenskin koptas had been turned back with severe losses. The only possible danger to the Imperial bastion was a sustained bombardment from orbit, but the horde's war camps were now so close to the island that calling down such a strike was more dangerous to the orks than to the Cassar itself.

Of course, the invulnerability of the island's void shields hadn't stopped the horde from continuing to fire at the Cassar with every weapon they had. Every day the orks consumed a huge quantity of ammunition for no appreciable effect, except perhaps as entertainment. Stocks of shells had run so low that the warbands had been forced to call for supplies from the orbiting fleet. Every day, transports landed at the edge of the city, outside the reach of the Cassar's guns, where convoys of ork trucks would be loaded with tonnes of weapons and ammunition for delivery to the warbands camped near the river.

The ambush Galleas had planned was an elementary one. The orks had grown careless, believing the surviving Imperials to be bottled up on the island. Surprise would be total, forcing the simple-minded xenos to behave in a straightforward, predictable pattern. If the Rynnsguard remembered their training and managed even a modicum of discipline, they would massacre the greenskins. If not...

Galleas had observed his intended target for more than a week. The convoy followed the same route through the city every time. In Zona Twenty-four the convoy's path wound through a narrow street clogged at intervals with piles of debris from the bombed-out buildings on either side. It transformed an otherwise straight road into a winding route pocked with shell craters that would force the vehicles to slow down almost to a crawl.

His squad was hidden in the rubble of three adjacent buildings that faced a stretch of road almost a hundred metres long. Their salvaged anti-tank mine rested at the bottom of a flooded shell hole at the northern end of the killzone to Galleas' right. The entirety of the Rynnsguard platoon, save Sergeant Kazimir, were in firing positions along the second floor of a burned-out residential building directly behind the Space Marines. The sergeant, armed with a scavenged ork rocket launcher, was hidden behind a debris pile covering the south end of the killzone to Galleas' left.

When the lead truck in the convoy hit the mine, Kazimir would knock out the rear truck with the rocket launcher, trapping the rest of the vehicles in the killzone. The Rynnsguard would then open fire, raking the surviving trucks. Galleas didn't expect much accuracy from Mitra's troops; they were, in fact, nothing more than a lure. When the orks got over the initial shock of the explosions, they would react to the gunfire as greenskins always did, leaping out of the relative safety of their trucks and charging into the ruins to attack their ambushers face-to-face. The xenos would be in amongst Galleas' brothers before they realised their peril, and then the real slaughter would begin.

The operation was almost foolproof. It was the sort of ambush that Space Marine Scouts were trained in, and one that a veteran Space Marine squad could carry off at the spur of a moment. All Mitra's troops had to do was sit and wait for the mine to go off, and then open fire with everything they had. The xenos would take care of the rest. Nonetheless, as Galleas listened for the sound of the greenskins' approach he found himself contemplating alternative plans in case the poorly disciplined troopers fired too early or too late.

Perhaps Royas and Olivar are right, the veteran sergeant thought. The very idea of a Crimson Fists squad depending on the support of a Rynnsguard unit verged on heresy. There was no question that he and his squad could move faster and operate more freely on their own – but in a situation as desperate as this, was he not obligated to use every asset available to fight the enemy?

If they can truly be called an asset, Galleas thought, recalling Juno's training session hours before. *That's the question.*

The veteran sergeant's reverie was broken by the distant

snarl of petrochem engines. Galleas listened, separating the mingled sounds into discreet sources. *Four trucks and a pair of escorts,* he reckoned, nodding in satisfaction. Their quarry was approaching.

He straightened slightly, using hand signals to alert his brothers. Tauros and Royas were hidden in the wreckage of the building to Galleas' left, while Juno and Valentus were situated in the ruins to his right. He held the centre, alongside Amador and Olivar. The Space Marines were pressed against fallen beams and heaps of rubble, their armour so thickly coated with ferrocrete dust that they blended almost perfectly with their surroundings. Wide puddles of filthy water stretched across the floors of the bombed-out buildings, and periodic flooding had coated the lower third of the interior walls with a foul layer of brownish-yellow slime. Even with the rains, the air was thick with the stench.

The veterans acknowledged Galleas' signal and prepared their weapons. Off to the far left, behind a two-storey mound of rubble, Kazimir raised the xenos rocket launcher to his shoulder.

The engines grew louder, echoing among the broken buildings. Galleas caught the sound of a deep voice murmuring intently over the engine noise; he glanced to the right and saw Olivar kneeling behind a broken ferrocrete ceiling beam, his forehead pressed to the stone, muttering the Litanies of Hate. For a moment the veteran sergeant contemplated reprimanding his brother for the breach of noise discipline, but decided to let it go. The orks weren't likely to hear anything but their own engines, and if the litany inspired Olivar and his brothers to greater acts of vengeance, then so much the better.

Galleas transferred the clumsy ork gun to his left hand

and drew Night's Edge. The weight of the ancient weapon in his hand was all the inspiration he required.

The snarl of engines swelled to a raspy growl, then a thunderous roar that Galleas could feel against the surface of his armour. Seconds later, a pair of ork warbuggies burst into view around the corner, their knobby tyres kicking up sprays of grime as they dashed up the road. The crews of the two buggies yelled oaths at one another as they raced around the shell holes in their path, some large enough to swallow a buggy whole.

Steady, Galleas willed to the Rynnsguard troops in the building behind him. *Let them pass.*

The buggies thundered past, oblivious to the trap laid in their path. They disappeared around the corner seventy-five metres to Galleas' right. The veteran sergeant relaxed slightly. *Just a few moments more.*

The first of the ork trucks lumbered into view. It was a towering, open-topped transport, with a huge engine and layers of crude, bolted-on armour. Garish tribal symbols were splashed on the truck's rusting flanks. Heavy guns bristled from mounts atop the vehicle's cab and along the upper rim of the cargo bed. The gunners paid their surroundings little mind, shouting instead at the driver to move faster and catch the swift-moving buggies. The truck rocked like a ship in a storm as it ploughed through one crater after another, drenching the surrounding ruins in gouts of filthy spray.

A second truck appeared, right on the tail of the first, followed by a third. Galleas reckoned the tail-end transport would be inside the killzone in another few seconds, just as the lead truck would hit the waiting mine.

The veteran sergeant bared his teeth in a mirthless grin

as the last elements of the trap began to slide neatly into place – then a furious shout rent the air, followed by a rattling burst of automatic fire.

Slugs sparked and rang along the flank of the second ork truck, raking it from front to back. An ork gunner pitched back into the cargo bay in a spray of blood and brain matter. The rest shouted in surprise, hosing the ruins with unaimed fire. Tyres howled as the driver of the second truck slammed on the brakes, bringing the transport to a screeching halt.

Heavy shells hammered into the walls and the piles of rubble surrounding the Space Marines. Furious, Galleas whirled, an oath rising to his lips as he looked back towards the Rynnsguard positions – but the fire hadn't come from them. It was Olivar, clambering drunkenly over the top of the fallen ceiling beam and charging at the ork trucks.

The lead truck in the convoy shuddered to a halt – well short of the crater holding the mine. Its heavy guns opened up, raking the buildings to either side of the transport. A moment later the third truck joined in, adding to the storm of fire. Orks leapt from the vehicles' cargo bays, brandishing guns and chainaxes as they charged, not at the still-hidden Rynnsguard, but directly into the Space Marines' positions.

The Imperials had lost the element of surprise, and now the battle threatened to spin completely out of Galleas' control. He reacted instantly, his instincts honed by more than a century of constant war.

'At them, brothers!' he roared, rising from cover. Night's Edge blazed in his hand. 'Vengeance for the fallen!' He unleashed a stream of slugs into the mass of charging orks, and then gestured with his power sword at the first truck. 'Valentus! Take out the leader!'

Valentus saw the danger as clearly as Galleas, and was already on the move. If the lead truck wasn't disabled, there was nothing to stop the convoy – save the xenos themselves – from hitting the throttle and racing away. The veteran Space Marine dashed through a hail of ork slugs, his skeletal face lit by the fiery glow of muzzle flashes. A slug struck his left pauldron, leaving a bright grey smear across the dusty metal, but Valentus scarcely missed a step. A burst from his own gun raked along the top of the truck's cargo bed, causing the ork gunners to duck behind cover. When they did, he lifted a tied-together bundle of greenskin stick bombs and lobbed them in a perfect arc into the back of the truck. The ork gunners had just enough time to bellow in terror before the armoured bed blew apart in a tremendous blast, scattering burning corpses and thousands of rounds of red-hot ammunition in every direction.

For a brief instant the killzone was bathed in orange light, throwing the chaotic melee into stark relief. Galleas counted almost thirty orks on the ground, rushing to surround the now-revealed Space Marines. Olivar was less than a dozen metres from the second truck, dividing his fire between the enemy gunners and the oncoming mob. His slugs tore through the front rank of charging greenskins, toppling three of them, before the heavy guns on the truck converged on him. Slugs battered Olivar, striking sparks from his shoulders, chest and legs. One round crashed into his helmet, snapping his head around sharply. The Crimson Fist staggered another step forward before he collapsed, his scavenged gun firing wildly as he fell.

The orks closed in around Olivar, their chain axes roaring. They did not see Titus Juno until the Space Marine leapt over a broken wall and landed in their midst, his short sword flashing. Orks fell in a welter of blood and severed body parts. The xenos gunners, just ten metres away, shouted in rage and brought their weapons to bear, but Juno stayed on the move, diving deeper into the mob and denying them an easy target.

Galleas charged forward, his scavenged gun hammering at the greenskins. Two of the xenos fell before the crude weapon jammed. The veteran sergeant flung it at a greenskin, crushing its skull, and then he was among the rest, slashing with his blade.

Off to the left, Amador charged into the teeth of the mob with an exultant shout, brandishing his combat knife in one hand and an ork axe in the other. A burst from an ork heavy gun stitched across his breastplate, staggering but not slowing him. His axe spun in a blurring arc, chopping through a greenskin's thick neck. Tauros and Royas were circling the mob, seeking to flank the xenos from the left, but concentrated fire from the third ork truck forced them into cover.

Tyres squalled at the far end of the killzone. The fourth truck had appeared, rushing forward at the sound of gunfire. The driver failed to stop in time, smashing into the back of the third truck with a crunch of metal and plastek.

Sergeant Kazimir had kept his nerve since the fighting began, waiting for his moment. As the fourth truck crashed to a halt he rose from cover and brought the greenskin rocket launcher to his shoulder. At such close range, even the crude xenos weapon could scarcely miss its target. The rocket burst from the launcher with a thunderous blast and smashed into the side of the fourth truck, detonating its cargo and consuming it in a roaring fireball. The explosion raked the third truck with molten shrapnel, killing most of its gunners and setting it ablaze.

More slugs snapped over Galleas' head – this time from the building behind him. The Rynnsguard had swung into action at last, firing down into the cargo beds of the surviving trucks. The fire from the heavy guns slackened, and the Space Marines pressed the advantage, carving their way into the mob. The veteran sergeant ducked the sweep of an ork axe and slashed deep into the greenskin's torso, severing its spine. Now the xenos were all around him, blades raking at the curved plates of his armour. Amador was surrounded as well, trading blows with the greenskins on every side. An axe caught him in the side of the knee and he staggered. An ork saw its chance and tackled him, knocking the Space Marine off his feet.

Galleas snarled an angry curse and pressed forward, trying to reach Amador. Royas closed in from the left, firing point-blank at the greenskins in his path. The Crimson Fists had unleashed a storm of carnage against the xenos, but their attack was losing momentum against the sheer numbers of the mob. They had to break the orks, and quickly, before the tide turned against them once more.

Then petrochem engines snarled to Galleas' right, followed by another ripping blast of gunfire. The ork warbuggies had turned around and come racing back to join the fight. Their twin-linked heavy guns blazed away, spitting slugs indiscriminately into the swirling melee. A burst of slugs sawed through a greenskin next to Galleas and struck sparks from the side of his armoured power pack.

Galleas spun to face the new threat, but Valentus was once again a few steps ahead of him. Valentus advanced on the warbuggies, trading shots with them across the cratered street. Slugs snapped back and forth through the foetid air, but his aim was true, punching into one of the gunners and knocking it from the buggy. The driver of the buggy roared a challenge and opened the throttle. Tyres howled, kicking up clouds of black smoke as the warbuggy raced towards Valentus. The Crimson Fist kept firing, slugs glancing from the buggy's front armour. He dodged to the right, putting a crater between him and the onrushing vehicle, but the ork driver matched his move and kept coming, bearing down on the Space Marine like a stampeding grox. The warbuggy plunged into the crater, kicking up a plume of scummy water before striking the anti-tank mine at the bottom. There was a thunderclap and a bright flash of red, and the buggy disintegrated in a cloud of molten debris.

The second warbuggy slewed to a stop, its heavy guns now tracking on Valentus. Galleas watched, powerless to intervene, as slugs clawed across the ferrocrete towards his battle-brother. But before the burst found its target there was an ear-splitting blast to Galleas' left, and an ork rocket flew past less than a metre over his head. Kazimir's shot threaded a narrow gap between a broken segment of wall and the wreckage of the lead ork truck. It struck the warbuggy at the base of its windscreen, blowing the vehicle apart.

Another fiery blast lit the sky to Galleas' left. Tauros had lobbed a grenade into the back of the third ork truck, detonating its cargo. Then came the sound of shouts at Galleas' back – human shouts, followed by the rattle of gunfire. He glanced over his shoulder to see Lieutenant Mitra and Corporal Ismail's squad firing at close range into the melee. Slugs struck Galleas' armour, but the sacred war-plate turned the rounds aside. The orks weren't so lucky – their makeshift armour was poor protection against the storm of fire. The Rynnsguard cut down half a dozen of the tightly packed greenskins, and the rest lost their courage at last. They fell back from the Space Marines, wailing in frustration.

'Kill them all!' Galleas ordered. Not a single ork could be allowed to escape and warn the rest of the horde that he and his squad still survived. He lunged forward, cutting down a fleeing ork, while Juno caught two more with precise thrusts from his heavy blade. The Rynnsguard kept up a steady stream of fire, emptying their guns into the backs of the greenskins. A bare handful of the xenos nearly made it to cover behind the last of the ork trucks, but were felled by aimed bursts from Tauros, Royas and Valentus.

Silence fell over the killzone. Galleas paused to offer a prayer of thanks to the Emperor. But for luck and the courage of the Rynnsguard, the ambush might well have ended in disaster. The veteran sergeant saw Royas pulling Amador to his feet. Juno knelt beside the prone form of Olivar, a few metres away.

Galleas went to his fallen brother, fighting a rising sense of dread. Olivar lay on his side. The Space Marine was alive and seemingly uninjured, but his limbs were twitching and he was muttering under his breath.

'Brother?' he asked, kneeling at Olivar's side. The veteran didn't seem to hear him. Galleas glanced at Juno. 'Help me get his helmet off.'

Working as swiftly and gently as they could, the two Space Marines undid the catches and removed Olivar's damaged helm. As the helmet came away the air turned sour with the stench of infection.

Galleas cursed under his breath. Olivar's face was livid with fever, and foul-smelling pus leaked from the raw wound of his eye. Blood poisoning had darkened the veins in a pulsing web-work along the Space Marine's cheek, forehead and throat. It was only due to Olivar's super-human constitution that he was still alive at all.

'By the Throne,' Juno hissed. 'What do we do?'

Mitra and Ismail's squad were working their way across the ruins to join the Crimson Fists, followed by Vega and Oros. The veteran sergeant studied the humans for a moment, and came to a decision. He beckoned Mitra over.

The lieutenant hastened to Galleas' side. When she saw Olivar she gasped and made the sign of the aquila.

'Tell me of this chirurgium,' Galleas said gravely.

CHAPTER NINE

HOUSE OF BONES

ZONA 23 COMMERCIA, NEW RYNN CITY
DAY 102

The cookfire was nothing more than a corroded metal fuel drum, raggedly cut in half by a chainaxe and filled to the desired depth with petrochem from whatever vehicle was close at hand. The orks stuck hunks of fatty meat on sawed-off lengths of steel bar scavenged from nearby rubble piles and charred them in the oily flames until the flesh was bubbling and black.

There were scores of such small fires scattered through the district surrounding the chirurgium, each tended by as few as three or as many as a dozen greenskins. They were fragments of larger warbands, wounded badly enough in the fighting that they were willing to risk the dubious skills of what passed for medics amongst their kind.

Even crippled orks were dangerous, Galleas knew, and if the raid on the chirurgium went badly, the hundreds of greenskins surrounding the building would come running, eager to win the favour of the medics that resided there. It was well known that ork medics would gladly trade their services for a clutch of prisoners they could experiment on. Space Marines were especially prized, because they could endure months of the worst tortures imaginable before expiring.

The cookfire Galleas observed now was situated in the hollow shell of a ruined building less than a kilometre from their objective. Eight greenskins sat around the hissing fire, each one marked by ghastly wounds that would have been the death of even the strongest human. There were crushed skulls and ragged stumps, fist-sized holes and gaping cuts. It made the greenskins sullen and wary, knowing that their injuries made them prey to others of their kind. They ate with their weapons close to hand and their good eyes struggling to penetrate the darkness surrounding them, searching for potential threats.

Galleas switched to thermal imaging and watched Corporal Ismail lead two members of her squad in a wide circle through the rubble to the far side of the ork encampment. It was late, well past midnight; the last of the rains had passed through, and the guns along the river had largely fallen silent. It had taken hours for the Imperials to work their way through the ork camps ringing the chirurgium, eliminating those they could not otherwise avoid. Tauros and Juno were a few hundred metres further east, scouting out the last leg of their route to the objective, while the rest of the squad waited with the balance of Mitra's platoon back to the west.

It had been a difficult decision to leave his brothers with the Rynnsguard, but a necessary one. Olivar's infection made him too unpredictable to operate stealthily, but the humans had no way of keeping him in check if his fever got the better of him again. Valentus, Amador and Royas would have to keep a close eye on Olivar and prevent him from doing harm to himself or anyone else until they could get him the medicine he needed.

There was no telling how long the infection had been working its way into Olivar's bloodstream. Vega had warned Galleas it might have already taken root in Olivar's brain. Even if he survived, there could be permanent damage. The possibility dogged Galleas, but he refused to consider what he might have to do if it proved to be true.

Ismail and her squad moved through the ruins with creditable skill, fanning out into a rough semicircle as they approached the ork camp opposite Galleas. The morale of the entire platoon had improved somewhat since the convoy ambush and given them a much-needed boost of confidence. Mitra had commended her troops at some length after they'd quit the ambush site, leaving a looted truck and a collection of crude booby-traps for greenskin scavengers to find later. After her speech, Galleas had offered his congratulations by selecting Ismail and two of her squadmates for the most dangerous part of the upcoming raid.

He wasn't certain the humans appreciated the magnitude of his gesture, but they had nevertheless risen to the challenge.

Ismail communicated to her troops with hand signals, assigning targets, then crept to the edge of the firelight. Galleas eased from cover behind a tumbled pile of bricks and slipped towards the orks, releasing his sword from its scabbard.

They had carried out this same sort of attack twice before, carving a safe route through the greenskin camps for the rest of the Imperials to follow. It unfolded now with almost mechanical precision. Ismail and her squadmates struck first, leaping out of the darkness onto the backs of their targets. Long knives flashed in the firelight, stabbing again and again into the orks' thick necks. The greenskins thrashed and choked, blood splashing across the stone.

The suddenness of the onslaught stunned the other orks. For a few crucial seconds they stared in shock at the blood-spattered humans, as if they couldn't quite comprehend what they were seeing. By the time they had recovered enough to reach for their weapons Galleas was upon them. Even without its power field activated, Night's Edge was a fearsome weapon. Two of the wounded xenos lost their heads in the blink of an eye; the warning cry of a third was cut short when Galleas lunged and stabbed the ork through the throat.

The last ork snatched up its gun. Its fanged mouth opened wide as it drew a bead on Galleas. '*WAA*–'

There was a sound, like steel thudding into thick wood. The ork's shout turned to a strangled wheeze. A moment later the greenskin fell backwards, Ismail's heavy combat knife jutting from its right eye.

The Imperials froze, listening intently for sounds of alarm. Off to the north a pair of guns hammered faintly, firing off a burst in the direction of the Cassar. Otherwise, the city was quiet.

'Quickly,' Galleas told the Rynnsguard. He went to the ork that Ismail had slain and pulled the Imperial's knife free, then grabbed the xenos by its collar and hauled it back into a sitting position against a crushed groundcar. Ismail and the others busied themselves arranging the other bodies, leaving the hulking figures slumped in a rough circle around the cookfire. Given enough distance and the orks' poor eyesight, the scene would look normal enough to fool any xenos skulking by.

Galleas gave the arrangement a cursory inspection and nodded in satisfaction. He flipped Ismail's knife end-for-end and returned it to the corporal hilt-first. 'A good throw,' he said.

Ismail accepted the knife with a grin. 'I could spit a rat at twenty paces,' she said proudly. 'It's how I fed myself most nights, when I was little.'

'I will keep that in mind in case our rations start to run low,' the veteran sergeant grunted. He beckoned to the humans. 'Let us go.'

They caught up with Tauros and Juno a few minutes later, crouched behind the burned-out remains of a Chimera personnel carrier. The Crimson Fists were studying the plaza that stretched in front of the chirurgium.

'How does it look, brothers?' Galleas inquired.

Tauros shrugged. The plaza was lit by two huge bonfires, one to either side of the chirurgium's imposing entrance. The leaping orange light highlighted the rough outlines of a score of greenskin transports parked haphazardly before the squat, Gothic building.

'Assuming those trucks were fully loaded when they got here, there could be more than two hundred greenskins inside,' he observed darkly. 'And that's not counting the medics.'

'Can we get in?' Galleas pressed.

Juno grunted. 'No sentries. Not even anyone guarding the vehicles. Getting through the door won't be a problem.'

Galleas turned to Ismail. 'Get back to the others. You know the route. Bring them here as quickly and quietly as you can.'

The corporal nodded and led her squad mates off into the darkness. When they were gone, Tauros turned to Galleas.

'Are you sure this is wise, brother?'

'We can't afford to wait,' the veteran sergeant replied. 'Olivar needs aggressive treatment, and the humans are getting sicker by the moment.'

The older Space Marine was unconvinced. 'If the orks catch us in there we're going to need a lot more than medicine to stay alive.'

Galleas settled down to wait. Nearly an hour passed before his ears caught the muffled rattle of Imperial wargear. A few minutes later Ismail came into view, followed by Mitra and Vega. The lieutenant eyed the collection of ork vehicles with obvious unease.

The veteran sergeant motioned Vega closer. He gestured at the chirurgium's entrance. 'What will we find once we're past those doors?'

The young human took a deep breath, gathering his thoughts. 'An entry hall with a tall dais at the end,' he said. 'Past the dais will be a set of doors leading to the examination chambers.'

'Where are the medicines?'

Vega gulped. 'Past the examination chambers lie the surgical arenas. Past the arenas lie the laboratories where the potions are mixed.'

Galleas studied the distant building as Valentus, Royas and Amador appeared, escorting a dazed-looking Olivar. Mitra's soldiers brought up the rear, weapons ready.

The veteran sergeant nodded. 'Corporal Ismail, return to your squad,' he instructed. To Mitra, he said, 'Tauros, Juno and I will take point and eliminate any orks in our path. Watch for my signals. And no gunfire once we're inside unless it's obvious we've been discovered. Understood?'

Mitra gave a curt nod. 'Understood, my lord.'

'Then remain here.' With that, Galleas turned, and as one the three Space Marines broke cover and crept silently towards the plaza.

The Crimson Fists moved through the darkness at a steady, measured pace, using their auto-senses to scan the area ahead for threats. The broken stone of the plaza was covered in filth and strewn with rubbish cast aside by roving ork bands. As Juno had said, the xenos had grown lax over the past few weeks – the transports were dark, their engines cold, and there were no guards about. Crossing the plaza, the Space Marines moved from one ork vehicle to another, until they were within twenty metres of the steps leading to the chirurgium's entrance.

The imposing, copper-clad metal doors of the chirurgium were decorated with towering bas-reliefs of legendary chirurgeon-saints. Their dour faces and upraised arms were pocked by heavy ork shells, and the doors themselves had been bent slightly inwards by the impact of a tremendous blow, as from some kind of battering ram. A gap just wide enough for a greenskin to pass through led inside.

Galleas edged forward. The steps to the chirurgium glistened dully in the light of the bonfires. He was close enough now to see they were coated in layers of filth and gore. Flies swarmed noisily over the clotted pools of blood and bits of tissue. The air stank with the reek of rotting blood.

Movement at the gap between the doors caught Galleas' attention. The veteran Space Marines crouched in the deep shadows cast by the ork trucks and froze. As they watched, a trio of scarred greenskins wearing stained leather aprons came shuffling out of the building, each one half-dragging, half-carrying a heavy, slopping bucket in their hands. At the edge of the steps they hefted the buckets and emptied their loads onto the ground to either side of where they stood. Blood, entrails and severed greenskin limbs scattered across the stones. Grunting to one another in their bestial tongue, the orks turned about and shuffled back inside.

The Space Marines held their position for a full minute, then crept warily up the steps. Galleas eyed the gap between the doors. The waste heat from the bonfires clouded his thermal vision, but he could still make out the telltale signs of living beings in the entry hall beyond.

Tauros saw it too. 'No telling how many are inside,' he said over the vox.

Juno shrugged, drawing his short sword and combat knife. 'Doesn't matter. The only way in is through them.'

Galleas nodded grudgingly, drawing his own sword. 'Assault pattern Omicron,' he said curtly. '*Go!*'

The veteran sergeant took the lead, rushing through the gap with his battle-brothers close behind.

Galleas emerged into a gloomy, high-ceilinged chamber, lit fitfully by a handful of failing lumen globes shining down from pillars running along the length of the room. Past the glow of the bonfires, his vision sharpened to its usual razor clarity. Galleas saw the dais at the far end of the hall, dominated by an imposing stone lectern.

The space between was crowded with orks.

For a fleeting moment, Galleas thought he had made a grievous mistake. The entry hall had been transformed into a festering greenskin nest. Dozens of xenos crouched or sprawled amidst weapons, loot and piles of rubbish. It seemed there were far too many xenos for the three Crimson Fists to deal with quietly – until Galleas realised that many of the greenskins were already dead. Every one of the orks was wounded, else they wouldn't have been in the chirurgium in the first place. The weakest and the most horribly injured had either died whilst waiting for a medic, or been preyed upon by the others and left to rot where they'd fallen.

The greenskins still alive and breathing were in ghastly shape: torn, punctured or scorched in dozens of odious ways. A few were alert enough to realise the danger in their midst, but the Crimson Fists were amongst them even as they reached for their guns. Blades flashed, spearing skulls and slitting throats. The orks died without so much as a shout.

When it was done, Tauros surveyed the scene. 'Maybe fifty here all told,' he mused, 'though some look to have died more than a week ago. Where are the rest?'

'Upstairs perhaps,' Juno suggested. He indicated the dais with the point of his bloody sword. Two broad staircases rose into the darkness at the far corners of the platform. 'This lot here are low-status scum. Look at how small their tusks are, and how few scars they've got. I expect the big bosses are up there with the rest of their mobs.'

Galleas paused, listening intently. Distantly, he could hear the sounds of machinery: buzzing drills and the high-pitched whine of bone saws, punctuated by deep-throated cries of pain.

The veteran sergeant gestured for Tauros and Juno to cover the far side of the hall. Then he went back to the chirurgium's entrance and signalled to the waiting Imperials.

Within moments, Valentus and the rest of the squad were slipping into the entry hall with Mitra's platoon close behind. By that time Galleas was across the hall and climbing the steps of the dais. Past the towering lectern lay a smaller antechamber dominated by another pair of engraved metal doors. Tauros and Juno waited to either side of the doorway, listening.

'What do you hear?' Galleas inquired.

'Sounds like a slaughterhouse,' Tauros replied. 'Knives and saws. Splintering bone. The greenskin medics are keeping busy.'

The veteran sergeant nodded thoughtfully. 'The noise could work in our favour. We'll clear the surgical arenas one at a time. With luck, the orks in the adjoining chambers won't notice any difference.'

Juno grunted. 'The way their medics work, I'm not sure there *is* any difference.'

Galleas put a hand to one of the metal doors and pushed it open a finger's width. Peering through the narrow gap, he saw a long, dimly lit passageway that stretched for forty metres to another arched doorway. Bits of debris – grisly castoffs from the surgical buckets – lay in puddles along the floor.

There were no signs of movement. From the far end of the corridor Galleas could now hear a muted cacophony of noise, like a cross between a melee and the screaming chaos of a field surgical station. Orkish curses and manic laughter rose and fell over the snarl of power saws and the dull thunk of cleavers.

Galleas pushed harder. The door swung open with a faint groan. Beyond, the air was humid and still, thick with the stench of old blood and festering decay. Narrow archways lined the walls at regular intervals along the passage, each one sealed shut by a crude door fashioned from a patchwork of welded steel plates.

The veteran sergeant crept silently into the corridor followed by Tauros and Juno. Tauros studied the archways. *'Examination cells,'* he noted over the vox. *'Or they were, before the invasion. What are the greenskins using them for now?'*

'It doesn't matter,' Galleas answered quietly. 'We avoid contact unless absolutely necessary. Keep moving.'

The Crimson Fists formed into single file and moved stealthily along the passageway, the faint sound of their footfalls masked by the gruesome noises from up ahead. Forty metres later they reached a pair of heavy double doors opening into another dimly lit corridor. Pale light flickered further ahead, casting thin shadows along the grimy floor.

Galleas crept through the doorway. Here the passage was narrow and low-ceilinged, almost claustrophobic compared to the lofty chambers at the front of the building. Bulky ultraviolet projectors stood in ranks to either side of the passageway, faintly outlined by the glow from the far end of the hall. Patients and chirurgeons alike would have passed along this corridor in solemn procession on the way to the surgical arenas, their clothes and skin purged of deadly bacteria by waves of cleansing radiation.

The entrance to the surgical arenas was through a thick, metal door that could have served as a hatchway on a battleship. It had been sealed by the chirurgeons when it was clear that the city would fall to the orks, in the hope of keeping the sacred space and its priceless machinery out of xenos hands. Greenskin torches had cut a jagged hole through it nearly three metres across. The flickering light of failing lumen globes shone through the opening, punctuated at times by showers of fat, blue sparks.

Galleas lowered himself to a crouch inside the corridor, just beyond the reach of the unsteady light. Through the hole he could see a large, high-ceilinged chamber, with a dozen chirurgical tables arrayed in a starburst pattern around a central column of monitors and logic engines. Still more monitors – many with shattered screens and their insides hanging in loops of torn cable – hung down over the tables in clusters. The veteran sergeant had seen similar arrangements before, back at the Arx Tyrannus. Here the patients would be brought in from the examination cells and made ready for surgery, under the electronic supervision of the senior chirurgeons.

The orks were making similar use of the space, though their methods were far cruder. Most of the tables were occupied, Galleas saw, but only four of the injured orks looked to still be alive. Each one was surrounded by four or five younger greenskins, who alternated holding the xenos down and attacking its injuries with saws, drills and knives. Shattered limbs were sawn away, eye sockets scooped out and displaced organs stuffed back into their original spots. The louder the wounded orks roared, the more gleeful the medics' apprentices became. Hunks of meat, bone and metal plate were tossed into the corners of the room, where a gaggle of runts skulked about, looking for teeth or other bits of treasure.

'I count close to thirty xenos, including the runts,' Galleas said over the vox.

Tauros grunted agreement. 'Too many for the three of us to deal with quietly.'

'Call for Royas and Amador,' Juno advised. 'Valentus can watch Olivar while the rest of us deal with the greenskins.'

Galleas nodded in agreement. He was just about to issue the order when a low babble of noise started up behind him, back towards the examination cells. At the same time, Valentus spoke over the vox.

'*Brother Galleas,*' the Space Marine's synthetic voice was clipped and urgent. '*We have a problem.*'

The veteran sergeant signalled to Tauros and Juno, and

the three Space Marines withdrew swiftly down the corridor. The noise – rattling metal, muffled pounding and a heated exchange of voices – grew louder by the moment, until it seemed the orks could not help but hear it.

Fighting his anger, Galleas dashed back through the double doors into a scene of confusion. Ismail and her squad were going from cell to cell, yanking on the crude doors and trying to pull them open. Hands pounded frantically against the thick steel from *inside* the cells. Muffled cries and desperate pleas for help rose on every side.

Lieutenant Mitra was at the far end of the corridor, surrounded by Sergeant Kazimir, Preacher Gomez and the rest of Galleas' squad. She was leaning close to one of the cell doors, speaking to whoever was on the other side in a low, urgent voice.

Galleas rushed down the corridor, scattering startled Rynnsguard as he went. He loomed over Mitra so abruptly that even Kazimir took a startled step back.

'What in Dorn's name are you doing?' the veteran sergeant hissed.

'There are people in these cells!' Mitra hissed back. 'Civilians!'

That explained the doors, Galleas realised. The chambers had been converted to cells in truth, holding prisoners for the ork medics' entertainment. No doubt one of the Rynnsguard had indulged his curiosity and tried one of the doors, alerting the desperate wretches inside.

'Get your troops under control, lieutenant,' Galleas warned. 'There is a large group of xenos less than sixty metres–'

'*For pity's sake, let us out!*' shouted a muffled voice on the other side of the cell door.

Mitra gave the veteran sergeant an entreating look. 'Help us get the doors open! I asked Valentus, but he said the decision was yours.'

'They are not the reason we're here!' Galleas snapped.

The lieutenant's eyes widened in surprise, but she refused to give in. 'I swore an oath to protect these people,' she shot back. 'As did you!'

The sheer audacity of Mitra's reproach took Galleas and the other Crimson Fists by surprise. All save Veteran Brother Olivar. The wounded Space Marine shrugged out of Valentus' grasp and lunged for Mitra, his combat knife gleaming in his fist. *'Insubordinate little worm!'* he raged, the words slurred by a scorching fever.

Mitra whirled. The blade plunged, aiming for her throat – but a gaunt figure in Ecclesiarchal robes leapt into its path. Preacher Gomez levelled an accusing finger at Olivar's livid face. 'Back, Angel!' he shouted in a surprisingly authoritative voice. 'I command you in the name of the Divine Emperor!'

The invocation of the Emperor's holy name brought the devout Olivar up short. The knife froze in mid-strike, scarcely a finger's width from the preacher's upturned face.

There was a moment of stunned silence. Even the prisoners grew still, wondering at Gomez's shout. And then, from back in the direction of the surgical arenas, came the guttural cries of greenskins.

Veteran Sergeant Galleas readied his weapons and commended his soul to the Emperor. Preacher Gomez's unexpected courage had doomed them all.

CHAPTER TEN

CHANGE OF PLAN

ZONA 23 COMMERCIA, NEW RYNN CITY
DAY 102

Galleas keyed the activation rune on his power sword and hefted a belt-fed ork gun in his left hand. His mind raced, forming a new tactical plan in the space of a few heartbeats. The situation was dire, but if they moved quickly and decisively, they might yet survive.

'Tauros, Juno, with me,' Galleas ordered. 'Escort pattern Delta. Valentus, take charge of Brother Olivar and fall in behind us.' The veteran sergeant searched amid the stunned Rynnsguard. 'Vega!'

'Here, my lord!' The young medic appeared, pushing his way past two of Corporal Vila's men.

Bestial shouts erupted from the far end of the corridor. The three apron-clad orks, wielding cleavers now instead of their gore-filled buckets, burst through the narrow doorway. Galleas, Tauros and Juno reacted as one, unleashing a stream of heavy slugs over the heads of Corporal Ismail's squad and dropping the greenskins in their tracks.

'You're coming with us,' Galleas said to Vega, hardly skipping a beat. 'Stay close to Valentus until we're past the surgical arenas.'

The young medic hesitated, casting an uncertain glance at Mitra. The lieutenant pretended not to have heard the exchange. She turned her back on Galleas and Olivar, drawing her laspistol with a slightly trembling hand and levelling it at the nearest cell door. The pistol barked, and a beam of ruby light carved through the crude bolt securing the door.

Galleas frowned in disapproval, but there was no time for debate. 'Move!' he commanded, shouldering past Tauros and heading for the surgical arenas. Juno and Tauros fell in at his heels, crude guns sweeping the doorway ahead, forming a wedge with Valentus and Olivar in the centre. Vega hesitated a moment more, his face a mask of indecision, then set his jaw and hurried after the swiftly-moving Space Marines.

'*What about Amador and me?*' Brother Royas called over the vox.

An injured greenskin lurched into the open doorway, gripping a battered gun in its hand. Galleas cut the xenos down with a quick burst. 'Form a rearguard and fall back to the entry hall,' the veteran sergeant ordered. 'Bottle up the stairways to the upper levels and keep a route open for us to withdraw once we've got the antivirals.'

'*Understood, brother,*' Royas said curtly. '*You may depend on us!*'

Of that, Galleas had no doubt, but the task was far easier said than done. Two Crimson Fists, even mighty veterans like Royas and Amador, would be hard-pressed to hold off as many as two hundred greenskins, but at the moment there was no other choice.

Galleas kicked aside the heap of greenskin corpses and plunged through the double doors leading to the purgation hall. At once he found himself confronted by a crowd of howling runts brandishing oversized pistols and wicked-looking knives. The xenos shouted in surprise and cut loose with their guns, filling the corridor with a hailstorm of unaimed fire. Slugs punched through the inert projectors and ricocheted from the walls. The veteran sergeant felt a barrage of impacts against his ceramite pauldrons and breastplate, leaving bright streaks of lead across their curved surfaces. The Crimson Fist responded with a long burst from his captured gun, blasting half a dozen of the runts apart. The rest stumbled to a halt, bawling in terror, and tried to run back the way they'd come, but by then Galleas was among them, scything through the mob with fearsome sweeps of his sword. Tauros and Juno added to the slaughter, snapping quick bursts into the backs of the retreating xenos. Barely a handful of the screaming runts made it through the melted portal into the surgical arenas beyond.

Galleas could now hear the sounds of gunfire and battle cries behind him. The greenskins on the upper floors had been roused and were moving to cut the Imperials off. He reached the far end of the purgation hall, skidding to a stop through a pool of spilled blood, and jammed the blazing point of Night's Edge into the scarred surface of the heavy door. The sword stuck firmly in the thick metal plate, sputtering angrily. With his free hand, Galleas snatched a pair of ork grenades from his belt, primed them and lobbed them through the jagged opening. There was a sudden babble of surprised shouts from the other side of the door, swallowed up by the double thunderclap of the bombs. The veteran sergeant pulled Night's Edge free and dived through the opening into the expanding cloud of red-hot shrapnel.

The torn bodies of greenskin runts and a pair of ork medics lay just inside the room. Six more of the xenos chirurgeons lay just a few paces away, stunned by the unexpected blasts. Galleas leapt at them with a furious oath, shooting one of the medics between the eyes. The gun's heavy bolt locked back on an empty chamber; Galleas spun on his heel, clubbing another medic across the face with the gun and chopping deep into the greenskin's chest with his power sword. The xenos fell with a choking cry and a welter of blood.

The surviving orks recovered quickly from the sudden assault, charging at Galleas with bloody cleavers and oversized syringes filled with a virulent green ooze. The veteran sergeant blocked a plunging cleaver with the barrel of his gun and stabbed the roaring medic in the chest. Another xenos crashed into him, stabbing for his armour's joints with a rusty needle. Galleas stunned the ork with a head-butt, splintering teeth and crushing bone, then cut the beast down with a backhanded swipe of his blade.

There was a roar of bloodthirsty shouts to Galleas' right. A crowd of medics and wounded orks came around the circle of surgical tables and rushed at him. Guns hammered, the shots going wide – and then Juno appeared, stepping squarely into their path. His short blade flickered, deftly stabbing, and greenskins toppled like threshed wheat.

Galleas felt a jab in the side of his left knee, followed by an explosion of pain so sudden and intense that it staggered him. The medic pressed his advantage, laughing maniacally and jabbing the syringe at Galleas' throat. The Space Marine jerked aside from the needle and smashed the ork's arm away with the barrel of his gun, then drove the point of his blazing sword through the ork's left forearm and on into its chest.

Heavy slugs buzzed through the air, and the two medics to Galleas' left spun and fell. Galleas pulled Night's Edge free and nearly collapsed himself as his knee almost gave way. Tauros appeared at his side, forcing another clip into his crude xenos gun. 'Are you hurt, brother?' he asked.

'I'm fine,' the veteran sergeant grated. With an effort of will, he forced his leg to straighten. The joint was stiff, the surrounding tissue feverish and swollen. He could feel the greenskin's poison burning its way along the veins of his thigh. Galleas tossed aside his empty gun, replacing it with one from a fallen xenos, and limped on.

The Crimson Fists pressed forward. Juno circled right around the surgical tables, while the others went left. Another mob of medics and injured orks appeared, but were driven back by a fusillade of shots from Galleas, Tauros and Valentus. As the greenskins fell back down a short passageway on the opposite side of the chamber, the veteran sergeant keyed his vox. 'Brother Royas! Report!'

'Orks are attacking on both stairways, and we've got more greenskins coming in through the main entrance,' Royas answered. 'They're trying to drive a wedge between Amador and me.'

'Can you hold?'

'We are the shield hand of Dorn,' Royas said grimly. 'We will hold.'

With a renewed sense of urgency, Galleas drove his pain-wracked body onward. The Space Marines linked up at the far side of the room, throwing grenades down the short passageway and then charging into the teeth of the blasts.

The surgical arena consisted of an octagonal staging area with six passageways leading off to separate operating rooms. A seventh passageway on the far side of the staging area led to the laboratory, where medicinal potions and unguents were prepared for the surgeries. There was almost a score of xenos gathered in the chamber: greenskin medics and their runt orderlies, plus a number of dazed and injured patients. The Space Marines raked them with fire and then charged, cutting down those who still stood.

'Clear the operating rooms,' Galleas hissed. His leg felt like a lump of fused metal, heavy and molten. 'Use the rest of the grenades. There is no time to waste.'

As Tauros and Juno went to work, Galleas limped across the staging area and down the corridor to the laboratory. He feared what he might find – smashed cabinets, overturned tables, drifts of broken glass and pools of precious fluids drying on the laboratory floor.

The laboratory, as it turned out, was a series of large, open rooms joined end-to-end and packed with ranks of cabinets interspersed with servitor stations. The servitors had all been hacked to pieces and some of the cabinets smashed, but many others had been left intact. Perhaps the medics had wanted to experiment with the potions inside, or perhaps they'd simply been distracted by some other bit of mayhem. With the xenos, nothing was certain.

Galleas limped to the closest servitor station and leaned against it for support. Valentus appeared, half-leading, half-dragging the delirious Olivar. 'Vega–'

'Yes, my lord.' The young medic was already hurrying down the debris-strewn aisles, boots crunching on broken glass as he squinted at the High Gothic lettering incised into each cabinet. At Valentus' urging, Olivar dropped to one knee with a discordant crash.

While Vega worked, Galleas devoted his full attention to the poison coursing through his veins. Using a series of mnemonic rotes, he marshalled his body's considerable resources to filtering the medic's vile potion from his system. He banished the molten pain with a measure of concentration and iron will, and stimulated capillary action to diffuse the fluid from around his knee and direct it to his Oolitic kidney. Within moments, he could feel the swelling start to ebb.

'*Operating rooms are clear,*' Tauros reported over the vox.

'Take Juno and reinforce Royas and Amador,' Galleas said. 'Our brothers must be hard-pressed by now.'

'*Understood.*'

Vega appeared from the depths of the laboratory with a bundle of glass vials cradled in his arms. He showed one, filled with an emerald-coloured liquid, to Galleas. 'The Emperor is with us!' he said triumphantly. 'How much should I give Lord Olivar?'

'What is a normal human dose?'

'One vial.'

'Give him eight.' Galleas pushed away from the servitor station with a low grunt. 'Then gather up as much medicine as you can and get back to Lieutenant Mitra.'

The veteran sergeant watched as Vega knelt beside Olivar and deftly fitted one vial after another into the armour's autodispensers. Satisfied, he glanced up at Valentus. 'Stay with him until he's in his right mind again,' Galleas said over the vox.

'*His humours should stabilise quickly once the antivirals take hold,*' Valentus assured him. '*Go. Deal with the xenos.*'

Galleas nodded curtly. Boots pounding on the slate tile, the veteran sergeant ran to the sounds of battle.

Mitra had managed to free the imprisoned civilians, Galleas saw at once, adding a degree of chaos to an already desperate situation. As he ran through the surgical staging area and into the pre-op chamber, Galleas encountered a growing crowd of panicked human prisoners who were trying to escape the sounds of fighting in the entry hall. Many of the humans were sick and injured, clad in little more than rags and layers of grime. The veteran sergeant spied Corporal Vila and his squad amongst the prisoners, making a half-hearted attempt to get the civilians under control. A few of the Imperials raised their hands beseechingly to Galleas as he went by, calling out to him in the name of the Emperor, but he paid them no mind.

The purgation hall was more crowded still. Men, women and children packed the corridor, cowering behind the derelict projectors. Some had simply collapsed where they stood, too weak to continue further. Galleas ignited his power sword, the angry crackle of the energy field cutting through the commotion, and the Imperials that could still move scattered quickly from the armoured giant's path.

Galleas found Lieutenant Mitra at the far end of the corridor, accompanied by Preacher Gomez. She was locked in a tense exchange with two former prisoners. One, an older man wearing stained labourer's coveralls, stood before the officer with bowed head and hands clasped nervously to his chest. The other stood at the labourer's shoulder, urging him on. He was a stocky man, wearing the remnants of an outfit that might have passed as fashionable on the wealthier hive worlds of the sector: a chromasilk blouse and cravat, ebon wool vest and knee-length trousers, Indiran cuffs and sark-skin slippers. A heavy, naval-style shoulder cape hung from his left shoulder.

The hammering of gunfire and the ripping snarl of ork chainaxes shook the air. *Too close*, Galleas thought grimly. *Too close by half.* It meant that his brothers were being driven back by the sheer weight of the enemy crowding into the entry hall, their hopes of escape dwindling with every backwards step.

Galleas loomed over Mitra and the civilians like a thundercloud. 'This is no time for idle talk,' he snapped, his booming voice cutting through the din. 'Lieutenant, rally your troops and get control of these prisoners *now*. If we don't force a path through the entry hall in the next few moments, we'll never make it out!'

The civilians jumped at the iron note of command in Galleas' voice. Mitra was still pale and unsettled from the confrontation with Olivar, but she bore up under Galleas' hard stare. 'We might not have to,' she said. 'This man here–' she gestured to the prisoner in the labourer's coveralls, '–says he knows another way out.'

'Indeed!' interjected the man in the shoulder cape. He turned to Galleas and gave him a courtly bow. 'Adalbert Bergand, void trader in good standing and master of the *Helicanum Dawn*, at your service. I had been leading the prisoners in planning an escape of our own for the past few weeks, and this man–' His confident expression faltered.

'Corvalles,' the man in the coveralls prompted.

Bergand snapped his fingers. 'Corvalles. Yes. Anyway, he says that there is an entrance to the storm tunnels at the rear of the building–'

'Where?' Galleas demanded, cutting the void trader off.

Corvalles pointed towards the laboratory with a bony

finger. 'There's a waste disposal system back of the lab, my lord,' he said in a dull voice. 'Leads straight down to the sluiceways and the sea. We can go through the maintenance access alongside.'

'Are you certain?'

The labourer nodded. 'I've worked the tunnels near fifty years, my lord, man and boy. I know 'em like the back of my hand.'

Galleas weighed the tactical permutations for a fraction of an instant. 'Go,' he commanded. 'My brothers and I will hold the greenskins for as long as we can to cover your escape, then rendezvous with you later.'

Mitra gave a curt nod. By now she knew better than to ask how the Space Marines would find them again. 'Bergand, you say you've been leading these people for the past few weeks. Take charge and get them moving to the labs.'

Galleas left the lieutenant to orchestrate the withdrawal as best she could. He would give them all the time he could. The rest was in the divine Emperor's hands.

Sergeant Kazimir and Corporal Ismail's squad were struggling to open the last of the examination cells as Galleas shouldered his way past the double doors and into the corridor. The Rynnsguard were working under sporadic fire, as stray rounds from the battle in the entry hall came buzzing down the narrow passageway. The bodies of escaped prisoners lay here and there along the slate tiles where a ricocheting slug had found its mark.

'Brother Valentus,' Galleas called over the vox.

'We're moving now,' Valentus replied at once.

'Negative,' the veteran sergeant said, picking his way past the corpses and breaking into a loping run. 'Stay where you are. We're coming to you.'

'*Acknowledged,*' the venerable Space Marine said, taking the sudden turn of events in stride.

Ork slugs buzzed past Galleas' helmet as he stormed down the corridor. Up ahead, the double doors leading to the entry hall were a third of the way open, and through the gap he could see the flicker of muzzle flashes and a heaving mass of roaring greenskins filling the chamber beyond.

Galleas emerged from the double doors into a maelstrom of gunfire, grenade blasts and guttural war cries. Royas and Tauros stood at the far end of the antechamber, their backs to the door, trading blows with a mob of orks trying to force their way past the Crimson Fists and deeper into the building. The two Space Marines had emptied their guns and were fighting with combat knives and looted chainaxes. Xenos bodies lay in heaps amid drifts of brass shell casings and spreading puddles of gore.

'About time!' Tauros called, glancing over his shoulder at Galleas. The greenskin in front of him saw an opening and lunged forward, chopping at the Space Marine's neck with a heavy cleaver. But the seemingly careless gesture was nothing more than a ruse. As the ork took the bait, the veteran Space Marine caught the greenskin's weapon arm on the point of his combat knife and slashed upwards with his looted chainaxe, ripping open the enemy's torso. Tauros kicked the ork's toppling body back into the crowd. 'I was starting to think you'd forgotten about us!'

Galleas surveyed the antechamber. 'Where are Amador and Juno?'

'Out there. Where else?' Royas answered, ripping his knife from the top of a greenskin's skull.

The veteran sergeant edged forward, searching the heaving sea of waving blades and snarling faces. There! A momentary gap in the crowd revealed the two Crimson Fists in the middle of the dais, fighting back-to-back against waves of bellowing orks.

Ten metres, Galleas reckoned. For all intents and purposes they were trapped behind a ten-metre-thick wall of blood-thirsty xenos.

Tauros ducked the swipe of an ork's chainaxe and cut the greenskin's legs off at the knees. 'What now?' he called.

Galleas raised his looted ork gun. 'Stay here!'

With a furious shout the veteran sergeant drove into the tightly packed mob. The crude greenskin weapon bucked in his hand as he unleashed a steady stream of shells point-blank into the crowd, carving a bloody path through the enemy. Night's Edge flared, sweeping in burning arcs that kept the xenos from closing in around him as he forced his way towards his trapped brothers. Slugs and grenade fragments raked at him from all sides, ringing against his sacred wargear. The orks, consumed with bloodlust, were firing indiscriminately, causing more harm to one another than to him.

Galleas emptied his gun and grabbed another off the floor, continuing to cut his way through the wall of green-skin flesh. Blows rained down on him from left and right, staggering but not stopping him. Warning signs began to flash from his damaged knee actuator as he shoved a burly greenskin corpse out of the way. He overrode the warning with a flick of his eye and pressed on.

An ork chainaxe shrieked as it raked against Galleas' left pauldron, its diamond-hard teeth kicking up a spray of hot sparks from the thick ceramite plate. The veteran ser-geant cut the xenos down with a backhanded swipe of his power sword and found himself face to face with Juno, less than three metres away. The Crimson Fist stood in a small, cleared space made by a mound of greenskin corpses, blood streaming from his twin blades. Behind him, Amador fought like a berserker, matching the greenskins shout for shout and hacking away with a pair of chainaxes.

'Amador!' Galleas bellowed. 'What in Dorn's name are you doing out here?'

'You said you wanted a path out of the building, didn't you?' Amador replied, bisecting a howling greenskin with a sweep of his twin axes.

Galleas frowned. From where they stood it was still another forty metres to the main doors, every square metre of it packed with angry xenos.

A pair of orks leapt at Juno. The Crimson Fist deflected one greenskin's axe into the face of the other, then dropped the second xenos with a precise thrust to the temple. 'Are we heading for the door?' he asked.

'We're falling back.'

'We're *what*?' Amador exclaimed.

'There's another way out!' Galleas replied. An ork crashed into his left side. Its bloodthirsty howl rang in his ears, and he felt the chisel point of the greenskin's cleaver punching again and again into his shoulder, seeking a way past the armoured pauldron into the weaker casing beneath.

Amador shook his head doggedly. 'We don't need another way out! Just a few more metres and we're through–'

The veteran sergeant pivoted on his heel, smashing an elbow into the ork's face, then finishing the xenos off with a sweep of his blade. 'If we stay out here too much longer we'll be overwhelmed!' He threw his empty gun aside and snatched another from the floor. 'Form up on me! Let's go!'

Galleas turned back towards the antechamber, raking

the greenskins with his looted gun. Looking ahead, he could see that the orks had driven Tauros and Royas apart through sheer weight of numbers, and a small mob was already charging through the doors towards the examination cells. Trusting that his brothers would follow, Galleas drove through the crowd back the way he'd come.

Seeing the Space Marines retreat, the greenskins gave a triumphant shout and renewed their assault. The xenos pressed in on either side of Galleas, raining blows upon his heavy armour – only to fall beneath the blades of Juno and Amador, who closed the gap and covered Galleas' flanks. It took nearly a full minute to cross the ten metres back to the antechamber and link up with Tauros and Royas, blocking the orks' route deeper into the building.

'Assault pattern Gamma!' Galleas called over the vox. At once, Tauros and Royas fell in beside Juno and Amador, forming an inverted wedge with Galleas at the point. Together, the five Space Marines fell back through the heavy antechamber doors.

The corridor along the examination cells was a scene of carnage. Sergeant Kazimir and Corporal Ismail's squad had stood their ground and were blasting away at half a dozen orks charging towards them. Four more greenskins lay dead, riddled by shotgun pellets and lasgun fire, along with two of Ismail's troopers and nearly a dozen civilians. Galleas emptied his gun into the backs of the charging greenskins, cutting down three of them and causing the rest to falter. Kazimir blasted the fourth at short range with his combat shotgun, and Ismail's squad finished the rest.

'The doors!' Galleas ordered. Tauros and Royas put their shoulders to the heavy doors, trying to force them shut in the face of the greenskin horde. The veteran sergeant grabbed a pair of grenades from the body of a fallen ork, primed them, and tossed them through the narrowing gap between the twin portals. The greenskins recoiled from the blasts, and the doors crashed shut. Before the enemy could recover, Galleas rushed forward, using his power sword to melt the hinges into solid lumps.

'Valentus! What's your situation?' the veteran sergeant called over the vox.

'Lieutenant Mitra has begun evacuating the civilians through the maintenance tunnel.'

There was a muted roar on the far side of the doors, and then a clangourous *boom* as dozens of greenskins threw their weight against them. Hot metal groaned under the blow, and Galleas saw the whole doorframe quiver. 'Tell her to hurry,' he said. 'We're heading your way.'

'Understood.'

Galleas and his brothers paused long enough to strip the dead greenskins of guns and ammunition, then ran down the hall to join the Rynnsguard. Kazimir, Ismail and the exhausted soldiers were fighting with the bolt on the last of the cell doors.

'Move!' the veteran sergeant barked, raising his sword. The Rynnsguard stumbled out of the way as Night's Edge fell, shearing off the bolt with a flash of actinic light. Galleas yanked the red-hot pieces free and then stepped back to let the Rynnsguard haul the makeshift door open.

A miasma of filth gusted into the passageway as the door swung open. Dull-eyed men, women and children stumbled out into the corridor, clutching weakly at their saviours.

There was a draconic hiss from the far end of the passageway. Galleas turned to see four tongues of intense flame burst through the heavy, metal doors. He bit back a curse. The orks had brought up several of their powerful, promethium-fuelled torches. When properly focused, their flames could cut through heavy hull plate – or Space Marine armour – with fearsome ease.

The Rynnsguard saw the danger, too. Sergeant Kazimir began barking instructions, and Ismail's squad got them moving. Some of the nearly catatonic prisoners had to be dragged along by the arm.

A pair of piteous wails rose from inside the cell. Galleas peered round the door and saw two young children, a boy and a girl, tugging weakly at an emaciated figure that might have been their mother. The woman was too sick and malnourished to stand, but the children refused to leave her.

'Sergeant Kazimir,' Galleas said.

Kazimir, his hands already full guiding a pair of prisoners, glanced back at the cell. His expression turned bleak. 'We can't carry her,' he said, his voice anguished. 'If she can't walk on her own–'

A tall shape shouldered past Galleas. Titus Juno stepped into the cell and swept up all three prisoners into his arms. The children stared in wonder at the blue-armoured giant as he carried them out of the cell and down the corridor.

A section of door fell to the tile with a clatter. Orks began forcing their way through the opening, heedless of the still-molten edges.

'Go!' Galleas ordered. The Rynnsguard herded the prisoners into the purgation hall with the Space Marines right on their heels. One by one the Crimson Fists ducked through the door, firing bursts back at the oncoming xenos as they went. Amador was the last one through, before Royas and Tauros slammed the double doors shut.

Once more, Galleas applied his power sword to the

hinges. 'Valentus!' he called, watching the thick, metal cylinders start to deform.

'*The last of the civilians have been evacuated, brother,*' Valentus replied.

'Not quite. How is Olivar?'

'*He has regained his senses.*'

'Good. I need the two of you to tear that laboratory apart. Anything flammable I want spread on the floor. Clear?'

'*Clear.*'

The Crimson Fists retreated down the corridor, pulling over the heavy radiation projectors in their wake. They were less than halfway along the passage before the greenskins' torches were cutting through the doors.

There was no way to block the hole that had been cut through the hatch leading to the surgical arenas. By the time Galleas reached the entrance to the laboratory he could hear the orks' bestial cries start up again as they broke through the doors.

Glass smashed loudly at the back of the lab. Olivar and Valentus had wasted no time, toppling entire cabinets and scattering their contents across the tiles. Galleas' multisensors detected a veritable witches' brew of potions, unguents and powders covering the floor.

The orks were gaining fast. Galleas led the others to the rear of the huge chamber, boots crunching over bits of broken crockery and glass. A trapdoor painted in yellow-and-black hazard bars leaned open along the far wall. Valentus stood nearby, ushering Kazimir and the last of the Rynnsguard through the hatchway. Several metres away, Olivar wrestled with a gas canister bolted to the wall.

The greenskins were in the lab now. Galleas turned to see their hunched shoulders and craggy heads rise over the tops of fallen cabinets. He raked them with a long burst. 'Down the hatch! Quickly!'

Juno, still carrying the woman and her children, went first, followed by Royas and Tauros. Amador hesitated, but at a stern look from Valentus the young veteran followed suit.

Heavy slugs droned through the air, ricocheting from the walls around Galleas. Still firing, he glanced back at Valentus. 'You're next! Go!'

The venerable Space Marine gave a curt nod and descended quickly through the hatch. Galleas fell back until he stood just next to the entrance. His gun's ammo belt was getting short. 'Olivar! Your turn!'

But Olivar did not reply. Instead, the veteran Space Marine redoubled his efforts to pull the canister free from the wall.

An ork slug caromed off Galleas' breastplate. Despite his suppressing fire, the xenos were getting closer. He glimpsed the distinctive twin tanks of a greenskin cutting torch, but the enemy carrying it had ducked into cover behind a cabinet before he could get off a shot. 'Olivar! *Now!*'

The veteran Space Marine let out an angry roar. Servo-motors whined, and the canister pulled away from the wall with an ear-piercing screech. Olivar staggered as the thing came free, a metal-clad hose spitting escaping gas and whipping about like an angry snake.

'I'll deal with the xenos,' Olivar said gravely. 'Go on. See to the others.'

'*Olivar!*'

The one-eyed Crimson Fist turned and broke into a trot, heading straight for the greenskins. Slugs ricocheted from Olivar's armour, striking bursts of orange sparks. As he went, Olivar began to chant the Litanies of Hate, the High Gothic words rolling like thunder in the echoing room.

A bulky figure rose from cover, a dozen metres in front of Olivar. Galleas saw the tiny blue flame of the torch's igniter as the ork levelled his weapon at the oncoming Space Marine.

'*NO!*' Galleas cried, as the ork triggered a blast from his torch and the laboratory erupted in a searing cloud of flame.

CHAPTER ELEVEN

THE WOUND THAT WILL NOT HEAL

ZONA 23 COMMERCIA, NEW RYNN CITY
DAY 102

Galleas was moving even as the ork triggered his flamer, crossing the space to Olivar in a single bound. Dropping his gun, Galleas grabbed the Space Marine's backpack and hauled him backwards just as the blast of burning promethium reached out to swallow them. Olivar hurled the gas canister at the same instant, sending it right into the expanding cone of flame.

There was a blaze of hungry orange light, followed by guttural shouts of surprise as the liquids on the floor ignited. And then the canister exploded with a loud, metallic bang, knocking Olivar and Galleas off their feet.

The veteran sergeant hit the tiles hard, glass and ceramics crunching beneath him. Burning potions splashed across his armour, wreathing him in multicoloured flames. Olivar twisted as he fell, landing on his side facing Galleas. His bare face was raw and blistered from the heat, and lacerations from razor-sharp pieces of the burst canister had flayed his forehead and cheeks to the bone. The one-eyed Space Marine glared at Galleas with undisguised rage.

Furious shouts rang through the lab as the orks tried to escape the surrounding flames. Then one of the shouts turned to a panicked yelp, and Galleas caught a glimpse of frantic movement. The ork with the flamer was on fire, staggering about as he struggled to rid himself of the heavy tanks filled with promethium on his back. With a convulsive heave the greenskin broke the thick, leather carry strap, letting the tanks fall to the floor. They hit the slate tiles with a *clang* and exploded, consuming the luckless ork and splashing burning fuel in every direction.

Galleas leapt to his feet. The rear of the laboratory was quickly becoming an inferno and the surviving greenskins were in full retreat, but he knew that could change at any moment. He seized Olivar by the arm and hauled him upright. 'Move!' the veteran sergeant yelled, propelling Olivar towards the trapdoor.

Below the trapdoor was a set of steep, narrow stairs that descended into darkness. Galleas followed right on Olivar's heels, dropping down below the level of the floor and pulling the trap shut behind him. Trickles of burning liquid dripped through the seams around the door, spattering across Galleas' armour and pooling on the steps by his feet.

Galleas searched for some way to secure the trapdoor. He could hear Olivar's ragged breathing in the darkness just a few metres below.

'What in Dorn's name were you thinking, brother?' Galleas snapped. He bared his teeth in frustration, seeing there was no bolt or latch and the hinges were on the opposite side of the door.

'I was covering your escape,' Olivar rasped. 'An honourable sacrifice on behalf of my brothers. There was a time you would have understood that.'

The trapdoor jerked in its frame. Galleas seized the handle and pulled it down. There was a muffled yell, and then a volley of ork slugs punched through the door and went ricocheting down the stairwell.

The veteran sergeant cursed. Apparently a little fire wasn't going to come between the greenskins and the prospect of battle. 'Go!' he shouted to Olivar.

The Space Marines retreated quickly down the stairs. After a moment they emerged through an archway into a large, vaulted room. The pale glow of a pair of lumen strips revealed darkened control panels along the wall to Galleas' right, and an open door in the wall opposite the archway. The rest of the squad were waiting at the far end of the room, their guns covering the bottom of the stairs.

'Mitra and her guide are leading the humans deeper into the sewers,' Tauros reported.

Amador managed a chuckle. 'They had to pry that mother and her children away from Juno. It seems he has the makings of a fine nursemaid.'

Galleas was in no mood for jests. 'How long?'

'They've only been gone for a minute,' Tauros answered. 'Perhaps less.'

'The orks are right behind us.' Galleas glanced around the room. 'Knock out those lumen strips. We'll ambush them here.'

Amador and Juno smashed the strips with their weapons, plunging the chamber into darkness. 'Switch to thermal vision,' Galleas instructed. 'Spread out. Fire on my command.'

The veteran sergeant switched over to the thermal imager in his helmet display, revealing the interior of the room in shades of pale green. They could move and act freely while the xenos, with their poor night vision, would be effectively blind.

They did not have long to wait. Boots pounded on the stairs, followed by guttural snarls and the scrape of metal on stone. A small mob of orks emerged into the room, their bulky forms glowing brightly in the thermal display. The lead greenskins stumbled to a halt in the darkness, cursing loudly as the others trod upon their heels. Still more emerged from the archway, crowding into the room.

The Crimson Fists were still as statues, waiting in disciplined silence only a few metres away. When the xenos filled the killzone, Galleas gave a mirthless smile.

'Vengeance for the fallen,' he spoke into the vox, and six guns spoke as one, muzzle flashes searing the darkness. Orks toppled, sawn apart by the storm of slugs. The survivors fell back, bellowing in rage, firing wildly as they retreated to the archway. A bare handful remained, stumbling blindly back up the stairs.

Galleas was moving the moment the orks had disappeared from sight. 'Weapons and ammunition,' he ordered curtly, looting the closest greenskin corpse. 'Quickly. The next thing coming down those stairs will be a bundle of grenades.'

The veterans moved swiftly, taking what they could and withdrawing through the door. Galleas was the last to leave, stepping through the doorway onto a narrow stone catwalk overlooking one of the city's deep storm drains. Water roared through the channel nearly thirty metres below, rushing its way out to sea.

A waist-high railing ran along the catwalk above the drain. After a moment's thought, Galleas activated his power sword and cut away the two-metre section just opposite the doorway. 'Put out the lumen strips,' he told his brothers, watching the red-hot pieces of metal tumble into the raging waters below.

Guns barked, and the strips over the catwalk went dark one by one. Moments later a series of grenade blasts hammered the chamber they'd just left. The orks had regrouped and were coming back for more.

'Back ten metres,' Galleas said, and the squad withdrew along the catwalk to create another killzone. Bloodthirsty shouts were already echoing down the stairwell as the greenskins charged at their foes.

This time the greenskins fired on the run, blazing away at everything in their path. Galleas watched slugs chip fragments from the side of the doorway and dig into the permacrete wall of the storm drain opposite as the xenos reached the bottom of the stairs and charged across the room. When the greenskins didn't find the Space Marines where they were expected to be, the beasts only grew more enraged, thinking the enemy was getting away. They charged through the doorway, navigating by little more than muzzle flashes alone.

Shouts turned to screams as the first few orks plunged through the gap in the railing and into the churning waters. The rest stumbled to a halt, bunching up on the catwalk as they tried to sort out the danger in their midst.

'Fire!'

Greenskins fell, raked by the Space Marines' accurate fire. A few of the xenos charged at the distant muzzle flashes, but were cut down before they'd covered more than a few metres. The survivors retreated back into the maintenance room, ducking out occasionally to fire a burst down the catwalk.

The Space Marines waited in the darkness, their armoured forms wreathed in streamers of spent propellant. Galleas fed another belt of shells into his gun. 'What do you expect they'll try next, brother?' he said to Tauros.

The veteran chuckled. 'The ork mindset can be boiled down to a single, basic concept – *when in doubt, get a bigger gun.* I expect they're sending a runt back to the surface for a rocket launcher right about now.'

Galleas nodded. 'This is our chance. We'll fall back to the first turning, taking out the lumen strips as we go.'

Moving silently and surely in the darkness, the Crimson Fists withdrew down the catwalk to the first branching tunnel, and then disappeared from the orks' line of sight. From there they went deeper into the labyrinthine sewer tunnels, putting distance between themselves and the ambush site. At one point Galleas and the others clearly heard the sound of explosions echo through the tunnels, followed by a chorus of distant greenskin war cries. The Space Marines paused, listening intently, but the sounds faded almost as quickly as they began, and there were no further signs of pursuit.

After nearly half an hour, the veteran sergeant called a halt. By his reckoning they'd covered just over a kilometre through the foetid tunnels.

'The orks will have given up by now,' he said. 'We'll wait an hour more, then backtrack and find our way to Mitra and the others–'

'No.'

Galleas turned. Olivar stood at the rear of the squad, fists clenched, one eye glaring balefully.

'What did you say?'

'It's time to put an end to this foolishness,' Olivar said. 'Your obsession with these humans not only borders on the heretical, it demeans us all. It is *shameful*.'

Galleas fought to control his anger. 'You're not in your right mind, brother,' he said in a tightly controlled voice.

But Olivar shook his head. 'Look at us,' he said, spreading his arms to encompass the squad and the noisome tunnel. 'When the tale of Snagrod's invasion is told back on Terra, hundreds or even thousands of years from now, would you have it said that the last of the Crimson Fists, mighty sons of Rogal Dorn, spent their final days knee-deep in filth, squandering their dignity and honour on a pack of hapless mortals? It's an affront not just to our fallen brothers, but to the God-Emperor Himself!'

Galleas' reply was cold as iron. 'And what would you have me do instead, brother?'

'Something *worthy*,' Olivar cried. 'If I am to die, let it be in a manner befitting a son of the Emperor! Let us be rid of these pathetic humans and do as we were made to do. We could strike a blow against the horde that would be a fitting epitaph for our Chapter.'

Amador stirred. 'Brother Olivar has a point–'

'It doesn't matter if he has a point to make or not!' Galleas snarled. 'We have our orders. Our *duty*. The Ceres Protocol binds us–'

'Damn the protocol!' Olivar shot back. 'The Chapter-monastery is gone. Our sacred relics are gone. Our history. Our gene-seed. All of it gone.' As he spoke, the anger faded from his voice, until there was nothing left but anguish. 'In the history of the Imperium, no Chapter has ever recovered from such a loss. *Ever.*' He regarded each of his brothers in turn. 'All we are doing now is avoiding our fate, instead of meeting it with courage, as sons of the Emperor ought. It is over. Let us at least choose the manner of our ending while we still can.'

Galleas did not reply at first. The veteran sergeant reached up and unlocked his helmet, removing it to reveal a face as hard as stone.

'My choice is made,' he said. 'It was made centuries ago, when I became an initiate in the Great Hall of the Arx Tyrannus. I chose to serve the Chapter Master unto my dying breath, and through him the Emperor of Mankind.' He stepped up to Olivar, meeting his ruined gaze unflinchingly. 'I will not throw away my life for the sake of pride. I will honour instead the commands of Chapter Master Kantor. I will fight the enemy with every weapon at my disposal, every warrior at my disposal, even if I have to create those warriors for myself.

'While I live, the Chapter lives. I am the shield hand of Dorn, and I. Will. Not. Yield.'

Silence fell. The two Space Marines stared at one another in silence, one indomitable will matched against another. Finally, it was Olivar who lowered his head in defeat.

'Forgive me,' he said in a haunted voice. 'The pain, it... sometimes it gets the better of me.'

Galleas laid a hand on Olivar's shoulder. 'There is nothing to forgive. The loss of the Arx Tyrannus... it is a wound that I fear will never heal.'

Olivar straightened to his full height. 'I will fight by your side until the last,' he said. 'But this can only end in death, brother. For all of us. Surely you see that?'

Galleas' silence was answer enough.

* * *

After an hour they made their way back to the site of the ambush and took what they could from the dead the orks left behind. Royas picked up the trail of the fleeing humans straight away, and the squad followed it deep into the sewer system.

The scent ran for kilometres, moving surely and steadily through the maze. It appeared that Corvalles, the labourer, was as good as his word. Eventually, the trail led the Space Marines to a darkened side tunnel that branched from one of the older sections of the network.

From the sight of it, the side tunnel seemed to have been abandoned long ago. Soon, Galleas saw why. After less than a hundred metres the passage ended in a heap of rubble.

The Space Marines came to a halt. Royas turned to Galleas. 'This doesn't make sense. The trail leads right into the rubble, but that cave-in looks to be years old.'

'Agreed,' Galleas said. He pressed forward, studying the collapse with every enhanced sense at his command.

'There is a draught here,' he observed. 'Faint, but steady.'

He approached the cave-in and switched to his thermal imager. Faint heat traces glowed amid the rubble. Galleas followed them cautiously and discovered to his surprise that the collapse wasn't a solid pile of rock as it first appeared. There was a winding path through the rubble that was nearly invisible from more than a few metres away.

Weapons ready, the Space Marines worked their way along the path. After several minutes, they emerged into a large, vaulted chamber, lit by a handful of flickering lumen strips. Galleas spied empty servitor stations and derelict monitor panels along the walls, and some kind of enclosed control room at the rear of the space.

Mitra rose from the floor as Galleas and his squad

appeared. Her platoon was tending to the liberated prisoners as best they could, checking their condition and sharing what little of their rations they could spare. Vega was moving amongst them, checking for injuries and administering his meagre store of medicine as needed.

'This was a stormwater monitoring station years back,' the lieutenant said. 'It was abandoned after the earthquake in 950. Corvalles was one of the team that dug through the rubble to rescue the labourers trapped inside.'

Galleas studied the layout of the chamber carefully. 'The path is nearly invisible to the naked eye. In the darkness, the orks would never find it.'

Mitra nodded. 'My thoughts exactly. And Corvalles says there are half a dozen ways to the surface within two hundred metres.' She managed a weary smile. 'We could stay here. Rest. Regain our strength. It's the closest thing to a secure base we'll find anywhere outside the Cassar. Gomez says it's the second miracle the God-Emperor has sent us.'

Galleas frowned. 'The second miracle? What was the first?'

'Why, when He sent us to find you, of course.'

The veteran sergeant looked away. All he could think of were Olivar's words, from back in the tunnel.

This can only end in death, brother.

For all of us.

PART TWO
THE SHIELDBEARERS

CHAPTER TWELVE

COUNCILS OF WAR

ZONA 9 RESIDENTIA, NEW RYNN CITY
DAY 160

One corner of the old hab unit remained, a crooked finger of scorched metal and broken permacrete rising four storeys through the yellow haze above the rubble of Zona Nine. Galleas studied it thoughtfully under full magnification for several long moments, then waved the scouting party forward.

Figures rose warily from the ruins around the veteran sergeant: point men first, then the flankers, hunched low and picking their way carefully across the treacherous piles of broken stone. Corporal Ismail was in the lead, clutching a battered ork gun low against her chest, her silhouette masked by a heavy cloak stained in layers of dirt and grime. The rest were a mix of troopers from her squad and four of the most promising civilians they'd rescued from the chirurgium, armed like the Rynnsguard with looted ork weapons and clad in camouflage cloaks and salvaged flak armour. Eyes searching the broken landscape for potential threats, the scouts continued their sweep northwards.

Fifty-eight days had passed since the battle at the chirurgium. The spring rains had given way to brutal summer heat. The filth that had flooded the city during Matiluvia now broiled under the glare of the system's twin suns, creating a pestilential smog that hung thickly in the humid air. Patches of yellow-green mould spread in vast colonies across shady patches of stone and broken pieces of flakboard. The haze caused respiratory ailments and skin infections amongst the Rynnsworlders, and even strained the limits of the Space Marines' filtration systems. The *greenskin blight*, Galleas had heard it called by the more venerable Space Marines of the Chapter. The vile xenos thrived in it.

Galleas waited until the advance party was at the limits of his line of sight before rising from cover and following in their wake. With him came Sergeant Kazimir, his lower face hidden behind the stained folds of a bandana to keep out the worst of the blight. They were joined a moment later by Tauros and Amador, covering the scout party's rear.

The veteran sergeant divided his attention between scanning the surrounding ruins for danger and evaluating the movements of the advance party just ahead. The humans were still too slow by Space Marine standards, too clumsy negotiating the broken terrain, but two months of training and patrols had improved their skills considerably. After some experimentation, Galleas had settled on a programme of instruction where Tauros, Valentus and Juno provided the knowledge and Sergeant Kazimir handled the actual training. Kazimir had ways of imparting the Space Marines' wealth of experience to the humans that didn't overwhelm or break them, and the new programme had produced swift results. The humans were becoming more than merely adequate; after much time and effort, they were now approaching the point of being actively *useful*.

The brassy rumble of jet engines swelled from the south-east, in the direction of the fallen spaceport. Galleas turned and caught sight of a gaggle of ungainly ork fighter-bombers thundering northwards towards the river. The blackened muzzles of their cannons flashed, spitting shells at the distant Cassar. Within moments the rattle of small-arms fire started up across the city as the orks on the ground were stirred to action by the roaring of the jets. Batteries of green-skin artillery quickly joined in, spitting unaimed salvoes at the besieged fortress. The paroxysm of destruction lasted less than a minute, culminating in a drumbeat of heavy bombs detonating against the Cassar's unyielding void shields. Then the fighter-bombers were gone, the sound of their engines dwindling to the north-east as they began a looping course back to the starport before night fell.

The veteran sergeant noted that he hadn't heard the Cassar's Hydra batteries fire once during the brief attack. *Saving their ammunition for actual threats*, Galleas hoped.

There hadn't been as many runts combing the wasteland since summer began, and the scouts reached the collapsed hab unit without incident. Up close, the surviving corner of the building looked like it was in a state of slow-motion collapse, held together by nothing more than twisted beams of structural metal. Planning each hand- and foothold with care, Galleas began to climb. Tauros watched his progress for several moments before joining in, followed by Kazimir.

The suns were setting in the west by the time Galleas and his companions settled onto an awkward perch some twelve metres above the ruined cityscape. From this vantage point Galleas could see the spire of the Cassar in the distance, shrouded by haze and partially obscured by pillars of dirty grey smoke rising from a sprawling ork camp in the foreground.

The camp sat at the northern edge of Zona Nine, festering amid the wreckage of a burned-out hab bloc. Shanties made of flakboard and scavenged girders sprouted in misshapen clusters amid winding lanes and sludgy cesspools. A handful of marginally wider paths allowed for the movement of vehicles, a great number of which were clustered with the warband's fuel and other supplies at the centre of the camp. The perimeter was loosely defined by half-finished walls and ramshackle sentry towers that covered most of the approaches to the camp. Ragged banners hung from the sentry towers, wrinkled and curling in the thick foetid air, their sigils masked by the haze.

Galleas had seen greenskin camps like these on a hundred different worlds. There were hundreds like it now on both sides of the river, well back from the killing ground around the Cassar.

Kazimir crouched beside Galleas, his gun balanced across his knees. He tugged the bandana down to reveal the rest of his lined face. 'What's it mean, my lord?' he asked hoarsely, nodding in the direction of the camp. 'For months they were thick as rats down by the river. Now they've mostly backed away.'

'Greenskins live to fight,' Galleas said grimly. 'If they don't have an enemy to kill, they'll just as soon turn on each other. It's been the downfall of many a Waaagh! in the past.' He gestured towards the camp. 'Snagrod is spreading out his warbands to keep friction to a minimum while looking for a way to end the siege.'

Kazimir spat at the mention of the warboss' name. 'Damned clever for a xenos.'

The veteran sergeant nodded. 'But not unexpected.' He glanced at Tauros. 'What do you think, brother?'

'Perimeter's full of holes,' the veteran Space Marine observed. 'Plenty of opportunities for a raiding party.'

Kazimir frowned. 'There's got to be hundreds of green-skins down there.'

Tauros chuckled. 'That's their problem, sergeant, not ours.'

'And the other camp?' Galleas interjected.

Kazimir nodded westwards, in the direction of a broken line of fallen buildings just over a kilometre away. 'Sitting on the grounds of the old schola urbis. A third as many greenskins, not much in the way of defences and few vehi-cles to speak of. A much easier target than this one, my lord.'

'Routes between the two camps?'

'Two,' Kazimir answered. 'The M-Twelve and the Cavalo-nian Way, an older secondary road connecting Zona Nine and Eleven.'

Galleas nodded thoughtfully. That matched his eidetic map of the city. 'Your knowledge of the area is exceptional.'

Kazimir's expression turned sombre. 'It ought to be, my lord,' he said quietly. 'I grew up here. Went to the schola urbis like my father, and his father before him.' He pointed to a field of rubble off to the east. 'My daughter and her family lived right over there. Nice little place on Chan-dler's Row.'

'What became of them?' Tauros asked.

The sergeant shook his head. 'The God-Emperor alone knows.'

A long silence fell. Galleas considered the odds of any civilian family surviving the ork onslaught, and found them almost too remote to calculate. 'I expect they're most likely–'

'I'm sure they're safe on the island,' Tauros interjected. 'Have no fear, sergeant. The Emperor protects.'

'Yes. Yes, of course.' Kazimir's tone was anything but certain, but he gave the towering Crimson Fist a faint smile. 'Thank you, my lord.'

Galleas frowned. The possibility sounded dubious in the extreme, but now was not the time for a lecture on statistics and probability.

'I've seen enough,' the veteran sergeant declared, turning his back on the greenskin camp. 'Call in the advance party, Sergeant Kazimir. It's time we returned to base. There is much work to be done.'

There were few sentries covering the approaches to the Imperials' subterranean base. With Snagrod's vast horde camped overhead, Galleas knew that secrecy was the base's best defence, and fixed points in the dark sewer tunnels would only serve to draw the greenskins' attention. Instead, grenade traps and scavenged land mines had been laid at strategic points along the approaches to the hidden chamber, where any explosion would echo a long way down the tunnels and provide early warning that the enemy was coming. With luck, it would provide enough time for the Imperials to evacuate, but Galleas was not eager to put the system to the test.

The traps were laid up to a kilometre from the entrance to the base, their locations marked by subtle signs that would be virtually invisible to the greenskins. Galleas and his brothers navigated the hazards with ease, moving through the near-total darkness by virtue of their enhanced senses and eidetic memories. The humans accompanying them were slower, but only marginally so, moving by the faint glow of red battle-lanterns salvaged from the battleground above. The scouts made little noise, speaking no more than necessary and choosing each step with care.

Several hundred metres later Galleas reached the listening post that covered the western approaches to the base. Little more than a pile of rubble that had fallen from the tunnel roof above, the mound of stones had been hollowed out on the reverse side and lined with a grimy tarpaulin to keep out the worst of the damp. As the veteran sergeant approached, he could see the silhouette of a small head and shoulders peeking over the top of the pile.

The girl was perhaps six or seven, Galleas reckoned, judging by her size. Her dirty, straw-coloured hair was pulled back and bound at the base of her neck by a rough length of cord, and her sallow cheeks were smeared with streaks of tunnel slime. A camouflage poncho covered the rags she wore, bound about her narrow hips by a utility belt. She looked up at Galleas with frank curiosity, one small hand resting on the hilt of the combat knife sheathed at her side.

The veteran sergeant paused next to the piled rubble and gave the post a cursory inspection. The girl's partner, an older child of perhaps fourteen, was huddled within the hollow of stones, a laspistol clutched loosely in his hands.

'Report,' Galleas said in a low voice. The deep tones echoed ominously in the confines of the tunnel.

The older sentry straightened. 'All's quiet,' he answered softly, his tone deferential. The young girl continued to stare silently up at Galleas, her face devoid of expression. Of all the survivors of the chirurgium, the children had adapted quickest to the demands of life in the tunnels. Their sharp ears made them excellent sentries, and their size allowed them to scavenge weapons and other gear from small spaces that adult humans couldn't reach. They were also proving to be adept hunters, stalking the tunnels for rats that continued to grow fat on the carrion above ground.

Some of them would have made worthy aspirants to the Chapter, Galleas mused, thinking back to his own childhood in the swamps of Blackwater, centuries past. The veteran sergeant nodded approvingly at the pair. 'Only in death does duty end,' he reminded the children. 'Carry on.'

The rubble-strewn tunnel leading to the base's entrance had been left exactly as the Imperials found it. Galleas picked his way amongst the debris with care and then along the hidden, winding path into the derelict monitoring station.

A heavy tent flap had been strung across the chamber's entrance to trap light and sound. Galleas pushed it carefully aside and emerged into a short passageway formed from sections of scavenged tent fabric and lit by the red glow of a battle lantern.

An old man wearing ill-fitting flak armour and clutching a lascarbine in his knobby hands struggled to rise from a stool set beside the entryway. A life of hard work in a manufactory had left him with leathery skin and deep lines at the corners of his eyes.

Galleas paused, recalling the man's name. 'Anything to report, Tomas?'

Tomas Zapeta considered the question carefully, his mouth working as though he'd bitten into something sour. 'Another day, another set of aches,' he grumbled hoarsely. 'It's the damp, I reckon, and being sat on that stool four hours at a stretch. Not one thing, it's another, Emperor knows. When my wife was still alive she knew how to make a poultice from mustard and bergwort–'

'Anything to report about the *tunnels*?' Galleas prodded.

Tomas gave the towering Space Marine a bemused look. 'Eh? The tunnels? No, no. Quiet as a tomb.' The old man shook his head gravely. 'Oh, I'm sure the orks will find us soon enough. Come howling in here and chop us all to bits. The rains always come, my old gran used to say. Rains always come.'

Galleas frowned. 'I fail to see how rain equates to the threat of a xenos attack.'

Tomas sighed. 'No. No, I reckon not. Will there be anything else, my lord?'

'Inform Lieutenant Mitra and Master Bergand that there will be an operations briefing in five minutes.'

'Very well, my lord.'

The veteran sergeant made a mental note to speak to Vega about Tomas' mental state as he crossed the makeshift passage and pushed past the flap at the far end into the space beyond.

The Crimson Fists had wasted no time transforming the derelict monitoring station into a functioning base camp. The rescued civilians had been put to work at once, emptying the chamber of refuse and debris. Galleas had given Enginseer Oros a small team of tradesmen to help strip the abandoned servitors of any useful parts, and then the servitors, too, were hauled away and dumped into the roaring storm waters outside. Scavenging parties had been sent out every night to comb the ruins for a long list of necessary supplies: clothes, bedrolls, blankets, energy cells, water flasks, field stoves, shelters and more.

The first few weeks had been hard. Food was scarce, and the supplies liberated from the chirurgium were barely enough to treat Mitra's surviving troops, much less the civilians. Several of the Rynnsguard, Kazimir included, had tried to refuse the antivirals and vitamin boosters for the sake of the others, but Galleas had sternly forbidden it. The soldiers were treated first, and then Vega was left to decide how to administer the rest, effectively choosing who would live and who would die. Before the first month was out, nearly a third of the former prisoners had perished. Preacher Gomez consigned their souls to the Emperor as their bodies were given to the raging waters and washed out into the bay.

Galleas and his brothers had evaluated the survivors carefully. Only half of the humans were fit enough for combat; the rest became servants, not unlike those who had walked the halls of the Arx Tyrannus. Shirking was not tolerated, and the veteran sergeant had made it clear that the punishment for disobedience would be swift and final. None doubted the Crimson Fist's resolve.

The humans had accepted their new roles without complaint, and the dank air of the chamber hummed with quiet, purposeful activity as Galleas emerged from the passageway into a rectangular commons created by walls of scavenged tent fabric. Men, women, and a few young children worked there, preparing meals, cleaning gear, or receiving instruction in the ways of war.

Galleas caught sight of Juno at the far side of the commons. He sat cross-legged on the permacrete floor, looming like a ceramite mountain over a small group of children who were learning how to disassemble and maintain the orks' crude firearms. Sitting front and centre before the veteran Space Marine were the eight-year-old brother and sister whom Juno had carried out of the chirurgium. They hung on the veteran's every word, mimicking his movements precisely as they worked on the oversized weapons laid across their knees. Their mother, Daniella, a former Administratum clerk who now managed the base's food supplies, sat close by, typing figures into a salvaged data-slate. The three had formed a tight attachment to Juno ever since their rescue, sticking close to the towering Space Marine whenever he was inside the base. Juno, for his part, treated them no differently. Galleas couldn't say for certain that the veteran Space Marine noticed their adoration at all.

Tomas shuffled into the commons behind Galleas, twitching aside the tent sections and peering into the sleeping cells on the other side as he searched for Mitra and Bergand. Juno caught sight of the veteran sergeant and began to hurry through the remainder of his lesson, reassembling his weapon in seconds while his perplexed students struggled to follow along.

The rest of the scouting party was arriving as Galleas crossed the commons and entered the narrow aisle on the opposite side. The aisle ended at a short flight of steps that led to the control room at the rear of the station.

The Crimson Fists had stripped the control room down to the bare walls and converted it into their own inner sanctum, complete with narrow meditation cells, armoury and a small, cleared area for close-combat practice. The commons area in the centre was dominated by a small, battered display console that Enginseer Oros had salvaged from the ruins of a commercial building nearby. The tech-priest knelt by one of the console's open access panels, affixing a data cable with his mechadendrites as he murmured a catechism in low, reverent tones. From one of the meditation cells at the far end of the chamber Galleas could hear another solemn chant; it was Olivar, his deep voice intoning the

Litanies of Hate. The rites wove together in the confined space, point and counterpoint, reason and emotion, the words heavy with the weight of millennia. For a moment it was as though Galleas was back within the Arx Tyrannus, and the Chapter was whole once again.

Oros turned at the veteran sergeant's approach, his yellow lenses gleaming. 'All is in readiness, my lord,' he said, bowing his hooded head. 'I require only the data to begin.'

Without a word, Galleas unsealed the mag-locks on his helmet and pulled it off. As always, there was the subtle shift in perception as the helmet's auto-senses disengaged and his genetically enhanced ones took over. The dank air of the chamber was rich with the smells of metal, dirt, stone and unwashed humans. The veteran sergeant handed the upended helm to Oros, who accepted it reverently and set it on a small stand at the foot of the console.

Tauros and Amador joined Galleas only a few moments later, followed by Juno, Lieutenant Mitra and Sergeant Kazimir. Valentus and Royas emerged from their meditation cells and took their place around the console. Royas, helmetless himself, watched Oros work with a disapproving glare. Vega came next, clutching a pair of data-slates and rubbing sleep from his eyes, then Bergand, the offworld merchant. Brother Olivar was last of all, joining the briefing only after the Litanies of Hate were complete. The ruined ocular of his helmet was a pit of shadows in the dim light.

As Olivar took his place around the console, Galleas began. 'Readiness update,' he said without preamble, sweeping his gaze across the assembled Imperials. 'Master Bergand?'

The void trader smiled. 'We have food enough for six weeks,' he declared. 'Mostly scavenged ration packs, plus... additional protein–'

'Sewer rats, you mean,' Kazimir corrected with a salty grin. 'Better flavour than the g-rats the Astra Militarum issues, even if they don't keep as long.'

Bergand gave a little shudder, but pressed on. 'Water is in ample supply, of course. Vega has certified that the storm water is sufficiently clean to drink.'

'That won't last once winter sets in,' Mitra cautioned. 'We should be storing up as much as we can while it's plentiful.'

Bergand's smile faltered. 'I see. Of course.' He drew a data-slate and stylus from his belt and began making notes. 'Our numbers?'

'One hundred and two,' Bergand replied without looking up from the slate. 'Including Lieutenant Mitra and the nineteen members of her platoon. That's not counting you and your six brothers, of course.'

'Of course,' Galleas echoed. He turned to Kazimir. 'Weapons and ammunition?'

'Sixteen lasguns, one lascarbine, one shotgun and six laspistols,' the sergeant replied. 'Plus another sixty ork guns, three dozen grenades and two rocket launchers with four rockets each. I can't vouch for the rockets, but everything else is in good working order. Thirty power packs for the las weapons, plus twenty-six hundred rounds of ammunition, give or take. Enough to last us a good long while if we're careful.'

'Vega?'

The field medic stirred, taking a deep breath as he gathered his wits. 'Everyone has been given the full course of antivirals at this point, which should be effective for as long as six months,' he said. 'Stocks of painkillers, anti-inflammatories and other potions are low. I barely have what I need to treat minor injuries, much less major trauma like a bullet wound.'

'We'll make that a priority for the search parties going forward,' Galleas replied. He turned to Mitra. 'What is the status of the training programme?'

Mitra straightened. She had changed during the weeks spent underground. The brittleness and barely-suppressed fear she'd displayed when she'd first met Galleas was gone, worn away to reveal the stubborn resolve that lay beneath. Her eyes were still haunted, though, and there was an edge to her voice when she spoke. 'Everyone capable of fighting has received basic training in weapons, fieldcraft and tactics. Some of the more promising individuals, including what's left of my platoon, are undergoing advanced training now.'

Royas and Amador exchanged disapproving looks, but kept their thoughts to themselves. Olivar listened impassively, his massive form as still as stone.

'Are they ready for battle?'

Mitra glanced at Kazimir. The Rynnsguard sergeant shrugged. 'As ready as we can make them.'

'How many effectives?'

'Sixty, including my men,' Mitra answered, 'broken out into fifteen-man squads. I'll take first squad, Kazimir will take the second, and Ismail and Vila will head up third and fourth squads.'

Galleas considered Mitra's dispositions, and nodded thoughtfully. Vila would bear watching, but otherwise the lieutenant's decisions were sound.

'Very well,' he said at length. 'The time has come to put our preparations to the test and strike back at the xenos.'

Galleas turned to Enginseer Oros, but Bergand cut in before the veteran sergeant could speak.

'Forgive me, my lord, but are you certain that's wise?'

The Crimson Fists turned as one to regard the offworlder.

A lesser man might have quailed under the stares of seven towering Space Marines, but Bergand stood firm. 'I mean no disrespect,' he continued hastily, raising a placating hand. 'I was just under the impression that the point of all this work was to improve our chances of escaping and reaching the safety of the Cassar.'

Royas snarled at Bergand. 'You imagine the Cassar is *safe*, do you?'

Mitra and Kazimir shifted uncomfortably at the contempt in Royas' voice, but the void trader was undeterred.

'Certainly safer than *here*,' Bergand countered. 'Any moment the orks could stumble over us, and then where would we be? How many of us would escape the greenskins' clutches?' He shuddered. 'You can't imagine what it was like, crammed into a cell in that dreadful chirurgium, wondering when your turn would come.'

Royas leaned over the console, his armoured hands clenching into fists. 'Mind your tongue, little man,' he spat. 'Who do you think you're talking to?'

'That's enough, brother,' Galleas said sternly.

Royas turned his angry glare upon Galleas. He locked eyes with the veteran sergeant for a moment, then lowered his head and drew back, muttering darkly.

Galleas brought his attention back to Bergand. 'Reaching the Cassar is impossible,' he said. 'Even if we could make it to the river undetected, we have no way of crossing over to the island, especially under the guns of Snagrod's horde.'

'But what about the tunnels?' Bergand pressed. 'I've been speaking to that fellow Corvalles, and he says there are tunnels that pass under the river and connect to the Zona Regis–'

'Collapsed,' Galleas said. 'Every one of them, along with

the bridges connecting the island to the rest of the city. That was the contingency plan in the event that the greenskins breached the last defensive wall. Otherwise there would be orks in the Zona Regis right now, and all would be lost.'

'But you can't mean–' Bergand faltered. The offworlder looked to Mitra and Kazimir for support, but the Rynnsguard returned his gaze coldly. He spread his hands entreatingly. 'Snagrod's horde is numberless. You can't mean to fight the xenos with less than seventy men!'

Galleas raised an eyebrow. 'Is that what you think, Master Bergand?' The veteran sergeant smiled mirthlessly. 'Nothing could be further from the truth. I intend for the orks to do most of the fighting themselves.'

The veteran sergeant gestured to Oros. The enginseer reached inside the console. There was a faint hum of power, and the display flickered to life. A map of Zona Nine appeared, drawn in phosphorescent lines from the data stored in Galleas' helmet.

'Over the past week, the enemy has altered their dispositions,' Galleas began. 'The battle for the city has reached a stalemate, with the orks unable to breach the Cassar's void shields. The longer this continues, the more frustrated and restless the greenskins will become. Ultimately, they will turn on one another to vent their mindless aggressions.'

Bergand frowned. 'Why then, all we have to do is wait–'

'Snagrod understands this as well as we do, Master Bergand. He has pulled the bulk of his force back from the riverbank and spread the warbands as much as possible to minimise friction while he looks for a way to break the siege.'

'Will it work?' Mitra asked.

'Most likely,' Galleas allowed. 'Unless someone were to provide the spark that would set the powder keg alight.'

His fingers moved across the display, dragging the map until it centred on the ork camp the scouting party had surveyed hours before. 'This is the largest warband in Zona Nine. Several hundred greenskins, possibly as many as a thousand, plus vehicles.'

'*What of the warboss?*' Valentus inquired.

Tauros shook his head. 'Unknown. But clearly powerful, to command such numbers.'

'The xenos are complacent,' Galleas continued. 'They believe their foes to be bottled up on the island, so the camp's defences are sloppy at best. A lightning raid, in the dead of night, would be explosive.' He rapped the top of the console with an armoured knuckle for emphasis. 'Sting the beast and it will lash out at the first thing it can reach. It's a strategy that my brothers and I have used against the greenskins on many campaigns across the Ultima Segmentum, and we know it well.' He nodded at Tauros. 'Veteran Brother Tauros alone broke up an ork horde at Cephalon with just an Astra Militarum regiment in support.'

Tauros folded his arms. 'It requires self-discipline, patience, and near-perfect coordination,' he said. 'We cannot afford to make a single mistake. But yes, it can be done.'

Mitra nodded thoughtfully, her gaze falling to the image on the display. Galleas could see the dread in her eyes, but when she spoke, her voice was steady.

'Can we really defeat Snagrod this way?'

'Defeat? No,' Galleas admitted. 'This horde is larger than anything the Segmentum has seen in thousands of years. The best we can do is sow chaos and confusion, drawing the warchief's attention away from the Cassar. But if we can delay the xenos an hour, a day or a week, it could make all the difference.'

Mitra studied the map in silence. Finally, she drew a long breath. 'When do we attack, my lord?' she said.

Galleas inclined his head in approval. 'Soon. But first–' His hand slid to the right, dragging the map eastwards, until it centred on the ruins of a schola urbis and the small xenos camp situated there. 'We must give them an enemy to fight.'

CHAPTER THIRTEEN

FORTUNES OF WAR

ZONA 9 RESIDENTIA, NEW RYNN CITY
DAY 162

Two nights later there was a new moon, and the scouts reported heavy clouds and the possibility of rain. Galleas passed word to Lieutenant Mitra that conditions were right, and the raid would commence at midnight.

Preparations began after the evening meal. The commons area bustled with activity as the Imperials gathered by squads and began the lengthy ritual of cleaning, inspecting and blessing their wargear. Children dashed back and forth from the makeshift armoury at the far end of the chamber, passing out ammunition and grenades. The would-be guerrillas said little, focusing instead on smudging their faces with foul-smelling mud to help blend with the shadows, or adjusting the fit of their battered flak armour. Wide, frightened eyes shone ghostly white in the gloom. Preacher Gomez walked among the squads, reading selections from the *Lectitio Divinitatus* in a funereal voice. It did not appear to be having the effect on morale that Gomez intended.

At precisely midnight, Galleas and his squad emerged from their inner sanctum. The commons fell silent as the Crimson Fists crossed the chamber in silent procession: grim, implacable gods of war, bristling with weapons, their ancient armour scarred by the marks of bullet and blade. The humans bowed their heads and made the sign of the aquila as the Space Marines went by.

Reaching the partition that led to the exit tunnel, Galleas stepped aside to let his battle-brothers file past, and beckoned to Lieutenant Mitra and her squad leaders. The lieutenant affected a calm demeanour, but Galleas knew her well enough by now to see the faint lines of tension in her face. Kazimir, the veteran, was stolid as ever. Corporal Ismail grinned up at Galleas, her face transformed by dirt and ash into a fierce-looking war mask. Vila, by contrast, looked like a man heading to his own execution.

'Are your troops ready, lieutenant?'

Mitra gave a curt nod. 'The sergeant and I have just completed a final gear inspection and reviewed the routes and timetables for each squad. We'll be ready to move out at the appointed time.'

The veteran sergeant regarded Ismail and Vila. 'You understand what is expected of you?'

Corporal Ismail's grin turned feral. 'Get into firing position, wait for the signal, and then unleash hell,' she said.

Vila gave Ismail a sidelong look and muttered something under his breath. Kazimir's eyes narrowed. 'Anything you want to add, corporal?' he said.

'No, sergeant,' Vila replied sullenly.

'Do you want to say a few words to the troops before you go, my lord?' Mitra interjected.

Galleas frowned. 'The operational details were explained

clearly in the briefing. Anything I would have to say at this point would be redundant.'

Mitra's brows knitted in consternation. 'I meant–' she started to say, then abruptly thought better of it. 'Perhaps I should just wish you good luck then.'

'Luck?' Galleas shook his head disapprovingly. 'Victory does not depend on luck, Lieutenant Mitra. That is what discipline and proper planning are for.' Without waiting for a reply, the veteran sergeant turned on his heel and disappeared behind the heavy tarp covering the exit.

The plan for the raid was a simple one, even by the standards of the Astra Militarum. While the Crimson Fists infiltrated the small ork camp and secured the raid's objectives, the Rynnsguard squads would emerge from the tunnels at four separate points around the camp and move into firing positions that had been carefully reconnoitred the previous night. When the signal was given, all four squads would open fire, unleashing a storm of ork rounds on the camp. Each soldier had been issued five reloads for his or her weapon – four would be expended on the camp, and the fifth one saved in case of encounters on the way back to the tunnels. The only challenge was getting all four squads in position to fire at the appropriate time. As long as the squad leaders followed the routes they were given and employed basic fieldcraft, it wouldn't be any more complicated than a routine night march. There was too little room for error to risk anything more complex.

The rest of the squad was waiting for Galleas in the main stormwater tunnel. At a nod from the veteran sergeant they set off in the direction of the greenskin camp. They would cover most of the three kilometres underground, emerging from a maintenance access just sixty metres from the enemy perimeter. By that point the Rynnsguard would be on the move as well, heading through the tunnels to their own exit points.

The Space Marines moved swiftly and silently along the darkened tunnels, weapons covering each side passage and potential ambush point with unconscious precision. It was the kind of manoeuvre the veterans could literally do in their sleep, allowing somatic reflexes to take over and freeing the conscious mind for more important tasks. Galleas was planning ahead, testing strategies for the larger raid on the second ork camp, when Royas intruded on his thoughts.

'You're putting a great deal of faith in these humans, brother,' he said. 'The Rynnsguard are bad enough, but that rabble we rescued from the chirurgium? I've seen their type on a thousand different worlds. Mark my words, they'll go to pieces once the shooting starts.'

'Perhaps,' Galleas admitted. 'Perhaps not. They have ample reason to hate the greenskins. Given an opportunity to strike back, I doubt they will hesitate.'

'The first taste of battle is different for everyone,' Valentus mused, the synthetic tones of his vox-speaker echoing discordantly from the tunnel walls. *'I remember my first live-fire exercise as a novitiate. The first time I came face-to-face with the enemy I froze for a full eighth of a second. I knew what I had to do, but I couldn't convince my body to actually do it.'* The veteran Space Marine chuckled, shaking his head. *'I was shot seven times. Captain Rigellus was so incensed he made me remove the slugs myself.'*

Tauros and Amador chuckled along with Valentus, but Royas wasn't mollified. 'Depending on them is foolish,' he persisted. 'And dangerous. We'd be better off leaving them to guard the other civilians while we do the real fighting.'

'The more firepower we use, the better the illusion,' Tauros pointed out. 'We need the orks to believe they're being hit by a warband, not a squad of seven Space Marines.'

'As long as we're spilling xenos blood, it's all the same to me,' Amador said. He turned to Tauros. 'Is this how you broke up the horde on Cephalon?'

The veteran Space Marine shrugged. 'More or less.'

'What is that supposed to mean?'

'When we were cut off at Cephalon, I had four veteran infantry regiments under my command,' Tauros explained. 'About forty thousand troops, centred on the planet's single continent.'

'And?'

'We broke up the horde with hit-and-run attacks over a five month period,' Tauros said. 'First we targeted their supplies. Then, when the greenskins were frustrated and hungry, we'd raid two or three neighbouring warbands at the same time. When they gave chase, we led them head-on into one another and disappeared in the confusion. Once the infighting started, it was all but impossible to stop. By the time Imperial reinforcements arrived, there wasn't much of the horde left.'

'It was a victory worthy of the annals,' Galleas said. 'Rigellus made all us novitiates study it during advanced training, but I suppose that was before your time.'

'How many survived?' Amador asked.

'The orks?'

'No. Your men.'

Tauros hesitated, until finally Amador turned to Galleas. 'Well?'

'Casualties were one hundred per cent,' the veteran sergeant replied. 'Not a single Imperial soldier survived.'

Amador considered this. 'We have considerably fewer than forty thousand men,' he observed.

Royas let out a snort. 'Maths always was your strong suit, Amador,' he said drily.

'And Snagrod's horde is many times larger.'

'*But there are seven of us,*' Valentus countered. '*That should more than make up the difference.*'

'He has a point,' Tauros said amiably. 'Why, a venerable old Dreadnought like Valentus here is worth at least five thousand Imperial soldiers all by himself.'

'*Five thousand? You insult me. I would think seven at the very least.*'

'Well, the codex teaches us to respect our elders, no matter how senile they may become, so we'll just leave it at seven,' Tauros agreed. 'Young Amador here still has much to learn, but is full of vigour, so let's say he's worth about four thousand or so.'

'Now look here–'

'As for the rest of us, well, we're in our prime. I'd say we're worth at least ten thousand apiece,' Tauros claimed. 'What do you reckon, Juno?'

'I reckon I could whip the lot of you blindfolded,' Juno replied. It wasn't clear if he was jesting or not.

'And there you have it,' Tauros said. 'We've got the Arch-Arsonist completely outnumbered. He just doesn't know it yet.'

'Regardless, it's the only viable strategy we have,' Galleas said. 'If we remain invisible and strike indirectly, we can fight the horde for as long as necessary, until Snagrod abandons the siege or Imperial reinforcements arrive.'

Royas shook his head in disagreement, but Galleas' tone made it clear that the topic wasn't up for further discussion.

A stony silence fell over the Crimson Fists as they continued to their objective.

Past the outer listening posts, the route to the surface was a straightforward series of tunnels that ran westwards for some four kilometres, crossing between Zona Nine and Zona Eleven. The Space Marines moved swiftly through the darkness, trusting their enhanced senses to warn them of any dangers ahead. Within twenty minutes they had reached a rusting metal door set into the side of the tunnel that opened onto a flight of rubble-strewn stairs leading to the surface. 'Royas, you're on point,' Galleas said over the vox. 'Juno and Amador, take the flanks. Let's go.'

The stairs led to the sub-level of a hab unit just a few hundred metres from the grounds of the old schola urbis. At the top of the stairs another metal door had been pulled open to reveal jumbled slabs of broken, scorched ferrocrete and half-melted girders. The hab unit itself was gone, blown apart by shelling and burned repeatedly by savage xenos warbands. The sub-level was now open to the humid night air.

The Space Marines slowed their pace, pausing amid the rubble for a moment and searching the darkness for threats. Nothing stirred amongst the wreckage, and the surrounding area was quiet. Darkness hung heavy over the ruins of the city. Satisfied, Galleas nodded to Royas, and the squad began climbing the tumbled slabs of ferrocrete to reach street level.

Zona Nine had been a prosperous, middle-class sector before the ork invasion. A two-lane boulevard ran westwards between the hab units, divided by a broad, tree-lined pedestrian space with stone pathways for families to walk their children to the schola. The boulevard now was lined

with crushed, burned-out vehicles and heaps of broken ferrocrete, presided over by the skeletal figures of scorched,
broken trees. Artillery shells had left deep craters here and
there along the route to the schola, offering good cover for
Galleas and his brothers.

The squad spread out and made their way carefully along
the boulevard, sweeping the ruins to the left and right in
search of threats. Another twenty minutes later and Galleas
was crouching against the slope of a shell crater, eyeing the
entrance to the grounds of the schola just a hundred metres
to the west. The main gate was long gone, knocked down
by artillery or maybe by the orks themselves, but the thick,
stone gateposts still stood. The low wall that bordered the
grounds was broken in a dozen places that Galleas could
see, and nothing had been done to repair them.

Two sentry towers rose from more or less the middle
of the ork camp, close to where the warband's few vehicles would be kept. A small mob of less than a dozen orks
slouched around a fire just beyond the open gate. Three
of the greenskins were amusing themselves by torment-
ing a screeching runt with a pair of red-hot tongs. The rest
appeared to be asleep.

'*Plenty of spots to slip past them,*' Tauros observed over the
vox.

Galleas shook his head. 'I don't want any potential wit-
nesses on the way out. We'll deal with them now and pick
up the bodies later.'

The veteran sergeant motioned Juno, Royas and Tauros to
go left, while he, Amador, Olivar and Valentus went right.
Like shadows, the Space Marines darted from cover to cover
along the boulevard, swinging wide of the open gate and
slipping through gaps in the wall to either side.

The grounds of the schola urbis covered a full city block, and in better times had been a tree-filled park where students could reflect on their studies. Now it was a wasteland of cinders and churned mud, dominated by the shell of the schola building at the far end. Ork shanties and reeking cesspools spread like fungus across the open space, outlined in places by the flickering glow of greasy cookfires. Nothing moved along the foul lanes running between the huts, the closest of which were more than a dozen metres from the main gate. Galleas crouched in the shadow of the wall and switched to thermal vision, scanning the tops of the sentry towers fifty metres away. There were a pair of heat signatures in each, but none of them were moving. *Most likely asleep as well*, the veteran sergeant reckoned. *The orks at the gate think the guards in the towers are watching out for them, and the ones in the towers are depending on the guards at the gate.*

Galleas waved his brothers forward. The Crimson Fists crept along the wall towards the gate. The runt's agonised cries covered the slight sounds the armoured warriors made as they closed the distance with their foe.

Ten metres from the xenos, Galleas lowered his ork gun to the ground and drew his sword. Combat knives slid silently from their sheaths. Though he could not see them, Galleas knew that Juno, Tauros and Royas would be doing the same. The three orks and their victim were on the side of the fire closest to Galleas, so their deaths were his responsibility.

The veteran sergeant exchanged hand signals with his brothers, assigning targets. Each Space Marine nodded curtly in turn. Satisfied, Galleas raised Night's Edge, and the four warriors bounded forward as one. Blades flashed, and the greenskins toppled without a sound, blood pouring onto the mud. Juno, Royas and Tauros appeared a heartbeat later, eliminating the sleeping greenskins on their side of the fire. The slaughter took only a few seconds to complete.

Working quickly, Galleas and the others propped up the dead orks who had been torturing the hapless runt, so that it would appear nothing untoward had happened. Then they gathered up their guns and made their way silently up the lane leading into the camp.

Galleas checked the chronometer on his display. It was an hour past midnight. Lieutenant Mitra and the rest of the guerrillas would be leaving the hideout on the way to their firing positions. If everything went according to plan, they would be in place in forty-five minutes.

The Crimson Fists slowed as they reached the first of the shanties. Here and there, muffled snores reverberated through the huts' thin, corrugated steel walls. The towers loomed against the dark sky up ahead. For a moment Galleas considered sending Juno and Tauros to climb them and eliminate the sentries, but just as quickly decided against it. The climb would expose the two Space Marines to view from pretty much every corner of the camp. He couldn't justify the risk. Instead, the armoured giants kept to the deep shadows and moved as quickly and as quietly as they dared towards the centre of the camp.

Like most ork camps, the greenskins kept their vehicles, fuel and ammunition at its core, where they could be easily reached in case of attack. Three hulking trucks were parked in a loose cluster next to a score of rusting fuel drums in a cleared space, surrounded by the shanties of the bigger orks in the warband. Galleas counted half a dozen smaller orks – the warband's tool-wielding engineers – sleeping in the stinking mud next to the vehicles.

The veteran sergeant pointed out the engineers to his brothers. They would be dealt with first. Engineers were prized by most ork warbands, so were valuable targets for a typical raiding party. The Crimson Fists spread out, blades ready, and silently despatched the sleeping greenskins. Then they gathered up the corpses and loaded them into the back of one of the trucks.

Tauros looked over the heap of bodies. 'How many more do you reckon we'll need?' he asked softly.

'I'd say not more than a dozen,' Galleas mused, 'including the ones left at the gate. You, Juno and Amador take care of it. The rest of us will deal with the trucks.'

Tauros nodded, gesturing to Juno and Amador and heading for one of the nearby shanties. Meanwhile, Galleas addressed Valentus, Royas and Olivar. 'Each of you take a truck and familiarise yourselves with the controls. Don't start the engines until I give the signal.'

The three Space Marines nodded and went to work, quietly climbing aboard the war machines. Galleas lifted himself into the troop compartment of Valentus' truck and worked his way forward to the twin-mounted heavy guns set in a pintle mount above the driver's cab. He took hold of the guns' oversized grips and steeled himself to wait.

This was the most dangerous part of the whole raid. It wasn't enough to hit the greenskins; they needed to grab 'prisoners' to taunt the orks further. Their corpses would be left behind during the attack on the larger camp the following night, to reinforce the illusion and enflame the situation even further. But a single mistake by Tauros or his brothers, a single shout of alarm, and the whole camp would be up in arms around them.

The minutes stretched, one after another. Galleas switched back to thermal and kept an eye on the towers to his left and right. After what felt like an eternity, Juno appeared from the open doorway of one of the greenskin shanties, lugging a dead ork over one shoulder. He laid the body in the back of one of the trucks and returned to the hut for another. Not long after, Tauros appeared with a corpse of his own and added it to the load.

Galleas eyed the chronometer. The diversionary squads should be approaching their firing positions east of the schola. Their fire would keep the orks occupied during the crucial minutes the Space Marines needed to get the trucks going and headed towards the gate.

Amador appeared off to the right, dragging a pair of orks across the mud. Galleas scowled at the Space Marine's carelessness, but before he could say anything he caught a hint of motion from the sentry tower overlooking Amador.

One of the orks in the tower was sluggishly stirring. Galleas slowly crouched, concealing his silhouette against the bed of the truck. His hands tightened on the guns' twin grips.

He watched the thermal image of the ork stagger upright and stand for a moment, scratching itself. Then it lumbered to the edge of the tower on the far side of where the trucks were parked. Galleas stole a quick glance at Amador. The younger Space Marine had spotted the danger and had dropped to a crouch, partially concealing himself behind the rear of one of the trucks.

The ork walked up to the edge of the tower and paused. Was he scanning the area? On the thermal imager the xenos was just a bright white silhouette, offering little in the way of detail. Moments passed... and then Galleas' enhanced senses caught a hiss of liquid as the beast relieved itself from the top of the tower.

The veteran sergeant started to relax – and then the ork, with typical greenskin humour, turned his aim on the shanties below. The stream hit the shanties' tin rooftops with a sound like a warning drum, reverberating across the camp.

Galleas cursed under his breath. 'Amador, get those bodies on board,' he hissed into the vox. 'Juno, Tauros, get back here now!'

An angry bellow rose from the far side of the tower, followed by shouting in the orks' crude tongue. The sentry in the tower laughed, continuing the downpour. Something flashed up from below, spinning end-over-end. It hit the side of the sentry tower with a metallic *crash*, knocking loose a piece of corrugated sheeting that landed on top of one of the other shanties with a furious clatter.

Grunts and growls sounded from several of the shanties surrounding the trucks. Across the camp another voice bellowed in fury. Galleas glanced over and saw Amador tossing the second greenskin corpse into the back of the nearest truck. Tauros and Juno had appeared with another pair of bodies, and were hurrying to load them as well.

'Get ready to move, brothers!' Galleas warned. He scanned the surrounding huts, expecting to see orks at any moment.

Up in the tower, the sentry finished his business and went back to where he'd been sleeping, still chuckling. There was another growled warning from the far side of the tower, then silence descended over the camp once more.

For several moments the Crimson Fists held absolutely still, their senses straining to catch the faintest sounds of movement. Finally Galleas allowed himself to relax. 'It seems our luck is holding, brothers–'

Gunfire erupted to the east, about two hundred metres back in the ruins of the hab district. More gunfire answered, until a full-fledged battle was raging just outside the ork camp.

Galleas bared his teeth in a snarl. It had to be one of Mitra's squads. Something had gone terribly wrong.

'Start the engines!' he shouted over the vox.

'*What about the bodies?*' Amador protested. '*There are a couple more–*'

'Forget them! We're out of time!'

There was a whine, then a grinding sound as Valentus stomped on the ignition. The truck's motor made a choking noise, then abruptly coughed to life, engulfing the war machine in a billowing cloud of exhaust. Galleas could hear the first angry shouts rising from the surrounding shanties as he brought up the twin guns and raked the sentry towers with fire. The heavy weapons bucked in their mounts, pounding like trip-hammers as they chewed the flimsy structures – and the orks inside – to pieces.

Gears gnashed, and the truck suddenly lurched forward, oversized tyres throwing up plumes of noxious mud. Valentus spun the wheel and Galleas was thrown to the right as the war machine sideswiped the stacked fuel drums and slewed around in a broad curve back towards the main gate.

The truck's armoured prow hit an ork shanty dead on, and the hut burst apart with a *bang* of rending metal, flinging wreckage in every direction. Valentus opened the throttle and hit another dwelling, then ploughed through the filth of a cesspool on the far side. Shouts and screams rent the air in the truck's wake as it smashed its way through the xenos camp. Galleas raised his head just enough to see the other two trucks moving as well, blazing their own trails towards the exit.

By now the entire camp was awake. Gunfire barked all around the trucks, growing more intense with each passing moment. Rounds thudded against the war machines' armoured flanks. A rocket streaked over the troop compartment, trailing smoke and a tail of bright orange flame.

Where was the diversionary attack? Galleas searched the ruins to the west, trying to make sense out of the chaos. The battle out in the ruins was still raging. From the volume of fire, it couldn't be more than one squad of guerrillas. What had happened to the others?

A trio of heavy impacts struck the right side of the truck. Three huge orks, bellowing in rage, had leapt onto the speeding war machine and were trying to climb into the open-topped troop compartment. Galleas wrenched the twin guns around and swept them away with a point-blank burst.

Another rocket struck the ground next to the truck, spraying it with mud. Ork rounds were hitting the war machine from three sides now in a steady hail. It was only a matter of time before they hit something vital. Galleas wondered how much longer their luck would hold out, then remembered his parting words to Lieutenant Mitra and angrily pushed the thought aside.

Galleas glanced back to the west. They were almost through the last of the ork shanties. The main gate was less than twenty metres away. Then a flicker of muzzle flashes caught his eye, off to the south-west. One of the squads had made it into position at last, and had opened fire on the camp. At this point there was so much confusion in the ork camp that Galleas wasn't certain the xenos would even notice.

The veteran sergeant looked back the way they'd come. The camp was swarming with angry orks now, trying to reach the fleeing trucks. The right side of Olivar's vehicle trailed smoke from a rocket hit, but the damage appeared to be minimal. A pack of xenos clung to the sides of Royas' truck, trying to climb aboard. Galleas brought his twin guns around and let off a long burst, scouring the xenos off the war machine's armoured flanks.

Valentus rocketed through the gate at full speed, clipping one of the stone gateposts in a spray of shattered ferrocrete. Galleas continued to fire at the pursuing greenskins until the other two trucks were past the gate and roaring down the boulevard, leaving the furious orks behind.

The gun battle was still raging amid the hab ruins as the stolen trucks sped past. The Crimson Fists had achieved their objectives, but the success of the raid – and Galleas' entire strategy of fighting the invaders – was still very much in doubt.

The Space Marines took their stolen trucks along a pre-planned route back into Zona Nine and hid them in the burned-out shell of a mercantile arcade that offered easy access into the storm tunnels below. There the war machines would wait until the attack on the larger ork camp the following night.

Galleas and his squad made their way back to base with all the speed their sense of caution would allow. Royas and Olivar were clearly seething at the failure of the guerrillas to fulfil their part of the battle plan, but they kept their counsel to themselves. Whatever they might have to say could wait until the full extent of the disaster was known.

Old Tomas Zapeta was still at his post when the Space

Marines arrived. He seemed genuinely shocked to see them. 'You're alive!' he blurted as Galleas emerged from the tunnel.

'Was there any reason to think we weren't?' The veteran sergeant said sternly.

Tomas frowned. 'Well, no. Not as such. Just the way our luck seems to run these days,' he said. 'Rains always come, my gran used to say. Rains always come.'

Galleas ignored the old man, continuing on into the commons area. Daniella was there, despite the late hour, her children curled about her, fast asleep. She smiled in relief as she caught sight of Juno, then busied herself with nudging the twins awake and leading them back to their bedrolls.

The veteran sergeant was surprised to find a squad of guerrillas already there, sat together and speaking to one another in hushed tones. At the sight of the veteran sergeant they fell silent, refusing to meet his penetrating stare.

'Where is your squad leader?' Galleas demanded, his voice ringing against the stone walls.

A partition to one of the sleeping cells twitched aside and Corporal Vila emerged with Bergand close on his heels. 'Here, my lord.'

'What is the meaning of this? You and your squad shouldn't be here for another fifteen minutes!'

The handsome young corporal plucked a cigarillo from beneath his flak vest and affected a contrite expression. 'Many apologies, my lord. Everything was going perfectly right up to the point the squads split up and we made our way to the surface. My compass malfunctioned, and we got turned around in the dark. By the time I realised my error, we could hear shooting coming from the hab ruins to our right, so I assumed that the attack had already begun. Since the orks were alerted, I thought it best to return to base.'

Galleas' first instinct was to kill the man. He was tired of Vila's cowardice and opportunism. On any battlefield anywhere in the Imperium, Galleas would have drawn his pistol and put a round in Vila's forehead. But this wasn't a typical battlefield, and Vila's mendacious response was just plausible enough to be believable. Executing the man in front of his squad and the rest of the civilians in the base would have far-reaching effects on morale.

Before Galleas could respond, the sound of breathless voices rose from the tunnel entrance. The tarp jerked aside to reveal Corporal Ismail and her squad, their grimy faces streaked with sweat. It looked as though they'd run the entire way back from Zona Eleven.

Ismail led her troops into the commons area and got them settled, then went to join Galleas. She eyed Vila and his squad speculatively as she approached.

'Corporal Ismail,' Galleas called out. 'Report.'

'Everything went more or less as planned, my lord,' she said, removing her helmet and wiping the back of a gloved hand across her forehead. 'We split up from the rest of the platoon and made our way topside to our firing position as directed. Then, just twenty metres short of the objective, all hell broke loose on the other side of the boulevard. It sounded like Lieutenant Mitra's squad had run into some kind of ambush, but there was no way to be sure.' Her eyes narrowed on Corporal Vila. 'We thought the corporal here was on our left, but we couldn't make contact with him, either.'

'And then?'

'By that point we could hear the shooting inside the ork

camp, so I ordered the squad to get to our firing positions double-quick and do our part.' She nodded to her squad. 'Fired three magazines or belts per trooper, as ordered, and then we got the hell out of there.'

'Casualties?'

'None, my lord.'

'What about Lieutenant Mitra?'

Ismail shrugged. 'As we were clearing out, we heard another big volley of gunfire, and then things tapered off quick after that. We got back here as quick as we could to see what we could find out. There were too many green-skins charging about to do any scouting on our own.'

Galleas considered this, and nodded. 'You did well, corporal. Go and see to your squad.'

'Aye, lord.' Ismail gave Vila a parting glare, then headed back across the commons area. As she left, Bergand came up alongside the veteran sergeant and cleared his throat.

'I, ah… I take it the raid wasn't successful, my lord?'

Galleas folded his arms. 'That remains to be seen, Master Bergand,' he said forbiddingly.

The void trader bowed his head and silently withdrew. The rest of the Crimson Fists were already gone, having disappeared into their sanctum to commence their post-battle rituals. The veteran sergeant stood alone in the commons, his gaze fixed on the tunnel entrance, and waited for news.

Twenty minutes later there was another commotion at the tunnel entrance, much louder than the one before. Within moments, Mitra appeared, followed closely by Vega, Preacher Gomez, and the rest of her squad. A bloody bandage was taped tightly against the lieutenant's cheek. The rest of her face was a mask of exhaustion, but when she saw Galleas she went to him at once.

'You're injured,' the veteran sergeant said by way of greeting.

Mitra waved her hand dismissively. 'Caught some stone splinters from a ricochet. Vega is being overprotective.'

'What happened?'

The lieutenant grimaced. 'We were fifteen metres from our firing position when we ran right into a mob of orks sleeping in the ruins.' She shook her head. 'No idea what they were doing there, so close to the other camp. Just bad luck, I suppose. Before I knew what was happening, a couple of the men panicked and opened fire. We killed a few of the orks, but the rest returned fire and drove us back into cover. They must have had us pinned down for ten minutes or more, until Sergeant Kazimir realised what was happening and brought his squad in on their flank. We wiped the greenskins out, but by then you and your squad were already gone.'

'Where is Kazimir now?'

'He held back to cover our withdrawal and make sure we weren't being pursued. I expect him here any minute.' She straightened. 'I take full responsibility for failing our part of the mission, my lord. If I hadn't been moving so quickly to get into position I might have seen the xenos in time–'

'I'm not interested in assigning blame, lieutenant,' Galleas interjected. 'Were there any casualties? Did you leave *any* of your troops behind?'

'Casualties?' Mitra smiled ruefully. 'Just me. Everyone else is fine, by the grace of the Emperor.'

'*Deus Gloriosa!*' Preacher Gomez said joyfully, raising his hands to the heavens. 'The God-Emperor has granted us victory over the xenos!'

The assertion took Galleas aback. Before he could correct

the preacher, however, the soldiers let out a ragged cheer that grew louder and more defiant by the moment. The sound drew many of the civilians from their sleeping cells, and soon the commons area was the scene of an impromptu celebration.

Galleas scowled at the jubilant faces. *A victory?* he thought. *Hardly.*

We were merely lucky.

CHAPTER FOURTEEN

BREAKING POINT

ZONA 9 RESIDENTIA, NEW RYNN CITY
DAY 163

Galleas spent the rest of the night and most of the next day in seclusion, meditating on the near-calamity of the attack the night before. For all that they had been successful in stealing the ork trucks and a number of greenskin bodies, as far as he was concerned, the raid had failed in its most important aspect: demonstrating that the Space Marines and Lieutenant Mitra's guerrillas could fight together as a single force. As matters stood now, it was clear that they could not.

The veteran sergeant considered the problem from every angle, bringing all of his experience and training to bear. He explored dozens of alternative campaign strategies and tactical schemes in search of one that might compensate for the humans' various deficiencies. Each one led to the same conclusion.

It was late in the afternoon when Galleas stirred himself from his meditative state. He found Enginseer Oros working on the display table in the sanctum's common area.

'Find Lieutenant Mitra and Sergeant Kazimir,' he said. 'Have them report to me at once.'

'Yes, my lord.' Oros retracted his mechadendrites from the display's inner workings and hurried from the chamber. After the enginseer was gone, Galleas went and summoned his brothers.

The Crimson Fists were waiting around the display table when the two Rynnsguard soldiers arrived. Both looked haggard, their eyes glassy from lack of sleep, but Mitra's voice was steady as she took her place at the table and addressed Galleas. 'You wished to see us, my lord?'

'The attack on the ork camp in Zona Nine is just eight hours away,' the veteran sergeant said without preamble. His stern gaze fell upon each of his battle-brothers in turn, then on to the weary humans standing in their midst. 'Time is short, which leaves us with few options to correct the failures that occurred during the raid last night.'

Mitra stiffened. 'You mean the failures of my platoon,' she said stonily.

'Indeed,' the veteran sergeant replied. 'Only one squad completed its objective. Another turned back under circumstances that would have merited a battlefield execution in a less desperate situation. Meanwhile, your squad's lack of proper vigilance forced Sergeant Kazimir to abandon his own objective to rescue you, and nearly compromised the entire raid.'

Kazimir cleared his throat. 'Begging your pardon, my lord, but my squad passed by that same mob and didn't see them either. It's not the lieutenant's fault–'

'As I said before, I take full responsibility for what happened during the raid,' Mitra said, fixing Galleas with a flinty stare.

'I would expect no less,' Galleas said. 'But that does nothing to address the fundamental deficiencies in the way your platoon operates. We are deep inside enemy territory, lieutenant. We cannot afford to make a single mistake, or else all our efforts will have been for nothing. Given what occurred last night, can you honestly tell me your troops are up to the demands of such a campaign?'

Mitra said nothing. Her silence was answer enough.

Galleas drew a deep breath. 'I have thought long and hard about this,' he said gravely. 'We find ourselves at a crossroads, lieutenant. Things cannot go on as they have before. Difficult decisions must be made.'

Galleas watched as his brothers reacted to his words. Outwardly they seemed stolid, impassive figures, but the slightest shift of the shoulders or tilt of the head spoke volumes to him. Royas and Olivar were suddenly very intent, expecting vindication at long last. Amador was tense, like a war hound straining at the leash. Tauros stiffened, clearly surprised at what he'd heard. Valentus was thoughtful, observing without passing judgement. Juno was impassive as ever, observing the whole exchange with stoic indifference.

'I see,' Mitra said coldly. 'And what have you decided, my lord?'

'Effective immediately, your sixty troops will be broken up into six nine-man squads. My brothers will take over as squad leaders. You, Oros, Vega, Preacher Gomez, and the remaining six troops will form a command squad on me.'

Mitra went pale. 'You can't do this,' she said. 'It's my platoon. You have *no right*–'

'I have every right, lieutenant,' Galleas countered. 'And you well know it. I want the new force organisation in place before we depart tonight. I'll have Enginseer Oros contact you presently with specific squad assignments.'

Kazimir stepped forward. 'My lord, if I may—'

'You may not, sergeant. The matter is not open for discussion. Pass the word to your troops. We'll form up in the commons area just before departure at midnight.' Galleas turned his attention back to Mitra. 'Any questions, lieutenant?'

'None, my lord,' Mitra replied, her voice tight with anger.

'Then you are dismissed.'

The two humans made a hasty exit from the Space Marines' sanctum. The instant they were gone, Royas rounded on Galleas. 'What manner of foolishness is this?'

'Easy, brother—' Tauros began.

'You stay out of this!' Royas snapped. To Galleas, he said, 'I told you last night that you were expecting too much from these humans. Olivar's said the same thing all along. Yet here you are, tying them even more tightly around our necks!' His fist rang against his breastplate. 'I've served our Chapter honourably for five hundred and fifty years, brother! I've fought campaigns longer than human lifetimes! I've commanded armies and conquered worlds!'

'And now you shall lead a squad of six against the greenskin horde,' Galleas told him, 'because that is what your duty demands, brother.'

'My *duty*?' Royas' fists clenched. 'I am a son of the Emperor. My duty is to him. Not this ignorant, ungrateful rabble. We fight for them, bleed for them, *die* for them... and for what? Humans are *weak*. They are arrogant, cowardly and *stupid*. They have cost us more worlds in the last ten thousand years than all the hosts of the enemy combined!'

'That's *enough*!' Tauros snapped. 'You're out of line, Royas!'

If the display table hadn't been between the two Space Marines, they might have come to blows. Royas started forward, but Olivar seized him by the arm and pulled him back. The Crimson Fist remained defiant, glaring at Tauros and Galleas.

'Perhaps so,' Royas snarled, 'but that doesn't make me wrong.'

'Right or wrong, Timon Royas, you will do as I command,' Galleas said, his voice ringing like iron. 'You will lead your new squad to the very best of your ability. You will guide them, teach them, and most importantly, you will fight alongside them against our common foe, or by Dorn, you will answer to me.' The veteran sergeant glared at the rest of his squad. 'Does anyone else care to challenge me on this? Anyone?'

No one spoke. Galleas caught a glimpse of Enginseer Oros as he quietly entered the chamber, sensed the tension in the air, and beat a hasty retreat. After a moment, the veteran sergeant gave a curt nod.

'The matter is settled. Begin your pre-battle rituals. We assemble in the commons in six hours, twenty-eight minutes for squad assignments. Dismissed.'

Galleas spun on his heel and returned to his cell. As he drew Night's Edge and began the Litany of Maintenance, he heard his brothers drift apart in silence, each lost in his own thoughts.

I ask too much of them, the veteran sergeant mused, brooding over the ancient blade. *The orks have taken everything except their pride. Now I'm asking them to cast that aside as well.*

Damn the xenos, Galleas thought bitterly. *There won't be anything left of us once this siege is done.*

* * *

Mitra's soldiers were ready at the appointed hour. When Galleas and his brothers emerged from their sanctum they found the humans formed up in ranks, as though on a parade ground. The rest of the civilians watched from the edges of their sleeping cells, despite the late hour.

There was a curious undercurrent to the gathering, a sense of ceremony that Galleas had not expected. Lieutenant Mitra stood before the assembled soldiers, her face a mask of aggrieved dignity.

When the Space Marines had taken position opposite the assembly, Mitra turned smartly about and faced her troops.

'Before Sergeant Kazimir reads out the new squad assignments, there are a few words I'd like to say to you,' Mitra began. 'I know some of you believe we're being broken up because we failed to carry out our mission during the raid yesterday. That's not true.'

Galleas frowned within the confines of his helmet. *It most certainly* is *the reason,* he thought. *Lying about it only compounds the error.* He drew himself up, preparing to correct the lieutenant, but Tauros stopped him with a slight shake of the head.

'For pity's sake, brother, let her talk,' he said over the vox. *'She knows what she's doing.'*

Galleas scowled at the lieutenant, but kept silent.

'In fact,' Mitra continued, 'we are being afforded a great honour. From this night forward we fight at the side of the Crimson Fists. They are the sons of the God-Emperor of Mankind, the shield-hands of Rogal Dorn – and we shall go into battle as their shieldbearers. Serve them, body and soul, and we will see our world free from the greenskin taint once more.'

The lieutenant drew a deep breath. 'As my final act as

commander of Second Platoon, let me say that I am proud of the soldiers you have become. For those of you who have been with me since the invasion began, let me say that it's been a privilege to lead you.' Then, with a curt nod to Kazimir, she turned about once again and went to stand beside Galleas.

As Sergeant Kazimir began the process of disbanding the platoon and re-assigning its troops, Galleas noted that a transformation had taken place amongst them. Their heads were high, and many were smiling proudly as they crossed the divide between their old unit and the waiting Crimson Fists.

Galleas glanced over at Mitra. The lieutenant was staring straight ahead, her expression inscrutable. The lie she'd told still rankled, but now he understood its intent.

I have underestimated her, Galleas thought. *Tauros was right. Perhaps I have underestimated them all.*

Galleas and his new squad took point, leading the raiders out into the tunnels an hour past midnight. The pace of march was slower than the veteran sergeant was accustomed to, but the combined force still managed to reach the cache of stolen ork vehicles in good time and without mishap.

The trucks' troop compartments were large enough to hold a dozen greenskins each. Even with the handful of xenos corpses loaded aboard there was just enough room for the Space Marines and their squads. The guerrillas stared at the dead xenos with equal measures of fear and hate, and clutched their looted weapons tight in anticipation of the fighting to come.

They drove through the darkness across Zona Nine until they came to the M12, the main throughway that led to

Zona Eleven. There they stopped just long enough for Squads Tauros, Royas and Amador to disembark. Sergeant Kazimir went with Tauros as part of his squad, while Corporal Vila and half of his former squad had been assigned to Amador. Galleas knew that Tauros and Kazimir together could function as a second command squad in the event that he and Mitra were killed. As for Amador, it was his hope that Vila's nature would curb the young veteran's impulsiveness – or eventually provide Vila an opportunity to die in service to the Emperor. Either outcome was acceptable, as far as Galleas was concerned.

The three squads headed north up the M12, making for the ork camp at the schola urbis. They would take up position outside the camp and, at Galleas' signal, open fire. Their objective was to draw the orks out of the camp and down the M12, where, if the operation went according to plan, Galleas and his force would have a reception waiting for them.

The trucks' petrochem engines roared hungrily as they turned west and headed for the larger greenskin camp. The ork sentries would hear them coming. Galleas, in fact, counted on it. They would be able to tell their warboss later that they'd heard the trucks coming down the road from the direction of the ork camp at the schola urbis. It didn't take a savant to guess what conclusion the bloodthirsty beasts would draw from that.

The bones of gutted hab units rose up on either side of the motorway as the trucks barrelled towards their objective. They made a path for themselves through piles of debris and the burned-out shells of civilian transports by ramming them head-on with their armoured prows. The passengers – human and Space Marine alike – were forced to crouch against the troop compartment's forward bulkhead to avoid the clouds of shrapnel kicked up with each bone-jarring impact.

The lead truck hit a wrecked car broadside, slicing the chassis neatly in two and flinging the halves to opposite sides of the motorway in a spray of shattered plasteel. The impact threw Galleas against the twin gun mount hard enough to leave a fresh scar across his breastplate. 'You hit that one on purpose, by Dorn!' he called over the vox.

'*Just trying to stay in character,*' Valentus replied. Not even the synthetic tones of his vox-unit could mask the mischief in his voice.

Galleas called a halt just five hundred metres from the enemy camp, in the shadow of a partially collapsed commercial building. At his signal, Mitra and the rest of his squad leapt from the troop compartment and dashed into the ruins. The veteran sergeant followed after them, vaulting easily over the truck's armoured side.

'Hold here until I give the word,' Galleas told Valentus and the rest of the raiders as he caught up to his squad and led them inside the building. 'We should be in position in less than twenty minutes.'

'*Affirmative,*' Valentus replied. '*Good hunting, brother.*'

Galleas keyed his auto-senses to low-light vision. At once, the darkened ruins sharpened into contrasting tones of green and black. Waving his squad forward, he led them into a rubble-strewn stairwell and headed upwards.

The veteran sergeant moved quickly, auto-senses strained to their limit. Given the state of the building, he was more concerned with a potential collapse than an encounter with the greenskins. Mitra and the others followed close at his heels, trusting that he would sense danger long before them.

They managed to climb a full four storeys before they found themselves looking up at a cloudy, moonless sky. Beyond an open doorway stretched a narrow tongue of ferrocrete that faced westwards in the direction of the ork camp. Galleas went first, testing the footing carefully, before beckoning to his squad. 'Gomez, Oros, Vega – stay where you are,' he ordered. 'The rest of you form a firing line to my right.'

Mitra and the four remaining members of his squad edged carefully onto the jagged strip of ferrocrete. In addition to their guns they carried the force's two rocket launchers and their entire store of eight rockets. Operating in pairs, the rocket teams each knelt beside a blown-out window frame and began to load their weapons under Mitra's supervision.

Galleas peered from his vantage point at the ork camp. Little had changed since his reconnaissance the day before. A mob had gathered at the barricade closest to the M12, drawn by the sounds of the truck engines. The veteran sergeant sought out the fuel stores located next to the warband's vehicles at the centre of the camp and keyed his helmet's auspex unit. 'The target is to the left of the cluster of cookfires,' he said. 'Range – six hundred and thirty-two metres.'

'I see it,' Mitra replied, peering through a pair of magnoculars. She relayed directions to the rocket teams as the gunners shouldered their weapons.

'Wait for my signal.'

Down in the street, the guerrillas had unloaded a pair of ork bodies and left them splayed on the pavement with weapons in their hands, where pursuing greenskins were sure to stumble across them. Galleas watched the humans clamber back aboard the trucks, and then checked his chrono. By now, Tauros and the others would be in position. They were too far away to risk confirmation by vox, but Galleas knew it wasn't necessary. He could count on his brothers to be where he needed them to be, no matter what stood in their way.

Dorn be with us, Galleas thought. He spoke the go-code over the vox. 'Retribution.'

At once, the engines of the three trucks roared, belching clouds of reeking exhaust. Spiked tyres raking the pavement, the war machines leapt forward, racing down the M12 towards the ork camp.

The greenskins at the barricade heard the swelling noise. Several stepped out into the open to get a better look down the motorway to see what was happening. They didn't have long to wait. At two hundred and fifty metres the trucks burst into view and the gunners manning their twin mounts opened fire, spraying the barricade and the camp beyond with shells. Two greenskins in the street were cut down and the rest scattered, firing wildly as they went.

Within moments, Galleas' enhanced hearing detected more small-arms fire off to the west. Tauros and his team were attacking the second ork camp, right on time. The veteran sergeant glanced over at Mitra and gave a curt nod.

The first rocket leapt from the building with an ear-splitting shriek. The shoddy xenos design began to corkscrew at once, falling into the camp well short and to the left of its target. The warhead detonated with a thunderclap, spraying the shanties nearby with shrapnel.

Mitra passed instructions to the second rocket team in low, urgent tones. Out on the M12, the trucks came to a screeching halt just a hundred metres from the barricade. Galleas watched as more ork bodies tumbled out into the street, followed by the guerrillas. As the twin mounts continued to hammer away, the humans fanned out to either side of the war machines and opened fire as well, unleashing a storm of lead on the barricade, the camp, and the sentry towers just beyond. Within moments, Juno, Olivar, and Valentus had made their way from the cabs into the backs of each of the trucks and taken over the heavy guns. Three seconds of concentrated fire later, the surviving greenskins had abandoned the barricade and were fleeing deeper into the camp.

The second rocket blasted clear of the ruined building. This one flew straighter, but went low and struck one of the parked ork trucks instead. There was a bright flash as it detonated in the truck's troop compartment, but did little else.

By now the entire camp was buzzing like a fire hornets' nest. Orks stumbled from their shanties, bellowing in confusion and anger. Their numbers swelled from one moment to the next, filling the spaces between the shanties and firing wildly into the night. Firefights erupted within the camp as greenskin mobs shot at one another in the confusion. For the moment, the greenskins were their own worst enemy, Galleas knew, but as soon as the warboss appeared and started cracking heads, the warband would go on the attack. And if they still had access to their vehicles, the guerrillas would be in grave danger of being overrun.

The third rocket fired. Galleas watched it streak through the darkness and go wide of the fuel stores, falling into the midst of a mob of greenskins near the cookfires.

'Lieutenant…'

'I know, my lord,' Mitra said tersely, hurrying to the next launcher team.

There was a furious bellow, louder and deeper than the

rest, which rose from the far side of the camp. The warboss was on the move. Already Galleas could hear other ork bosses shouting in reply. The warband was recovering quickly.

A rocket fired – not from the ruins beside Galleas, but from one of the sentry towers near the barricade. It missed Juno's truck by less than a metre, blasting a crater in the pavement just behind it. Juno spotted the launch and shifted his fire, punching holes through the tower's flimsy metal sheeting.

Inside the camp, hundreds of bestial voices joined together in a single, hungry roar. '*WAAAAAAGHHHHH!!!!*'

Mitra's fourth rocket fired. The shriek of its rocket motor was almost lost amid the din of the orks' war cry. Galleas watched the projectile arc like a fiery arrow into the centre of the camp and plunge into the midst of the fuel stores.

WHOOOMPH.

For a split-second, the camp was bathed in yellow-orange light, throwing sharp-etched shadows and outlining every xenos and every crude structure within a hundred metres. A fireball twenty metres across blossomed at the point of impact, swallowing the ork vehicles and hurling burning debris high into the air. Shanties disintegrated, raking the greenskins with red-hot shrapnel. The skeletal structures of the sentry towers shuddered violently in the shockwave, their banners flapping in the hot wind and catching alight.

The banner of a burning human, outlined in flame.

Galleas' eyes widened. *Rottshrek!*

The warboss bellowed again amidst the carnage. Galleas dialled his helmet's vision to maximum magnification, searching for the beast.

Down in the camp, the greenskins were on the move.

Backlit by the fire consuming the fuel stores, the xenos surged towards the barricade. First by the dozen, then by the score, firing at the muzzle flashes atop the trucks as they came.

Galleas keyed the vox. 'Valentus, it's time to move.'

'*Understood.*'

One by one the twin mounts fell silent as the Crimson Fists abandoned the trucks. Galleas watched Valentus, Olivar, and Juno leap from the troop compartments and begin issuing orders to their squads. At once the guerrillas started falling back, firing as they went.

A hundred metres away, the greenskins were swarming over the barricade. One of Mitra's rocket teams fired, scoring a direct hit on the barrier and scattering ork bodies in all directions. The blast halted the enemy charge for a couple of moments, buying more time for the men on the ground to escape.

Mitra's gunners fired two more rockets, one after another, into the midst of the greenskins on the far side of the barricade. Dozens were torn apart in the blasts. The mob reeled – but this time they surged forward, baying for slaughter and pouring like a flood into the street. Then, as the pent-up warband dispersed into the open, Galleas saw the hulking figure of Rottshrek following in their wake. The warboss looked just as he had during the breach at Zona Thirteen – except now there were five Crimson Fists helmets hanging from his banner pole instead of three.

Rodrigo and Caron.

Mitra's gunners were preparing to loose their last rocket. Galleas acted without thinking, driven by an all-consuming rage. He plucked the launcher from the startled gunner's hands and raised it to his shoulder.

Rottshrek was nearly at the barricade, bellowing orders

at the greenskins. The grinning engineer with its heavy gun and force field lurched along at the warboss' side. Bodyguards surrounded Rottshrek, partially concealing the beast from view. Galleas settled the launcher's crude sight where Rottshrek's chest would be and waited.

The rocket might not fly true, he told himself. It might explode harmlessly against the damned engineer's force field. A bodyguard might step into its path instead. *Dorn guide my blow*, he willed. *Not for me, but for my brothers, who have fallen by this monster's hand.*

The mob shifted around Rottshrek. Galleas could sense the opening a split-second before it occurred. His finger tightened on the trigger.

'Vengeance for the fallen,' he said, and let the rocket fly.

Backblast buffeted Galleas. The flare of the rocket motor dazzled his eyes, but he forced himself to follow its fiery trail as it stabbed down through the darkness. The rocket flew in a perfect arc, flashing through a narrow gap between two of the warboss' bodyguards and striking like a thunderbolt. There was a bright, blue flash as the rocket hit the engineer's force field – followed an instant later by a searing thunderclap and an angry flash of red as the weapon detonated. Rottshrek was cut off in mid-bellow by the blast, disappearing in a cloud of shrapnel and debris. The warboss' huge axe, its notched blade glinting in the fiery light, flew into the air and vanished into the darkness.

Galleas bared his teeth in triumph. *Rest well, brothers. You have been avenged.*

Outside the barricade, the ork onslaught momentarily faltered. He'd managed to buy Valentus and the others a few more moments to pull back. 'Time to move,' Galleas said, handing over the smoking launcher.

By the time they negotiated the stairway and reached ground level the sounds of gunfire and the howls of pursuing orks were very close. Galleas ordered the guerrillas into cover amidst the rubble facing the M12. The veteran sergeant anchored one end of the line and Mitra the other, with Vega and Gomez in the rear, out of the line of fire. Charging bolts clattered as the guerrillas readied their weapons.

Less than a minute later, Juno and Olivar came into view, surrounded by their squads. They bounded past Galleas' position and found cover amidst the debris scattered across the roadway. Galleas did a quick count as they went by. *No casualties yet,* he noted with satisfaction. The plan was working.

The sounds of gunfire grew louder. Stray rounds began whipping by overhead, or striking the ruins behind the guerrillas. Valentus and his squad appeared, retreating at a measured pace and firing back the way they'd come. Galleas could feel the pounding of hundreds of heavy feet along the motorway and hear the guttural shouts of the greenskins over the rising thunder of the guns.

The veteran sergeant raised his weapon. 'Wait until I fire,' he told the command squad. 'Aim for the muzzle flashes, but don't waste time lining up a shot. Volume of fire is what matters now. Understood?'

Heads nodded in reply. Galleas switched to thermal imaging and began marking targets.

The orks were coming on in a vast mob, charging blindly after the retreating Imperials. With their poor night vision the greenskins couldn't see much further than the glare of their own muzzle flashes, but they were too lost in bloodlust to care.

When Valentus reached Galleas' position, he gave a curt order to his squad and they picked up their pace, bounding past Olivar and Juno and heading further down the motorway. Once they were clear of the killzone, Galleas turned his attention back to the greenskins. At fifty metres, he opened fire.

The storm of fire from the three squads savaged the oncoming greenskins. Nearly every shot found a mark in the tightly packed mass of orks, and dozens fell under the sudden onslaught. The headlong charge faltered, reeling back in panic from the withering fire.

Galleas emptied his weapon in less than two seconds. 'Move!' he snapped, rising from cover and falling back. Mitra repeated the order and the rest of the squad followed. As they bounded past Juno and Olivar, the other squads broke cover and fell in alongside them.

They continued like this for almost a kilometre, moving in squads down the M12 in an alternating series of ambushes that just barely held the orks at bay. Meanwhile, the sounds of fighting were growing louder from the east, in the direction of the schola urbis. Tauros and his detachment had drawn out the orks there as well.

An hour and a half after the attack began, Galleas caught sight of Tauros and his squad falling back down the motorway towards him. He checked his position on his map display; they were exactly where he expected them to be, just fifty metres from their escape route. As Juno's and Olivar's squads took their turn holding off the orks, he and Valentus rushed to link up with Tauros.

'Status?' Galleas called to Tauros over the vox.

'Amador and Royas are with their squads fifty metres to the east,' Tauros reported. *'Ammunition is at twenty per cent.'*

'And the orks?'

'*Right behind us. We fired a few shots and the whole damned camp came rushing out at us.*'

'Excellent. Pull in the squads and make for the egress point. We'll let the beasts take things from here.'

Within minutes, Tauros and Valentus had their squads moving south, cutting through the ruins in the direction of a storm tunnel access a few hundred metres away. Galleas held position until the ambushing squads appeared, then ordered them to the egress as well. The evolution happened smoothly, aided by the Space Marines' ability to penetrate the darkness with their auto-senses and herd the guerrillas across the blasted landscape.

Galleas and his command squad were the last to move. As the greenskins came roaring in from east and west, the Imperials withdrew silently out of their path. The two enraged ork warbands crashed together in a crescendo of gunfire, chainaxes and slaughter.

The sounds of ork killing ork echoed across Zona Nine as the Imperials disappeared into the night. Galleas was already thinking ahead to his next set of targets.

The fire has been lit, he thought, smiling in grim satisfaction. *Now we feed it until Snagrod himself is caught in the flames!*

CHAPTER FIFTEEN

GRIM REALITIES

ZONA 18 COMMERCIA, NEW RYNN CITY
DAY 353

Outside of combat, orks were often creatures of habit. Galleas knew this was because the xenos were stupid and lazy – once they'd worked out the quickest and easiest way to do something, they stuck to it, even if it courted disaster.

Especially if it courts disaster, Galleas amended, peering over the jagged lip of ferrocrete at the approaching greenskin mob.

The largest ork camp in Zona Eighteen was situated in the centre of a ruined industrial block, surrounded on all sides by a wasteland of shattered ferrocrete and twisted metal. A single road led to the camp's entrance, largely clear of debris and offering good sight lines for a unit on the move – but it was a long and roundabout route, built when the sector was crowded with low, squat manufactoria. It wasn't long before the orks discovered a much quicker and more direct path, cutting through the ruins from the west. They'd been at it for so long that they had created a

clearly visible path through the wreckage, one that Galleas'
scouts had been watching for nearly a week.

The ambush had been timed with care. It was approaching early evening, and twilight was coming on, filling the
hollows of the debris field with deep shadow. The ork raiding party was in a hurry, perhaps tempted by the nauseating
smell of the camp's cookfires and eager to show off the trophies they'd won. Judging from the bloodstained bags of
teeth hanging from the belt of the lead ork, Galleas reckoned their raid had been a successful one indeed.

Even now, just a few hours short of full darkness, gunfire and occasional explosions continued to echo across
the southern sectors of the city. The fire the guerrillas had
lit months ago had taken hold and continued to burn
throughout the long, hot summer, spreading from one
warband to another despite Snagrod's efforts to contain
it. Though the Arch-Arsonist had managed to keep things
from escalating into full-blown warfare, the constant spate
of raids, counter-raids, feuds, and usurpations were killing
a few hundred orks a day and spreading hairline fractures
through Snagrod's horde. And it was taking pressure off the
Cassar, Galleas knew. There hadn't been any major attacks
from the south against the Zona Regis for the past two
months.

The ork boss – the one in the lead with the bags of teeth –
was nearly parallel to Galleas' position. Slowly, deliberately,
the veteran sergeant raised his weapon. When the beast's
misshapen head filled his sight, Galleas squeezed the oversized trigger and blew the ork's bony skull apart.

The greenskins reeled back at the sound of the shots,
bellowing in anger and alarm. Galleas ducked behind the
ferrocrete slab as a few of the orks recovered their wits and

opened fire. Slugs cracked against the thick composite, kicking up puffs of dust and buzzing angrily through the air.

Galvanised by the sound, the rest of the mob let out a bloodthirsty roar and began to spread out, searching the ruins to the right of the path for Galleas' position. That was the moment Tauros' squad opened fire from the left, hitting the greenskins in the back. Half the mob was cut down, and the rest wavered, caught between two attackers and unable to decide which was the greater threat. Three different orks tried to assert control and get the survivors moving, but the conflicting orders only added to the confusion.

Galleas raised his scarred, red fist. To his left and right, Mitra and the rest of his squad rose from their concealed positions and opened fire, catching the orks in a withering crossfire. More greenskins fell, and the rest panicked, running for the dubious safety of the camp. Galleas and Tauros picked them off one by one as they fled, the last falling just ten metres from the killzone.

The guerrillas were moving before the final greenskin fell, clambering over the treacherous piles of rubble and descending on the fallen xenos. They were masters at this sort of ambush now, each step unfolding with gruesome precision. Single shots rang out as the humans put a bullet in each ork's skull, then, while Galleas and Tauros kept watch, they closed in to start stripping the corpses of weapons, grenades and ammunition.

Months of privation and the harsh demands of combat had transformed the Imperials. They had the hard look of veterans now, their bodies rendered down to little more than leather, sinew and bone. The humans scarcely noticed the carnage around them as they drew their knives and began cutting away bandoliers and grenade pouches. If a xenos weapon looked particularly desirable they didn't hesitate at sawing off fingers as well.

Galleas and his brothers had demanded much of the humans. Royas and Olivar had been particularly unsparing, pushing their squads to the edge of their endurance, but the Imperials had persevered. After a time, they had *thrived* under pressure. In fact, it had become a badge of honour. Lieutenant Mitra's words had left an indelible impression on them. She had made them more than soldiers. They were now shieldbearers to the sons of Rogal Dorn.

He caught sight of Mitra, head down and hands stained with xenos blood, shouldering heavy belts of ork shells and following the rest of the squad to the next greenskin corpse along the path. Where others had prospered under the reorganisation, she had become quiet and withdrawn, even refusing the company of stalwarts like Sergeant Kazimir and Preacher Gomez.

'Four minutes,' Tauros warned.

Galleas frowned, castigating himself for the momentary loss of focus. He dialled up his auto-senses and scanned the approaches from the ork camp. 'No signs of movement,' he said at length. 'We'll hold for another sixty seconds.'

'We've been here sixty seconds too long already,' Tauros observed. *'The humans are too exposed, and the orks could be on us any moment.'*

'Another minute means more grenades and ammunition we'll have for the raid tomorrow night,' Galleas said stubbornly. 'It's a calculated risk.'

'A gamble, in other words,' Tauros countered.

The mild reproof surprised Galleas. 'If you think there's a flaw in my tactical thinking, brother, I'd like to hear it.'

'There's nothing wrong with your tactics. Your conduct of the

campaign so far has been flawless. Better even than I managed at Cephalon, much as it pains me to say it.'

'Then what's this about?'

Tauros considered his reply carefully. *'You know as well as I that we can't afford a single misstep. Not one. And the odds against us increase with each mission we undertake. We can't keep this up forever.'*

'Forever? No. Just until the relief force arrives.'

Tauros sighed. *'It's been nearly thirteen months since* Crusader *left for Kar Duniash.'*

'Twelve months, thirteen days, eighteen and a half hours,' the veteran sergeant said. 'Your point?'

'My point is that the relief force should have been here a long time ago.'

Galleas bristled. 'The Imperial Navy could be fighting Snagrod's fleet at the edge of the system even as we speak.'

'Or Crusader *might have been lost in the warp and never reached Kar Duniash at all,'* Tauros countered. *'I don't think the humans have realised it yet – except perhaps Bergand, who knows the warp routes better than most – but something's clearly wrong.'*

There was movement along the pathway. The guerrillas had gathered all they could and were scattering back into the rubble.

The Crimson Fists waited in silence until the humans withdrew. Tauros regarded the veteran sergeant gravely.

'What if there is no aid coming from Kar Duniash, brother?' he said at last. *'What then?'*

The receiver cover snapped into place on the ork gun with a dull *clack*. Galleas cycled the xenos weapon's bolt several times, testing the action. He raised the gun to the light, turning it this way and that as he inspected his handiwork. Years of propellant fouling had been methodically scoured away, and the moving parts gleamed with a thin coating of oil. The whole process, stripping down the gun, cleaning it and reassembling it, had taken him just over twenty minutes.

The veteran sergeant frowned. A similar process for a boltgun took a skilled practitioner nearly three hours. It was a part of the pre-battle ritual he'd always found meditative and calming. But the blunt simplicity of the ork weapon, the lack of sacred Litanies of Maintenance, its absence of a machine-spirit – it all felt unseemly to him, and if anything, left him more troubled than before. The conversation with Tauros at the ambush site the day before still weighed heavily on his mind.

If there was no aid coming from Kar Duniash – and the possibility grew more and more likely with each passing day – then Rynn's World was doomed, and he and his brothers along with it. It wasn't the prospect of certain death that troubled him. The Adeptus Astartes knew no fear, least of all the fear of death. It was the prospect of total defeat – and with it, the extinction of his Chapter – that filled Galleas with dread.

He could hear his brothers stirring in their cells, making final adjustments to their wargear. With a deep breath, Galleas walled away his doubts and loaded the gun with one of the fresh magazines stacked neatly on the cloth before him. The remaining magazines, eight in all, were packed into utility clips around his waist. Next came four heavy ork stick bombs, clipped to rings on his right hip. Finally, Galleas reached for Night's Edge, its scarred metal scabbard and hilt gleaming faintly in the dim light. He set the relic

blade before him, point-down, and bowed his head, pay-
ing respect to the ancient weapon's machine-spirit, and to
the long line of heroes who had wielded it before him.

'For the glory of the Emperor and the souls of the
fallen,' he intoned. Then he rose to his feet and locked the
scabbard to the magnetic stays at his hip. When the relic
blade snapped into place, his mind grew calm and his sense
of purpose was restored.

His brothers were gathering in the sanctum's common
area as Galleas left his cell. Enginseer Oros stood by the
scavenged display table. As the veteran sergeant approached,
he sank to his knees and offered up the Crimson Fist's battered helm. Galleas accepted it without comment, lifting
the helmet one-handed and locking it into place. As his
displays came online, he checked the chronometer. It was
approaching midnight.

'We move out in five minutes,' Galleas said without preamble. 'Final checks. Any questions?'

Galleas studied each of his brothers in turn. Olivar and
Royas were stiff and sullen as always, and Amador radiated
impatience. Juno and Valentus were calm and inscrutable,
ready to get on with the job at hand.

His gaze fell last on Tauros. The veteran Space Marine
stared back in silence, keeping his own counsel.

After a moment, Galleas nodded curtly. On impulse, he
said, 'There is only the Emperor!'

A stir went through the Crimson Fists. They replied without hesitation, *'He is our shield and protector!'*

'Do not forget,' Galleas told them. 'Even here. Even now,
in our darkest hour. We are not alone.' Then he turned on
his heel and headed from the sanctum. 'Gather your squads,
brothers. We move out in five minutes.'

The guerrillas were waiting for them in the larger commons area beyond, talking in low tones and making last-minute adjustments to their gear. Where once they had gathered in a single, homogenous group, now they divided themselves by squads, each one shaped by the character of the Space Marine who led it. Juno's squad had taken to carrying heavy cleavers and strings of greenskin tusks as trophies. Tauros and Valentus had transformed their squads into quiet, capable professionals, steady under fire and able to react to the unexpected with resourcefulness and skill. Olivar's and Royas' squads were a dour bunch of penitents, always conscious of their leaders' disapproving stares. Only Amador's squad had failed to gel into a unified whole, caught between the opposite poles of the Crimson Fist's impetuousness and Vila's malingering. The result was an uneasy balance that – so far – had kept everyone's worst impulses in check.

Galleas sought out his own squad, waiting near the base's exit. They rose to their feet as he approached – all except for Preacher Gomez, who paced the length of the commons area, reading aloud from the *Lectitio Divinitatus*. Lieutenant Mitra stood near the rocket teams, her ork gun slung from her shoulder. She avoided the veteran sergeant's gaze as he approached.

Gomez finished his sermon hurriedly and tucked the small, tattered book into a pouch on his web harness. His lips moved in silent prayer as he made the sign of the aquila, and a number of the guerrillas joined in. By then, it was time to move. Galleas readied his weapon and led the way, each squad following in line behind his own. They left in silence, and no one marked their passing. The nightly raids had become routine now, and the exhausted civilians were huddled in their bedrolls, gathering their strength for the day to come.

Old Tomas Zapeta was at his post as the raiders filed past. The guerrillas treated the man as a sort of touchstone, wishing him well or reaching out to pluck at his sleeve as they went by. Zapeta accepted the gestures with a dolorous nod and commended their souls to the Emperor, for surely this would be the night that disaster would strike and he would never see them again.

Their target was a large ork camp in Zona Fourteen, nearly ten kilometres away. The plan called for the raiders to cover most of the distance underground, a more roundabout route that would take just over four hours to complete. Galleas led them through the labyrinth of tunnels by memory, auto-senses dialled to maximum gain in the unlikely event that there were xenos prowling through the darkness ahead.

They reached the egress point, a ruined pump station that had once served a cluster of hab units, without incident and precisely on time. Past the pump station's crumpled metal door was a treacherous slope of piled debris that led Galleas and the others up into the open air.

A heavy overcast hung over New Rynn City. Winter's chill was coming on early, and a biting wind whistled through the skeletal ruins of the hab block. The moons had set in the west, and darkness filled the cracked and rubble-filled streets.

Galleas paused at the top of the debris pile, listening intently. Other than the sound of the wind, the city south of the river was eerily quiet. Frowning, the veteran sergeant scanned the nearby ruins for heat sources, wary of a potential ambush, but as far as he could tell, they were alone. Finally, he raised his hand and waved the squad forward. They moved cautiously, clearly as unnerved by the quiet as he.

The plan was for the squads to break off at the egress point, with Galleas, Olivar, Royas and Valentus moving up to firing zones overlooking the ork camp, and Juno, Amador and Tauros setting up ambushes along the guerrillas' egress route to slow down any ork pursuit. The stillness in the air left Galleas uneasy, but that wasn't enough to justify a change of plan. Nevertheless, while the whole force was still in range, he spoke over the vox. 'Something's not right,' he told his brothers. 'Stay vigilant.'

The target was two kilometres away, across a wasteland of jagged rubble. Galleas lost sight of the other attacking squads almost immediately as they fanned out and headed for their firing positions. His squad made for an artificial ridge of broken ferrocrete some two hundred metres from the centre of the greenskin camp. Switching to light intensification, Galleas could just see the tops of the ork sentry towers appear in the distance as he and his squad dashed from cover to cover up to the rear slope of the ridge.

With practised skill, the squad shook out into a loose firing line, with the rocket teams in the centre, Galleas to the left, and Mitra to the right. Vega, Gomez, and Oros formed a second group at the rear of the line, ready to lend support if needed.

Galleas checked his chronometer. Another five minutes, and the other squads would be in position. He strained his senses to the utmost, searching the surrounding ruins for signs of danger. The seconds ticked by, and with each passing moment he grew more convinced that something was very, very wrong.

The chronometer flashed. It was time to move. Galleas drew a deep breath and waved his squad forward.

The guerrillas scrambled to the top of the ridge, now trading silence for speed. Galleas reached the top ahead of them, falling prone against the slope and rising slowly to peer over the summit.

The veteran sergeant froze. At first, he couldn't make sense of what he saw. Forcing himself to focus, he scanned the xenos camp from one end to the other, cycling his auto-senses through the visible and invisible spectrum. Each time, the result was the same.

The camp was deserted.

Galleas scanned the entire site again. It was situated in a bowl-like depression formed by the collapse of a cluster of hab units, and took up a full city block. Just two days before, his scouts had found more than a thousand greenskins there, plus dozens of vehicles and stores of ammunition. Now they were nowhere to be seen. The shanties and sentry towers were empty, and the barricade covering the main entrance had been dragged aside. All in a single day.

Suddenly, the silence hanging over the city took on an entirely different cast. Galleas felt his pulse quicken. His words to Tauros came back to him in a rush. *The Imperial Navy could be fighting Snagrod's fleet at the edge of the system even as we speak.*

Had the hour of their deliverance arrived at last?

Galleas checked the vox. Jamming still howled across the long-range bands. He searched the sky for signs of Imperial craft, but the overcast covered the city like a shroud. Then he saw it – a faint glow reflecting off the clouds along the horizon to the south.

The guerrillas were staring at the camp with bemused looks. Mitra rose hesitantly to her feet. 'What is this?' she asked. 'What's going on?'

Galleas turned about, searching the surrounding area. 'We need to get to higher ground,' he said. His gaze settled on a broken finger of steel and ferrocrete rising from the wasteland to his right. 'This way!'

He set off across the rubble at a trot, leaving the guerrillas scrambling to keep pace. In moments he was at the foot of the spire, a corner of a hab unit that had refused to collapse with the rest. Without waiting for the others, he set down his weapon and began to climb.

Minutes later, Galleas was three storeys in the air, the cold wind keening in his audio receptors. Switching to maximum magnification, he turned his gaze to the south.

He was still staring into the distance when Lieutenant Mitra lifted herself onto the narrow ledge beside him. Shoulders heaving with exertion, she fumbled one-handed with the magnocular case at her hip. 'What is it?' she gasped. 'What do you see?'

The vast majority of the orks south of the river had abandoned their camps and withdrawn, en masse, to a dense swathe of industrial sectors several kilometres outside the city walls. Even now, at this late hour, they swarmed around the vast factories, labouring under the hot glow of work lights and the occasional bonfire. Debris was being cleared away and new camps were being built with feverish intensity.

Galleas felt his hopes turn to ash. Snagrod and his horde were far from beaten. Instead, the siege of the Cassar had taken a grim new turn.

CHAPTER SIXTEEN

A FIGHT TO THE DEATH

ZONA 9 RESIDENTIA, NEW RYNN CITY
DAY 378

'My lord?'

It took several seconds for the enginseer's voice to reach Galleas in the depths of his meditative rite. Like a dormant machine coming online, his mind and body responded to the outside stimulus in stages. Heart rates quickened, increasing circulation, which in turn stimulated brain activity and sharpened sensory input. A full second later, the veteran sergeant drew a deep breath and opened his eyes. Enginseer Oros was standing at the entrance to his cell, head bowed and hands clasped nervously at his waist.

'What is it, enginseer?'

'The scouting mission h-has returned,' Oros said.

The veteran sergeant frowned. 'What time is it?'

'Not yet eleven, my lord.'

Galleas straightened. Tauros and his squad weren't supposed to return for hours yet. 'All right. I'm coming.'

The veteran sergeant took another deep breath and rose

from the hard ferrocrete floor. As he did so, his armour's damaged right knee actuator gave a thin whine of protest and momentarily locked up, causing him to stagger.

Oros made the sign of the Omnissiah and murmured a hasty prayer. 'The actuator has degraded nearly thirty-two per cent, my lord,' he said gravely.

Galleas gritted his teeth. The momentary display of weakness galled him. 'You fancy yourself a Techmarine now, enginseer?' he growled.

Oros jerked as though he'd been stung. 'No! Certainly not!' he exclaimed, holding up his hands in a placating gesture. 'When I connect your helmet to the table, I have to run a diagnostic rite. The armour status is part of it.'

Galleas waved away the enginseer's protest. 'It's nothing, Oros. Put it out of your mind.'

'Y-yes, my lord.' The enginseer started to turn away, then paused. Hesitantly, he glanced back at Galleas. 'I could perhaps repair it, if you wish.'

Despite himself, Galleas gave the enginseer a scandalised look. '*Repair* it? You?'

'I'm no expert, of course,' Oros said quickly. 'Nothing like that. But when I wasn't attending my studies on Mars, I spent much of my time – well, all of it, really – poring through the archives. I studied everything about the Adeptus Astartes wargear that my meagre access level would allow.'

'Why?'

Oros shifted uncomfortably. 'Because I wanted to be like you,' he said in a small voice. 'Ever since I was a child. I wanted to be a Crimson Fist. One of the shield hands of Dorn.' He sighed. 'My father said I wasn't worthy. But I didn't listen.'

The words conjured memories in Galleas from more than three hundred years ago. Feverish and shivering, his pale body streaked with mud and gore, clutching a dead boy's knife in his hand while angry voices raged around him.

'Did you undergo the Trials of Selection?' he asked.

Oros shook his head ruefully. 'Oh, no. No. I didn't even make it through the initial screening. But the tests showed I had an affinity with machines, so I was given to the Adeptus Mechanicus instead.' He spread his hands. 'I am no hero, my lord. But if you would allow it, I could still be useful.'

Galleas reached for his helmet. He stared down at its scowling features for several moments, unsure how to respond. 'There's nothing to be done, Oros,' he said at last. 'It's not that I question your skill. We simply don't have the parts to repair it.'

'Yes, we do. My servo arm uses the same actuator system. I could disassemble it and give you one of mine.' Oros bowed his head. 'It would be the greatest privilege of my life.'

The sincerity of the enginseer's offer moved Galleas. For a moment, he wasn't sure how to respond. 'I… am honoured, Enginseer Oros. Truly. But don't concern yourself about me. I've managed with much worse in the past.'

The young enginseer seemed to shrink in on himself. 'Yes, my lord. I understand.'

Just then, Galleas heard Tauros climb the steps to the Crimson Fists' sanctum. Moving past Oros, the veteran sergeant stepped out into the commons area as his brother came into view.

'I didn't expect you for another six hours,' Galleas said. 'You must have turned back the moment you reached the observation point.'

Tauros nodded. His manner was grave. 'We need to talk, brother.'

'As bad as all that?'

'Worse.'

A sense of foreboding settled over Galleas like a shroud. 'I'll summon the others,' he said, then turned to Oros. 'Fetch Lieutenant Mitra, Sergeant Kazimir and Master Bergand,' he said. 'They should be a part of this as well.'

For almost four weeks after the orks began their undertaking south of the city, there was nothing the guerrillas could do but wait. With the greenskins slaving night and day to clear out the industrial centre, there wasn't the time or energy to fight amongst themselves, and the new camps they were building were better sited and more heavily fortified than before, making the raids of the previous summer too risky to contemplate. The Imperials would have to switch targets – but until Galleas had a better idea of what Snagrod was up to, he couldn't begin to guess where to strike next.

So the Imperials busied themselves in the final days of autumn by sending out scouting parties to probe further and further southwards, searching for routes out of the city and vantage points from which to observe the greenskin positions. They soon learned that, with the exception of a large force still threatening the Zona Regis from the southern riverbank, the rest of the city's southern ruins were deserted, allowing the guerrillas to move freely through the wasteland. While the scouts kept watch on the orks, Galleas took advantage of the situation by sending out scavenging parties to search far and wide for supplies. Temperatures above ground were dropping with each passing day. The amount of ash and debris blown into the atmosphere by the destruction of the Arx Tyrannus had wrought havoc on the planet's weather patterns, and the veteran sergeant suspected that the coming winter would be a bitter one.

In the meantime, Galleas listened to the reports the scouts brought back and meditated upon them, trying to divine the Arch-Arsonist's plans.

Now he had his answer.

'Zona Sixty-two was a heavy industry sector before the invasion, building mega-harvesters for agri-combines across the planet,' Tauros explained as the display table came to life. The image, composited from data gathered by multiple scouting missions, showed a complex of massive one- and two-storey manufactories covering more than five square kilometres. The squat cooling towers of a high-output power plant loomed above the manufactories near the centre of the complex.

'Though we do not have access to the records, we can assume the manufactories were shut down during the general mobilisation in the weeks prior to the invasion,' the veteran Space Marine continued. 'Located well outside the city's outer wall, the complex was overrun during the first wave of ork landings. It was subjected to heavy shelling during the early spring. From our estimates, the complex suffered moderate to heavy damage to most of its structures in that time.

'As the ork assault drove deeper into the city, the outer zones were largely abandoned, save for packs of scavengers and greenskin engineers. It's a pattern we've seen many times across the Loki sector. That changed six weeks ago, when Snagrod withdrew almost two-thirds of his forces south of the river and concentrated them in and around Zona Sixty-two.'

Tauros nodded to Enginseer Oros. The tech-priest twitched a mechadendrite inside the table's casing, and the image on the display began to change.

'Over the past several weeks, the greenskins have cleared the debris from the complex and used it to create twenty-four large camps and scores of smaller camps in and around the area.' Large, rough squares dominated by sentry towers and a rash of smaller circles sprang up in and around the giant manufactories. 'The bigger camps are built more like forts, and contain anywhere from one to three large warbands.

'At the same time, large mobs of ork engineers have been observed making crude modifications to several of the manufactories.' Six of the massive structures on the display changed colour from blue to a sullen green. 'Similar work recently began on the power plant as well.'

Galleas observed his brothers' reactions as Tauros delivered the news. From the tension in their armoured forms it was clear they understood the grim implications of what they'd been told. It was Lieutenant Mitra, however, that put their concerns into words.

'The orks are getting the manufactories back online,' she said, folding her arms across her chest. She shook her head. 'I don't understand. What would they want with mega-harvesters?'

'A mega-harvester uses a lot of the same parts as a battle tank,' Sergeant Kazimir pointed out.

'The greenskins have plenty of trucks and tanks,' Mitra countered. 'That's not what's holding them back. It's the river and the Cassar's void shields.'

'And Snagrod wouldn't need to shift thousands of orks just to build tanks,' Tauros said. 'This has to be something else. Something huge.' He nodded to Oros, and the display shifted again. 'During the course of the reconnaissance mission tonight, we discovered these.'

New structures sprang up next to each of the manufactories. At first glance they looked like the skeletal structures of large towers, frameworks made of salvaged girders that rose even higher than the cooling towers of the power plant nearby.

Oros straightened, peering over the rim of the table. 'Construction gantries,' he observed, the display image reflecting eerily in the lenses of his respirator mask. 'Big ones. If the scale is correct, they m-must be thirty metres high.'

'Gargants,' Amador said in disbelief. 'Dorn's blood. Snagrod's building *gargants.*'

Mitra glanced from Amador to Galleas, a bemused expression on her face. 'What in the Emperor's name is a gargant?'

Once again, Oros provided the answer. 'Massive ork war machines. Crude mockeries of the Omnissiah's blessed Titans.'

Kazimir blanched. 'I saw a Titan once, during the Purge of Lemnos,' he said, shaking his head in awe. 'If a gargant is anything like that–'

'They are engines of pure destruction,' Galleas explained. 'Huge, ponderous and very, very heavily armed. This is how Snagrod intends to break the siege of the Zona Regis and the Cassar.' The veteran sergeant turned to Valentus. 'You have the most experience with these monstrosities, brother. Are they capable of bringing down the Cassar's void shields?'

Valentus considered the question for a moment, his polished metal face inscrutable. *'The citadel's void shields are strong enough to withstand orbital bombardment,'* he mused, '*but if the gargants concentrated all their firepower on a single point… Yes. It's possible.*'

'How many gargants would it take?' Galleas said.

Valentus gave a slight shrug. '*I can't give a precise answer, brother. No two gargants are alike.*'

'Your best guess?'

'*I would say three at minimum, though it might take them hours to wear down the shields.*'

'Three,' Tauros echoed grimly. 'Snagrod's building *six.*'

The news shook Galleas to the core. 'If they reach the Cassar, they'll bring the shields down in minutes.'

Mitra's expression turned grave. 'Can the forces at the citadel stop them?'

Valentus shook his head. '*The gargants are heavily armoured, and protected by crude force fields of their own. The Cassar's guns might account for one, perhaps two at most, before they are overwhelmed.*'

'What about the factories?'

'The complex is beyond the range of the guns at the Zona Regis,' Galleas said. 'And a raid from our brothers in the citadel would be impossible, given the thousands of orks still threatening the island's defences.'

Mitra stared angrily down at the images on the display. Galleas watched her anger give way to a look of grim determination.

'What about us? What can we do to stop them?'

'*Us?*' Bergand exclaimed. The offworlder stared at her in horror. 'Are you mad? If the forces at the Cassar haven't got a chance, what do you think *we* could possibly do?'

'What then would you suggest, Master Bergand?' Mitra said coldly. 'That we sit by and do nothing?'

Bergand drew himself up haughtily. 'I've been trying

to persuade everyone to see reason for months now,' he declared. 'The fact of the matter is that Rynn's World has fallen. With the exception of a small island in the middle of the River Rynn, the entire planet is in greenskin hands, and nothing we do is going to change that.' He turned to Galleas. 'With all due respect, my lord, we tried things your way and it availed us nothing. I say we need to take advantage of the current situation and find a way to reach the island before it's too late.'

'Too late?' Mitra exclaimed. 'Too late for what?'

'To get off this damned planet!' Bergand snapped. 'Come now, lieutenant. I know your family. You know as well as I do that there are ships hidden at the Zona Regis to evacuate the nobility in the event of disaster.'

Mitra stiffened as though she'd been struck. The colour drained from her face, and when she spoke, her voice trembled with barely-contained rage.

'I know of no such thing,' she answered. 'The very idea is *obscene*.' She took a step towards Bergand. The void trader backpedalled, eyes widening, only to fetch up against a wall of scarred ceramite in the form of Titus Juno.

'If you *ever* again suggest that me and mine are cowards, Master Bergand,' Mitra continued, her hand falling to the sabre at her hip, 'then by the Golden Throne it will be the very last thing you do.'

Bergand went pale. 'F-forgive me,' he stammered. 'I didn't mean–'

Galleas spoke, his voice cutting through the sudden tension like a phase knife. 'On the contrary, Master Bergand. Your meaning was quite clear. Leave us.'

The offworlder fell silent. He looked to Kazimir, hoping for a sign of support, but the sergeant's face was pitiless.

Drawing himself up with as much dignity as he had left, Bergand turned on his heel and strode quickly from the sanctum.

When the void trader was gone, Mitra drew a deep breath and turned back to Galleas. 'My question still stands, my lord. How do we stop them?'

'We can't,' Galleas replied. The words tasted bitter on his tongue. 'Once the gargants become operational they will be nearly unstoppable.'

'Then we kill them while they're still in their cradles!' Mitra said, pointing to the glowing skeletons of the construction gantries. 'Plant some demolition charges and let gravity do the rest!' The lieutenant's voice took on a desperate edge.

But the veteran sergeant shook his head. 'Any damage we inflicted would be quickly repaired. Snagrod's labour force is huge, and he has a whole city to scavenge for resources, not to mention a fleet in orbit.'

Olivar let out an exasperated growl. 'Dorn's blood!' he snapped. 'You're all ignoring the obvious.' He leaned forward, tapping the centre of the display with an armoured fingertip. 'The power plant.'

Enginseer Oros shuddered and made the sign of the Omnissiah. 'M-my lord Olivar is right,' he said. 'A reactor overload would produce a thermal pulse that would level the entire complex.'

Galleas folded his arms. 'What Brother Olivar neglects to point out is that the power plant is virtually surrounded by fortifications and large ork warbands. An attack on the plant would be a suicide mission.'

'So be it then!' Royas cried. 'What other choice do we have, brother? If we don't act, the Cassar is doomed!'

Galleas was tempted. He imagined the fiery blast that

would consume the manufactories and the thousands of orks inside. It would be a devastating blow, one that Snagrod's horde might not recover from, and a fitting vengeance after the destruction of the Arx Tyrannus.

It took all of his will to remember his duty and push such thoughts aside.

'A raid on the power plant would be the death of us,' he declared. 'I won't countenance it except as a last resort.' He glanced at Tauros. 'Especially not when the relief force from Kar Duniash could arrive at any time.'

Tauros returned the veteran sergeant's stare and let the comment go unchallenged.

'Constructing the gargants will consume the efforts of thousands of orks,' Galleas continued. 'More importantly, it will take *time*. Snagrod has committed such huge numbers to the project because he knows that he has to resolve the siege before the Navy arrives.

'So we will harass the greenskins at every turn. We will create so many disruptions that the process slows to a crawl. Even as little as a week's delay might make the difference between victory and defeat.'

It was clear that Royas and Amador disagreed, but they kept their thoughts to themselves. The challenge to Galleas' plan came from Juno instead.

'This won't work like before,' the Crimson Fist pointed out. 'We won't be able to fire a few wild shots in the dark and let the orks take things from there. This means direct action. It'll be us against the horde.'

'Indeed,' Galleas said. 'We'll have the advantage of surprise for our first strike. After that, we will have tipped our hand, and the orks will know we're here. Once we begin, it will be a fight to the death. I expect few, if any of us, will survive.'

The veteran sergeant paused to let that sink in. As he expected, his brothers were unmoved. To their credit, neither Mitra nor Kazimir seemed dismayed by the prospect either.

It was Valentus who finally broke the silence. *'Then we must make the most of our first strike,'* he observed. *'If not the power plant, then what?'*

Galleas considered the display. They were committed now. The prospect of life and death could be put aside, leaving him to focus on the matter at hand.

'Our target must be something that the orks have in short supply, and will find very difficult to replace,' he mused.

Kazimir chuckled. 'Brains?'

The suggestion drew a laugh from Juno and Tauros. Galleas glanced up from the table and gave Kazimir a penetrating stare.

Kazimir's grin faded. 'Sorry, my lord,' the Rynnsguard sergeant said sheepishly.

'Don't be,' Galleas said. Kazimir's jest had sparked an idea, and a battle plan was already forming in his mind.

'That's exactly what we are going to do.'

CHAPTER SEVENTEEN
ACCEPTABLE LOSSES

NEW RYNN CITY
DAY 380

The raiding force kept to the tunnels as far as they were able, working their way from Zona Nine to the outer districts of the city. The further they got from the river, the emptier the stormwater channels became. The air grew colder and quieter, causing every step, every rattle of harness to echo and re-echo from the walls. The funereal stillness reminded Galleas of the Hall of the Ancients beneath the Arx Tyrannus, where the old Dreadnoughts once slept.

Within an hour they were crossing the Via Tempestus, the great underground aqueduct that separated the old city from the new. Past the ancient watercourse, the tunnels grew progressively rougher; the curving walls were carved from tightly joined blocks instead of fused ferrocrete, and the lumen network was sparse and weak where it functioned at all. Icy water pooled on the tunnel floors, and the air was thick with the stench of rot and old death.

Galleas knew they were getting close to the outer walls

when they came upon the first corpses. Most were slumped against the tunnel walls or face-down in the reeking muck, their uniforms covered in mould and their bodies reduced to bone and sinew by the damp air. Preacher Gomez muttered a prayer over each one as they passed, consigning the spirits of the fallen to the grace of the Emperor's holy light.

The numbers of the dead grew quickly as the guerrillas pressed on. Where the tunnels widened they found the dead lying in rotted heaps, their skulls split and bones scattered by the blows of frenzied ork axes. Every intersection contained a makeshift barricade of corrugated metal and flakboard piled with grisly remains. The majority of the dead were Imperials, but here and there the guerrillas came upon a greenskin corpse as well. Unlike the humans, the xenos were still more or less recognisable, but their waxy bodies had started to soften and were covered in thick patches of sickly-looking fungus. Not even the sewer rats would touch them.

Once they came upon the body of a Crimson Fist. He lay on his back at the narrow part of a tunnel, not far from the foundation of the city's inner curtain wall, and a passage full of xenos corpses stretched for nearly a hundred metres before him. The fallen warrior's head had been taken, along with his weapons, and his many battle honours had been ripped away. Neither Galleas nor his brothers could say who he was, or how he'd come to die there, alone and cut off from the rest of his squad.

Past the inner curtain wall and its death-choked tunnels, the guerrillas found their way to a maintenance access shaft and climbed the freezing metal rungs to the surface. They emerged into a burned-out wasteland beneath a heavy, overcast sky.

A bitter wind whistled through the ruins. Lieutenant Mitra hunched her shoulders against the cold and wiped a hand against her cheek. She stared at the tiny crystals glittering on her palm. 'What in the Emperor's name?'

'Snow,' Galleas explained. On Rynn's World, with its twin suns, such a thing was nearly unheard of. Mitra shivered, wiping her hand against the front of her flak armour.

Once on the surface, Galleas ordered Juno's squad to take point, and sent Tauros and Valentus to cover the flanks. The city's outer districts had seen very heavy fighting in the first stages of the invasion, and had been transformed into a blasted hellscape of shattered buildings, shell craters and scorched vehicles. At every crossroads they came upon a makeshift barricade, each one smaller and more desperate the closer they came to the outer curtain wall, where the city's defenders had tried to slow the advance of Snagrod's horde. Thousands of Rynnsguard had sacrificed their lives in these brutal rearguard actions, buying time for their fellow soldiers to retreat. All that remained of them now were heaps of charred bone and melted bits of armour.

The city's outer wall loomed above the ruined outer districts like a mountain range, its towers and crenellations splintered by hundreds of shell hits. A crashed ork transport had created a breach nearly fifty metres across. From the top of its broken hull, Galleas could see the orange glow of the tractor works reflecting off the low clouds some five kilometres further south.

They descended the broken back of the crashed transport and left the city behind, marching silently into a desolate wasteland of shell craters and splintered trees. The earth had been burned black for as far as the eye could see, and the sight of it left the Imperials deeply shaken. The ruin of

New Rynn City had been hard enough to bear, although buildings could be rebuilt given time. But an entire *world*…

For more than an hour, the guerrillas crossed the ravaged landscape in silence. Galleas was thinking ahead, reviewing the tactical plan for the assault on the tractor works, when a faint sound behind him attracted his attention. Lieutenant Mitra had closed the gap between them and was walking at the Space Marine's shoulder. Her expression was troubled. Before Galleas could reprove her on her poor march discipline, she spoke in a low voice.

'It isn't true, my lord.'

'What?'

'There aren't any ships hidden on the Zona Regis,' Mitra insisted. 'No plan to evacuate the nobles if the void shields fall.'

'I know.'

'I don't know what kind of world that snake Bergand is from, but here the old families would never stand for such a thing. *Never.*'

'There is no need to convince me, lieutenant,' Galleas replied. 'I'm familiar with every square metre of the Zona Regis. If there was a ship hidden there, I would know it.'

Mitra nodded, but her expression remained troubled. She walked in silence for a while, struggling with her thoughts.

'When my father heard that Snagrod was coming, he summoned the entire family back to the estate,' she said. 'Aunts, uncles, cousins… absolutely everyone. Many of them were city-bred, and had never set foot on an agri-combine in their life, but that didn't matter. They had an obligation to return and defend the land from the xenos, my father said. It was a debt of blood we owed to our ancestors, and if we failed to honour it then we were no longer worthy of our name.'

Mitra stared off at the barren hills to the west, her eyes distant. 'Not four hours after my father's call, the first family members started to arrive. They came from the far corners of the world, with nothing but what they could carry on their backs, until the old house was full of them.' She shook her head. 'They could have come here instead, taken refuge behind the city walls, but they wouldn't hear of it. They were Rynnsworlders, and they knew their duty.

'It was madness. I said as much. My father and I fought like bull grox up to the day I had to leave and join my regiment.' She wiped the back of a grimy hand against the corners of her eyes. 'Now I'm the only one left.'

Galleas frowned, uncertain how to respond. 'Duty… is a difficult thing to bear sometimes,' he said.

Mitra nodded. The two walked on in silence for a time, scanning the desolate landscape. Then the lieutenant drew a deep breath and stared up at the Space Marine.

'Do you grieve, Lord Galleas?' she asked.

The question shocked him. An uneasy silence fell between them. Mitra glanced away. 'That was impertinent. I'm sorry.'

They walked on a while longer, the scorched earth crunching beneath their feet. Mitra started to turn away, heading back to her place in the file, when Galleas suddenly spoke.

'I was born on a planet not far from here, called Blackwater,' he began. 'A feral world, covered in primordial swamps and filled with savage beasts. It is a place where the strong prey on the weak, and the human clans exist in a constant state of war with their neighbours.

'I never knew what clan I was born to, or who my father was. My mother was taken in a raid, and gave birth to me in the slave pens. Not long after, she disappeared. Perhaps she was sold to another clan, or was killed – all I knew was that one day she was there, and the next she was gone.' He shrugged his massive shoulders. 'After that, I was on my own. If I ate, it was because I managed to wrestle a meal away from the other children. If I stayed dry during the rainy season, it was because I scavenged a scrap of oilskin to cover me while I slept.

'Eventually I was put to work, cleaning the longhouses and taking out the scraps,' Galleas recalled. The memories were still sharp and clear, centuries later. His nose wrinkled as he remembered the foetid air inside the clan buildings, and the way the muck clung to his feet as he dashed through the dimly lit rooms on one errand or another. 'Every day was a new set of torments, but the more the master and his people tried to break me, the more I hated them for it. I stole food for myself to keep up my strength, and when the master's children singled me out for a beating I made sure to spill a little of their blood in return. Several times I tried to escape, but the swamps were dense and difficult to traverse, and I never got far before the master's people found me.

'The older slaves warned me that if I made too much trouble, the master would lose patience and have me fed to the marsh krakens.' Galleas thought for a moment. 'I wasn't deterred. In fact, part of me welcomed the prospect.'

Mitra frowned. 'How old were you?'

Galleas shrugged again. 'It's difficult to say. We paid little attention to such things. Eleven years old, perhaps. Possibly twelve. That was the year of the festival.'

'Festival?'

'The Festival of the Burning Fist,' Galleas said. 'A celebration of the sky gods' favour, and a chance to win glory as one of the Chosen. For the space of a single month, once in a generation, the clans would put their raiding aside and gather at the foot of a great mountain in the north, where they would welcome the coming of the gods and offer up their sons as tribute.

'In the weeks before the festival I was put to work cleaning the master's finery and polishing his weapons and armour. His sons practiced their martial skills outside the long-house and boasted how the gods would accept them into their ranks. I worked, and listened, and a plan took shape in my mind. It was a foolish scheme, born of desperation and anger, but I didn't care. What did I have to lose?

'The night after the clan left for the great mountain, I slipped from the slave pens and fled the village. But instead of fleeing into the swamp I followed the clan northwards, along the ancient trail.

'I watched from the edge of the swamp as the clans gathered and laid their banners of blue and red upon the stone dais at the foot of the mountain. I watched their celebrations and their sacrifices. And then came the night when the gods descended from the sky in thunder and fire.

'The clans assembled around the dais as the thunder faded. Soon the gods appeared – giants in dark blue armour with hands the colour of new blood. There was a long ceremony as the clanlords offered lavish gifts and renewed their oaths of fealty to the gods. And then came the procession I had been waiting for, when the sons of the gathered clans marched to the dais to begin the Trials of the Chosen.

'When I raced from the shadows and fell in behind the procession I fully expected to die. I never for a moment believed that the clanlords would let me undergo the trials. It was a final act of defiance, nothing more. And so, when the procession reached the dais, I slipped through the ranks, up to the very front, and before anyone could speak I raised my fist to the gods and demanded the right to join the trial.'

Galleas chuckled ruefully. 'I had barely got the words out before the blows started falling. The clanlords surrounded me, clamouring for my death. I was ready. All I cared about was taking as many of them with me as I could.

'But then a strange thing happened. One of the gods stepped forward, his boots ringing on the stones. He spoke in a voice that cut through the noise of the mob like a knife. He told the clanlords, *it is not for you to decide whether the boy lives or dies now. He has demanded the trial. Let him prove his worth.*

'The clanlords and their sons withdrew. It took me a moment to realise I was free. Free to prove myself worthy of the gods, or die in the attempt. In that moment, I was reborn.

'The trials that followed were terrible. Aspirants died every day, or were too maimed to go on. To make matters worse, the sons of the great clans fought me at every turn. There were times I was certain that I would be the next to die. But I did not yield. I suffered. I endured. And in the end, I was victorious.

'I was the only one to survive the final trial. The clans watched in silence as I emerged from the swamp and laid the head of the barb dragon on the dais at the god's feet. And he raised his blazing fist to the crowd and proclaimed me, a nameless slave boy, one of the Chosen.' Galleas raised his chin proudly. 'His name was Pedro Kantor.'

Mitra's eyes widened. 'The Chapter Master himself?'

'He was captain of Fourth Company at the time,' Galleas said, 'but by then everyone could see he was destined for greatness. He gave me a life of purpose, a life of honour. He made me a brother to angels. He even gave me my name, which I have borne with pride for centuries. I have travelled the stars, fought mighty battles and wrought great deeds, all because of him. Because he spoke for me when no one else would.'

Mitra nodded slowly. 'Was he at the Arx Tyrannus when–'

'He was,' Galleas said. 'I expect he was on the battlements with the rest of my brothers when the missile fell. There is little reason to believe he survived.'

The Space Marine raised a scarred, red fist and rapped at the battered aquila on his breastplate. 'But as long as I keep to my oaths, as long as I can keep fighting and keep my squad alive, a part of him lives on as well. The Chapter, gravely wounded as it is, will live on a while longer.

'I will continue to do my duty, lieutenant. I will continue to prove my worth, as I have done every moment of every day since Kantor first spoke for me. I will suffer. I will endure. I will fight on, beyond all hope, until my final breath. Not for my sake, but for the fallen, so that their deaths will not be in vain. If that is not grief, lieutenant, then it is the nearest I can come to it.'

The activity at the tractor works carried for kilometres, a rumble of machinery and bestial voices that was more felt than heard. Galleas could feel it reverberate through the soles of his boots and against the curved surfaces of his armour. The guerrillas sensed it too, growing warier and more apprehensive the closer they came to their objective.

An hour after leaving the city, the guerrillas came to a halt in a burned-out industrial centre on the other side of a cratered motorway from the tractor works. As the humans made last-minute checks to their wargear, the veteran sergeant spoke to his brothers.

'Once we separate, you will have one hour to get your squad into position,' he said. 'No more. No less. By that point, Enginseer Oros will have rigged the transformer to overload. You will have between eight and ten minutes to complete your objective.' He surveyed the assembled Space Marines. 'Stay focused. As soon as the lights fail, begin your withdrawal to the rally point.'

'We all know the plan, brother,' Amador said impatiently. 'You covered it in great detail just a few hours ago.'

'Think of your elders, young Amador,' Tauros chided in a deadpan voice. 'Old Valentus is getting a bit feeble and needs reminding from time to time. Why, he thought I was Royas just the other day.'

'*You all look the same with your helmets on,*' Valentus quipped.

'It bears repeating,' Galleas interjected sternly, 'because we will be operating by squads against six separate targets, with no way to support one another if something goes wrong.' He gave his brothers a forbidding look. 'Remember, we're here for the engineers. They're the one resource Snagrod can't easily replace, and without them the whole effort will grind to a halt. We must kill as many as we can find and then get out before we're cut off and destroyed.' The veteran sergeant's gaze fell squarely upon Amador. 'Understood?'

Amador folded his arms and growled, 'Get in, kill the engineers, and get out. Simple enough that a human could do it.'

'Indeed,' Galleas replied pointedly, hoping that the impulsive Amador would take the message to heart. The image of their fallen brother in the tunnels lingered in the back of the veteran sergeant's mind. He wasn't ready to lose another. 'There is only the Emperor,' he intoned.

'*He is our shield and protector,*' the Crimson Fists replied in unison.

Galleas nodded in approval. 'Return to your squads. We move out in three minutes.'

At the appointed time, the guerrillas slipped silently from the ruins along separate paths leading to their targets. Each squad was assigned one of the six factory buildings to attack. The seventh squad, led by the stolid and dependable Valentus, remained behind; he was tasked with launching a diversionary attack against one of the outlying greenskin forts, drawing as many of the orks as possible away from the strike teams' escape route.

Galleas' squad had the shortest route to travel, but the most to accomplish before the attack began. They worked their way single file through the ruined industrial centre, and then crossed beneath the motorway through a rubble-choked drainage culvert.

From the lip of the culvert the squad had an unobstructed view of the terrain between them and their objective, the tractor works' main factory building. Two large ork camps, built using scavenged ferrocrete slabs and rusting metal girders, covered the approaches to the building from the north. Tall, ramshackle sentry towers swept the dead area between the camps with powerful searchlights, seeking targets for the heavy gun emplacements mounted on the camps' crude walls. Beyond the killzone, much of the broken tarmac surrounding the factory building was bathed in the white glare of salvaged floodlights, illuminating the greenskin work gangs as they went about their tasks. Where

there were large gaps in the floodlights' coverage, the orks
had built towering bonfires instead, throwing long, leaping shadows across the tarmac. At the western end of the
factory rose one of the massive construction gantries. Orks
swarmed over it like ants, assembling the skeleton of one
of Snagrod's fearsome gargants.

Galleas paused at the culvert and scanned the area carefully, covering the full spectrum available to his auto-senses.
The approach to the factory across the featureless killing
ground seemed impossible to the untrained eye.

After a moment, the veteran sergeant turned to his squad.
'Stay close,' he said in a low voice. 'When I move, you move.
When I stop, you stop. Understood?'

Mitra and the others nodded. They were tense, their faces
taut with fear.

Galleas turned back to the killing ground, his attention
focused on the interlocking patterns of the searchlights.
When the moment was right, he leapt silently from the
culvert.

The veteran sergeant crouched low and dashed across
the stony ground. He cut to the right, past the reach of the
searchlight beam on his left, then forward again, finally
dropping onto his chest in a shallow depression just slightly
lower than the surrounding terrain. An instant later, another
searchlight, this time from the fort on the right, swept past.
Its beam cut an arc less than a hand span above the Space
Marine's head.

Galleas stole a quick glance over his shoulder. Mitra
was right behind him, her chin pressing into the ground.
Her breath came in shallow gasps, making tiny gusts of
vapour in the freezing air. The rest of the squad was spread
out behind her, exactly where they were supposed to be.

Satisfied, he turned his attention back to the searchlights, waiting for the beams to synchronise again.

For the next half hour, Galleas led his squad across the killing ground, weaving a careful path around the reach of the orks' searchlights. The closer they came to the factory, the louder the heavy machinery became, effectively covering the sound of their movements. They avoided the glare of the floodlights, sticking to the deep shadows at the edge of the crackling bonfires. Ork mobs crouched around the flames, grunting at one another in their bestial tongue and peering idly out at the darkness. As Galleas suspected, the greenskins were unaware they were in any danger. The forts surrounding the complex were a way to separate the larger warbands and keep them from fighting one another, not to defend the tractor works from an outside attack.

That would change after tonight, Galleas knew.

The going became more dangerous once they were past the bonfires. Galleas signalled for the guerrillas to follow single file, lest they be backlit by the flames and have their shadows thrown against the side of the factory building. Twice they had to flatten themselves against the cold ground and wait as a greenskin work party lumbered by, urged on by a cursing overseer and his lash. Both times their luck held, and the xenos went past without realising the threat in their midst.

Finally, they had come within ten metres of a side entrance to the factory building. Galleas paused, scanning the area for a full three seconds before giving a quick hand signal. On cue, Enginseer Oros scrambled to his feet and dashed for the door, his robes flapping around his heels. This was potentially the most dangerous part of the insertion. If he found the door was locked, the enginseer was the only one equipped with the tools to bypass it, but he would have to do so in full view of any ork passing by.

Oros reached the door in moments. The guerrillas watched from the shadows, scarcely daring to breathe. Galleas waited, prepared to act at the first sound of alarm.

The door slid open with scarcely a pause, and Oros disappeared inside. Someone, perhaps Mitra, let out a quiet breath. Galleas waved the guerrillas forward.

The noise level inside the factory was nothing short of thunderous. Forges rumbled, and automatic hammers pounded red-hot metal into structural pieces for the gargants taking shape outside. The engineers had prioritised repairing the banks of work lights directly over the forge and assembly areas, leaving the edges of the cavernous building in darkness.

Galleas checked his chronometer. Twenty-two minutes left. He nodded to Oros. The tech-priest hurried off down the length of the massive building, sticking closely to the dark hulks of idle hydraulic presses and dashing quickly across the lanes in between. Galleas and the others followed, trusting to the Space Marine's enhanced vision to lead the way.

Less than a minute later, Oros reached his goal: a massive, industrial-grade transformer set against the building's outer wall. The tech-priest studied it for a moment, his mechadendrites twitching thoughtfully, then made the sign of the Omnissiah and opened a pair of access panels and went to work.

Galleas and the others formed a rough perimeter around Oros, facing outwards, alert for potential threats. The veteran sergeant caught glimpses of orks moving between the heavy machinery in the centre of the building, but none of them came close enough to pose any danger to the guerrillas.

A few minutes later, Oros crouched down next to Galleas. 'It's done,' he said, shouting to make his voice heard over the roar of the machines. 'May the Machine-God forgive me.'

'And you are certain it will knock out the power to the entire complex?' Galleas said.

The enginseer nodded. 'Oh, yes. When the transformer overloads, the power surge will force the reactor into standby mode. It will take a minimum of ten minutes to reset and get the grid back online. Possibly longer.'

'How long until the overload?'

'There's no way to say for certain, my lord,' Oros replied sheepishly. 'My best guess is fifteen minutes.'

Galleas nodded curtly. The other squads would be in position in five minutes. That gave them just enough time. He gestured with the muzzle of his gun at a series of five window-lined offices connected by a series of catwalks that ran down the centre of the building's ceiling. 'The engineers will be up there, in the overseers' posts,' he said. 'Follow me. If any orks get close enough to see us, cut them down.'

He set off at a swift pace through the darkness, back the way they'd come. The guerrillas followed at a run, gun muzzles sweeping the aisles as they went past. At the far end of the building, Galleas found what he sought: a metal stairway climbing the inside of the wall up to the overseers' catwalks. Guttural voices echoed from above. The veteran sergeant switched to thermal vision and spotted four greenskins working their way down the stairs towards them.

Galleas felt his pulse quicken at the prospect of battle. 'On me,' he said to his squad. 'Watch your spacing. Once we get to the catwalks, kill anything that moves.'

Mitra and the others growled their assent. Weapon ready, Galleas took the stairs at a run.

Over the pounding of his boots, Galleas heard the guttural voices stop. One made a quizzical sound, and then called out a question. A moment later, the Crimson Fist gave them his answer, rounding a switchback halfway up the wall and spotting the xenos on the stairs less than three metres away. The four engineers gaped in shock at the sight of the oncoming Space Marine.

Galleas fired on the move, unleashing a series of short bursts into the greenskins. The engineers fell one after another, their bullet-riddled bodies rolling wetly down the stairs. The veteran sergeant leapt easily over each corpse and kept going, the thirst for vengeance quickening his pace. Mitra and the others cursed and stumbled around the falling bodies and struggled to follow.

Seconds later the Crimson Fist rounded the stairway's upper landing. The first overseers' post was ten metres away, at the far end of a narrow catwalk. Three ork engineers, drawn by the sounds of gunfire, had emerged from the post and were peering curiously over the catwalk's railing.

Galleas drew Night's Edge. Lit from below by the hellish glow of the forges, he was the living image of the Emperor's holy wrath.

The veteran sergeant keyed the power sword's activation rune. 'Vengeance for the fallen!'

The engineers scarcely had time to register their shock before Galleas was upon them. Night's Edge flashed, and bodies tumbled from the catwalk. Mitra and the others reached the top of the stairway and raced after him, taking up the war cry as they went.

'Vengeance for Rynn's World! Vengeance for the fallen!'

Galleas burst through the doorway of the overseers' post, gun blazing. The room was filled with consoles monitoring the systems running on the factory floor, and nearly a dozen ork engineers were turning away from the windows or rising from their chairs, weapons in hand. The Crimson Fist never stopped moving, carving his way from one end of the chamber to the next through a hurricane of lead. Slugs rang from the curved plates of his armour, ricocheting into consoles and through the grimy windowpanes. A pair of engineers bolted for the opposite doorway, bellowing in alarm, and Galleas ran them down, splitting their skulls with a sweep of his blade and shouldering the bodies aside. In the space of a few seconds he was gone, leaving the surviving enemy to Mitra and the rest of the squad as he raced for the next post down the line.

Galleas was halfway down the second catwalk when a small mob of ork engineers came charging out of the office ahead of him. Guns blazed, slugs snapping back and forth down the narrow catwalk. The veteran sergeant fired one-handed, dropping a pair of orks in the front rank as he closed the distance. Answering fire struck sparks off the catwalk railing or rang from the surface of his breastplate. A sputtering grenade went spinning past his head and fell in a long arc to the factory floor below.

He crashed into the oncoming orks with a roar of righteous anger, firing point-blank into the mass of bodies and hacking away with his sword. When he'd emptied the gun's clip he used the weapon as a club, smashing skulls and staving in ribs. The catwalk's metal grating grew slick with gore. The mob slowed his charge for the space of a few seconds before the greenskins broke, scrambling back down the catwalk the way they'd come.

Galleas paused for a moment to reload his weapon. Boots pounded on the catwalk behind him. The guerrillas were breathing hard, faces stained with propellant from the close-quarters battle. At the rear of the group, Preacher Gomez was gasping out a savage prayer from the *Lectitio Divinitatus*.

One of the squad was missing. Galleas gave Mitra an interrogatory look and she shook her head. *Our first casualty*, he thought grimly.

Shots rang out from the overseers' post. Glass shattered as orks fired through the windows at their attackers. 'Grenades!' Galleas ordered, firing a burst through the doorway ahead.

Mitra dug into a satchel at her hip and produced two ork stick bombs. Pulling the pins, she took a few quick steps past Galleas and drew back her arm for an overhand throw. At the same moment another fusillade of shots rang out. Mitra let out an explosive grunt and toppled forward, just managing to hurl the grenades as she fell.

The grenades bounced across the threshold and blew up, shattering more windows and filling the office with screams and dirty, grey smoke. Galleas grabbed Mitra by the arm, pulling her back. The lieutenant was pale and gasping for air, one arm wrapped tightly across her chest. By a stroke of luck, it appeared her flak armour had stopped the heavy ork slugs.

Vega was already forcing his way past his squadmates towards Mitra. Galleas left her in the medic's hands and dashed forward, into the shattered overseers' post. Two engineers were fleeing the room as he entered, leaving behind half a dozen dead or injured greenskins. The veteran sergeant gave chase as the rest of the squad charged into the room and began finishing off the wounded enemy.

As fast as Galleas was, the panicked engineers had good reason to be faster. They were more than halfway down the catwalk by the time the veteran sergeant made his way across the second overseers' post. The third and largest of the five was just ahead. If the engineers intended to make a stand, Galleas reckoned it would be there.

Galleas charged down the catwalk through a hail of enemy fire. The fleeing orks were aiming over their shoulders as they ran, and now the greenskins on the factory floor had seen what was happening and were taking shots at the Space Marine as well. Slugs rang off the catwalk rails and punched jagged holes through the plating at his feet, but Galleas pressed on through the storm.

The veteran sergeant gained ground on the retreating orks with each passing second. Orks from the post ahead were firing now too, blazing away from the few windows that faced along the catwalk. Galleas was already past the halfway point and less than five metres from the closest of the panicked greenskins. He brought up his gun and centred it on the xenos, but before he could pull the trigger there was an intense flash of light from the doorway ahead, and a blue-white arc of energy incinerated the leading ork.

Heavy blaster! Galleas felt his blood turn to ice. It was the same weapon that had wrecked his squad's Rhino during Rottshrek's attack.

Visions of the breach in Leonidas Square flooded into his mind. He saw the leering face of the ork engineer as it turned its weapon on the transport, and Salazar's body hurled into the air by the blast. His lips drew back in a snarl.

The remaining ork was braying in terror, caught between Galleas and the heavy blaster. The beast hesitated, uncertain which was the greater danger. Galleas seized the xenos by the back of its thick neck and shoved it with all his strength through the doorway. The ork had barely crossed the threshold when another blue-white bolt cut the engineer in half.

Galleas dived through the doorway right on the hapless engineer's heels and rolled left behind a bank of consoles. Almost at once, he fetched up against a press of stinking, green bodies. His tactical analysis had been correct – the office was packed with engineers, eager to repel the enemy raiders. Blows from axes and cleavers rained down on his shoulders and back. The veteran sergeant lashed out with his power sword, killing a pair of greenskins, and the surviving xenos were forced back.

A blast of energy struck the console above his head with a thunderous explosion, raking Galleas and the surrounding orks with red-hot shrapnel. Greenskins bellowed in fury and confusion. Galleas added to the carnage by emptying his gun into the packed crowd, then forcing his way through the falling bodies and around the corner of another set of consoles. Only then did he risk a quick look over the top of the machine to find the source of the blasts.

The boss engineer stood near the centre of the room, flanked on both sides by a small mob of engineers armed with a chaotic assortment of modified guns and blasters. The greenskin leader caught sight of Galleas at the same moment and spun about, bringing his cumbersome weapon to bear. The Crimson Fist ducked just in time, the searing bolt passing close enough to leave a glowing scar across the surface of his right pauldron. The blast carried on through the wall of the office, blowing a jagged hole through the flakboard and glass.

The engineers surrounding Galleas had scattered in terror now that he was the boss' target. He dashed to the next console down the line, changing clips as he went. Another blast tore through the spot where he'd crouched a moment before, turning the console into blazing fragments. The other engineers quickly joined in, blazing away at any sign of movement. The far wall of the office was riddled with bullet holes and blast marks, throwing up a shower of debris.

Galleas kept low and kept moving, working his way down the room. An engineer leapt into view ahead of him, snarling in triumph; the veteran sergeant shot the ork in the face, then seized its corpse and dragged it towards him.

At just that moment, a clutch of grenades came bouncing through the doorway into the centre of the room. The concussion from the guerrillas' stick bombs shook the entire chamber, filling the air with a sleet of razor-edged steel. As the orks reeled from the blasts, Galleas surged to his feet, lifting the dead ork before him as a shield, and charged the stunned engineers.

Many of the greenskins were down, killed or wounded by the grenades, but the boss and those immediately around him were unhurt thanks to the boss' personal force field. The beast saw Galleas and let out a deranged laugh, sweeping his heavy blaster around in a sizzling arc. The beam shredded an unsuspecting engineer, clawed molten furrows through a bank of consoles, and then tore into Galleas' greenskin shield. As the engineer's body was ripped into burning fragments, the veteran sergeant launched forward into a shoulder roll, crossing the distance between him and his prey in the space of a heartbeat.

His armour registered the ork's force field as a wash of charged particles across its surface. The defensive barrier reacted to energy bolts and high-velocity projectiles, but couldn't cope with a large, slow-moving object like Galleas. The Crimson Fist rolled to his feet and slashed at the boss engineer in a single motion, slicing through the bundle of power cables feeding the boss' heavy blaster. Roaring in fury, the ork boss swung the huge weapon like a club. Galleas parried the clumsy stroke with Night's Edge, the power sword biting deep into the side of the blaster. Then he jammed his gun into the boss' belly and held down the trigger.

The huge greenskin collapsed to its knees, its spine severed by the burst. Galleas drew back his glowing blade and looked the beast in the eye.

'This is for Salazar,' he said. Night's Edge hissed in a burning arc, and the boss' head bounced wetly across the floor.

More gunfire tore through the room as the guerrillas burst through the doorway. The surviving engineers turned and fled, firing as they went. Few made it to the door at the far side. Galleas kicked over the big engineer's headless body and was about to start after them when there was a thunderous *boom* from the other side of the factory and everything went dark.

Galleas checked his chronometer. *Fifteen minutes exactly.* Whatever his shortcomings, Enginseer Oros knew his machines.

Lieutenant Mitra appeared in the doorway, leaning on Vega for support. Her eyes were glassy from whatever painkiller the medic had given her. 'Orders, my lord?' she said through clenched teeth.

Galleas stared after the fleeing engineers. Reason warred with bloodlust.

Oros cleared his throat. 'We have ten minutes before the reactor resets.'

The words had the desired effect. Galleas drew a deep breath. 'We've done all we can,' he said heavily. 'Fall back. We're getting out of here.'

Galleas and his squad emerged from the factory into the midst of bedlam. Valentus had begun his diversion precisely on time, attacking two of the greenskin forts to the east. The orks responded with predictable aggression, blazing away at anything that moved in the sudden darkness. The guerrillas added to the chaos as they fled, firing at one group or another and prompting another frenzy of unaimed fire. One group ran headlong into a mob of charging orks, prompting a sudden, vicious melee. The battle lasted for just a few seconds, until another passing mob of greenskins heard the sounds of fighting and opened fire into the crowd. The orks scattered in every direction and the guerrillas fled into the night.

They were the first squad to reach the rally point, in the shadow of the crashed transport at the city's outer wall. They had lost another member of the squad during the escape, hit by a stray burst of fire just as they were crossing the complex's outer perimeter. Two other guerrillas besides Mitra had minor wounds, and Vega set about tending them as the squad settled into cover to wait.

Juno's squad was the next to arrive. They had taken no losses, and several of the squad members, including Corporal Ismail, wore several sets of fresh ork teeth around their necks. Juno himself was covered in gore. He sat down next to Galleas without a word and began tending to his blood-soaked blade.

Fifteen minutes later Tauros appeared, leading a bedraggled squad of eight men. Kazimir joined Mitra and spoke to her in low, almost fatherly tones. He had a nasty cut on his forehead and there was a jagged scar across the front of his flak armour, but the grizzled old soldier seemed otherwise unhurt.

Half an hour passed. Royas and Olivar appeared with their dour squadmates in tow. Then came Amador, helmetless and grinning, his armour splashed with xenos blood. Vila and his former squadmates stumbled along in the young Space Marine's wake, their faces pale from stress and exhaustion.

Valentus had kept up his attack until the very last moment, providing as much time as possible for his brothers to make their escape. He and his squad arrived a full hour after Amador, their magazine pouches empty and their clothes reeking of propellant. One of their number was missing, killed during the running battle with the orks.

Five dead, Galleas mused, including the two men lost from his own squad during the attack. In purely tactical terms, it was a small price to pay for scores of Snagrod's best engineers. Construction of the gargants would come to a grinding halt while the survivors fought with one another and established a new hierarchy. Still more engineers would die, and more valuable time would be lost.

The raid might have bought them a few weeks, Galleas thought. Perhaps as much as a month. But Snagrod would ultimately replace his losses and the effort would continue much as it had before.

Galleas turned his face to the overcast sky. The Navy had

to come soon. The guerrillas would be lucky to last through the winter.

CHAPTER EIGHTEEN
THE HUNTED

The snow lay thick on the ground across Zona Fifty-seven, filling the shell holes and covering the rubble fields with smooth mantles of ghostly white. The sky was the colour of lead, blocking the light of the twin suns and casting the city into a state of perpetual twilight.

The long winter had been pitiless and cruel, unlike anything the people of Rynn's World had ever seen. The temperatures had plunged a week after the raid on the tractor complex, and the snow had started falling not long after that. Cold became an enemy every bit as relentless and deadly as the greenskins, sapping the guerrillas' strength when they needed it the most. They wore layers of clothes and cloaks made from repurposed tarpaulins, ate what they could, cursed and shivered and prayed for an early spring that no one believed would ever come.

If there was any consolation to be had, it was that the orks didn't care for the cold either. It made them a little more sluggish in body and mind, a little less active and a little more inclined to seek the warmth of their bonfires at night.

Galleas and his squad crouched on the second floor of a ruined manufactory and listened to the rumble of distant petrochem engines. Lieutenant Mitra hunched low against the wall to try to keep out of the wind, her arms tucked inside the layers of a makeshift cloak. Her head was wrapped in rags, leaving only her eyes exposed. She cocked her head, trying to gauge the distance of the convoy. After a moment, she shook her head in disgust.

'Can't tell how close they are,' she said. Her voice was raspy, like rusted iron. Sickness had returned with the cold temperatures, and Vega was growing desperate for more antivirals. No one had died yet, but the exhausted medic had confided to Galleas that it was only a matter of time.

The veteran sergeant knelt beside Mitra, his ork gun resting across his knee. He sampled the sounds through his auto-senses, adjusting for the dampening qualities of the heavy snow. 'Two kilometres,' he reckoned. 'Perhaps a bit more.' He keyed the vox. 'Ten minutes. Squads, prepare for contact.'

The ambush had been laid out in a classic L-pattern. His squad, as well as those of Tauros, Olivar and Valentus, were hidden in the upper storeys of a line of buildings that looked across a rubble field at a narrow section of the M35 motorway, less than two hundred and fifty metres distant. Squads Juno and Amador were in cover at the near edge of the field. Squad Royas was positioned in the upper storey of a building perpendicular to the field, forming the base of the L. He and his men would be the first to see the greenskin vehicles entering the killzone from the west.

The attack on the tractor works had disrupted the

construction of the gargants for more than a month, but the greenskins had been far from idle. Packs of runts had continued to scour the ruined city for metal that would be used to craft everything from internal skeletons to armour plate. In their wake would come huge convoys of excavators and transports that would strip the bones from collapsed buildings and carry them back to the tractor works to be melted down and re-used.

There were also the hunting parties. Now that Snagrod knew there were Space Marines and human fighters hiding in the city, he had sent entire warbands into the streets to try to root them out. So far the hunters had limited themselves to searching the ruins at street level, giving the guerrillas almost unrestricted movement through the tunnels below. As tempting as it was to turn the tables on the hunters and lure them into deadly ambushes, Galleas knew that doing so would serve Snagrod's purpose just as well. He could not afford to waste men and ammunition fighting skirmishes with greenskin mobs. Instead, he was forced to play a game of cat-and-mouse with the hunting parties, looking for gaps in their coverage where he could slip through and strike at the salvage convoys instead.

For the past week and a half, Galleas had been waiting for another such opportunity to arise. This morning, his scouts had reported that a large warband had shifted its search a kilometre further north, creating a small gap along one of the greenskins' main convoy routes. By the afternoon, the strike plan had been devised and the guerrillas were in place.

Now, with just two hours left before sundown, the orks were on the move, hauling their salvage back to the tractor works before darkness and bitter cold set in. From the sound of the engines, they were moving fast, not realising the hunting party in the area had gone, and that the road ahead wasn't safe. The xenos were in for a bitter surprise.

Galleas did not have long to wait. Five minutes later, Royas called over the vox. '*Vanguard approaching.*'

The roar of petrochem engines swelled, echoing across the rubble field as a line of fast-moving warbuggies appeared, followed by a pair of heavily armed trucks. This was the advance force, ranging a kilometre or two ahead of the convoy to search for potential ambushes. Galleas' suspicions were confirmed when the vanguard scarcely slowed down as it entered the killzone. Thinking the area had been cleared hours before, the greenskins didn't so much as slow down as they passed through the choke point and continued along the motorway.

A wolfish smile crossed the veteran sergeant's lean face. 'Five minutes,' he called over the vox. 'Wait for the signal.'

Mitra shifted her stance, bringing up her gun and resting it atop the edge of the window frame. A few metres to the right, the squad's sole remaining rocket team readied their weapon. Gomez began to mutter a prayer, his teeth chattering in the cold. Vega, glassy-eyed with exhaustion, took up position near Oros, whose Mechanicus robes seemed to insulate him completely from the cold.

The sounds of the convoy drew closer. Exactly five minutes after the vanguard had gone past, the first heavy truck came into view. The massive vehicle was packed with orks and armed with a twin heavy gun on a ring mount over the cab, and was equipped with a blocky-looking crane and an earthmoving blade. Part war machine, part excavator, it was the first of three similar trucks rolling at a steady clip along the motorway. Behind them came three equally massive flatbed haulers, their beds stacked with tons of salvaged structural metal ripped from a hab unit nearby.

Galleas reached down and unclipped a small box from his belt. As the lead truck approached the far end of the killzone, he keyed a rune on the box's display.

There was an ear-splitting crack as the explosive charge buried in the road detonated, lifting the truck's front end off the ground and tipping the vehicle onto its side. It came to rest in a billowing cloud of snow and dirt, blocking the narrow motorway.

At the signal, the ambushers facing the motorway opened fire. The rocket team next to Mitra went into action, sending a sputtering missile across the rubble field and into the side of the second truck. The blast ripped through the vehicle's troop compartment, hurling burning bodies high into the air. A second rocket, this time fired from Olivar's squad, struck the flatbed hauler at the rear of the column and turned its cab into flaming wreckage.

The convoy was now trapped inside the killzone, but Galleas knew the clock was ticking. Even now the vanguard was turning around and rushing back to deal with the ambushers. They had four minutes, maybe less, to complete the ambush and escape.

The greenskins were leaping from the flatbed haulers and the surviving truck and charging across the rubble field towards them in a howling mob. As they crossed the open terrain in front of Royas' position, his squad opened fire. Streams of red and green tracers clawed across the field and tore into the running greenskins as the squad cut loose with a pair of heavy stubbers that had been salvaged from the ruins of the outer wall and put back into service. The automatic fire scythed through the orks, catching them in a withering crossfire and forcing the survivors back towards the motorway.

Slugs chewed the ferrocrete in a ragged line across Galleas' position. Preacher Gomez screamed and fell backwards, clutching his arm. Down on the motorway the third truck was turning to face the line of buildings across the field. Its twin guns hammered away, raking the second storey windows and forcing the guerrillas to take cover. Royas shifted the fire of his heavy stubbers onto the truck, drawing the ork gunner's attention long enough for Olivar's rocket team to put a missile into the front of the vehicle's cab. The truck came to a shuddering stop and burst into flames.

The surviving greenskins had retreated behind the flatbed haulers. Galleas searched the line of vehicles for the ork warboss. The beast ought to be out at the front, bellowing at the orks to get back in the fight.

Galleas had just enough time to realise that something was wrong before he heard the throaty snarl of jet engines approaching from the west.

'Airstrike!' he shouted, just as the ork fighters came roaring into view.

The two planes were dark, blunt-nosed shards of metal, built around a single massive engine and loaded with as many guns as the airframe could handle. They came up parallel to the motorway, racing along at rooftop height, guided to their target by the convoy's warboss. As Galleas watched, flames danced along the fighters' wings and nose, and a hail of explosive shells tore into the building containing Royas and his squad.

The thunder of the jet engines rose to a crescendo and then the planes were gone, disappearing behind the column of dust and smoke rising from their target. The heavy shells had riddled the building from the ground up, practically chewing it to rubble.

'Royas!' Galleas shouted over the vox. 'Royas! Answer me!'

There was no reply. The sound of the jets shifted, echoing through the ruins from west to south-west. The ork planes were coming around for another pass.

There was no time to think. If they stayed where they were, the fighters would cut them to pieces. Galleas rose to his feet and drew Night's Edge. 'Charge the convoy!' he shouted over the vox. 'Now!'

The Space Marines understood the danger at once. Juno and Amador burst from cover with their squads strung along behind them, charging across the open field towards the burning trucks. Tauros and Olivar quickly followed suit, sliding down piles of rubble and closing the distance with the enemy. Galleas waited until his own squad was moving before leaping from the second-storey window and heading for the nearest enemy truck.

The guerrillas were most of the way across the field by the time the fighters appeared again, this time roaring in from the south. Their guns hammered the buildings where the squads had been hiding just moments before, blasting the upper floors apart.

Gunfire and grenade blasts echoed along the length of the convoy as the guerrillas charged into close combat with the orks. It was a desperate move, but Galleas reckoned the ork pilots wouldn't risk firing into the melee and destroying the convoy itself.

He wasn't prepared to risk it. The veteran sergeant reached the burning truck that had tried to force its way into the field. He clambered atop the ruined cab, pushed the dead gunner out of the ring, and raised the twin guns to the iron-grey sky.

Flames licked around him as he traversed the guns from right to left, tracking the sound of the jets. They were coming back again, coming back up the motorway on the same heading as when they'd first appeared. Galleas tightened his hands around the weapon's grips and peered through the crude sights down the length of the road.

The jets were upon the convoy in the blink of an eye. Even with his enhanced reflexes, Galleas barely had time to react. The guns thundered, spitting a stream of shells into the fighters' path. One of the planes was hit hard, belching flame and smoke from its engine as it flashed overhead. The second plane pulled into a tight turn, vanishing from sight off to the south. Moments later a thunderous boom rolled over the city from the direction of the stricken plane.

One down, Galleas thought, searching the sky for the second plane. Would the other pilot break off, or would the beast come looking for revenge?

A rising roar from the west gave him his answer. Galleas slewed the guns around just as the fighter came into view, cannons blazing. Explosive shells raked the length of the convoy, tearing into the stricken trucks. The veteran sergeant fired back, unleashing a long burst that shredded pieces from the plane's right wing and tail. The fighter shuddered under the blows, even as its own shells ripped into the truck upon which Galleas stood. The vehicle's fuel tank blew as the enemy plane flashed overhead, hurling the Crimson Fist through the air.

Galleas landed on his back in the snow, steam hissing from the plates of his superheated armour. He recovered at once, struggling to his feet. The roar of the ork fighter was dwindling fast, heading off in the direction of the spaceport. The sounds of fighting around the convoy were tapering off as well. The ork's strafing run on the trucks had panicked the surviving greenskins, driving them back into the ruined buildings on the far side of the motorway. The guerrillas had fallen back as well, placing the line of trucks between them and the xenos and hurriedly stripping the enemy dead of weapons and ammunition.

Engines were approaching from the east. *The vanguard.* Belatedly, Galleas realised the airstrike hadn't been an accident. The fighters had been waiting above the clouds, ready to pounce when the guerrillas sprung their ambush. The shifting of the hunting party hadn't been the opportunity Galleas had thought, but a carefully laid trap, and he had walked right into it. Now, if they didn't move fast, the vanguard would swoop in and cut his disorganised force to pieces.

First, he had to see about Royas. 'Squads, form on me!' he shouted over the vox. Then he turned and ran across the field to the building where he'd positioned Royas' squad.

A pall of dust still clung to the ruined structure like a shroud. Fresh rubble choked the entrance to the building, but Galleas was able to force his way through a ground-level window frame and reach the stairs leading to the second storey. 'Royas!' he called as he dashed up the stairs.

Galleas emerged from the stairs into a scene of carnage. Blood and fragments of cloth were splashed everywhere, coating the floor, walls and ceiling. The only recognisable pieces of equipment were the mangled wreckage of the heavy stubbers. Everything else, including the ten men and women of Royas' squad, had been literally torn apart by the fusillade of shells.

There was a groan from the far side of the room. Rubble shifted, and Galleas saw Royas struggling to get up. The front of the Crimson Fist's armour was covered in blood.

'Royas!' Galleas rushed to his brother's side, already dreading what he would find. 'Where are you hurt?'

The veteran Space Marine shook his head slowly. 'Not mine,' he said dazedly. A bright streak on the side of his helmet showed where a cannon shell had struck a glancing blow, knocking him senseless. 'The fools... the damned fools...'

'Come on,' Galleas said, reaching for his arm. 'We've got to get out of here.'

Royas seemed not to hear him. 'They threw themselves on me when the planes came in,' he said dumbly. 'Tried to shield me from the shells. Why in the Emperor's name would they do such a thing?'

Galleas pulled Royas to his feet. The Crimson Fist surveyed the room much as Galleas had done, and shook his head in horrified wonder. 'The damned fools!'

'Foolish or not, they gave their lives for you,' Galleas told him. 'And if we don't get out of here right now, their sacrifice will have been for nothing. Now move!'

The guerrillas were waiting as Galleas led the shell-shocked Royas down the stairs. The veteran sergeant surveyed the haggard force. Gomez was pale and trembling with shock, a bandage cinched tightly around his upper arm. Juno's squad was missing two men, and it looked like Olivar had lost a soldier as well. *Thirteen dead*, Galleas thought. *Eighteen since the raid on the tractor works. Nearly a third of my force, and we've delayed the gargants barely a month.*

With an effort, Galleas pushed such bleak thoughts aside. 'Olivar, come take your brother,' he said. 'Vega, stick close to Royas. I fear he has a severe concussion, and it may be an hour or more before he regains his senses. Tauros, Juno, Valentus, form a rearguard. Don't engage unless absolutely necessary. Let's move.'

The predatory roar of the engines was very close now, less than half a kilometre away. Galleas and his squad took the lead, heading out into the snow. The nearest tunnel entrance was just a few blocks away. By the time the greenskins thought to look for their trail, it would be too late.

As Galleas marched beneath a leaden sky he could not help but feel the tide was starting to turn. For the first time since the invasion began, the veteran sergeant began to contemplate the possibility of defeat.

CHAPTER NINETEEN

ONE MORE DAY

RYNNLAND TRACTOR WORKS, NEW RYNN CITY
DAY 496

Seen at maximum magnification, the gargant resembled nothing so much as a child's caricature of an ork. It was brutish and crude, potbellied, misshapen and clumsy-looking, complete with beady portholes for eyes and a massive, oversized jaw that served no useful purpose whatever. The xenos war machine was a mockery of an Imperial Titan's cathedral-like grandeur, but its appearance made the patchwork of thick armour plating bolted to its hull and the massive weapons jutting from its arms, shoulders and bulging abdomen no less effective.

'*Patrol closing from the west,*' Tauros warned over the vox. '*Four minutes.*'

Galleas dialled back his helmet's visual receptors to normal magnification, and the sneering face of the gargant and its construction gantry faded into the distance. He lay prone atop a low hill almost two kilometres from the tractor works, the closest he and his brothers dared to approach the complex in daylight. Ork patrols around the factories had doubled as spring approached and winter's icy grip on the hemisphere weakened. Snagrod was taking no chances now that his war machines were nearing completion.

The veteran sergeant looked to the west. A mob of orks mounted on warbuggies and fast-moving bikes was heading their way. Months of brutal cold had killed what little of the vegetation hadn't been burned by orkish wildfires, and the melting snow had left behind bare hills and wide plains of thick, clinging mud. The ork vehicles slewed through the muck, tyres spinning, exhaust stacks belching plumes of poisonous black smoke.

Galleas reckoned there were thirty or so greenskins in the patrol. He had brought only Tauros and Juno with him on the scouting mission, because a smaller team stood a better chance of evading the countless ork hunting parties now combing the city, and after the brutal winter the humans had to conserve their strength for when it could be put to the best use.

Part of him wanted to stay and wait for the patrol, to spill the blood of the xenos who had brought ruin to his Chapter. It took all his will to push the urge aside.

'I've seen enough,' he said to his brothers, who waited in cover at the base of the hill. 'It's time the others heard the news.'

The Crimson Fists returned to the city in fits and starts, sometimes taking an hour or more to cover a mere hundred metres of terrain. The threat of greenskin patrols was ever-present, not just on the ground, but in the air. Twice the Space Marines had to quickly find cover as a flight of ork fighters or koptas passed low overhead. Each movement required absolute concentration and superlative skill.

The going became no easier once darkness fell. The warmer temperatures allowed the xenos hunting parties to remain in the city at night and watch for signs of their hated enemy. Every few kilometres the Space Marines would pause and wait, scanning their back trail with their full range of auto-senses for the slightest hint of pursuit. Only when they were absolutely certain there was no risk of observation did they make for the nearest tunnel entrance and head below ground.

Winter still held sway in the dark tunnels beneath the city. Ice rimed the edges of the storm channels, and the air was dank and cold. Where once they moved with impunity, now the Space Marines were forced to tread with caution, as the greenskins had lately begun to extend their searches underground as well. As they crossed the Via Tempestus they came upon piles of spent torches and crude markings etched upon the walls where the xenos were attempting to map out the extent of the tunnel network.

It was well into the night by the time Galleas and his brothers turned down the rubble-choked tunnel leading to the hideout. They hadn't passed a single living soul since leaving the city above. The network of listening posts that had once covered the approaches to the base had been abandoned more than a month ago as the guerrillas' strength had waned.

The tent flap across the base's entrance was heavy with frost. As Galleas pushed it aside, Tomas Zapeta stirred from his wooden stool. The old man was wrapped in a mouldy blanket over a ragged oilskin cloak, and a dirty rag was tied about his scrawny neck. His grey hair was long and lank, his eyes sunken and his cheeks sallow, but his knobby, arthritic hands were steady as they gripped the lascarbine in his lap.

'Anything to report?' Galleas inquired, more out of respect for the old man's dedication than anything else.

Zapeta's rheumy eyes shifted, looking up at the towering Space Marine. 'Not dead yet,' he said in a thin voice. 'I expect it's just a matter of time, though.'

The veteran sergeant nodded. 'The rains always come,' he said gravely.

'They do indeed, my lord. They do indeed.'

Galleas continued on, pulling aside the second tent flap and entering the commons area. The air was somewhat warmer here, with so many bodies huddled in so small a space, but the air was foul with the smell of sickness and unwashed flesh. Food had been an issue before the coming of winter; as the snows fell, supplies dwindled to almost nothing. Rationing had been in effect for months, prompting fierce struggles between Master Bergand and Field Medic Vega over who would eat on a given day and how much they were allowed. Hunger had weakened the humans, and the cold had unbalanced their already fragile humours, leading to sickness. The scourge of disease fell hardest on the non-combatants, most of whom hadn't experienced fresh air or sunlight in months. Despite Vega's tireless efforts, people began to waste away and die.

The guerrillas were finishing their evening meal just as Galleas arrived. Soldiers shared cups of thin gruel thickened with gritty flour and containing thin strips of cured rat meat. The non-combatants, who were forced to subsist on far less, huddled against the damp walls and watched the guerrillas eat with glazed, desperate eyes. At Vega's insistence, the sick were confined to the sleeping cells in a vain attempt to prevent the spread of disease, while the still healthy were turned out into the commons area to sleep as best they could.

Galleas took in the room with a glance. Lieutenant Mitra was helping Preacher Gomez change the bandage on his arm. An ork slug had punched through his biceps during the ill-fated ambush a few weeks before. Vega had managed to keep the wound clean despite the conditions inside the base, but it was healing slowly, keeping Gomez from performing any duties more stringent than evening prayers.

Kazimir was sitting with his squad, methodically licking the last drops of gruel from his cup. Nearby, Ismail and the survivors of Juno's squad had finished their meal and were tending their weapons. Next to the corporal sat Daniella's two children, Patrik and Annaliese, who were listening to Ismail expound on the proper way to sharpen a knife. The siblings were among the handful of scouts and scavengers that Galleas had left – the rest had fallen prey to ork hunting parties over the past few weeks as they searched the ruins for food. The risks had grown so great that Galleas had been forced to end the scavenging efforts and restrict the survivors to base, lest one finally be taken alive and tortured into revealing the location of their hideout.

Master Bergand, Galleas noted, was sitting with Corporal Vila and his squad. The offworlder had gravitated to Vila after his falling-out with Lieutenant Mitra, and he called upon them often to help inventory the base's dwindling supplies. Despite being classed as a non-combatant, Bergand always seemed healthy and well fed, though if he was hoarding food meant for the rest of the civilians Galleas had yet to see any evidence of it.

Heads turned as the Crimson Fists arrived. Lieutenant

Mitra met the veteran sergeant's gaze and rose to her feet along with Sergeant Kazimir. They fell in behind the Space Marines as Galleas crossed the room and entered the inner sanctum.

The rest of Galleas' battle-brothers had already stirred from their meditation cells as the veteran sergeant arrived. Enginseer Oros sat at a makeshift work table in the corner of the sanctum, his mechadendrites delicately exploring the circuits inside Royas' helmet. The veteran Space Marine had surprised the tech-priest with a request to re-calibrate the helmet's auto-senses after the hit he'd suffered during the ambush. Seeing Galleas, Oros withdrew his mechadendrites and solemnly made the sign of the Machine-God before the damaged helm, then rose and went to activate the darkened display table.

Galleas unsealed his helmet and handed it to Oros. As Kazimir and Mitra took their places around the table, he spoke.

'We now know why the salvage convoys stopped running two weeks ago,' he said grimly. 'The construction of the gargants is nearly complete.'

The magnified image of the gargant in its construction gantry took shape on the display. The Crimson Fists accepted the news in stoic silence. Kazimir closed his eyes, his lips moving in what appeared to be a silent prayer. Mitra drew a deep breath. Tears shone in her sunken eyes for a brief moment, but she ground them away with the heel of her hand. She straightened her spine and accepted her fate with as much dignity as her weakened condition allowed.

'At this stage, all that remains is to arm the gargants and test their motive systems,' Galleas continued. 'Their power fields and super-heavy weapon systems are being ferried down from orbit even as we speak.' The veteran sergeant gestured to Oros and the display image shifted, focusing on a broad, muddy plain next to the tractor works.

'Instead of landing the ordnance and ammunition at the starport and transporting them overland to the factories, Snagrod is landing the cargo haulers and unloading them less than half a kilometre from the tractor works.'

Kazimir opened his eyes and stared up at Galleas. 'How long until the gargants are fully armed?'

'As you can see from the display, the process is already well under way.' Galleas folded his arms. 'Barring interruption, I expect the gargants will be ready to march in just three days.'

Three days. That was all the time Rynn's World and the Crimson Fists had left. The realisation was difficult to take, even for veteran Space Marines. Amador shook his head angrily. 'We are forsaken!' he spat. 'The Emperor has turned his back on us!'

Olivar glared at Amador. 'Do not blaspheme in this dark hour,' he said sternly. 'If Rynn's World falls and the Chapter is no more, the failing is ours, not the Emperor's!'

'*Our* failing? We've fought Snagrod's horde alone for the past fifteen months!' He pushed past Royas and stood nose-to-nose with Olivar. 'We put aside our honour. Our dignity. Our traditions. We gave up *everything* to keep our brothers on the Zona Regis alive! What more could we have done? Tell me!'

'Both of you are wrong,' Galleas said in a hard voice. 'Only in death does duty end, brothers. We are far from finished.'

Mitra looked up at Galleas. A faint glimmer of hope had returned to her eyes. 'We're with you, my lord,' she said. 'What can we do?'

'We attack the landing site,' Galleas declared. 'Destroy as much of the munitions as possible, and cripple or destroy the transports.'

Mitra studied the display, a scowl forming on her face. 'How? We're out of rockets, and we lost the heavy stubber during the strafing attack.'

'We still have a crate of melta charges the scavengers found over the winter,' Galleas explained. 'While the greenskins are focused on unloading the transport, we'll approach by stealth, plant the charges, and withdraw.'

Tauros folded his arms. 'It's an obvious target,' he observed. 'Perhaps the most obvious target left at this point. The orks are bound to expect an attack.'

'That is a risk we will have to take,' Galleas said stubbornly.

'To what end, brother?' Amador snapped. 'What will this possibly gain us?'

Galleas felt a flash of anger. 'What if the Navy is here right now, brother? What if they are fighting their way across the system to reach us, even as we speak? What would you give to hold back Snagrod for a single day if it meant the difference between life and death for Rynn's World?'

Amador clenched his fists, but said nothing. Galleas gave a curt nod and continued.

'Gather your squads,' he ordered. 'We march in one hour.'

It was well past midnight by the time the guerrillas reached the landing field. Galleas brought his force around in a wide circle to the east of the field, observing the activity there as the Imperials made their way across rolling hills to approach the target from the south. Even at this late hour, work gangs were loading crates onto trucks for transport to the construction gantries at the tractor works. The guerrillas got into position, settled down into the mud, and waited for the next cargo hauler to arrive.

Hours passed. The Imperials wrapped themselves in their cloaks and shivered. Vega went from one squad to another, checking on the sick and helping in any way he could. Galleas, meanwhile, kept a careful watch on his chronometer. They had to be back inside the city before dawn, or the ork patrols would cut them to pieces.

The veteran sergeant was on the verge of aborting the attack when a faint rumble of thunder rose from the south. Within moments the sound grew until it vibrated through the Space Marine's bones and set the earth to trembling. A smudge of fiery light appeared behind the overcast. Down on the landing field, the orks were shouting orders and running about, clearing a path for the oncoming ship.

The ork cargo hauler wallowed out of the clouds like a drunken grox, its thrusters belching clouds of smoke and flame. Humpbacked and clumsy, the transport plunged towards the landing field and flared its engines at nearly the last moment, settling onto its landing struts with a heavy thud that the guerrillas felt half a kilometre away.

As the cargo hauler's hatch began to open, the ork crews picked themselves up off the ground and closed in on the transport from all directions. While they went to work, Galleas surveyed the field one final time.

The ork ship had landed on the western side of the field, the veteran sergeant noted. Any cargo it carried would be unloaded and added to a scattering of crates at the centre of the field, where some would be placed onto trucks for immediate delivery to the tractor works. The rest would be sorted into a much larger collection of crates at the field's north-east corner. Galleas suspected those contained ammunition for the gargants' heavy weapon systems.

The veteran sergeant spoke over the vox. 'Tauros, Juno and Olivar, place your charges on the crates to the north-east. Valentus, Amador and I will take the cargo hauler. Royas, you go with Tauros.'

'What about those low structures along the eastern edge of the field?' Tauros asked.

Galleas knew what Tauros was referring to at once. The two rectangular buildings had the look of bunkers, each one perhaps fifty metres long. It was clear that both had been built very recently, but their purpose was unclear. 'Most likely underground storage for fuel or explosives,' Galleas mused. 'If you have charges to spare, destroy them as well.'

'Affirmative.'

The veteran sergeant checked his chronometer. 'Forty-five minutes, twenty seconds until extraction. Move out.'

As one, the squads rose from their hiding places and crept forward, working their way across the dark, rolling terrain towards the field. The orks had set up clusters of blazing work lights, but they were all turned inwards, focusing on the landing sites and leaving pools of deep shadow amongst the stacks of crates. The greenskin work parties were moving at a frantic pace, shoulders bent under their taskmasters' lash. They paid no mind to the forbidding darkness beyond the reach of the lights.

Within minutes, the guerrillas had reached the southern edge of the field. The orks were already at work unloading crates from the cargo hauler's prodigious hold. Galleas signalled to Tauros, Juno and Olivar. The three squads went into action, racing low to the ground towards their objective to the north-east. Then the veteran sergeant turned his attention to the grounded transport.

'Amador, you and I will fix our charges on the crates at the centre of the field,' he murmured over the vox. 'Valentus, you'll take the transport. Place your charge where it will breach the plasma reactor.'

'Understood.'

'Trucks coming from the west,' Royas interjected.

Galleas could hear the grumble of approaching engines, but the vehicles were hidden behind the bulk of the cargo hauler. 'How many?'

'Four,' Royas answered. 'Coming up fast.'

'Most likely coming to pick up a load of crates for the tractor works,' Galleas reasoned. 'Carry on.'

'Affirmative. We're a hundred metres from the objective now.'

Galleas nodded curtly and then waved his squad forward. Valentus and Amador followed, the squads spreading out into a shallow arc as they crept across the landing field. Weapons ready, they kept the stacked crates between them and the work parties as much as possible to hide their movements.

The roar of truck engines grew louder as Galleas dashed across the field. Orks bellowed orders as the vehicles came to a screeching halt just on the other side of the crates. The guerrillas reached the containers and pressed themselves against their grimy, plastek sides, scarcely daring to breathe.

Galleas scanned the stack of crates before him, determining the best place to put his melta charge. A quick check to his left showed that Amador had already fixed his charge in place. Valentus, several metres away, was peering around his stack of crates and gauging the right moment to make a dash for the cargo hauler, just fifteen metres distant.

The veteran sergeant glanced to the right, over the heads of his squad. He could just see the towering stack of crates to the north-east. He couldn't see Tauros and Olivar, but Juno and his squad had broken from cover and were heading to the nearest of the two low structures off to the east.

Galleas checked his chronometer. Eighteen minutes left. Satisfied, he reached back for the melta charge hanging beneath his power pack.

A chorus of guttural shouts rent the night air from the direction Juno had gone, followed by a furious exchange of gunfire.

Galleas felt his blood turn to ice. The melta charge forgotten, he looked back to the east and saw Juno and half his squad falling back from a mob of axe-wielding orks. The greenskins were erupting from the two low buildings that Galleas had taken for warehouses. *Not warehouses,* the veteran sergeant thought savagely. *Barracks.* The orks had set up a garrison to cover the landing field in case of attack.

Bedlam erupted across the field. Tauros and Olivar opened fire on the orks that had suddenly appeared on their flank. The charging xenos caught up with Juno and his squad, and a wild melee broke out. On the far side of the crates, the orks unloading the cargo hauler shouted in fury and went for their guns, while the trucks' engines roared back into life. And then, without warning, there were greenskins charging down the aisles between the crates and into the midst of Galleas' squad.

Mitra shouted a warning and shot an ork point-blank, blowing the xenos off its feet. Galleas shot two more, and then a third lunged in and drove a chisel-pointed blade into the Crimson Fist's chest. The point scraped across his breastplate. Galleas stunned the ork with a blow from his gun, then drew his sword and opened the beast's throat.

Galleas spun on his heel and found Mitra and another guerrilla facing off against an ork armed with a chainaxe. As he watched, the ork caught the guerrilla with a backhand stroke, splitting the screaming Imperial open in a spray of blood and bone. Mitra lunged forward with a shout, driving her sabre into the greenskin's neck, but the xenos hardly appeared to notice. The beast gripped its axe and rounded on Mitra, lips drawing back in a bloody-toothed grin. Galleas shot the ork through the eye and covered Mitra while she yanked her sabre free.

The pounding of heavy guns rose over the screams of battle as the ork trucks roared forward, heading for Tauros' and Olivar's positions to the north-east. Galleas saw streams of tracer fire chewing into the crates as the ork gunners drove the guerrillas into cover. Juno and what was left of his squad were caught out in the open, surrounded by bloodthirsty greenskins. For the moment Juno was getting the better of the xenos, piling ork bodies at his feet, but that would change in moments once the trucks had a clear field of fire.

Galleas set Night's Edge alight and cut down an onrushing ork. Nearby, he could see Enginseer Oros and Field Medic Vega fighting with their backs to the crates, firing at any ork who got near. He watched as two orks pulled another guerrilla off his feet and chopped him to pieces with their cleavers. Mitra shot one of the greenskins in the back, then hacked at the other with her sabre. The ork drove her back with a swipe from his bloody cleaver, then lunged for her with a roar. To the greenskin's surprise, the lieutenant stood her ground, letting the onrushing ork impale itself on her outstretched blade. Human and xenos went down in a tangle of thrashing limbs.

A pair of orks crashed into Galleas. An axe rang against the back of his helmet, followed by a blow from a cleaver just above his left knee. The veteran sergeant spun, slicing one ork's head from its shoulders. The second greenskin recoiled with a shout, and Galleas shot the beast in the face. As the ork fell, Valentus called over the vox.

'We're going after the transport! Be ready to move in ten seconds!'

Galleas glanced to his left. Amador and his squad were in the middle of a melee with another ork mob. Beyond them, at the edge of the crates, Valentus and his squad had formed up. As Galleas watched, they broke cover and raced for the cargo hauler.

There was a sudden whine of heavy-duty servos from the ork ship. Galleas felt his hearts clench. He shouted a warning, but the words were lost over the roar of autocannons as the transport's dorsal turret opened fire.

Galleas watched as Valentus and his squad were engulfed in a hail of explosive shells. More than half the squad was torn apart, and Valentus fell, hit in the right arm and the left leg. The stunned survivors were driven back into cover, their armour spattered with gore.

'Valentus!' Galleas cried. He started towards his fallen brother, but a trio of orks blocked his path, chopping at him with their axes.

Amador ripped his combat knife from the front of a dead ork's skull and spun at the sound of Valentus' name. Incredibly, two of the Space Marine's surviving squad mates had leapt back into the line of fire to try to drag Valentus to safety. Another burst from the cargo hauler's autocannon stitched explosive rounds across the Crimson Fist's breast-plate and cut one of the struggling guerrillas in half.

Galleas watched Amador go very still. He glanced back at the veteran sergeant, and for a moment the two locked eyes. Then Amador wrenched his melta charge free from the crate where it had been placed and broke into a run, disappearing down a nearby aisle in the blink of an eye.

'*See to Valentus*,' Amador told Galleas over the vox. The young hothead's voice was strangely calm. '*I've got the transport.*'

'Amador, wait!' Galleas clubbed an ork with the barrel of his gun, then broke its leg with a savage kick to the knee. As the beast fell, he pumped two rounds into its knobby skull. An axe crashed into the side of his helmet, sending static coursing across his display. The veteran sergeant shoulder-checked the xenos and spilled its guts with a sweep of his blade. The third ork fell back, its courage wavering, and Galleas emptied his gun into the greenskin's chest.

By then, it was too late. Galleas heard the turret servos whine as Amador leapt from the far end of the aisle and charged at the cargo hauler. The autocannons opened up, blowing a line of craters across the field as the weapon swept towards the onrushing Space Marine.

Galleas leapt for Valentus. He passed Vila and the rest of Amador's squad in a blur of motion, and broke cover just as Amador reached the shadow of the transport. The veteran Space Marine stumbled as an autocannon shell smashed into his left shoulder. A mob of orks on the cargo ramp were firing as well, battering Amador's midnight-blue armour with a hail of slugs.

The autocannon turret twitched a fraction of a degree to

the right, anticipating Amador's next move. But instead of running for the cargo hauler's reactor grating, he dodged in the opposite direction, charging at full tilt up the cargo ramp into the packed hold. The orks at the top of the ramp shouted in terror and started to run, but it was already too late.

Galleas seized Valentus by the back of his gorget and hauled him into cover. 'Everybody down!' he shouted, throwing himself to the ground.

The explosion shook the earth like a hammer blow, ripping the guts out of the transport and spewing a cone of flame and shrapnel for a hundred and fifty metres through the open cargo hatch. The concussion hurled heavy crates through the air like toy blocks, touching off secondary explosions as they slammed into the ground.

Galleas struggled to his feet. The cargo hauler was burning fiercely, and the stacked crates had been scattered the length and breadth of the landing field. The surviving guerrillas were struggling to rise, their faces blackened and their armour smouldering from the blast. The orks were in even worse shape, given that they had been standing when the explosion occurred. But even now, Galleas could hear the distant snarl of engines from the tractor works as more greenskins rushed to join the fray.

A few shots rang out across the landing field, and more shouting could be heard to the north, but it sounded like the surviving orks were falling back to regroup. 'Tauros!' Galleas called over the vox. 'Report!'

'Here, brother. What happened to Amador? Did he–'

'He did,' Galleas answered through gritted teeth. *Another of us gone forever,* he thought bitterly, then pushed the thought away. 'What is your status?'

'*Looks like Juno and his squad caught the worst of it. We've got three dead and another four injured. The charges were set, but Dorn alone knows where they are now.*'

Galleas got his arms under Valentus and hauled him to his feet. 'Did any of those ork trucks survive the blast?'

'*One looks fairly undamaged.*'

'Secure it. We're getting out of here.'

Valentus stirred weakly in Galleas' grasp. '*I'm fine… brother. Let me go. I… can walk…*'

'Your left knee's gone, and your arm's in tatters,' the veteran sergeant growled. 'I doubt you can crawl, let alone walk.'

Vega was up and moving, checking on the walking wounded. Enginseer Oros came running when he saw Valentus. Muttering a prayer to the Omnissiah, he deployed his servo arm and gripped the Space Marine's power pack, taking most of the weight off Galleas.

Mitra had kicked free of the greenskin's corpse and was rising to her feet. Blood coursed down her cheek from a gash across her forehead. She wiped it away with the back of her hand. 'Wh-what now?' she asked, a little shakily.

'Get everyone moving and follow me,' Galleas ordered. 'Vega! See to the lieutenant!'

The veteran sergeant lurched between tumbled piles of crates into the centre of the field. Greenskin bodies were strewn everywhere, shredded by the blast. Two of the huge ork trucks had been flipped over, and a third was engulfed in flames. Even the two bunkers at the far end of the field were on fire. Between them and the trucks were heaps of xenos corpses. There had been perhaps as many as two hundred greenskins waiting in the barracks for the guerrillas to try an attack. Once again, Snagrod seemed to be one step ahead of them.

But the Arch-Arsonist hadn't counted on the reckless courage of Claudio Amador, veteran brother of the Crimson Fists.

Tauros' and Olivar's squads were already aboard the surviving truck, dragging the bodies of dead orks to the rear and dumping them over the tailgate. Juno and the three survivors of his squad were picking their way across the field of bodies towards them. Corporal Ismail dogged the towering Space Marine like a shadow, her gore-stained knife still clenched in her hand. Her face and chest were splashed with greenskin blood, and she had a devil's smile on her delicate face.

Galleas helped Valentus board the truck, and then waited until the last of the guerrillas had climbed into the troop compartment. Less than a third remained, gaunt and hungry and wounded to one degree or another.

The veteran sergeant turned and surveyed the destruction they'd wrought. Amador's angry words came back to him. *What will this possibly gain us?*

'One more day,' Galleas said softly, raising Night's Edge before the pyre of his fallen brother. Then he turned his back on the flames and climbed aboard the truck.

'Onward,' he said in a leaden voice.

They reached the city's outer wall just at the break of dawn. Galleas ordered the guerrillas to abandon the truck, and they headed into the ruins on foot. Taking a calculated risk, he made for the nearest tunnel access and got the survivors below ground before the greenskin hunting parties were out combing the streets in force.

Nevertheless, the march through the tunnels was painfully slow and fraught with danger at every turn. Many times Galleas and his brothers caught the distant sounds of movement and the rumble of greenskin voices echoing through the tunnels. It was only thanks to the Space Marines' enhanced senses and their superior knowledge of the tunnel network that they were able to slip past the hunters at all.

It was almost ten hours later when Galleas found himself at the entrance to the base's commons area. At once, the veteran sergeant could sense that something was wrong.

Master Bergand rose from his bedroll and picked his way nervously across the commons area towards him. 'You can't blame me!' he blurted, wringing his hands. 'I tried to stop them, but they wouldn't listen!'

Galleas scowled at the void trader. Around them, tired and wounded guerrillas staggered silently into the room. Vega, his face pale and eyes sunken with fatigue, started organising the civilians to set up a makeshift aid station in one corner of the room.

'Tried to stop whom, Master Bergand?' the veteran sergeant growled.

Bergand came to a stop and took a deep breath, collecting himself. 'The children. Patrik and Annaliese. They slipped out last night, after you left. No one knew they were gone until morning. When their mother found out, she became very upset and went after them. Gomez went with her.'

Galleas bit back a curse. 'How long?'

'It's been hours, my lord. I told Daniella not to go–'

'Corporal Ismail!'

Across the commons area, Ismail pushed herself to her feet and limped over to Galleas. The explosion at the landing field had blistered the skin on the left side of her face and singed much of her short hair. 'My lord?'

'You were with Daniella's children yesterday. Did they say anything to you about going out looking for food?'

Ismail sighed and tried to concentrate through a haze of exhaustion. 'The boy, Patrik, said something about ration packs. I don't remember exactly what. Annaliese seemed to know what he was talking about.' She frowned. 'The girl might have mentioned Zona Twenty-eight, but I can't be sure.'

Galleas checked the ammo load on his ork gun. 'Juno! Olivar! On me!'

Mitra stepped up beside Galleas. 'I'll go with you,' she said, shouldering her weapon.

'No,' Galleas said flatly. 'We'll have to move fast, and you won't be able to keep up. Stay here.'

The veteran sergeant spun on his heel and raced from the commons room, his brothers silently falling into step behind him. His mind was already rushing ahead, planning out the fastest route from the hideout to Zona Twenty-eight.

It was possible the children could have avoided the ork hunting parties all this time. It was even possible their mother and Preacher Gomez could have found them and brought them into hiding until darkness, when it would be safer to head back to the tunnels.

Galleas hastened through the darkened tunnels and refused to consider the other possibilities.

The Crimson Fists emerged from a maintenance access at the bottom of a ruined hab unit near the centre of Zona Twenty-eight. By the time they made their way to ground level, Galleas could hear the rough laughter of orks in the distance and knew that they were too late.

He led his brothers further up into the ruined building,

climbing from one treacherous floor to another until they found themselves a full six storeys above ground. From there they had a commanding view of the gruesome spectacle playing out in a stretch of burned-out parkland just a few hundred metres away.

There were at least two hundred greenskins in the park, laughing and jeering and jostling one another to get a better view of the captives. They formed a turbulent circle around a scorched marble dais where Gomez, Daniella and her children had been tied to jagged girders and tormented. They still lived, Galleas saw, but were clearly hurt and scared.

As he watched, a pair of leering orks unwrapped the wire loops around Preacher Gomez's bleeding wrists and let him fall onto the polished stone. Laughing, they grabbed him by his tattered robes and dragged him like a sack of meal to the edge of the dais, where he lay almost within reach of the howling mob.

A massive figure was pacing across the dais behind the dangling captives. As the orks dropped Gomez and stepped away, the beast emerged into view. The ork was huge even by greenskin standards, owing much of its bulk to a massive exoskeleton covered in salvaged armour plate. One of the ork's arms had been replaced by a savage-looking pneumatic claw, and its lower jaw was nothing more than a curved slab of deck plate with a wicked set of sharpened iron teeth. What remained of the beast's face was a mass of scar tissue and misshapen bone, but Galleas recognised it at once.

Rottshrek.

The warboss stared down at Gomez, beady eyes glittering with madness and hate. It said something to Gomez.

Galleas could not make out the words, but the meaning was clear. Rottshrek was toying with the Imperial, savouring his fear and pain.

Gomez shuddered. With an effort, the priest slowly, painfully pushed himself to his feet. Ignoring the shouts and laughter assailing him from all sides, he turned to Daniella and the children and raised a trembling hand in benediction as Rottshrek brought up his combi-weapon and bathed Gomez in flame. The priest staggered across the dais, arms flailing, until he finally collapsed a few metres away.

The orks continued to laugh and shout, demanding more. Rottshrek laughed along with them, glancing back at the remaining captives. The warboss bellowed a question at Daniella and the children. When they didn't answer, Rottshrek gestured, and the warboss' retainers went to fetch young Annaliese.

Olivar whirled and made to head for the stairs, but Galleas seized him by the arm. 'Where do you think you're going?'

'You expect me to stand here and watch them suffer?' Olivar's voice was choked with emotion. 'By Dorn, we've got to do something!'

'That's just what Rottshrek wants,' Galleas said, struggling to keep his own emotions in check. 'It's a trap, brother. Can't you see? They refused to give up the location of the base, so Rottshrek is trying to draw us out instead!'

'Let go of me, brother, or I swear–'

The gunshots rang out in the space of a single second, so close together that the sounds nearly overlapped one another. Galleas turned. Down on the dais, Daniella and her children were free from their tormentors at last.

Titus Juno lowered the ork gun from his shoulder. Without a word, he brushed past his brothers and disappeared down the stairs.

CHAPTER TWENTY

THE LAST FULL MEASURE

ZONA 9 RESIDENTIA, NEW RYNN CITY
DAY 497

Enginseer Oros peered into the ruin of Valentus' augmetic arm and sighed, shaking his head. 'I can save either the arm or the leg,' he said sheepishly. 'I am sorry, my lord. If my skills were greater, or I had more resources...'

The Crimson Fists were gathered in their sanctum, waiting on the verdict from the tech-priest. Valentus lay on the floor of his cell, his mangled augmetics leaking fluids onto the ferrocrete slab. His death's-head face was inscrutable, but his synthesised voice was light.

'A difficult decision, enginseer. An arm to fight with, or a leg to walk on?' He raised his head slightly and addressed his brothers outside the cell. *'Perhaps Tauros and Royas can build me a palanquin, and carry me into battle as my station deserves?'*

'Best check that polished dome of his for dents,' Royas shot back. 'Sounds like brain damage to me.'

'Then perhaps good brother Juno will let me ride upon his shoulders?'

Juno pretended not to hear. He sat cross-legged on the far side of the sanctum, methodically cleaning his wargear. The veteran Space Marine had been quiet and withdrawn since returning from Zona Twenty-eight.

After a moment, Valentus lowered his head and stared up at the grimy ceiling. *'It wouldn't do for a warrior of the Adeptus Astartes to crawl into battle like a crippled bug,'* he said in a more sombre tone. *'Do what you can for the leg, enginseer. I'll fight the enemies of the Imperium single-handedly if I must.'*

Oros made the sign of the Omnissiah and returned to his table for tools. After he had gone, Valentus looked up at Galleas. *'The day we gained at the landing field is almost done,'* he observed.

A day our brother bought with his life, Galleas thought. The bloody battle at the landing field and the deaths of Daniella and the children had left him in a bleak mood. The atmosphere in the dank little hideout was rank with misery, and worse, a sense of defeat.

Valentus felt it too. All of them did. He regarded the veteran sergeant gravely. *'We must decide what to do with the time we have left.'*

Galleas nodded. 'I know, brother.'

In fact, he had thought of little else since Amador had died. The answer to the question was obvious, but it was a step that Galleas found surprisingly difficult to take.

He turned to find the rest of his brothers staring at him expectantly. They knew the answer too. All that remained was to hear him say it.

'There will be a briefing at midnight,' he told them. 'Until then, see to your meditations. Remember the fallen, and prepare yourself for what is to come.'

* * *

The hours passed all too swiftly. Galleas knelt on the floor of his cell, Night's Edge held before him, holding vigil for Amador and all those who had gone before him. But the solemn ceremony did nothing to ease his turbulent spirit. The contemplation of sacrifice and death left him more troubled than before.

His focus guttered like a candle flame, and his mind began to wander. Outside the sanctum, one of the injured guerrillas moaned softly in his sleep. Another shifted weakly on her bedroll and let out a wet, wracking cough.

Closer, Galleas could hear the patient hum of his brothers' power armour as they pursued their meditations. Rising faintly above the sound, just loud enough to be heard, was a single, murmuring voice. The veteran sergeant listened for a time, trying to make out the words. Finally he sheathed his sword and rose to seek out their source.

Brother Olivar sat on the floor of his cell, facing the rough, ferrocrete wall. He had set aside his helmet and was reading aloud from a tiny, battered tome resting in his gauntleted hand.

'I didn't know you carried a copy of the *Lectitio Divinitatus,*' Galleas said quietly.

Olivar glanced over his shoulder at Galleas, then gently closed the book and set it aside. 'It belonged to Preacher Gomez,' he said. 'I found it here in my cell. He must have left it before he went out with Daniella.' He sighed. 'I suppose he trusted me to keep it safe until he returned.'

'Or he didn't expect to return at all.'

The one-eyed Space Marine nodded gravely. 'Perhaps so.'

'He was a brave man.'

Olivar shook his head. 'He was a fool. A wide-eyed,

bombastic fool. But,' he added grudgingly, 'his faith in the Emperor was strong. I'll grant him that.'

Galleas stepped inside the narrow cell and sat beside Olivar. 'I was thinking of Amador just now,' he said. 'Hardly the Hero's Vigil I'm sure he dreamt of, with his name scribed in the Annals and his wargear resting in state inside the Great Chapel.'

Olivar nodded solemnly. 'We remember his sacrifice. It will have to be enough.'

'And who will remember us when we are gone?'

Brother Olivar shifted his armoured bulk around until he faced Galleas. His ruined eye socket was a pool of shadow, depthless and forbidding.

'The Emperor will know,' Olivar assured him. 'He sees all that transpires within His holy light. The *Lectitio Divinitatus* tells us so.'

Galleas considered this and nodded. 'It will have to be enough.'

At five minutes to midnight, Galleas woke Enginseer Oros and sent him to fetch Lieutenant Mitra and Sergeant Kazimir. Then he went to join his brothers, who were already waiting in the sanctum's commons area.

The humans arrived within minutes. Neither Mitra nor Kazimir looked as though they'd slept a single moment since returning from the landing field. From the looks on their haggard faces it was clear they had been expecting a summons at any time.

Galleas regarded each of his brothers in turn. They understood as well as he did what had to come next.

'The raid on the landing field inflicted considerable damage,' the veteran sergeant began, 'but at most it gained us a single day. I expect more weapons and supplies have already been ferried down from orbit and are in the process of being fitted to Snagrod's war machines.' He stared down at the outlines of the tractor complex glowing on the display table. 'We have a day, perhaps two, before the gargants are fully operational.'

He drew a deep breath. 'We have only one course of action left. An attack on the complex's power plant.'

Galleas nodded to Oros. The display expanded, zooming in on the reactor building at the centre of the tractor works. It was a stepped, hexagonal structure forty metres across, topped by a dome of double-reinforced ferrocrete nearly four storeys high. A rank of squat, hourglass-shaped cooling towers behind the plant sent thick columns of steam hundreds of metres into the air.

'Our tactical options are limited. The plant is a high-security facility, with a single entrance sealed by interlocking blast doors. We will be forced to carry out a frontal attack, depending on speed and shock effect to penetrate the greenskin defences. Upon reaching the blast doors, we will use our remaining melta charges to create a breach, then fight our way inside to the reactor control room.'

The veteran sergeant folded his arms. 'Upon reaching the control room, we will cause an overload and then keep the orks away from the controls until the reactor goes critical. The resulting explosion should level the complex and destroy or severely damage the gargants.'

Kazimir rubbed his stubbled chin. 'What do we know about the defences?' he asked hoarsely.

Galleas indicated the plant's entrance. 'We know the orks have set up heavy guns on the level overlooking the doors, and there is a mob of greenskins standing watch outside at any given time. Once the shooting starts, however, it is certain to draw the attention of every ork in the complex. There will be hundreds more surrounding the plant within minutes.'

Kazimir sighed. 'And inside?'

'Given the danger posed by the reactor, we can assume that Snagrod has put one of his best lieutenants in charge of its defence. We'll be facing an entire warband, with some of the toughest troops in the Arch-Arsonist's horde.'

Mitra stared up at Galleas. 'You're talking about a suicide mission.'

The veteran sergeant nodded. 'One with only a slim chance of success. Now you understand why I was reluctant to attack it before.'

Tauros shook his head. 'The problem is that the orks will know exactly where we're heading once we breach the doors. They'll head right for the control room and fight us every metre of the way.'

There was a rustle of robes. Enginseer Oros peered over the rim of the display table. 'Then don't go to the control room,' he said.

Royas glowered at the tech-priest. 'How else do you expect us to overload the reactor?'

'I can think of half a dozen ways, off the top of my head,' Oros said archly. 'The simplest would be to disable the primary intercoolers for the magnetic flux couplings. They're in the sublevel below the reactor core.'

Galleas leaned over the display table. 'Once these intercoolers are disabled, how long until the reactor goes critical?'

'A few minutes at most,' the enginseer replied. 'And if the damage is done properly, there will be no undoing it.'

'Can you show us how to disable these intercoolers?'

Oros rose to his feet. 'The process is a delicate one, and requires the attentions of a priest,' he said with as much dignity as he could manage. 'I shall have to accompany you and perform the work myself.'

Tauros gave Galleas a sidelong glance. 'While the orks run to defend the control room, we go to the sublevel instead. That just might work.'

The veteran sergeant considered the tactical ramifications of the plan and nodded in agreement. 'We'll make our way into the complex using the truck we stole from the landing field. If we strike early in the morning, while the daily patrols are heading out, we might make it all the way to the plant before we're challenged.'

Mitra and Kazimir exchanged glances. 'When do we depart?' Mitra asked Galleas.

The veteran sergeant waved the question away. 'This is a matter for me and my brothers,' he said gravely. 'You and the others will remain here and guard the civilians.'

Spots of colour darkened Mitra's pale cheeks. She drew herself ramrod-straight and glared up at the Crimson Fists. 'The hell we will. Our world hangs in the balance, my lord. We're your shieldbearers, and we'll be damned if you leave us behind.'

Galleas sighed. 'Very well, lieutenant. If you insist on sharing our fate, I won't try to stop you. But I want volunteers only, and Vega will remain behind to tend to the sick and injured. Understood?'

'Understood, my lord. Thank you.'

The veteran sergeant gestured to Oros, and the display table darkened for the last time.

'We leave in four hours,' Galleas said with grim finality.

'Brothers, make ready your boltguns. We'll go to our last battle armed with the weapons of our sacred Chapter, in the name of Dorn and the God-Emperor of Mankind.'

CHAPTER TWENTY-ONE

NECESSARY SACRIFICES

RYNNLAND TRACTOR WORKS, NEW RYNN CITY
DAY 498

At the appointed hour, Galleas completed his Rites of Maintenance. With solemn ceremony he hefted the fully loaded drum and locked it into the boltgun's magazine well, then cycled the sacred weapon's action. Telltales on his helmet display blinked from red to green, and a grim sort of peace stole over him.

He could hear his brothers gathering in the sanctum's commons area. All was in readiness. Galleas adjusted the bolt pistol at his hip and made certain his sword was locked in its scabbard. Reflexively his fingertips brushed across his breastplate and pauldrons, checking the positioning of his battle honours, only to remember that they had long since been torn away. All he found were battle scars, etched deep into the ceramite plate.

Master Bergand was waiting outside the entrance to the sanctum when Galleas emerged from his cell. The offworlder rushed to the Space Marine's side, wringing his hands nervously.

'I beg you, my lord, please don't do this,' Bergand entreated in a low voice. 'Think of the men, women and children you are leaving behind! What will become of us after you're gone?'

'If we do not act, the Zona Regis will fall, Master Bergand, and the Crimson Fists will be no more.'

'But there's no guarantee the mission will even succeed!' Bergand protested. 'Would… would it not be better to try to reach the Zona Regis and warn them of the impending danger?'

Galleas scowled at him. 'They already know, Master Bergand. They've known for months. I expect Snagrod went to special effort to make certain that my brothers at the citadel could see what was being built at the tractor works.'

The void trader's tone grew more desperate. He gripped Galleas' broad forearm. 'Listen to me! The food's almost gone. There's no medicine. How will we survive?'

The veteran sergeant gave Bergand a forbidding glare. 'If we succeed, Master Bergand, the orks will have lost their best chance at breaking the siege. It will take months to rebuild the gargants, if they can be rebuilt at all. And Snagrod knows the Navy is coming, even if you do not.' Galleas pulled his arm from Bergand's grip, nearly yanking the man off his feet. 'Have faith, Master Bergand. If not in the Emperor, then in those who fight in His name.'

Galleas beckoned to his brothers. Bergand was forced to shrink aside as the Crimson Fists marched to war.

Lieutenant Mitra, Sergeant Kazimir, and Field Medic Vega were waiting in the commons area. Almost the entire surviving force – twelve guerrillas, including Corporal Ismail – stood with them.

Mitra straightened as Galleas approached. 'Corporal Vila and four of his cronies declined to volunteer,' she said, disdain evident on her face.

Royas snorted in disgust. 'Lucky for them Amador is gone. He'd have likely killed them all out of shame.'

Vega stepped forward. 'My lord, I must protest–' he began, only to succumb to a series of wracking coughs. His fist trembled as he pressed it to his mouth, and a sheen of sweat glistened on his cheeks and forehead.

Galleas placed a hand on Vega's shoulder, gripping him firmly until the coughing spell had passed. 'This is no reflection on your courage,' he said. 'Remain here, where you can still fulfil your oath and serve the Emperor. Your skills would be wasted on the likes of us.'

Vega took a shuddering breath and managed a reluctant nod. 'What will we do once you're gone?' he said, his voice little more than a whisper.

'If we succeed, there will be chaos in the greenskins' ranks,' Galleas replied. 'Snagrod will have suffered a tremendous blow, and will find himself struggling to control his horde. The orks might withdraw from the city, or they may even depart the planet entirely. Watch for an opportunity to reach the riverbank and join the survivors at the Zona Regis.'

Galleas paused. 'If we fail, then the Zona Regis is doomed. The gargants will bring down the citadel's void shields and the orks will sweep over the island like a tidal wave, destroying everything in their path. Find a way out of the city while the horde is preoccupied. Head for the mountains to the west. There are deep caves there, some with ample sources of water. With spring coming on, you could last for weeks. Long enough, perhaps, for the Navy to arrive.'

Vega turned his weary gaze to the huddled forms sleeping across the commons area. His expression was bleak. 'I don't know how many would survive such a journey.'

Galleas nodded grimly. 'Such is war. Do your utmost. Remember your oaths. The rest is in the hands of the Emperor.'

Mitra and the rest of the volunteers fell into step with the Crimson Fists as they picked their way across the crowded commons area. Most of the civilians were asleep. A few, tormented by sickness or hunger pangs, huddled on their filthy bedrolls and watched dazedly as the raiders went past. Vila and his squad mates had gone to the far opposite corner of the room, as far from their fellow guerrillas as they could get. Vila himself was already asleep, his face turned to the wall. The others formed a miserable knot beside the corporal, heads down and shoulders hunched, and wouldn't meet their former comrades' eyes.

Tomas Zapeta was sitting in his customary place as Galleas slipped past the partition and made for the base's exit. The gloomy old man was fast asleep, leaning upon his stool at a precarious angle, as though he might topple onto the ferrocrete at any moment. He clutched his blanket tightly around his chest with one claw-like hand, and his breath came in a bubbling wheeze.

The veteran sergeant loomed over Zapeta. The old man stirred faintly, lost in the depths of a dream. The ghost of a smile crossed his seamed face.

The guerrillas exchanged glances. One by one they filed silently from the room, fingertips brushing lightly against the old man's shoulder in a wordless farewell.

* * *

Hours later, the guerrillas emerged from the tunnels and made for the gap in the outer wall. Both moons had set, and the sky to the east was just starting to pale with the first light of dawn. The early morning air was silent and eerily still, as though the whole world was holding its breath, dreading what was to come.

They crossed the outer wall without incident, and in less than half an hour they had reached the burned-out warehouse where they'd abandoned the ork truck just twenty-four hours before. Galleas put Royas behind the wheel and Tauros on the twin mount, while the rest found places in the vehicle's troop compartment. Belching clouds of petrochem smoke, the truck rumbled out into the early-morning light and gathered speed, making its way cross-country towards the waiting tractor works.

As the truck bounced over the rough ground the guerrillas were quiet and withdrawn, each one preparing for what was to come in their own way. Corporal Ismail sat next to Juno, holding her necklace of trophies in her hands and fingering the yellowed tusks as though they were prayer beads. Enginseer Oros busied himself by making a last-minute inspection of repairs to Valentus' augmetic leg, and the crudely welded stump of his arm. Sergeant Kazimir had separated himself from the others and sat at the rear of the troop compartment, where he could look back at the ruined city receding in the distance. The faint glow of an antique silver holo-locket shone in the palm of one calloused hand. From time to time he would stare wistfully into its depths.

Lieutenant Mitra leaned against the side of the troop compartment next to Galleas, squinting through the dirty clouds of exhaust at the complex up ahead. 'The greenskins in the outer forts are bound to stop us long before we hit their perimeter,' she observed.

'Perhaps,' Galleas allowed. 'Perhaps not. An ork's hyper-aggressive nature makes it poorly suited for defensive war-fare. That's why their perimeter has so many holes – the idea of keeping an enemy at bay is anathema to them. Remember that the forts' primary purpose is more to keep the big warbands apart than to keep anyone out of the complex. On a subconscious level, the greenskins would rather invite an enemy to attack, then surround him and destroy him. If we move quickly enough, we will be inside the power plant before they can muster such a response. Then it will just be a matter of holding them off until our mission is complete.'

She turned, giving him a searching look. 'Is this easy for you?'

Galleas frowned. 'I didn't say this would be easy. The tactical constraints–'

Mitra gave him an exasperated look. 'That's not what I'm talking about. Don't you fear death?'

The veteran sergeant straightened. 'The Adeptus Astartes know no fear,' he said proudly. 'Least of all the sons of Rogal Dorn.'

'How do you do it?'

Galleas considered the question. 'It is simply how we are made,' he said at last. 'I told you the story of how I earned my place in the Chapter. From the moment we embark on this path, death is our constant companion. It is never a matter of *if* we will die in service to the Chapter – only *how.*' He glanced up at the brightening sky. After many days, the overcast had finally parted, revealing a vault of deep blue that was nearly the colour of the armour he wore.

'Death is a simple matter, lieutenant. It is duty that sometimes weighs heavily on our souls.'

Tauros, up in the cupola, growled a warning. 'We're fifteen hundred metres from the outer perimeter.'

Galleas calculated speed and distance to the objective. 'Five minutes,' he called to the guerrillas. 'Everyone get behind cover.'

Mitra ducked down into the troop compartment and the rest of the humans pressed themselves against the truck's thinly armoured flanks. The Space Marines slumped their shoulders and hunched over, trusting to the plumes of exhaust and the speed of their passing to disguise any details of their appearance.

Three minutes, twenty seconds later they had crossed the outer perimeter and were passing between the greenskin forts covering the north-west quadrant of the complex. Galleas glanced up at Tauros. 'How does it look?'

Tauros had lowered himself as far as possible into the cupola, until only the top of his helmet was visible as he peered over the twin mount. 'No challenge from the forts,' he reported. 'There's heightened activity around the gantries. Huge numbers of orks are clustering around the feet of the gargants.'

'That can't be good,' Mitra said grimly.

A few seconds later, Galleas could hear the greenskins over the roar of the truck's engine. The air shook with the thunder of thousands of xenos voices, baying for human blood. Time was running out.

'Royas, increase speed,' Galleas said over the vox.

At once, the greenskin vehicle growled and leapt forward, tyres crunchling on the broken tarmac. Galleas resisted the urge to look up at the nearest gargant as they sped past.

Then they were in the shadow of the main factory building, and the power plant was coming up fast.

'Tauros?' Galleas inquired.

'I count fifteen orks with heavy weapons outside the plant's entrance,' Tauros reported. 'Another eight, perhaps ten, in the gun positions above.'

'Have they seen us?'

Up ahead, a heavy automatic weapon ripped off a stuttering burst, spewing a fan of tracers a few metres over the top of the oncoming truck.

'It seems likely.'

Galleas reached for a pair of grenades at his belt. 'Target the gun positions,' he told Tauros. 'We'll deal with the orks on the ground.'

'Understood.'

Galleas held one of the grenades out to Mitra. 'For your father,' he said solemnly.

The lieutenant's gaunt face tightened. She nodded. 'For your brothers,' she said, accepting the weapon.

Tauros opened fire, raking the ork gun positions with the twin mount. Galleas surged to his feet. 'For Dorn and the Emperor!' he shouted, priming the grenade and flinging it at the bellowing ork mob in their path. The greenskins opened fire at the same moment, unleashing a storm of heavy slugs from their shoulder-mounted guns.

'*Death to the xenos!*' the Crimson Fists answered, and the battle for the power plant began.

The truck shuddered and rang as ork slugs glanced from its armoured front and sides. A few struck where the plating was thinner and punched through, buzzing like hornets through the cab and troop compartment. Juno grunted as a slug hit him full in the breastplate, leaving a dent in the battered aquila on his chest. The impact rocked him slightly as he rose, throwing a grenade of his own and then vaulting over the side of the still-moving truck. Olivar was right behind him, boltgun thundering, his stentorian voice intoning the Litanies of Hate.

Twin blasts tore through the ork ranks, felling a pair of greenskins. The rest scattered left and right, still firing at the oncoming truck. The power plant was less than fifty metres away now; Tauros was still sweeping the gun positions over the main entrance, killing the orks manning the guns and forcing the rest into cover. The plant's heavy blast doors, as thick as any to be found on a Navy battleship, were sealed up tight.

Royas plunged into the midst of the ork mob and slammed on the brakes, kicking up a shower of dirt to either side of the truck. Galleas anticipated the move, bracing against the sudden deceleration and dropping one of the greenskins with a shot to the head. As the truck was still skidding to a stop the veteran sergeant vaulted over the side into the enemy's midst.

An ork less than two metres away swung to face Galleas. Before the muzzle of its shoulder-mounted gun could be brought to bear, he shot the xenos in the neck. Night's Edge blazed as he drew it from its scabbard and sliced through a greenskin's chest.

Slugs tore past the Space Marine as Mitra and the others joined the battle. A grenade went off on the far side of the truck, and gunfire drew more screams from the surprised orks. Valentus leapt from the back of the troop compartment, landing heavily, with Oros and another guerrilla behind him. Royas struggled from the truck's bullet-riddled cab, shooting an ork that had fallen back towards the power plant's entrance.

Juno and Olivar charged into the midst of the greenskins, wreaking bloody havoc with their blades. Galleas turned to Mitra and pointed to the gun positions over the entrance. The lieutenant understood his meaning at once, pulling the pin on her grenade. She took two quick steps and flung it end-over-end, up and over the orks' makeshift barricades. A panicked greenskin lurched out of cover, gripping the sputtering bomb, but before the xenos could throw it back Galleas shot the beast through the eye. The blast followed half a second later, silencing the surviving gun teams.

The ork gunners on the ground were falling back, over-whelmed by the ferocity of the Space Marines' assault. The air rang with distant shouts, but Galleas could see no imme-diate signs that more xenos were on their way. He levelled his blade at the entrance. 'Royas! Tauros! Prepare to breach!'

Royas reached the heavy doors first, pulling a melta charge from his back and clamping it to the door. Tauros was next, then Galleas himself. As the rest of the raiders took positions to either side of the entrance, the veteran sergeant affixed the last of their charges and tapped its acti-vation rune. Stepping to one side, he readied his weapons. 'Three! Two! One! Breach!'

Galleas triggered a rune on his helmet display and the world dissolved in a flash of white light.

The concussion was deafening. Galleas felt the foundation of the power plant tremble under the triple blast. When his helmet's vision returned, the building's entrance was hidden behind a cloud of grey smoke, and the air was shimmering with heat.

'Move!' Galleas ordered, switching to thermal vision and ducking into the cloud.

The melta charges had blown an opening two and a half

metres high and a metre and a half wide though the blast
doors. Galleas ducked beneath the still-molten upper edge
of the breach and into the midst of a charnel house. Beyond
the blast doors was a wide entry hall almost ten metres in
length. A moment before, it had been packed with orks,
eager to come to grips with the enemy on the other side.
They had taken the full force of the melta bombs and the
superheated fragments carved from the blast doors, leaving
behind heaps of charred flesh and twisted wargear stretching two-thirds of the way down the hall.

Residual heat from the blast interfered with the thermal
display, but Galleas could still make out the hulking shapes
of more greenskins gathering at the far end of the hall.
He charged forward, crushing the grisly remains of dead
orks beneath his boots. His boltgun blazed, sowing death
amongst the xenos. The greenskins bellowed in rage and
rushed to meet him, plunging blindly through the smoke.

Galleas greeted the orks with fire and sword, shooting two
of the xenos point-blank, then ducking the cleaver of a third
before slicing the greenskin in two. The rest crashed against
the veteran sergeant like a wave, pressing him from three
sides and hacking at him with their crude blades. Hatchets
and saw-edged knives grated against the curved plates of
his armour, seeking a weak spot where they could tear into
the flesh beneath. The Crimson Fist fought back blow for
blow, his power sword severing arms and splitting skulls.

Still, the pressure mounted as the greenskins threw
the full weight of the mob against him. An ork drove a
chisel-pointed knife into a crack in his breastplate, touching off warning runes in Galleas' helmet display. He blew
off the ork's right kneecap with his bolter and opened its
throat with his sword as it fell.

And then Tauros and Royas were beside him, firing into the mob and stabbing the xenos with their knives. Kazimir was right behind Tauros, firing his combat shotgun as fast as he could cycle the weapon and scourging the orks with a storm of heavy shot. The mob wavered under the sudden onslaught – and then started to fall back.

Galleas buried his blade in a greenskin's chest. The smoke in the hall was beginning to clear, and beyond the thinning mob he could see an open threshold just five metres away. Beyond that was a smaller mob of orks, clad in garishly ornate heavy armour. The lenses of augmetic rangefinders glowed like baleful eyes in the thinning murk. As the veteran sergeant watched, the mob bared their gilded tusks in evil glee. A fearsome assortment of customised guns glinted in their knobby hands. Before Galleas could shout a warning the hall shook with the roar of automatic weapons.

The ork mob poured fire into the chaotic melee, not much caring who or what they hit. Greenskins fell, riddled by a combination of solid slugs, explosive shells and armour-piercing rounds. The ork in front of Galleas was hit a dozen times. Some of the rounds passed through the greenskin's thick torso and flattened themselves against the veteran sergeant's armour.

As the orks fell, more shots found their way to the embattled Space Marines. A burst of incendiary rounds struck sparks across Galleas' breastplate and left pauldron. An explosive shell cracked against Royas' helmet, forcing him a step back. Then Tauros staggered as a pair of armour-piercing rounds punched two neat holes in the left side of his breastplate.

An ork, maddened by bloodlust and bleeding from numerous bullet wounds, leapt for Galleas. Royas was hit by a burst of greenskin fire, then tackled by another wounded ork. Tauros had sunk to a knee and Kazimir was standing over him, blasting away at the ork firing line with his shotgun.

There was a blur of motion behind the ork line. Galleas caught sight of a lone greenskin lumbering for the far side of the threshold. At once, the veteran sergeant understood – the xenos was trying to reach the controls for an inner set of blast doors! Galleas tried to bring his boltgun to bear, but the ork grappling him forced the edge of a knife underneath his chin and started sawing away at the gorget beneath, spoiling his aim. He staggered a step, trying to bring the point of his blade around to drive it into the greenskin's chest, but the xenos locked a bloodstained hand around his sword wrist.

And then a figure passed between him and Tauros, advancing on the ork firing line. It was Valentus, firing one-handed at the greenskins as he charged for the threshold.

Bolter shells struck the orks, detonating against their heavy armour plates in an arc that swept across the left-hand side of the line. Valentus had seen the danger and was trying to blast his way through the intervening orks to reach the greenskin behind them. Snarling in fury, the orks focused their attention on the advancing Space Marine, savaging him with a torrent of fire.

Galleas roared in wordless rage as Valentus staggered under the barrage. Still, he kept firing, switching his boltgun to three-shot bursts. One of the orks in the firing line toppled as its skull blew apart. Another reeled sideways as a mass-reactive shell found a weak spot in the greenskin's armour and blew a crater out of its shoulder. A fraction of a second later, the lumbering ork crossed into the gap.

Valentus lurched to a halt as an explosive shell struck his already damaged knee and fused the joint. More shells struck his breastplate and pauldrons. Unmoved by the storm, the Crimson Fist took careful aim.

At the opposite end of the line, an ork took a step forward. Bellowing in its foul language, the xenos levelled its customised blaster at Valentus.

Tauros and Kazimir shouted a warning at the same time. Both fired at the blaster-wielding ork, but the greenskin's heavy armour turned aside shot and shell.

'Valentus!' Galleas cried.

The Crimson Fist and the ork fired at the same moment. Both found their mark. Valentus sank slowly to his knees, smoke rising from a hole burned into the side of his polished metal skull, then fell face-first onto the floor.

There was a flicker of adamantine, and the ork grappling with Galleas collapsed, stabbed neatly through the base of the skull. As Juno charged past, the veteran sergeant kicked the greenskin's body aside and cut down the blaster-wielding ork with five rounds from his boltgun.

Royas had despatched his attacker and was rising to his feet, as was Tauros. Juno had already reached the ork firing line and was killing every greenskin he could reach. Consumed with fury, Galleas rushed to join him. He scarcely felt the slugs ringing against his armour as he closed with the orks and the slaughter began.

A heartbeat later, the greenskins were dead. Mitra and the rest of the guerrillas rushed past him, into the chamber past the threshold, firing at a few ork stragglers that were fleeing towards a staircase in the far right corner of the room. Olivar followed a moment later, escorting Enginseer Oros.

Galleas moved to the left, searching for the controls to

the blast door. Valentus had stopped the ork less than a metre from its goal. Another second, two at most, and all would have been lost.

As the veteran sergeant activated the blast doors, his gaze went to Valentus' lifeless form.

'God-Emperor of Mankind, bear witness,' he said softly, remembering what Olivar told him back at the sanctum. 'Remember Brother Valentus, a veteran brother of five hundred years' service. He honoured his oaths, and did not falter when death beckoned. Remember him, when we are no more.'

As the massive doors boomed shut, Galleas joined the surviving raiders. Juno, Royas and Olivar were covering the stairway to the far right, while Oros was working feverishly on an access panel to a sealed door at the far left. Other doors on either side of the room led to ransacked offices and workspaces for the power plant staff. From the stench and the refuse piled in the doorways it was clear the orks had been using them as living quarters for months.

Tauros was standing next to Mitra and Kazimir in the centre of the room. Dark blood streaked the left front of his breastplate.

'Brother?' Galleas inquired.

'I'm fine,' Tauros said tightly. 'It's just a couple of slugs. Nothing to worry about.'

The veteran sergeant scowled at Tauros, but had little choice other than to take him at his word. 'Juno?'

'Lots of shouting from far up the stairwell,' the veteran brother replied. 'Oros says it climbs the inside wall of the dome and leads to the reactor control room. Sounds like the warboss is up there digging in.'

'Good. Enginseer Oros?'

'Almost there!' Oros twitched a mechadendrite and the access panel lit up. The door opened with a grating hiss. 'Got it! The intercooler control node is one level below!'

'Tauros, you're with me,' Galleas said, heading for the door. 'Mitra, you and the others cover Enginseer Oros. Royas, Juno, Olivar, you're rearguard.'

Beyond the door was a narrow spiral stairway, dimly lit by flickering lumen sconces. Almost at once, Galleas heard faint sounds of movement below. Blade and bolter ready, he descended the stairs.

A few moments later, he emerged into a large, rectangular chamber packed with chattering logic engines. A bank of control consoles faced a cage-like wall of steel supports that looked out onto a huge, hexagonal space filled with arcane machinery connected by a complex webwork of pipes. In the centre of it all was the base of the reactor itself, a ring of ceramite supporting a massive, three-storey polyhedral sphere. The deep, almost sub-aural hum of the reactor and its hyperconducting torus reverberated in Galleas' bones.

There was a flash of movement and the bark of gunfire from behind the control consoles, and a trio of slugs dug into the ferrocrete wall to his left. Galleas swept into the room, bolter tracking along the arc of fire, seeking targets. A chorus of panicked shrieks rose above the background note of the reactor, and the veteran sergeant caught sight of a small pack of greenskin runts fleeing through an open doorway and scattering amongst the bulky machines in the reactor chamber.

Tauros had entered the room and taken position just to the left of the stairway. Seeing the runts take flight, he beckoned to Mitra and the others. The guerrillas dashed into the room, crouching low, weapons at the ready. Oros came last. The tech-priest stopped just past the stairs and surveyed the room, his hands unconsciously making the sign of the Omnissiah.

Galleas swept around the far end of the control console and searched the reactor chamber for threats. The runts had plenty of cover to hide behind, and might decide to start shooting again at any time. Through the metal wall of supports he could peer up into the reactor dome and see the stairway that curved along the inner wall until it reached the main control station. About halfway along the stairway was a landing, and there, just out of bolter range, Galleas spied a massive ork and a mob of equally huge greenskins in heavy armour. The ork warboss was leaning against the railing, peering down into the depths of the reactor chamber. Galleas could almost imagine the crude gears turning in the ork's tiny mind.

'Tauros, cover the reactor chamber,' Galleas said. 'Choose your shots carefully. We can't risk damaging anything that might prevent the reactor from going critical. Mitra, you and the others stand by to support the rearguard on the stairs. I estimate we have two to three minutes before the warboss realises where we've gone.' He turned to the enginseer. 'Oros, begin your rites. We'll hold them off as long as we can.'

The tech-priest nodded. After a moment's thought, he crossed to the control console and studied its layout carefully. Then, with a murmured prayer, he leaned forward, resting his hands on the console's metal surface.

There was a whine as the enginseer's servo-arm unfolded. It rose above Oros like a scorpion's tail, its pincer-like clamp opening slightly. Then, with surprising speed, it plunged downwards, punching through the console's front panel and driving deep into the machine's vitals. There was a tortured squeal of metal and the crackle of shorting circuits. Bright, blue sparks reflected in the tech-priest's lenses as the servo-arm slowly withdrew, gripping a metre-long metal cylinder wrapped in copper wire and trailing a pair of severed cables.

Oros straightened, studying the cylinder for a moment, then nodded in satisfaction. The servo-arm's pincer tightened, crushing the sides of the cylinder, until finally it shattered, scattering coils of wire and shards of crystal all over the room.

Galleas and the others stared at Oros as he folded his servo-arm back into place. Smoke began to rise from the innards of the console.

'I thought you said the process was a delicate one,' Galleas said.

Oros hung his cowled head in shame. 'If I'd told you the truth, you would have left me behind,' he said in a small voice.

Krrump.

The floor of the power plant trembled beneath their feet. Galleas took a step towards Oros. 'I thought you said it would take several minutes for the intercoolers to fail.'

'It does! It will!' Oros exclaimed. 'Whatever that was, it wasn't me!'

Krrump. The concussion shook the floor again, like the heavy beat of a drum.

Or the footfall of an angry god.

Krrump.

Galleas felt his blood run cold. 'We're too late,' he said. 'The gargants are on the move.'

CHAPTER TWENTY-TWO

THE MARCH OF THE GARGANTS

RYNNLAND TRACTOR WORKS, NEW RYNN CITY
DAY 498

Mitra paled at the sound of the gargants' tread. 'This can't be happening,' she groaned. 'Not after everything we've done...'

'Can the gargants get away in time?' Kazimir asked, a glint of desperation in the old sergeant's eye.

Galleas gave Oros a hard look. 'How long do we have?'

'Ten minutes before the intercooler matrix fails,' the enginseer said ruefully. 'Maybe a little less.'

The veteran sergeant shook his head. 'Gargants are slow, but they're not *that* slow. They'll be far enough away for their power fields to weather the blast.'

Mitra's face twisted into a snarl. 'I'm not giving up now,' she growled. 'I *can't*. There has to be some way to stop them!'

'The gargants are operational, lieutenant,' Galleas said

flatly. 'At this point, the only thing on Rynn's World that can stop them…'

Galleas' eyes widened.

'…is another gargant.'

His mind raced. 'Sergeant Kazimir! How many explosives were left back at the base?'

Kazimir frowned. 'Enough to bring down half the city. Thanks to the orks, that was the one thing we never lacked.'

'If an exploding reactor won't stop the gargants, what do you expect a few hundred pounds of high explosive to do?' Mitra exclaimed.

Before Galleas could answer, Tauros interjected. 'We've got more pressing concerns at the moment,' he said grimly. 'The warboss is on the move, and he's heading this way.'

The veteran sergeant was already dashing for the staircase. 'We've got two minutes, forty-five seconds to fight our way out of the building,' he snapped, 'or we'll never make it out of the blast zone in time. Let's go!'

Juno, Royas and Olivar were waiting halfway up the curving stair, blocking the path with the bulk of their armoured forms. Olivar, in the back, stared at Galleas in bemusement as the veteran sergeant came bolting up the stairs.

'What's going on?' Olivar demanded. 'The reactor–'

'Change of plans,' Galleas said curtly. 'We've got to stop the warboss before he makes it off the upper stairway. Move!'

The iron tone of command in Galleas' voice spurred the Crimson Fists into action. Juno led the way, taking four steps at a time as he raced up the twisting stairway.

As fast as the Space Marines were, the orks were faster. Juno leapt from the staircase into the path of a mob of howling greenskins heading their way.

Howls and screams rang off the ferrocrete walls, followed by the deafening roar of gunfire. Juno did not hesitate for a single instant, plunging like a thunderbolt into the midst of the mob. His short sword flickered like lightning, and everywhere it touched, an ork fell in a welter of blood. Royas and Olivar plunged into the maelstrom at Juno's back, keeping the greenskins off his flanks with murderous fire from their boltguns. The greenskins reeled from the ferocity of the sudden assault, falling back towards the stairway from whence they came.

A thunderous bellow from beyond the far doorway froze the retreating orks in their tracks. Galleas emerged from the stairway and fired one-handed, sending a boltgun shell past Olivar's shoulder and dropping another of the greenskins. 'Forward!' he roared. 'Don't let them surround us!' Then, as Mitra came up the stairs behind him, he pointed at the blast doors to his right. 'Get those open and get to the truck!'

Mitra's eyes widened. 'But the orks outside–'

'Just do it!'

Without waiting for a reply, Galleas rushed to join his brothers just as the ork warboss came charging into the room.

The greenskin was massive, its stupendous bulk covered in a clanking harness of heavy, armoured plates. Chains strung with desiccated human heads covered the beast's broad chest, and its tusks were tipped with sharpened caps of polished adamantium. The warboss gripped a huge axe in one hand and a belt-fed, twin-barrelled gun in the other. It scattered the hapless orks in its path with a stuttering burst, and then plunged into the midst of the Space Marines like a maddened grox.

Juno dodged out of the warboss' path, sidestepping just enough to avoid a backhanded swing of the greenskin's axe. His blade flicked back in response, plunging deep into the ork's arm, but the warboss didn't seem to notice. Still roaring, the giant ork ploughed into Olivar, knocking the Space Marine off his feet, and then brought its gun around to fire a burst point-blank at Galleas. But the veteran sergeant was already moving, dodging to the right as the gun began to fire. The burst missed Galleas by millimetres, striking a pair of guerrillas as they emerged from the stairway behind him.

Galleas and Royas fired as one, hammering the warboss with single shots from their bolters. The range was so close that the shells' rocket motors scarcely had time to ignite before striking their target, and the shells flattened harmlessly against the ork's armoured plates. Furious, the greenskin turned on Royas and lashed out with his axe, carving a notch out of the Space Marine's right pauldron and driving him back.

The warboss' personal mob was forcing their way into the room now, blazing away with their guns at anything that moved. The surviving guerrillas were firing back as well, covering Mitra as she ran for the blast door's control panel. Tauros reached the top of the stairs and rushed to join his brothers in the melee, firing as he went.

Caught amidst this vicious crossfire, Galleas watched the warboss' axe smash into Royas' shoulder and saw his opportunity. Lunging forward, he drove Night's Edge through the ork's left forearm and on into its torso, pinning its gun arm against its chest. The greenskin staggered, bellowing in rage, and chopped down at Galleas with its axe, but the veteran sergeant was already inside the weapon's considerable reach. The haft of the axe came down heavily on Galleas' shoulder as he shoved his bolter underneath the warboss' chin and blew its head off.

The rumble of sliding metal caught Galleas' attention. As he planted a boot in the warboss' chest and ripped his blade free, he chanced a look over his shoulder to see the blast doors starting to open. 'Go!' he shouted at Mitra. 'Get moving!'

More orks were forcing their way into the room, driven by the sheer weight of the greenskins crowded on the stairs behind them. Juno had brought down a pair of orks in heavy armour and was trading blows with a third, while Royas despatched another with a pair of shots to its head. A fifth greenskin rushed at Galleas, swinging a cleaver at his head. He reeled back, outside the sweep of the ork's blade, then blew off the greenskin's weapon hand with a shot from his boltgun. The ork staggered, howling in rage, and the veteran sergeant split its skull with an upward stroke of his power sword.

Galleas glanced over his shoulder again to see Oros disappearing through the widening blast doors. Only Kazimir and Corporal Ismail remained, covering the guerrillas' retreat.

'Fall back!' he shouted over the vox. 'Now, brothers! Before it's too late!'

With flawless discipline, the veteran Space Marines switched from offence to defence, blasting away at the swelling horde as they tried to fight their way clear of the melee. Juno was the furthest away, beset by orks on three sides. Royas, Olivar and Tauros poured fire into the mob, blasting open a path for him to withdraw. Juno's blade lashed out, crippling two of the orks and giving him time to disengage.

Kazimir retreated through the doors, dragging Ismail with him. With no one but the Crimson Fists left behind, Galleas spun and fired a single round into the blast door's access panel. There was a flash as the mass-reactive round exploded, followed by a shower of sparks. At once, the power plant's security protocols went into action, and the doors began to grind shut again.

'Tauros! You're first! Go!'

There was no time to argue. Tauros felled another ork with his boltgun and ducked through the narrowing gap between the doors.

'Olivar! Royas! Move!'

The Space Marines were falling back into a tight knot, surrounded by a bloodthirsty sea of green. Olivar and Royas raked the horde with burst after burst until their backs were to the blast doors, then disappeared through the gap.

Howling in frustration, the orks pressed in from all sides, trying to cut off their last two foes. Galleas drove them back with fiery sweeps of his blade. Juno was almost to the doors, leaving a trail of bleeding corpses in his wake.

The gap between the doors was barely wide enough for a single Space Marine. Tossing his boltgun through, Galleas grabbed the back of Juno's power pack with his free hand and leapt through, dragging his brother behind him.

The orks' bloodthirsty howls were cut off as the blast doors clanged shut behind Juno. The two Crimson Fists found themselves alone in the entry hall, save for the bodies of the dead. Outside, Galleas heard the truck engine roar into life.

The veteran sergeant snatched up his boltgun. Juno had sheathed his blade and was standing over Valentus' body. 'Help me with him,' he said.

Galleas could only shake his head. 'There's no time, brother.'

'We can't just leave him here with the orks,' Juno protested.

'In a few more minutes he'll have a pyre fit for the Emperor Himself,' Galleas replied. 'And the orks will burn with him. Now move.'

Galleas broke into a run, and Juno reluctantly fell into step behind him. Seconds later they were through the breach in the outer blast doors. Outside, Royas was waiting behind the wheel of the truck, and Tauros was back on the twin guns. There wasn't a single live ork in sight.

Royas gunned the engine as Galleas and Juno clambered into the troop compartment. Tyres squalling, the big truck sped across the tarmac. Mitra staggered across the compartment and sat down heavily next to Galleas.

'I don't understand,' she gasped, shoulders heaving with exertion. 'What happened to the rest of the greenskins? I thought they would've had us surrounded!'

'That changed when the gargants went on the move,' Galleas explained. 'Right now they're racing ahead of the war machines to be in position when the citadel's void shields fail. The beasts don't want to miss out on the slaughter that will follow.'

Moments later, Galleas' assertion was proven correct. As the truck emerged from the tractor works, the Imperials caught sight of a vast horde of greenskins, some in vehicles, some on foot, all racing north towards the city. Behind them came the towering forms of the gargants, their exhaust stacks belching clouds of thick, black smoke as they marched in a ragged line towards the distant citadel.

Galleas and Juno could not help but stare in awe at the

behemoths. Even for the battle-hardened Crimson Fists, the sight of the massive war machines was terrible to behold.

As soon as they were clear of the complex, Royas altered his course, intending to give the behemoths a wide berth. Galleas climbed to his feet, observing the gargants and comparing their course and speed against the layout of the southern half of the city.

Mitra joined him, staring up at the distant war machines with a look of undisguised dread. 'You still haven't explained how we're going to stop them,' she said.

Galleas glanced down at her. 'Isn't it obvious? We're going to capture one of the gargants and turn its guns on the rest.'

They had left the slow-moving gargants behind and were almost to the outer wall when the plasma reactor blew. For a fraction of an instant, the southern horizon flashed a searing white, brighter than the twin suns combined, and transformed the gargants into sharp-edged silhouettes against the deep, blue sky. Once again, the earth shook under a mighty hammer blow, followed by a thunderous, apocalyptic roar that rolled over the city like a harbinger of doom.

The Imperials followed in the wake of the rampaging horde, remaining far enough behind that their battered truck drew little notice from the orks. Daring greatly, they trailed behind a ragged band of trucks and battlewagons that veered east as they approached the outer wall and sped through one of the ork-held gates. The greenskins holding the strongpoint bellowed curses and scattered as the lead battlewagon smashed through their crude barricades and barrelled down the ruined motorway towards the river. By the time the raiders reached the gate, less than a minute later, there was no one left to stand in their way.

Royas pushed the truck as far as it would go, gaining them almost two more kilometres before the fuel ran out. Time was of the essence. Galleas estimated they had less than two and a half hours before the gargants were in position for them to spring the trap.

They took to the tunnels at once, moving as fast as they dared through the near-darkness. The tread of the gargants could be felt even there, sending ripples through the scummy pools and shaking dust from the ancient stones with every step, urging the Imperials on.

While his brothers watched their flanks and listened for the sound of ork hunting parties, Galleas' mind was ranging far ahead, refining the next steps of his plan. Every civilian that could lift a pack would be put to work carrying explosives. Combined with the surviving guerrillas, they could have everything in place with half an hour to spare.

The veteran sergeant was so preoccupied with his thoughts that he was halfway down the base's entrance tunnel before he caught the smell: the telltale stench of fyceline propellant and the reek of spilled blood.

The outer partition had been torn halfway from its mountings, its folds streaked with red. Beyond, Tomas Zapeta still sat at his post, lascarbine clenched in his hands. The blanket wrapped around his shoulders was riddled with bloody holes, and his cloudy eyes stared sightlessly into the gloom. Near the inner partition, just a metre away, one of Vila's squad mates lay face down on the ferrocrete amid a scattering of spent casings and a pool of drying gore.

They found Vega's body near the entrance to the commons area, with a dozen dead civilians at his back. The healer had died fighting, a heavy ork pistol on the floor by his side. Beyond, the carnage inside the commons was terrible. Nearly two-thirds of the non-combatants – the old, the sick and the very young – had been slain, their bodies torn apart by automatic fire. The rest were simply gone.

The guerrillas picked their way through the room, stunned and sickened by the sight of the massacre. Mitra's face was stricken. 'The orks–'

'If the xenos had done this, they would still be here,' Galleas said, his voice tight with rage. 'This was done by someone else.'

'That faithless coward Bergand is missing,' Royas spat. 'Along with Vila and most of his squad.'

Galleas' lips drew back in a grimace. 'The void trader must have been planning this for some time,' he said. The signs, he realised, had been there all along. 'He won Vila over, and some of the civilians, and once we'd left for the power plant, he made his move. When Vega and the others tried to stop him...'

Tauros shook his head. 'The fools,' he said, his voice thick with emotion. 'The damned fools. Rottshrek must have them by now.'

The veteran sergeant nodded. 'If any of them lived long enough to be tortured, then the warboss knows the location of the hideout,' he said grimly. 'The orks could be here at any moment.' He turned to Mitra and the rest of the humans. 'Grab as many explosives as you can carry. Hurry!'

The guerrillas put aside their horror and grief and went to work, filling sacks with explosives, detonators and wire. Within minutes, nearly a third of their stockpile was loaded and ready to move. It was little enough, Galleas thought with a frown, but it would have to do. He turned to Mitra, who was bent like a crone with the heavy bag of explosives on her back.

'Get back to the Via Tempestus as quickly as you can,' he ordered. 'Set charges on every third column from the M Twenty-six junction to Chandler's Square. If the orks come, we'll buy you as much time as we can. Now go!'

The guerrillas left without a word, saving their breath for the arduous trip back to the old aqueduct. As soon as they were gone, Galleas wired the rest of the explosives with a handful of detonators and synched them to his helmet display. 'Let's go,' he told his brothers, and led them back out into the tunnels.

The Crimson Fists had no sooner left the hideout than their enhanced hearing picked up a distant murmur of sound. The noise grew in volume with each passing moment, echoing down the main tunnel like the rumble of a spring flood.

'*WAAAAAAAAAGHHHHHHHHH!!!*'

Tauros sighed, readying his boltgun and drawing his combat knife. He glanced at Galleas. 'Sometimes I hate it when you're right, brother.'

'On the bright side, it means Bergand and that traitor Vila got what they deserved,' Royas muttered.

'Leave it to you to find the silver lining,' Juno observed drily.

The orks were coming up fast. Galleas gestured down the tunnel with his sword. 'Back to the next major junction,' he said. 'Formation Omicron.'

The Space Marines withdrew thirty metres down the tunnel and took up position. By now the xenos' bloodthirsty shouts were almost deafening. Galleas switched to thermal imaging and saw the leading edge of the warband a hundred metres distant, charging headlong down the main tunnel from the north.

The greenskins knew exactly where they were going. Gal-leas watched grimly as they turned off from the main tunnel into the base's entrance, brandishing cleavers and axes, their toothy jaws agape at the prospect of slaughter. More than a hundred orks disappeared down the side tunnel. Still more followed, baying at their heels.

'Vengeance for the fallen,' he said softly, and keyed the detonator rune on his display.

There was a muted roar, and the main tunnel seemed to lurch beneath the Space Marines' feet. A plume of dirt and debris jetted from the side tunnel, flinging greenskin bod-ies against the far wall and dropping them into the empty storm channel below.

For several long moments, chaos reigned. Orks howled in frustration and pain. Then, a small pack of runts emerged from the billowing clouds of dust. Their long, pointed noses sniffed the air. One of them drew back its lips in a feral grin and screeched in triumph, pointing down the tunnel where the Space Marines waited.

'They've got the guerrillas' scent,' Galleas snarled. 'Open fire!'

Five boltguns thundered, spitting a stream of mass-reactive shells down the length of the tunnel. The pack of runts was torn apart, spraying the curved walls with blood, and more dead greenskins tumbled over the rail into the depths of the storm channel. But the sound of the gunfire energised the rest of the warband, giving them an enemy to focus on at last.

'*WAAAAAAAAAGHHHHH!*' the greenskins bellowed, the noise swelling as more and more of the xenos took up the shout.

As the first orks came charging out of the murk the

Crimson Fists fired again, cutting down the front rank and creating an obstacle for the rest. Galleas signalled to his brothers and the Space Marines swiftly and silently withdrew, drawing the furious greenskins after them.

For the next half an hour they led the xenos on a bloody chase, using their intimate knowledge of the tunnel network to confound the greenskins and hit them from unexpected directions. Galleas and his brothers would fire a few well-placed shots, kill the closest orks, then withdraw to the next junction down the line. They had rehearsed such tactics for months in case their base was discovered and they were forced to relocate, and now they put their plans into brutal effect.

But the orks were relentless, and with every ambush, the distance between them and the Space Marines dwindled, until finally there was no room left to run.

Galleas knew the moment was coming, and had planned for it. By the time it was down to blades and point-blank fire the Space Marines were in a long, narrow tunnel a little over a kilometre from Chandler's Square. The Crimson Fists worked in pairs, alternating to keep up their strength and making the greenskins pay for every metre in blood. For almost another half an hour they held the warband at bay, tangling the feet of the xenos with the bodies of their dead.

Slowly, stubbornly, the Space Marines withdrew. After three hundred metres of brutal, close-quarters fighting, Galleas risked a glance over his shoulder and spied a dark side tunnel just a couple of metres away. The timing had worked out just as he'd planned. Juno and Royas were trading places at the front with Tauros and Olivar, falling back past Galleas for a moment's respite. The veteran sergeant stowed his bolter and pulled his last grenade from his belt. Another few moments, and it would be time to disengage.

'Get ready!' he called over the vox as the group came within reach of the side tunnel. 'When I give the signal–'

The rest was lost in a chorus of triumphant howls as a mob of greenskins burst from the side tunnel into the Space Marines' midst.

A pair of orks crashed into Galleas, driving him back against the side of the tunnel. A blade glanced off his helmet's cheek, narrowly missing his eyes. Without thinking, the veteran sergeant smashed one of the orks across the face with the grenade in his hand and drove the point of Night's Edge into the other greenskin's chest.

Seeing their ambush sprung, the orks in the main tunnel renewed their assault, pressing Tauros and Olivar hard. Still more greenskins were pouring from the side tunnel, creating gaps between the Crimson Fists and driving them further apart. In the space of seconds, their orderly withdrawal had dissolved into five separate battles, each one just a metre or two apart.

There was barely any room to swing a blade. Night's Edge was trapped in the torso of the dead ork, which was still standing upright amidst the press. Juno was having better luck with his short sword, the blade darting like a needle into green throats and snarling faces. He was working his way left to try to link up with Royas, who was fighting with his back against the far wall.

A cleaver crashed against the side of Galleas' helmet. Snarling, he hooked the pin of the ork grenade with his thumb and pulled it, flipping the sputtering bomb over the heads of the mob and into the mouth of the side tunnel. Then he dropped his hand and went for the bolt pistol at his hip.

To his right, Olivar and Tauros had been separated, beset both from the front and from behind. Olivar had turned, trying to cover Tauros' back, and the greenskins had driven him against the tunnel wall. Galleas watched the one-eyed Space Marine open an ork's throat with his combat knife, then twist suddenly as a greenskin blade found a weak spot in the side of his breastplate. Blood poured from the puncture for almost a full second before Olivar's Larraman cells could seal off the ruptured blood vessels.

Tauros was now almost six metres away, standing alone against the onslaught of the ork warband. Rather than retreat, the veteran Space Marine advanced into the teeth of the enemy attack, fighting to create room for his brothers to free themselves from the ambush. His boltgun swept across the mass of greenskins, the explosive shells sowing death amongst the enemy.

The grenade detonated, its lethal blast almost smothered by the crowd. Orks screamed in agony, and the press of bodies against Galleas suddenly ebbed. He pulled the bolt pistol from its holster and shot the two closest orks through the belly, then snapped a quick shot into the head of the greenskin that had stabbed Olivar.

Juno had reached Royas' side, and the two Crimson Fists began to work their way towards Galleas. Another few seconds and they would be able to withdraw.

'Tauros!' Galleas shouted over the vox.

There were now almost eight metres between Tauros and the rest of the squad. The Crimson Fist fought like the hero of legend that he was, and the orks howled in dismay as he carved his way through their ranks.

But the veteran Space Marine was losing speed, his precise shots and his deadly blows fractionally slower by the moment as the bullet wounds he suffered at the power plant began to take their toll.

It was at that moment that the tunnel shook with a furious shout, and the greenskins facing Tauros were crushed against either wall as Rottshrek bore down upon his foes.

The hulking warboss was a terrifying sight, filling the tunnel before the embattled Tauros. Sneering a challenge in the greenskins' savage tongue, Rottshrek lunged at Tauros with its fearsome power claw.

The orks surrounding Galleas bellowed in triumph at the sight of the warboss. Olivar was still beset on two sides, and Juno and Royas were three metres further down the tunnel. Desperate, Galleas twisted at the waist and ripped Night's Edge free from the greenskin's corpse.

Tauros met the warboss' charge with one of his own, sliding past the outstretched power claw and stabbing at Rottshrek's throat. The blow struck the ork's metal gorget and glanced aside, leaving no more than a bright scratch across its curved surface.

Rottshrek responded to the blow with one of its own, dropping its horned head and butting Tauros full in the face. The force of the impact stunned the veteran Space Marine, driving him back a step.

The power claw lunged for Tauros again, reaching for his throat. At the last moment, the Crimson Fist realised his peril and dodged to the right – but again, his wounded body betrayed him, and the move was a fraction of a second too late. With a malevolent hiss of hydraulic fluids, the scythe-like blades of Rottshrek's claw snapped shut around Tauros' neck. For a terrible moment, he struggled in Rottshrek's grip, uttering a choked cry of defiance and firing his bolter point-blank into the warboss' chest. Then, with a shriek of parting metal, Tauros' head separated from his neck, dropping his decapitated body to the tunnel floor.

A wordless, feral cry of rage tore its way from Galleas' throat. Night's Edge flashed in a burning arc, slicing through a pair of orks in his path. Consumed with fury, he cut and stabbed at every greenskin he could reach, driving the survivors before him until finally they broke and ran, retreating down the tunnel to where their warboss was stooping to collect his new trophy.

Within moments, Galleas had reached Olivar's side. Juno came up beside them, his short sword gleaming with greenskin blood. His eyes never left the gloating warboss.

'This beast and I have unfinished business,' the Crimson Fist said calmly. 'You three go on now. I'll deal with this lot.'

'You'll not go alone!' Galleas snarled.

'Don't be stupid, brother.' Juno stowed his boltgun and plucked an ork cleaver from the floor. 'You clumsy oafs would just get in my way.'

'Juno–'

The Crimson Fist turned to Galleas. 'I said get out of here, brother. Mitra's waiting. You don't expect her to take that gargant all by herself, do you?'

Before Galleas could reply, Juno was gone, striding swiftly down the tunnel towards the greenskins.

Royas gripped Galleas' arm. 'He's right, brother. This is our only chance. We've got to go.'

Tormented by grief, Galleas spun on his heel and led Olivar and Royas down the tunnel. Seeing the Space Marines retreating, the orks howled like daemons and broke into a run. Titus Juno was waiting, his arms spread wide as if to welcome them, twin blades glinting in his hands.

* * *

The Crimson Fists reached Chandler's Square without a minute to spare. The gargants were very close now, the thunder of their footfalls reverberating through the ancient tunnels.

Mitra and the others were waiting. A flicker of pain shone in her eyes when she saw that Tauros and Juno were missing, but she made no mention of their absence. 'Charges are set,' she reported, her voice cracking with exhaustion. She handed Galleas a remote detonator with its safety engaged.

The veteran sergeant accepted the device with a curt nod. 'Follow me,' he said, and led his battered force a dozen metres east along the high, arched tunnel, where a rusting metal ladder offered access to the world above.

They emerged from beneath a heavy street cover on the far side of the square. Galleas searched the ruined skyline from east to west, getting his bearings. The gargants were almost upon them, their misshapen hulls towering over the burned-out structures less than a hundred metres to the south.

The veteran sergeant saw at once that the ork war machines were not where he'd expected them to be. Their rough battle line now stretched almost five hundred metres further east than he'd expected. Only a single gargant, anchoring the western end of the line, was heading into the trap they'd sacrificed so much to create.

Fifteen metres at a stride, the nearest gargant ground its way through the ruins towards the distant citadel. The guerrillas crouched amongst the ruins as the war machine bore down on them, scarcely daring to breathe.

Galleas switched off the detonator's safety. The ready light flashed from red to green. He had no idea what to expect once they were aboard the gargant. Absently, he thought to ask Valentus, and then remembered his brother was no more.

The veteran sergeant's grip tightened on the detonator. A hundred metres away, the gargant crushed the old bones of a hab unit beneath its feet, then took a single, ponderous step into the wide avenue beyond.

Galleas drew a deep breath. 'God-Emperor of Mankind, bear witness,' he whispered, and thumbed the detonator's trigger.

CHAPTER TWENTY-THREE

THE PATH OF STORMS

ZONA 13 COMMERCIA, NEW RYNN CITY
DAY 498

Brrrrrrmmmmpppp.

The explosive charges blew in a rapid chain of sharp detonations, marching in a line down the avenue above the Via Tempestus. Half a second later the gargant's massive foot came down on the tarmac with a hollow boom that sent cracks racing in both directions along the rubble-strewn street. Galleas heard the faint rumble of collapsing stone, and the towering war machine seemed to teeter slightly on the suddenly unstable ground. But if the orks realised their peril, it was far too late. The gargant brought its rear foot forward, completing its clumsy stride – and as the entire weight of the ponderous construct settled on its front foot the street beneath it gave way with a grinding roar.

The gargant's stubby leg dropped into the ancient aqueduct up to its knee. Slowly at first, the pyramidal war machine began to topple forward, gathering speed as it went. It crashed against the face of a ruined commercia building on the opposite side of the street and leaned there like a drunkard, weapon-arms dangling limply at its sides. Dust and powdered ferrocrete billowed from beneath the gargant's skirts in an ever-expanding cloud, lit from within by arcs of electricity as the particles interacted with the machine's force field.

Galleas rose to his feet. 'This is our chance!' he shouted over the thunder of the gargants. 'Brothers! Shieldbearers! Follow me!'

The veteran sergeant broke into a run, crossing the square and making his way over the uneven pavement along the southern side of the street. The curtains of dust fell over him like a shroud, all but concealing him from sight. The massive ork war machine still hadn't moved. Galleas hoped the crew was too stunned by the sudden fall to search for threats or get the gargant's weapons into action. The hundred metres of open ground between him and the behemoth set his teeth on edge.

Nine long seconds later, Galleas reached the back foot of the giant construct. There were still no signs of movement, but the gargant's exhaust stacks were belching clouds of smoke, and he could hear a chorus of high-pitched shouts echoing back and forth from the lower half of the machine. Royas and Olivar arrived right on his heels, and the guerrillas caught up a few seconds later.

The gargant's legs had no knees, Galleas found. They appeared to pump up and down like a piston, giving the machine its characteristic waddle. The back leg was retracted nearly the entire way into the lower hull, with only the truck-sized foot and part of the lower leg visible. Peering through the clouds of dust, Galleas tried to find an access hatch on the gargant's bottom hull. After searching in vain for several precious seconds, he turned to Enginseer Oros. 'How do we get inside this thing?'

'Ah...' The tech-priest wrung his hands nervously as he studied the massive machine. Finally he pointed to a line of metal rungs that climbed the outside of the gargant's foot and up the leg. 'There! Follow the ladder up through the l-leg well!'

Sheathing Night's Edge, Galleas picked his way quickly across the partially collapsed avenue and clambered up the side of the machine's massive foot. Bolt pistol in hand, he climbed the ladder as quickly as he dared, searching the shadows above him for threats.

The noise inside the gargant's lower hull was nearly deafening, reverberating like a bell underneath the construct's massive petrochem engines. Galleas had expected the space around the legs to be mostly empty, but in fact it was crammed with giant magazines that fed rockets and shells up tracks along the inner hull to the weapons along the gargant's shoulders and arms. Narrow metal gantries criss-crossed the space around the giant legs, providing access to the magazines and to the war machine's middle decks.

Galleas heard a startled shriek from the gantry behind him. A gun boomed, the slug striking sparks from the gargant's massive leg. The veteran sergeant turned, still hanging from the ladder, and saw a greenskin runt clad in crossed tool belts taking aim at him from the canted surface of the gantry. He blew the xenos apart with a round from his bolt pistol and leapt from the ladder onto the gantry next to where it had stood.

No sooner had his boots hit the metal grating than the air resounded with a chorus of screeching, and Galleas found himself caught in a crossfire as a mob of runt mechanics opened fire from the shadows of the lower hull. Slugs ricocheted from his armour and went buzzing off into the gloom, sometimes striking sparks from one or more of the fully stocked magazines.

Galleas traded fire with the runts as Olivar and Royas clambered up into the hull, followed by Mitra and the rest of the guerrillas. The veteran sergeant spied a runt scampering like a spider along the curved inner hull and took careful aim, killing the fast-moving xenos with a single shot. 'We've got to keep moving!' he shouted over the vox. 'Every second we waste down here, the other gargants are moving out of range!' He pointed with his pistol at a pair of wide ladderways leading up to the war machine's middle deck, one forward and one aft. 'Olivar, Royas! Take Oros and four shieldbearers up the aft ladderway and clear out the engine room! I'll take Mitra and the others forward and secure the belly cannon!'

The two groups split up, braving the harassing fire from the runts and dashing up the ladderways. One of the guerrillas in Galleas' team was hit in the neck at the base of the ladderway and fell, choking on his own blood. Ismail spotted the runt who shot him and blasted the xenos before it could scuttle back into cover.

The veteran sergeant leapt through the open hatchway at the top of the broad steps and dodged to the right, searching for targets. Kazimir came next, moving left, combat shotgun at the ready. As Galleas expected, they had reached the gun deck for the gargant's massive belly cannon, a cramped, claustrophobic space containing the gun's enormous breech, plus the huge, grease-stained gears of its aiming system.

The gun captain and crew met the Imperials head-on, charging at Galleas and his team with pistols, knives and wrenches clutched in their clawed hands. The veteran sergeant shot the captain twice in the chest, then drew his sword and cut down one of the gunners in mid-stride. Another ork gunner fell to a shotgun blast from Kazimir, just as Mitra and Ismail came charging through the hatch, guns blazing. Another gunner and a pair of ammo runts fell under the withering fire, and the rest fell back, retreating behind the cover of the cannon's breechblock.

'Covering fire!' Galleas ordered, moving left to get a line of sight on the surviving orks. Ismail and one of the guerrillas followed while Mitra, Kazimir and the rest kept up a steady harassing fire from the far side of the gun. Slugs buzzed like angry hornets in the cramped space, posing as much danger to the Imperials as the xenos, but the storm of lead kept the gun crew pinned until Galleas and the two humans could work their way around and finish off the greenskins with a few carefully-aimed bursts.

No sooner had the last runt fallen than Galleas was heading for the next ladderway. 'Olivar!' he called over the vox. 'Report!'

'Engine deck is clear,' the Crimson Fist reported. *'Two casualties. We've found another ladderway leading up to the next deck.'*

'Understood. We'll link up there.'

The ladderway ran upwards at a steep angle to another set of gantries that serviced the guns on the gargant's shoulders and arms. At the centre of the gantry, just below the war machine's bulbous head, was a larger space with a spiral staircase winding up to the command deck. An ork engineer wearing an ornate coat and peaked officer's hat stood at the railing, pistol in hand, shouting questions in a stentorian voice. Galleas shot the ork through the neck as he dashed up the steps, then crossed to the spiral staircase without breaking stride.

The staircase ended in a small landing at the rear of the command deck. In the centre of the space rose the war machine's command dais, a crude throne that sat before a stout-looking console bristling with levers, switches and dials. A quartet of brass speaking tubes flanked the dais on either side, ostensibly so the war machine's captain could shout orders to the crews below decks. Before the dais were another four control stations that faced the gargant's gridded viewport. From the collection of rangefinders, dials, levers and triggers, the veteran sergeant reckoned they were the war machine's primary gunnery stations.

There were almost a dozen dead and wounded greenskins scattered about the control station, and splashes of blood were smeared across the sharp metal brackets and the thick crystalflex of the viewport. The command crew had suffered the brunt of the damage from the gargant's fall, having been thrown from their stations face-first as the toppling war machine crashed against the front of the building.

Galleas made short work of the injured orks, then took stock of the situation as the rest of the Imperials reached the command deck. As he had feared, the remaining gargants were still on the move, heading for the Zona Regis. The lead war machine was already coming into range, firing a series of ranging shots from its arm-mounted super cannon that kicked up plumes of water just short of the island.

The veteran sergeant turned to his companions. 'We've already cost the orks one gargant,' he told them. 'By Dorn, perhaps we can stop a few more!' He pointed to Oros.

'Enginseer! The command throne is yours. See if you can get us moving again. The rest of you, man the gun stations. It's time to see what this monstrosity can do!'

Mitra and Ismail went to the gunnery stations at the far left, along with three of the surviving guerrillas. Kazimir and the rest of the Imperials took the right. Royas supervised the stations to the left, Olivar the right. While Oros tried to decipher the orks' bewildering control systems, the gunners began to tentatively pull levers and twist dials under the Crimson Fists' guidance.

Thirty seconds later the lead gargant unleashed a stream of heavy rockets at the citadel, followed by a barrage of super cannon shells that hammered the fortress' void shields. With each successive shot, the ork gunners adjusted their aim, concentrating the explosions on a single quadrant.

Galleas knew that if they didn't act soon, the citadel had only minutes to survive. 'Oros, status report!'

The tech-priest jumped in his seat. 'Ah, main power online! Force field at sixty-three per cent! Motive systems operational!'

'Can you get us under way?'

'Ah... Yes. I think so.'

'Start with getting us back upright, and we'll take things from there.'

The veteran sergeant turned to Olivar. 'Status?'

'We've identified the controls for the right arm super cannon and the shoulder heavy rockets, more or less. Ready to engage targets.'

'Royas?'

'We're ready, brother, but the building is blocking our guns.'

'Oros!'

'Ah! Yes! One moment!' Oros rubbed his hands together and muttered a quick prayer, then reached out and grabbed a large pair of levers directly in front of the throne. As he drew them back, the gargant lurched violently to the right, throwing several of the gun crew from their seats. A segment of the ruined building broke apart under the war machine's weight, sending tons of broken ferrocrete cascading to the ground.

'Beg pardon, my lord!' the tech-priest exclaimed. 'The controls are more sensitive than I thought! I believe I have it now.'

The enginseer made a slight adjustment to the levers. The pitch of the war machine's engines changed, and the gargant shifted back and to the left, pulling away from the building. The deck tilted beneath Galleas' feet, returning to level.

'Well done, Oros,' Galleas said. 'Royas?'

The Space Marine shook his head. 'We still don't have a shot.'

'Then bring down the building instead! Olivar, target the nearest gargant and fire at will!'

Olivar passed orders to Kazimir, who relayed them to the gun crews. Seconds later the gargant shook as four massive rockets roared from the launcher on the gargant's shoulder.

At little over half a kilometre away, the enemy gargant made for an easy target. Galleas watched the projectiles streak over the ruined city on plumes of dirty, grey smoke and detonate in a series of thunderous explosions against the war machine's powerful force field.

The deck trembled under Galleas' feet as autoloaders began feeding a new set of rockets into the launch tubes. Meanwhile, there was a grinding of massive gears as the gargant's right arm elevated and fired a salvo from its super cannon.

Boom. Boom. Boom. The muzzle flashes lit the interior of the control room with fiery orange light. The massive shells, each one weighing as much as a ton, were coated with a chemical that caused them to blaze in flight like giant tracer rounds to make it easier for the gunners to adjust their aim. The first salvo was high, arcing over the gargant's right shoulder and falling like thunderbolts across the wasteland beyond.

Olivar and Kazimir bent over the gun crews, calling out adjustments to the range. On the left, Royas and Ismail swept the barrel of their super cannon across the façade of the building, smashing through the thick ferrocrete as though it were no more substantial than a sand castle. Galleas bared his teeth in a feral grin. As crude and clumsy as ork engineering was, there was no denying its power.

Boom. Boom. Boom. The right-hand super cannon fired again. This time the salvo was on target, battering the enemy gargant's force field with a trio of earth-shaking explosions. The enemy war machine had come to a halt, wreathed in waste heat and swirling clouds of propellant, and was starting to turn and face its attacker.

'Oros, can we get the force field back to full power?' Galleas inquired.

'We'd need engineers for that,' the tech-priest said absently. 'And I think we killed them.'

'We're going to be taking fire in approximately eight seconds.'

'Yes. Thank you. I can see that,' Oros muttered testily, wrestling with the controls.

Mitra glanced up from her controls. 'We have the target!'

'Open fire!'

The massive gargant rocked backwards as its left super cannon and shoulder-mounted launchers all fired in unison. Rockets and shells pummelled the enemy war machine in an apocalyptic roll of thunder, culminating in a dazzling flash of blue-white light.

'Their force field is down!' Royas declared.

The enemy gargant vanished behind a billowing column of dust and petrochem exhaust. Moments later, Galleas heard the muffled boom of a super cannon, and three blazing shells came arcing out of the murk towards them, followed by a hissing stream of rockets.

'Incoming!' the veteran sergeant yelled.

The cannon's first salvo went wide, one shell striking the edge of their force field and the rest plunging into the cityscape on their left. The rockets, however, by accident or design, were right on target. The gargant rang like a massive bell with each detonation. For a sickening instant the deck tilted again, and Galleas thought the behemoth was going to topple onto its back, but Oros grabbed a series of levers and righted the machine in the nick of time.

'Enginseer, get us moving!' Galleas snapped.

'I'm trying!'

Five hundred metres away, the enemy gargant was still hidden behind the column of dirt and debris, but Galleas was certain it was turning, bringing its guns to bear. 'Royas, keep engaging the target,' the veteran sergeant ordered. 'Olivar, shift your fire to the next gargant along the line!'

The fourth enemy war machine was now seven hundred and fifty metres away. The lead gargant and its two closest companions were all pouring fire into the citadel's void shields. The air around the spire was already starting to distort as the first shield layer strained under the pounding of shells and energy beams. Galleas could see that the guns on the Zona Regis had gone into action as well, battering the ork war machines with Earthshaker shells and carefully hoarded Deathstrike missiles. It was a fierce and stubborn defence, but it was too little, and too late.

Olivar unleashed another salvo of super-heavy rockets. The weapons streaked downrange but fell short of the target, blasting a line of craters fifty metres behind the gargant. Kazimir barked out a sulphurous stream of curses and the rocket crew began frantically twisting the elevation dials.

Boom. Boom. Boom. The right-side super cannon spat another stream of massive shells. At the same time, shells from the closest enemy gargant detonated against their force field, causing it to momentarily incandesce under the load of waste heat. Three-quarters of a kilometre away, plumes of dirt and dust erupted around the feet of the fourth gargant as Olivar's gun crew found the range.

'We're losing the force field!' Oros warned.

Four hundred and eighty metres across the blasted cityscape, the fifth gargant lumbered out of the dust. Catching sight of its prey, the enemy war machine lurched to a halt. The stubby barrel of its belly cannon began to move, elevating slightly.

'Royas!'

'I see it!'

The left-side super cannon unleashed a salvo at the enemy gargant, stitching a line of explosions across the behemoth's chest and shoulders. Multi-ton armour plates flew skyward, rough edges curled and molten. The gargant staggered under the blows, but did not fall. Then came a titanic flash of orange flame as the war machine's belly cannon fired.

The giant shell was slow enough to be visible to the naked eye – a blur of dark metal that seemed to arc lazily in the air towards them. It fell short, hitting the ruined building in front of them, and the earth quaked beneath the blow. The enemy gargant vanished behind a wall of pulverised ferrocrete and fragments of twisted metal.

Royas fired the left-side rocket launcher blindly into the smoke, aiming for the gargant's last known position. The right-side launcher fired a second later. Galleas could track the flight of its salvo as it plunged down upon the fourth gargant, now almost eight hundred metres distant and moving into firing range of the citadel. This time the rockets were on target, detonating in blooms of red and yellow against the behemoth's force field.

Kazimir gave a whoop of triumph. He glanced over at Galleas, his seamed face split in a wolfish grin. 'We got them that time, by the Emperor!'

The sound of the near gargant firing its super cannon was lost in the thunder of the Imperials' own weapons. The blazing shells burst from the dust cloud and struck the war machine dead on. There was a tremendous, world-shattering crash, and everything vanished in a blaze of yellow-white.

Galleas landed hard on his back, fetching up at the foot of the command dais. As the glare from the blast faded, he heard the crackle of sparks and smelled the stench of smoke and spent fyceline. The veteran sergeant blinked, trying to clear his eyes.

The command deck was littered with shattered crystalflex and chunks of twisted metal. Smoke curled in thick eddies across the floor. To the right, pale sunlight shone through a huge, jagged hole in the gargant's viewport.

Olivar lay on his back a few metres from Galleas, the front of his armour scorched and smoking from the blast. The right-hand gun stations were gone, reduced to twisted wreckage, along with Sergeant Kazimir and the gun crews.

With an effort of will, Galleas forced himself onto his feet. On the left, Royas was doing the same. Mitra and the surviving gunners were struggling to get back to their stations, clearly dazed by the blast.

'Damage report!' Galleas snapped. 'Oros, get us moving! Another hit like that and we're dead!'

The veteran sergeant turned to the command dais just as a massive figure burst through the hatchway at the rear of the deck. Streaming blood from a dozen wounds, Rottshrek bellowed like a maddened grox and lunged for the command throne with a gore-stained power claw.

CHAPTER TWENTY-FOUR

BROTHERS IN ARMS

ZONA 13 COMMERCIA, NEW RYNN CITY
DAY 498

Galleas shouted a warning, his hand reaching for his bolt pistol as Rottshrek's claw seized the command throne and squeezed, its curved blades crushing inwards. Oros writhed in the warboss' grip, shrieking in pain. The control levers jerked in his hands and the gargant groaned, pitching to the left.

The veteran sergeant was flung across the deck, the bolt pistol flying from his hand. Laughing maniacally, the warboss tightened its grip on the command throne and blazed away at the tumbling Space Marine with its belt-fed gun. A stream of explosive shells chewed the deckplates and raked across Royas and the left-side gun stations.

Olivar surged to his feet with a furious oath, boltgun in his hands. The weapon thundered, stitching a burst of mass-reactive shells along the ork's arm and chest, but could not penetrate the warboss' fearsome mega armour.

Galleas fetched up against the bulkhead on the left side

of the command deck. He rolled to his feet, Night's Edge blazing in his fist. A couple of metres away, Corporal Ismail slid from her chair onto the floor. Her left shoulder was soaked in blood, the arm hanging limply at her side, but her blue eyes were hard and her pale face was twisted into an icy mask of fury. She drew her broad-bladed knife with her good hand and struggled to reach her feet.

Rottshrek whirled, gripping the throne for support, and fired a long burst at Olivar. An explosive shell struck the Crimson Fist in the leg, punching through the armour and knocking him to the deck.

Snarling in rage, Galleas lunged to his feet and charged the warboss, aiming for its bloodstained claw. Ismail moved at the same time, crouched low and circling wide to the right.

But no sooner had Galleas begun his charge than Rottshrek spun again, a cruel smile splitting its toothy face. Hydraulics hissed and the claw tightened, cutting the throne and the dying tech-priest in half.

Laughing, the warboss flung the grisly wreckage into Galleas' path. The veteran sergeant dodged to the left, narrowly avoiding the attack, but Ismail wasn't so lucky. The wreckage struck her in the chest, smashing her diminutive form back against the curved bulkhead. She hit the deck hard and didn't rise again.

More shells hammered along Rottshrek's side. Olivar lay where he'd fallen, harassing the ork with fire and hoping to divide its attention. But Rottshrek was too cunning for such a ruse. Ignoring Olivar, the warboss lunged at Galleas, twin guns blazing.

The veteran sergeant was caught in a rain of explosive shells. By ill luck, one round burst against the side of his right knee, and the damaged actuator seized. He pitched headlong, crashing into the giant ork's chest.

A massive fist crunched into the side of Galleas' head, smashing him to the deck. Night's Edge slipped from his fingers, skating just out of his reach. Half-dazed, he groped for the weapon's hilt just as the ork's power claw seized him by the neck.

Rottshrek bent over Galleas, scarred lips drawing back in a sadistic grin. The claw tightened slowly, its gory blades forcing their way under his chin and pressing against the thinly armoured gorget. The beast hissed something in its foul tongue. Galleas could not be sure if it was a promise or a threat. His fingers fumbled against the pommel of his sword, just a few centimetres out of reach.

The claw tightened, forcing Galleas' head back. There was a pounding in his ears. He thought it was his pulse, until he felt it vibrating along the surface of the deck.

Boots ringing on the deckplates, Titus Juno leapt the last two metres onto Rottshrek's back. His bloody short sword plunged downwards, avoiding the ork's massive armour and stabbing deep into its muscular neck.

The warboss shuddered, bellowing in rage and pain. Galleas twisted in the warboss' grip, reaching for Night's Edge with all his strength. The claw sliced through the gorget, leaving a ragged gash along his throat, but his fingers closed about the power sword's hilt. With a shout, he twisted back and drove Night's Edge into Rottshrek's chest.

The giant ork screamed, bloody spittle spraying from its lips. Its savage face twisted into a grimace of hate. The claw tightened. Galleas forced his blade deeper, driving its burning point through the great beast's heart.

At last, the life went out of Rottshrek's eyes. The claw's

hydraulics gave a final hiss, and the blades seized, locking in place.

Juno pulled his sword from the warboss' corpse and slid wearily to the deck. His armour was covered in fresh scars and plastered in gore. Grabbing the blades of the power claw in his hands, the Space Marine applied his superhuman strength and pried them far enough apart that Galleas could pull his head free.

'Sorry for not coming sooner,' Juno said laconically. 'This green bastard left me to the mercies of his warband and ran off after you. Took me an age to finish them off.'

Galleas made no reply. His attention was drawn to the thunder of the guns echoing across the ruined city. Climbing to his feet, he limped to the hole in the gargant's viewport.

Streamers of dust from the destroyed building hung in the air, but Galleas could see the outline of the fifth gargant, damaged but still functional, making its way through the ruins towards the citadel. The remaining four war machines had come to a halt a few hundred metres from the riverbank, and were battering away at the spire's void shielding with every weapon they had. Several layers of shielding had already failed, and the remaining defences were weakening fast.

Grief stabbed deep into Galleas' heart. They had given all they had. There was nothing left but to bear witness to his Chapter's final stand.

A flicker of sunlight on metal caught the veteran sergeant's eye. He glanced up to see contrails against the blue sky, coming from the direction of the starport. Scores of them, flying in tight formation and heading for the river. Moments later, the rumble of their engines reached his ears.

Galleas felt his hearts clench. *Those weren't ork planes.*

Then came the trumpeting of mighty horns, sounding in the east. Galleas knew the sound at once. 'Imperial Titans,' he said, hardly daring to believe his ears. 'Imperators and Reavers, by the sound.'

Across the city, the gargants were moving, turning to face the sudden threat. Overhead, Imperial bombers dived like eagles, beginning their attack runs.

The Navy had arrived. At long last, the deliverance of Rynn's World was at hand.

Galleas turned, his elation tempered by the carnage on the command deck. Juno was kneeling next to Olivar, examining the wound in his leg. Ismail lay unmoving, partially covered by the command throne's broken back.

Lieutenant Mitra knelt on the deck beside the shattered gun station, bent over Royas' prone form. The bodies of the gun crews slumped in their chairs, wreathed in smoke.

The veteran sergeant limped over to his fallen brother. Royas lay on his side, his armour marked by the bright scars of shell hits. A single round had punched through his helmet, just above the temple.

Mitra glanced up at Galleas, her cheeks damp with tears. 'He shielded me with his body when the warboss opened fire,' she said, shaking her head in disbelief. 'It doesn't make any sense. He *hated* us.'

The veteran sergeant knelt beside her and placed a hand on Royas' chest, against the battered silver aquila.

'Perhaps,' Galleas answered sadly. 'But at the end, he was also your brother.'

EPILOGUE

THE ZONA REGIS, NEW RYNN CITY
DAY 532

The garden lay at the end of a path that wound about the base of the Upper Rynnhouse, not far from the spires of the Silver Citadel. Small and secluded, it sat atop a grassy knoll that afforded a sweeping view of the River Rynn as it ran west to the sea.

Little remained of the garden's former glory. The ornamental trees had been cut down for firewood during the siege, and the delicate flowers uprooted and eaten by the starving Rynnsworlders. All that remained were curved marble benches and an elegant fountain that murmured sadly to itself amid the desolation.

Antonia Mitra was sitting alone in the afternoon sunshine, watching the dark ribbon of the swift-moving river. She had gained back a bit of weight in the month following the end of the siege, but her face was still gaunt, and the dress uniform she wore seemed two sizes too large. Yet she managed a smile as Galleas came walking down the gravel path towards her, and when she spoke, her voice was still strong.

'I had almost given up on you,' she said. Mitra straightened; a faint wince hinted at wounds that had yet to heal. 'It's been weeks. I was starting to think you hadn't got my messages.'

Sandor Galleas made his way across the ruined garden. He cut an imposing figure, his scarred and battered armour covered by a flowing red tabard, and Night's Edge gleaming at his hip. The veteran sergeant had left his helmet at the Cassar, and the cool breeze plucked at his curly hair.

They had not seen one another since shortly after the battle aboard the gargant. As the Imperial relief forces stormed into the city, the orks' vox jamming had finally stopped, and Galleas had managed to contact the Silver Citadel. Not long after, a transport from the Zona Regis had come to collect them. The last he had seen of Mitra, she had been in the hands of Rynnsguard medics on the way to a field hospital being set up on the other side of the island.

'I was occupied elsewhere,' Galleas replied. 'The siege of Rynn's World has been broken, but the battle for the planet rages on.'

Overhead, scores of contrails cross-hatched the azure sky as transports ferried troops and supplies from Navy ships in orbit. The plains around the starport now played host to a massive military encampment, and would likely continue to do so for months to come. The Imperial relief force had arrived from Kar Duniash in overwhelming force: two thousand warships, plus elements of four Titan Legions and six Space Marine Chapters, backed by hundreds of thousands of Astra Militarum troops. They had routed the ork fleet at the edge of the system and smashed Snagrod's forces at New

Rynn City, though it appeared that the Arch-Arsonist and a significant portion of the greenskin horde had nonetheless managed to flee the planet and escape into the warp. Untold numbers of greenskins had been left behind, and were even now being hunted across the face of the planet by detachments of Imperial troops. There was no counting the number of orks that had been slain. Estimates were in the tens of millions, but such numbers mattered little to Galleas. Orks were vermin. No matter how many the Imperium exterminated, there would always be more. The same could not be said for the people of Rynn's World, much less the fallen brothers of the Chapter.

Mitra nodded. She was silent for a moment, staring out at the river. 'How are Juno and Olivar?'

'Olivar is healing, though the Apothecaries believe it will be some time before he can be fitted with a new eye. Juno is... Juno.' Galleas stood beside the bench, clasping his hands behind his back. 'As soon as Olivar is fit for duty, the Chapter Master says we will be deployed to hunt ork warbands in Magalan.'

The mention of the Chapter Master caught Mitra's attention. 'I heard the news about Kantor. Everyone says it was a miracle.'

Since returning to the Cassar, Galleas had heard the tale of Kantor's escape from the destruction of the Arx Tyrannus, and his epic journey through enemy territory to reach his brothers in New Rynn City. It was Kantor whom Huron Grim had been waiting for at Jadeberry Hill, and his arrival had rallied the spirits of the city's defenders during their darkest hour. He had led the defence of the Zona Regis during the terrible months afterwards. With Imperial relief forces en route, Kantor had led a desperate mission to reach the starport and disable the orks' orbital defence network, allowing the Titan Legions to land and march to the Cassar's aid.

'If anyone can lead us out of these perilous times, it is Pedro Kantor,' Galleas said. 'I do not envy the weight that rests on his shoulders.'

Mitra's expression turned grave. 'I've heard rumours... Is it truly that bad?'

There are less than a hundred of us left, Galleas thought bleakly. The Chapter had suffered such grievous losses before, but now they had lost their Chapter Monastery and their store of gene-seed as well. Despite everything they had done, everything they had sacrificed, the Crimson Fists now stood upon the brink of extinction. Kantor was considering the extraordinary step of sending a delegation to appeal directly to the High Lords of Terra and the Fabricator General of the Adeptus Mechanicus for aid. Restoring the Chapter to even a portion of its former strength would require the release of gene-seed that had been tithed to Mars for centuries, and would occupy the industries of scores of forge worlds scattered across the Imperium. It would be a monumental effort, akin to the founding of an entirely new Space Marine Chapter. But the Crimson Fists had served the Imperium with honour and courage for ten thousand years. They had fulfilled their oaths, time and time again. It was inconceivable that Terra and Mars would not do the same.

But one did not discuss such things with those outside the Chapter. 'We will endure,' Galleas said gravely. 'What of you?'

'I'm fine,' Mitra said. She smiled again, fleetingly. 'Just tired. Sleep is hard to come by these days.'

'And Corporal Ismail?'

'Ismail is… Ismail,' she answered wryly. 'The chirurgeons say she's making a rapid recovery. Once she's released, she'll be joining my staff as regimental sergeant major.' Mitra sighed. 'She's no Sergeant Kazimir, but I suppose she'll do.'

Galleas nodded approvingly. 'I think she will serve you well. Congratulations on your new commission.'

Mitra unconsciously plucked at the hem of her dress tunic. She wore the uniform and rank pins of a colonel in the Astra Militarum, and a peaked cap with gold braid rested on the bench beside her. 'More regiments are needed to help liberate the worlds Snagrod conquered, and Rynn's World must do her part.' She glanced up at Galleas. 'I'm told someone spoke for me. Someone that High Command held in great regard.'

Galleas glanced away. 'You are a fine warrior and a capable leader, Antonia Mitra. The Astra Militarum needs officers like you, now more than ever. Once I explained my reasoning to the General Staff, they were in full agreement.'

Mitra chuckled. 'I expect they were. You can be very persuasive when you want to be.' Turning, she took up her cap and then rose stiffly to her feet. 'I leave to join my unit in the morning. Word is we're heading to Blackwater next. Will I see you there?'

The veteran sergeant drew a deep breath and shook his head. 'The Crimson Fists have been placed in the strategic reserve,' he said, trying to keep the bitterness from his voice. 'We will remain behind and focus on cleansing the ork filth from Rynn's World. At the moment, it is the best we can do.'

Mitra put on her officer's cap and stood beside Galleas for a moment, uncertain how to proceed. After a moment, she said, 'I have another meeting to attend. I did some checking, and it turns out that Kazimir's daughter and her family survived. They're still here on the island.'

'Indeed?' Galleas said.

'I'm going to see them. Tell them a little about what we did out there in the city.' Her expression grew haunted again. 'Not all of it, of course. Not everything. They wouldn't understand.'

'No. I suppose not,' Galleas agreed.

She glanced up again at the towering Space Marine. 'Farewell, Veteran Sergeant Galleas.'

The Space Marine stared down at her for a long moment. Then he reached out and laid a blood-red hand upon her shoulder. 'Farewell, shieldbearer. Until we meet again.'

Galleas watched Mitra limp away, across the garden and down the path, until she was lost from sight. Alone, he stared down at the river and the ruined city beyond, and pondered the future.

ABOUT THE AUTHOR

Mike Lee's credits for Black Library include
the Horus Heresy novel *Fallen Angels*, the
Warhammer 40,000 title *Legacy of Dorn* and
the Space Marine Battles novella *Traitor's Gorge*.
In the Warhammer world he is well known for
his Warhammer Chronicles trilogy *The Rise of
Nagash* and, together with Dan Abnett, he wrote
the five-volume Malus Darkblade series. An avid
wargamer and devoted fan of pulp adventure,
Mike lives in the United States.

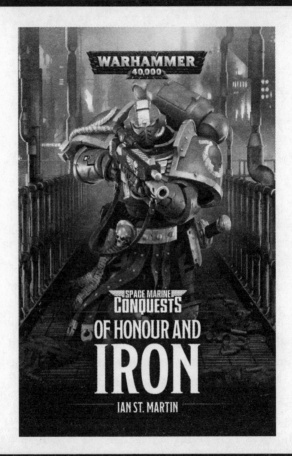

OF HONOUR AND IRON
by Ian St. Martin

As Roboute Guilliman's Indomitus Crusade drives across the galaxy, Ultramarines Chaplain Helios is tasked with a mission of vital importance to the reborn primarch.

An extract from
Of Honour and Iron
by Ian St. Martin

Jovian ran through the streets of Dinath, which was now a city of the dead.

Slaughter and atrocity reached out to him on all sides. The sound of crackling flames and collapsing foundations was muted, drowned out by his pounding boot steps. His failure to have held the walls against his enemy's assault was now compounded by being forced to double back through the city they had been built to defend.

Jovian's mind checked the term almost immediately. Few would possess a perspective generous enough to name where he found himself – even before it had been razed – a city. There were hive cities on this planet, great abandoned monoliths of its relative past left to rot or swallowed by massive sinkholes. Where he stood now was the world's present, one of a scattered few threadbare settlements that housed the people who still called this world home.

No building stood intact, their skeletal frameworks

gutted and jagged like broken teeth reaching out from the pulverised rockcrete. The ground was littered with bodies and their severed component parts. Jovian passed the twisted forms of men and women who had become trapped in their flight when the heat of the firebombing had rendered the streetways molten. They were hunched, trapped and sunk to their elbows and knees inside the road, their clothing baked onto their flesh, their final fates sealed by the blistering heat or any of the other myriad agents that had surrounded them when they died.

Others lay in hideous repose, victims of the after-effects of firestorms and thermobaric detonations. Jovian's enemy was cunning enough to have known they needed only expend enough munitions to allow for nature to step in as the chief force of destruction. Start enough fires within close enough proximity to one another, and they would merge into a single mass conflagration. Such a drastic shift in air temperature withdrew the air from the area with explosive violence, just as it did within a human body. All that remained afterward was a shrunken, leathery thing, barely recognisable as having ever been human.

Jovian saw these corpses, thinking they resembled the dolls he had witnessed children carry, drowning in clothes that were now bizarrely oversized.

He blink-clicked a rune on his retinal display, searching the vox-network for active transponders, for any sign of his brothers holding key positions and aiding in evacuations across the planet. Only static replied.

Jovian slowed to a halt, pivoted around and brought his bolter up. The few breathless auxiliaries that had fallen back with him staggered past, ducking at each heavy bang of fire from their pursuers. Jovian fired single shots from his boltgun, mindful of every shell. The soldiers recoiled at his own shots just as much as those of the enemy.

One of the last mortals limped in exhaustion towards Jovian, struggling with the weight of his sniper-variant las-rifle. He was within five metres of the Space Marine when a bolt-round struck him in the meat of his right thigh. He cried out as he crashed to the broken road. It was a ricochet and a glancing wound, but still contact with the mass-reactive warhead had been enough to nearly sever his leg.

He reached for Jovian, squirming in a quickly expanding pool of crimson that could only mean the destruction of a main artery. He began to speak when a second round penetrated the carapace armour on his back. His muscles twitched and seized, feigning life, but Jovian knew better.

The Apothecary fired, staggering one traitor and sending the others scattering in search of cover. Two more shots found the more elastic armour between the ceramite plates and removed the heretic's arm at the elbow. The flamer he was clutching fell to the dust with it. Suppressing fire lashed at Jovian as the wounded traitor's foul kin bought him the time to scramble away.

Jovian could not hope that the Iron Warrior he had wounded was suffering with the effects of haemorrhage. He had seen the distinctive puff of black fluid when the limb was severed. An augmetic.

Jovian wondered just how much of the twisted men they once were remained of them at all. He doubted that all of his foes combined would amount to a single man. They were just hate and iron, and had been so for a very long time.

He spared a glance at the dead marksman as he turned.

Jovian recalled the man's name. Rask. He had watched him as an aspirant, striving like so many youths of Newfound to be deemed worthy to join the ranks of the Genesis Chapter. He had borne witness first-hand when Rask had failed in his quest for ascension, as his body rejected the surgeries Jovian laboured to complete upon his flesh during the first implantation cycle. From that day Rask became just another man. One more whom Jovian and his brothers had failed here on Quradim.

The moment passed, and after checking the vox again to no avail, Jovian plunged back down the flame-distorted road. He wondered if perhaps the droves of scorched wretches he passed were in fact the most fortunate of this world's citizenry. Those who had survived, with the Chapter garrison shattered and unable to protect them, had been led into bondage in Olympian chains. The heresy of expending one's life-force in service to Chaos, even against one's will, was unfathomable to Jovian. It was far better to die than be forced into apostasy.

Another two of the soldiers with Jovian were cut down by bolter fire as the Iron Warriors renewed the chase. Only one of the auxiliaries remained, a man cowering behind a waist-high mound of broken rubble.

'Rise,' Jovian said as he stopped beside him.

'I, I cannot, lord,' he gasped.

Jovian smelled the sour reek of fear mixed with his exhaustion. The Apothecary tasted his despair, and it stoked a rage within him.

Jovian loomed over the soldier and seized him about the arm. He was careful not to crush the limb into uselessness or dislocate it from the shoulder as he made to throw him to his feet. The brassy clank of a frag grenade landing behind them widened the man's eyes, filling them with an animal panic.

Jovian did not think. He only reacted. He crouched, positioning his armoured bulk between the auxiliary and the grenade. He released the man's arm as his own swept out to draw him to his chest just before it detonated.

Light and sound drowned Jovian for an instant and then vanished, replaced by a lightless silence as his helm's sensory cancellation systems recalibrated. The rubble the soldier had been sheltering behind had absorbed a portion of the blast, yet still Jovian felt it with the force of a thunder hammer against his spine. His armour's systems lagged and flickered as his powerplant endured the brunt of the detonation.

The smoke and shrapnel cleared, and Jovian drew back from the man. The soldier's form was twisted awkwardly in the throes of panic, his terror so great and his body so fragile that he was dead, crushed within Jovian's embrace, while the Apothecary himself was unharmed.

What good am I, as protector of humanity, the thought rose unbidden in his mind, *if I outlive it? What good is a wall left standing over ruins?*

Jovian let the dead soldier go. He slumped bonelessly to the dust. Another bolt-round spanked off the Apothecary's shoulder pauldron, sending his brothers' harvested gene-seed bound to his armour spinning on their chains. He felt what was left of his kin slosh inside the armourglass. His adrenaline spiked, and he launched forward, sprinting deeper into the city.

JOIN THE FIGHT AGAINST CHAOS
WITH THESE COMIC COLLECTIONS

WARHAMMER 40,000
VOL 1 / WILL OF IRON

GEORGE MANN
TAZIO BETTIN
ERICA ANGLIOLINI

WARHAMMER 40,000
VOL 2 / REVELATIONS

GEORGE MANN
TAZIO BETTIN
ERICA ANGLIOLINI

WARHAMMER 40,000
VOL 3 / FALLEN

GEORGE MANN
TAZIO BETTIN
ERICA ANGLIOLINI

WARHAMMER 40,000
DEATHWATCH

AARON DEMBSKI-BOWDEN
WAGNER REIS

BLOOD BOWL
MORE GUTS, MORE GLORY!

NICK KYME
JACK JADSON
FABRICIO GUERRA

DAWN OF WAR III
THE HUNT FOR GABRIEL ANGELOS

RYAN O'SULLIVAN
DANIEL INDRO